Now it was ...
the space b... y
me."

Her smiled died faster than it had ignited, falling from her mouth. She stared back at him, eyebrows drawing slightly closer together. "I think I misheard you."

"Look," he said, spreading his hands wide as he watched her. "If you married someone like me, you would have access to the best medical treatments, and you could stay in New York without any worries."

She did a slow nod. "Funnily enough I've been joking with my friends for weeks that I need to find a wealthy husband. Not that I would ever be some kind of gold digger," she added quickly. "I'm used to having a successful career and standing on my own two feet."

Blake shrugged. "What if we did it? If we got married so you could stay in New York? I could pay for any specialist treatment you need to get you dancing again."

Her gaze was uncertain, maybe even cool. He couldn't figure out exactly what she thought now that her smile had disappeared. "I know why it would be good for me, I just don't get why you'd want to do it. What's in it for you? Why would you want to help me?"

"Marriage to a beautiful ballerina?" he suggested.

"Blake, I'm serious. Why would you marry me unless there's something in it for you?"

MARRIED FOR THEIR MIRACLE BABY

BY
SORAYA LANE

First Published in Great Britain 2016
By Mills & Boon, an imprint of HarperCollins*Publishers*
1 London Bridge Street, London, SE1 9GF

© 2016 Soraya Lane

ISBN: 978-0-263-91970-7

23-0316

Our policy is to use papers that are natural, renewable and recyclable products and made from wood grown in sustainable forests.The logging and manufacturing processes conform to the legal environmental regulations of the country of origin.

Printed and bound in Spain
by CPI, Barcelona

As a child, **Soraya Lane** dreamed of becoming an author. Fast-forward a few years, and Soraya is now living her dream! She describes being an author as "the best job in the world." She lives with her own real-life hero and two young sons on a small farm in New Zealand, surrounded by animals, with an office overlooking a field where their horses graze.

For more information about Soraya, her books and her writing life, visit www.sorayalane.com.

For my mother, Maureen.
Thank you for everything.

CHAPTER ONE

BLAKE GOLDSMITH TOOK a slow sip of whiskey, enjoying the burn of the straight liquor as he swallowed. He wasn't a big drinker, but he'd fast developed a taste for whiskey on the rocks to help get him through the torturous task of attending cocktail parties and gala events. He gazed down at the ice sitting forlorn in the glass. *Darn.* He either had to go without or brave the crowd mingling near the bar again. Neither option appealed to him right now.

Instead he decided to stretch his legs and head outside. If anyone stopped him, he could blame his departure on needing some fresh air. As soon as the auction was over, he was heading home anyway. He craved the solitude of flying, the closeness of being with his unit when he was serving. If he had half the chance, he'd be hightailing it to wherever they were stationed and not coming back. *If only that were an option.*

"Excuse me," he muttered, touching a woman's elbow as he passed, eyes downcast so he didn't have to engage.

After a while, everyone started to look the same—

a sea of black tuxedos and white shirts mixed with elegant women in sparkly dresses. He should have been used to it by now, but playing the black sheep turned good wasn't a part he'd ever wanted, and neither was being part of glittering society parties.

Wow. Blake squared his shoulders, stood a little straighter as he stared across the room. She was standing alone, back to the large windows that overlooked a twinkling New York City below. Her dark red hair was loose and falling over her shoulders, lipstick bright in contrast to her pale skin. She was like a perfectly formed doll, her posture perfect, one hand holding a full glass of champagne, the other clasping a tiny purse. In a room where all the women were starting to look scarily similar with their perfectly coiffed updos and black dresses, she was like the breath of fresh air he'd been so desperately craving only moments before.

Blake didn't waste time. She was alone, which meant she was either waiting for her date to return or actually solo. Either way, he wanted to get to her before anyone else did. He might be avoiding the pressure to settle down, but introducing himself to a beautiful woman would make the night a whole lot more interesting.

He excused himself past a few more people, striding across the room, eyes locked on her. *So much for a boring night out to buy some art and make the company look good.* His evening was looking better by the second. Blake cleared his throat and smiled when dark brown eyes met his.

"I'd ask if you want another drink, but it doesn't look

like you've even touched this one," he said. "Unless you don't like champagne."

The redhead laughed, tipping back a little so her hair tumbled over her shoulders, the unblemished skin of her neck on show. "I love champagne. I'm just…"

Blake laughed. "Bored?"

She grimaced, and it only made him like her more. "Yeah," she said softly. "You could say that."

"I'm Blake," he said, holding out a hand. "Blake Goldsmith."

She reached hers out and he shook it, her skin warm against his. "Saffron Wells."

"So what's a girl like you doing here alone?"

"A bored girl?" she asked.

Blake raised an eyebrow. "No, a beautiful one."

Her smile was sweet. "I promised a friend I'd come, but it's not really my thing." Saffron shrugged. "She's an artist—one of her pieces is being auctioned tonight, so I couldn't really say no. Besides, I don't get out much."

She might feel out of place, but she sure looked the part, as if it was exactly her scene. Blake glanced down when she looked away, eyes traveling over her blue satin dress, admiring her legs. It was short and strapless, and it took every inch of his willpower to stop staring. She was a knockout.

"So what do you do?" he asked.

"I'm having some time out right now," she replied, her smile fading. "I'm just making coffee and…"

Blake cringed, wishing he'd asked something less invasive. He hadn't wanted to put her on the spot or make her uncomfortable. "I love coffee. The barista at my local café is my favorite person in the world."

"How about you?" she asked.

Now Blake was really regretting his line of questioning. He'd walked straight into that one. "Family business. I'm here tonight because no one else would take my place."

"Poor you."

"Yeah, something like that." Blake hated talking about himself, and he liked the fact that this beautiful woman seemed to have no idea who he was. If he read another tabloid or blog article about his most-eligible-bachelor status, he'd lose it. And the lies surrounding his dad's death were driving him to drink. So to chat with a woman like Saffron and not deal with any of that was refreshing to say the least.

A waiter passed and Blake held up a hand, beckoning him over. He smiled and placed his empty whiskey glass on the tray, taking a champagne and putting it into Saffron's hand. He removed her other one, ignoring the look of protest on her face, and then he took another glass for himself.

"I was perfectly happy nursing that," she said.

"Nothing worse than warm champagne," Blake told her. "Want to get some fresh air?"

Saffron's smile was small, but it was there. "Sure. Any excuse to get out of here."

Blake grinned back and touched the small of her back as she turned, guiding her to the only exit he could see. There was a large balcony, which was probably full of smokers, but the room was stifling and he didn't care.

"Excuse me." A loud voice boomed through the speakers, making him turn. "May I have your attention please?"

Blake groaned. Just as he'd been about to escape… "Want to make a run for it?" he murmured, leaning down to whisper into Saffron's ear. Her hair smelled like perfume, and it was soft against his cheek when she tipped her head back.

"I think we need to stay," she whispered in reply, dark brown eyes locked on his for a second. "As much as I'd love to disappear."

Blake shrugged. He would have happily disappeared and made a phone bid, but he wasn't about to leave the most interesting woman he'd seen all evening. Her dark red hair stood out in a sea of bright blondes and raven-haired heads, the color subtle but stunning. And in a room full of slim woman, she seemed even smaller, but not in a skinny way. Blake had noticed the way she was standing when he'd first seen her, her posture perfect, limbs long yet muscled, her body even more sculptured up close than it had appeared from afar. He was intrigued.

"Thank you all for being here tonight to raise funds for underprivileged children right here in New York City," the host said. Blake was tall, so even from the back of the room he could see what was going on, but he doubted Saffron would be able to see a thing. She was almost a head shorter than him. "Funds raised tonight will help to provide a winter assistance package for under-twelve-year-old children who don't have the basics to help them through our harsh colder months.

They will receive a warm coat, shoes, hat, pajamas and other things so many of us take for granted."

Blake glanced down at Saffron. He watched her raise the slender glass to her mouth, taking a sip. He did the same, even though champagne wasn't his usual drink of choice.

"This is my friend's piece," Saffron said, meeting his gaze for a moment. "She's been working on this on and off all year, as part of her latest collection."

Blake pulled the brochure from his inside jacket pocket and stared at the first painting on the crumpled paper. He wasn't the type to get superexcited over art— all he cared about was making a sizable donation to a worthy cause—but he didn't dislike it. The bright swirls of multicolored paint looked interesting enough, and a quick scan over the bio told him the emerging artist could be one to watch. If he got a worthwhile, long-term investment for his donation, he'd be happy.

"We'll open the bidding at five hundred dollars," the auctioneer said, taking over from the host.

Blake raised his hand just high enough for the spotter to see. The bidding quickly moved up to five thousand dollars, and Blake stayed with it, nodding each time now that he was being watched. He didn't like drawing attention to himself, and from the look on Saffron's face when the bidding stopped at just over ten thousand, even she had no idea it was him pushing the price up. He was buying on behalf of the company, so to him it was small change, but he was certain it would be exciting for an emerging artist trying to make a name for herself.

"She'll be thrilled!" Saffron said, eyes bright as she

connected with him. "All the other artists are so well-known, and..." She narrowed her gaze and he laughed.

"What?"

"Why are you smiling like that?" she asked.

Blake grinned. "I bought it," he said simply. "Hopefully she'll be superfamous one day, and I'll have a good story to tell and a decent investment on the wall of my office."

Saffron raised her glass and clinked it to his. "You're crazy."

"No, just in a generous mood." Blake had done his good deed, and now he was ready to go. The auctioneer started all over again, and he placed a hand to the small of Saffron's back. "Meet me outside? I just need to sign for the painting." He'd intended on buying two pieces, but he decided to make a donation with his purchase instead.

He watched as she nodded. "Sure."

Blake paused, hoping she wasn't about to walk out on him, then decided it was a risk he was just going to have to take.

"You never did tell me which café you work at."

She just smiled at him. "No, I don't believe I did."

When she didn't elaborate, Blake walked backward a few steps, not taking his eyes off her before finally moving away. He was used to women throwing themselves at him, wanting his money, being so obvious with their intentions. Saffron was different, and he liked it. There was no desperation in her eyes, no look as though she wanted to dig her claws in and catch him, and it only made him want to get to know her all the more. If she genuinely didn't know who he was right now, then he could be himself, and that was a role he hadn't been able to play in a very long time.

Saffron watched Blake from across the room. She'd been dreading coming out, not looking forward to making small talk and having people ask about her injury, but so far no one had really bothered her. Until Blake. She had no idea who he was or if she was supposed to know who he was, but he'd purchased Claire's painting as if it were no big deal, so he either had money or worked for a company that had told him to spend up. Either way she didn't care, but she was definitely curious.

The night air was cool when she moved out, but the large balcony was virtually empty. There was a couple kissing in the corner, obscured by the shadows, so Saffy walked closer to the edge, admiring the view. She'd never tire of New York. The vibrant atmosphere, the twinkling lights, the fact the city never seemed to sleep. It had a vibe about it that she'd never known anywhere else in the world, and for the first time in her life she felt as if she belonged, as though she was where she was supposed to be.

"Am I interrupting?"

The deep rumble of a voice behind her pulled her from her thoughts and made her turn. Blake was standing a few feet away, his champagne glass hanging from one hand and almost empty, his bow tie no longer perfectly placed against his shirt. The black satin tie was messed up, his top button undone and his jacket open.

Saffy thought he looked sexy and so much more interesting than the rest of the suits she'd seen inside.

"Not at all. I was just admiring the city."

"You're not from here, are you?" he asked, moving
closer and standing beside her, gazing down at the city
as she glanced at him.

"Is my accent still that obvious?" Saffron frowned.
She'd lived in New York for almost ten years now, since
she was sixteen, and to her own ears she sounded more
like a local than a girl from a small town in Kentucky.

"It's just a little twang every now and again. I can't
quite put my finger on it, but…" Blake laughed. "Small
town?"

Saffy gave him a stare she hoped looked evil before
bursting out laughing. "A little place called Maysville,
in Kentucky. But I haven't even been back in—" she
sighed "—forever. You can take the girl out of the small
town, but not the town out of the girl, right?"

Blake leaned against the railing and stared at her,
his smile slow and steady as it spread across his face.
She should have shrunk away from his stare, from his
attention, but instead she bravely faced him. All the
years she'd focused on her career, dancing from her
childhood through her teens and then through almost
all her twenties, she hadn't had time for boyfriends.
But flirting with Blake felt good, and it wasn't as if she
had anywhere else she needed to be or anything else
she should be doing.

"So what's a girl from Maysville doing in New
York?" he asked.

Saffy raised her glass and took a sip, wondering how much or little to tell him. "It's a long story."

His grin was infectious, the way it lit up his dark eyes and made a crease form at each side of his mouth. The man was gorgeous, textbook handsome with his dark hair and even darker features, his golden skin sexy against the white of his shirt.

"It just so happens," he said in his deep, raspy voice, "that I have all night."

"I'd rather hear about you," Saffy said, clearing her throat and trying not to become lost in his stare, hypnotized by his gold-flecked dark eyes.

"I'm guessing you want to open up about yourself about as much as I like talking about *myself*," Blake said with a chuckle.

Saffron raised her glass again, realizing she was drinking way more than usual. She was usually too busy training to drink or socialize. Unless it had been with other dancers, she'd hardly seen anyone else, and she'd had to be so careful with her calorie count and her energy levels to waste on alcohol. She felt good tonight, though—alive and buzzing, even if it was due to the champagne and the smooth talker charming her.

"How about we agree to no personal questions then? I don't want to talk about work or my life," she admitted. She'd lived her work all her life as a ballerina, but every night she flexed her leg, only to be rewarded by ongoing shoots of pain, and she was reminded of what had happened. How little time she had left in the city she loved, and how quickly her dream had ended.

"It just so happens that I don't want to talk about

work, either," Blake said. "Want to go somewhere less…" His voice trailed off.

"Dull?" she suggested.

"Yeah, dull," he agreed, knocking back the rest of his champagne. "I hate these kinds of parties."

"I always thought it would be incredible to be asked to amazing parties, rubbing shoulders with the city's elite," Saffron admitted. "But I quickly realized that the part I liked was getting all dressed up. The parties weren't exactly as amazing as they looked from the outside once I'd attended a few."

"So you'd rather be somewhere more fun?" he asked with a chuckle.

"Ah, yes. I guess you could say that."

Saffron passed Blake her glass, not bothering to drink any more. She liked to stay in control, and if she was going somewhere with a man she hardly knew, she wasn't going to get drunk. Blake took it, turning his back for a moment as he found somewhere to leave them. She quickly pulled out her phone to text Claire.

Hey, you did great tonight. I'm heading out with the guy who bought your painting! If you haven't heard from me in the morning…

Saffy grinned as she hit Send. Claire would flip out, or maybe she'd just cheer her on. Her friend was always telling her to have more fun and stop taking life so seriously, but she wasn't the one in danger of having to pack her bags and go back to Maysville if she didn't get her job back. Saffron was serious because her job had demanded it, and she'd been happy to make it her life.

Her phone pinged back almost instantly.

Have fun. I'll track him down if I need to. xoxo

"Shall we go?"

Saffron put her phone back into her purse. "Sure thing."

Blake held out his arm and she slipped her hand through, laughing to herself about how absurd the evening had turned out. She wasn't the girl who went on dates with strangers or disappeared with men and left her friends at a party. But nothing about the past month had gone according to plan, so she had nothing to lose.

"Do you like dancing?" Blake asked as they walked around the back of the crowd. He was leading her around the room, and she could feel eyes on them. Either because they were leaving too early or because of who he was. Or maybe she was just being overly sensitive and imagining it.

Dancing. When in her life hadn't she loved dancing? "Sometimes." If her leg didn't hurt like hell when she tried to dance, she'd love to.

"I was hoping you were going to say no."

Saffron laughed. This guy was hilarious. "It's a no. For tonight, anyway."

"Then why don't we go back to my place?" He must have seen the hesitation written all over her face, because he stopped walking and stared down at her. "Sorry, that came out all wrong."

"It's not that I don't want to..." Saffron actually didn't know what she thought, but she wasn't about to jump into bed with him. Maybe that's what he was used to? She hoped she hadn't read the situation wrong.

"I just meant that if we don't want to dance and we're bored here, it might be nice to just chill with a drink. Or we could find a nice quiet bar somewhere. It wasn't supposed to sound like that."

Saffy looked deep into his dark eyes, didn't see a flicker of anything that alarmed her. "Why should I trust you?" she asked.

He cleared his throat. "United States Army Officer Blake Goldsmith," Blake said, giving her a quick salute. "One of the only things I'm good at in life is keeping people safe, and that's about the only good reason I can give you."

She was more shocked that he was an officer than the fact he'd asked her back to his place so fast. "You're in the army?"

"Was." Blake grimaced. "So much for not talking about my work life, huh? But yeah, you can trust me."

Saffron knew that just because he was a former officer didn't make him trustworthy on its own, but she wasn't actually worried about Blake. She felt as though she could take him at face value. What worried her was how he was making her feel, how desperate she suddenly was to know what it was like to meet a man and go home with him. Not that she could actually go through with a one-night stand, but the thought was making her tingle all over.

"So what do you say?" Blake asked. "I have a car

waiting, so we can either jump in and head to my place or duck into a nearby bar."

Saffron passed a number over and collected her coat, snuggling into it before they stepped out into the chilly night air. On the balcony she'd been so busy admiring the view that she'd hardly noticed it, but now she was feeling the cold.

"Yours," she finally said. "It had better be warm, though."

Blake was holding a black scarf, and he tucked it around her neck, his hand falling to her back as they walked. "I promise."

She walked until he pointed out a black town car, and within seconds he was opening the door for her and ushering her inside.

"Tell me—how does a former soldier end up at a glitzy charity gala with a plush town car at his beck and call?" she asked, curious.

"Goldsmith Air," Blake said, pulling the door shut as he slid in beside her, his thigh hard to hers. "Family business, one I tried to steer clear of but somehow ended up right in the thick of."

Saffron knew what that felt like. "Sorry, I know we promised no work questions."

They only seemed to travel for a few blocks before they were outside a pretty brick building that looked old but had been renovated and kept immaculate. A huge glass frontage showed off a contemporary-looking café inside, the lights still on but the signs pulled in. She guessed he lived upstairs.

"So this is your local coffee place?" Saffron asked.

"I wake up to the smell of their coffee brewing, and by eight I've usually ordered my second cup for the day."

"They deliver to you?"

Blake gave her a guilty look before pushing the door open. "One of the perks of being landlord."

She didn't show her surprise. He was definitely not your average US Army veteran! Saffron stepped out and followed Blake as he signaled his driver to leave before taking her in through a locked security door that required him to punch a code in. They went in, and it locked behind them before he was punching in another code and ushering her into an elevator. Saffy admired the old-fashioned metal doors he pulled across, and within moments they were on the second floor.

"Wow." They stepped out into one of the hugest loft-style apartments Saffron had ever seen. Interior brickwork was paired with high-gloss timber floors, a stainless steel industrial-type kitchen taking center stage. She had to fight to stop her jaw from hitting the floor.

"So this is home?" she asked.

Blake shrugged. "For now."

He closed the door behind them and touched her shoulders, slipping her coat off and throwing it over the arm of a huge L-shaped sofa. Saffy spun around to ask him something and ended up almost against him. He must have moved forward, his arms instantly circling her, steadying her. She stared up at him, touched his arm, her fingers clasping over his tuxedo jacket as she became hypnotized by his stare.

Blake was handsome and strong and intriguing… all of the things that sparked her interest and made her want to run in the opposite direction but at the same time want to throw herself hard up against him.

"Are you okay?" he asked, the deep timbre of his voice sending a shiver down her spine.

Saffron nodded. "Uh-huh," she managed, still not pulling away, not letting go.

Blake watched her back, his eyes never leaving hers, and just when she thought she was going to step back, his face suddenly moved closer to her, *dangerously close*. Saffron's breath halted in her throat; her heart started to race. What was she even doing? In this man's apartment? In his arms? She barely even knew his name!

"Can I kiss you?" he murmured, his whisper barely audible, his mouth so near.

Saffy felt herself nodding even though she knew she shouldn't. But he clearly wasn't going to ask her twice. Blake's lips connected with hers, just a gentle, soft caress at first, his mouth warm to hers, unbearably gentle. She lifted her arms and tucked them around his neck as Blake deepened their kiss, his lips moving back and forth across hers as his hands skimmed down her back.

"I think we should get that drink," he muttered, barely pulling his lips from hers.

"Me, too," she whispered back. But her body had other ideas, pressed tight to him as he cupped her even tighter against him. Saffron had never been with a man she didn't know, her only experience from the one relationship she'd had with a dancer she'd performed alongside. But right now she wanted Blake, and no amount of willpower was going to let her move away.

Blake's groan was deep as he scooped her up, lifting her heels clean off the ground and walking her backward to the closest sofa. She only had a second to gaze up at him, a bare moment to wonder what the heck she was doing as he ripped off his tie and discarded it, staring down at her, his big body looming above.

And then he was covering her, his body over hers. Saffy lifted her mouth up to his, met his lips and hungrily kissed him back. She knew it was all types of wrong, but tonight she was going to be bad. If this was one of her last weekends in New York, then she was going to make the most of it. Her career might be over, but it didn't mean her life had to be.

CHAPTER TWO

SAFFRON OPENED HER eyes and quickly closed them. She groaned and pulled the covers over her head. She'd never had firsthand experience with what to do the morning after, and nothing clever was springing to mind. What had she been thinking?

"Morning."

She took a deep breath and slowly slipped the covers down, clutching them tight to her chest as she sat up. Blake was standing in the doorway, looking just as chiseled and sexy and gorgeous as he had the night before. No wonder she'd ended up in his bed. He crossed the room and sat on the bed beside her.

"Ah, morning," she finally stammered, clearing her throat and trying to pull herself together. She didn't usually lack in confidence, but then again she didn't usually have to deal with handsome men so early in the morning. Saffron ran her tongue over her teeth, wishing she could have had ten minutes in the bathroom before having to face Blake.

"So I need to show you something," he said, eyebrows drawn together as he leaned closer.

It was only then she realized he was holding an iPad. Curious, she reached for it.

"What is it?"

"You know how we didn't want to talk about our personal lives or our work?"

Saffy nodded. She didn't understand what he was trying to tell her. Until she looked at the screen.

"Oh," she blurted.

"I think we probably *should* have had that conversation," Blake muttered. "Maybe we could have taken a back exit and made sure no one saw us."

Saffy kept hold of the covers with one hand and swiped through the photos with the other. There was Blake with his hand to her back, Blake laughing, her laughing with her head tipped back and her eyes locked on his, and there was them getting into his town car. Paired with headlines screaming that Blake was one of the city's most eligible bachelors and naming her as one of ballet's finest forgotten stars. The description stung.

She swallowed away the emotion in her throat, the familiar burn behind her eyes that always hit when she thought about her career. When she passed the iPad back and glanced up at Blake, she wished she hadn't.

"Hey, it's not so bad," he said, discarding the iPad and leaning over. He reached for her hand and lifted it, kissing the soft skin on the inside of her arm.

Saffy smiled. *This* was how she'd ended up in his bed! He was so smooth yet seemed so genuine at the same time, although hearing that he was such a prized bachelor only made her wonder if he'd expertly played her to get her into bed.

"You're really upset about it, aren't you? I was hoping you wouldn't think it was that big a deal being papped."

She shrugged. "I don't care about being seen with you, or the photos. It's the headlines that sting," Saffy admitted.

Blake looked confused. "I'm not sure I'm following. You do realize that the whole bachelor thing has been completely blown out of proportion, right? It's rubbish."

Saffy shook her head. "It hurts to read that I'm a washed-up former ballerina. Sometimes the truth stings more than we realize."

Blake kept hold of her hand, staring into her eyes. "You look far too young to be washed up, surely."

"I'll give you points for being kind, but I'm not too young, not in the ballet world. My body broke down on me, so I'm out."

He chuckled. "By out, you mean injured, right? Taking some time out? From what I've read this morning, you're pretty incredible."

Now it was Saffy chuckling. "You've been googling me?"

He shrugged. "Yeah. I'm an early riser. I saw this, and I've been reading up about you ever since."

She liked that he was at least honest. He could have lied and not admitted to it, but he was obviously curious about who he'd spent the night with. And if she was honest, she was starting to get pretty intrigued about him, too.

"What did it say?" Saffy wasn't clutching the sheet quite so tightly now, not as concerned as she had been about him seeing her.

"From what I've read, you came to New York as a teenager, wowed all the right people and eventually landed your dream role as lead in *Swan Lake* last year."

Saffron smiled. "Sounds about right." She wasn't sure she wanted to talk about it, not anymore. For years ballet had been her life, since she was a little girl in love with the idea of being a pretty dancer to a determined teenager and a dedicated adult. She'd lived and breathed her dream all her life, which was why she was at such a loss now. How did anyone move on if they'd lost the one thing that meant more to them than anything else?

Blake surprised her by stroking her face, his thumb caressing her cheek as he stared into her eyes. "I know the feeling."

She smiled, but it was forced. There was no way he knew how she was feeling. "You don't happen to have coffee, do you?" she asked, hoping he'd say *yes* then go and make her a cup so she had a little privacy.

"Sure do." Blake pulled back then rose, and the moment was over. He looked down at her, his height imposing. He was already dressed, barefoot but wearing dark jeans and a plain white tee.

Saffy waited for him to go then quickly scanned for her clothes. She hardly even remembered how they'd gotten to the bedroom. From what she could recall, her dress was in the living room wherever he'd thrown it, but her underwear was somewhere in the bedroom. She jumped up, taking the sheet with her. It wasn't until she had her underwear back on that she relaxed. Saffy looked around the room but he didn't have any clothes scattered, so she opened his closet and grabbed a sweatshirt. It was fleecy on the inside with a zipper, and given the size on her, she had to zip it all the way just to cover her body. Then she dashed into his bathroom, splashed some water on her face and ran her fingers through her hair to tame it. Given the fact she'd just woken and didn't have all her usual things with her, she didn't think she looked too terrible.

"So I—" Blake's deep voice cut off. "You look cute in my hoodie."

"Sorry." Saffron spun around, feeling guilty. "I should have asked first, but I didn't want to walk out half-naked."

Blake's laugh made her smile. He waved her toward him and turned, and she followed him out to the living area. He had music playing softly, just audible, and she tried not to gape at the apartment all over again. It was incredible, and it oozed money. He pointed to the coffee machine.

"I can make an okay black coffee, but if you want something fancy, I'll call downstairs."

Saffron shook her head. "I don't need fancy café coffee. Just give it to me however it comes, with a heaped teaspoon of sugar."

"Not what I expected from a ballerina. I thought all dancers would think of sugar as the devil and have eating disorders." Blake turned straight around then, his face full of apology. "Sorry, that was in bad taste. I didn't mean it."

She was used to it. "It's fine, and it's kind of true. There are plenty of dancers with problems."

"Yeah, still. Bad form. Want to tell me what happened?" he asked, pushing a big mug of steaming coffee across the counter and shoving his hands into his jean pockets as he stood watching her on the other side. "Sounds to me like you've had a rough year."

"Yeah, you could say that again," Saffy muttered.

"I have waffles and bacon on their way up, so you can tell me over breakfast."

She groaned. "Do I have to?"

His laugh made her smile. "Yeah, you kind of do."

Saffron hated talking about what had happened, didn't want to have to explain what she'd been through and what it meant for her, but breakfast did sound good and she wasn't about to run out. Especially not if there were paparazzi waiting outside to see if she'd spent the night.

"We could talk about what happened last night instead," he suggested, giving her a smile that made her want to slap him.

"Um, how about no?" she quipped straight back, heart racing.

"So let me guess," Blake started, walking away from her when a buzz rang out. She tracked him with her eyes, admired how tall and built he was. His hair was thick and dark, a full mop of it, and whereas last night it had been styled, this morning it was all mussed up. She liked him even better less groomed, although he had looked pretty hot in a suit the night before.

The next thing he was pressing a button. "Just give me a sec," Blake called over his shoulder before disappearing from the apartment.

Saffy let out a breath she hadn't even known she was

holding. She reached for her coffee and took a slow, long sip. It was hot, but the burn felt nice down her throat, helped her to calm down somehow.

She could run. It wouldn't be her stupidest idea, and she could just grab her dress and bolt for it. Make up an excuse and dash past him. Get out of Dodge and never have to see him again or talk about what happened. She could even mail him back his hoodie, forget what she'd done. Only she wasn't sure she wanted to. The last few months, after the worst of her pain had passed, she'd been bored and miserable. She was working on autopilot, making coffee and serving people food, seeing her dreams disappear. It hadn't mattered what she'd done or how hard she'd tried, her leg hadn't healed fast enough, the ligaments badly torn, and with arthritis on top of it making the pain debilitating at best.

Blake had reminded her she was alive. If she hadn't met him, she'd have stayed another hour at the party, chatted with her friend, then gone home alone. Almost all her friends were dancers, and she wasn't in that world anymore.

So she stayed put, only leaving her seat on one of Blake's leather bar stools to retrieve her purse. It was tiny so she didn't have a lot in there, but she did have her foundation stick and some lip gloss, and she was keen to use both to make herself look half-decent. Plus she needed to text Claire.

She laughed. Her friend had already sent her three text messages, first wondering where she was, then asking how fab her night had been after seeing the article on some lame website. Then asking if she needed to send out a search party. Trust Claire to be scanning those types of pages as she ate her breakfast in the morning.

She sent her a quick message back.

I'm fine. He's gorgeous. Do you know anything about him?

The door clicked then, and she shoved her phone back in her purse. She hadn't had time to google him, and not being a native New Yorker, she didn't know the company name he'd mentioned the night before. He didn't strike her as a spoiled rich kid—more like a man who'd made his own money or his own way in the world, and she wanted to know more. Especially how he'd come to be listed as an eligible bachelor worthy of paparazzi.

"Breakfast is served," he announced.

Saffron stood and made her way back to the bar stool. "Mmm, smells delicious." Now she had clothes and some makeup on, she was a lot less self-conscious.

"Waffles with whipped caramel cream and fresh fruit. I went with sweet." His grin was naughty and she laughed at him.

"Can I just set the record straight about last night," she said, cringing at the way the words had come out.

"Sure. But you don't have to explain anything, if that's what you're worried about."

She sighed, taking the plate he held out to her. It did look delicious, the waffles thick and square, with pineapple and blueberries piled beside a swirl of the cream. "I just don't want you to think I do this sort of thing all the time."

He joined her around the other side of the counter, sitting down and passing her a knife and fork. "I kind of got that impression when you were peeking out at me from beneath the covers this morning with a horrified look on your face."

"Really?" She had to give it to him—he hadn't turned out to be a jerk the morning after.

Blake leaned over, smiling before dropping his mouth to hers, not giving her a second to hesitate. His lips were warm and tasted of coffee, his hand soft as he cupped the back of her head. He kissed the breath from her then pulled back, lips hovering as he stared down at her. Saffy felt the burn of heat as it spread up her neck, every inch of her body tingling from the unexpected kiss.

"You're too cute," he said with a grin, digging into breakfast like he hadn't just kissed her as if it was their last kiss on earth.

"And you're too suave for your own good," she muttered, stabbing her waffle with the fork, irate that he'd had such a visceral effect on her. "I'm guessing most of the women you bed are happy to drag you into bed the moment they lock eyes on you."

She had no idea why she was so mad with him when all he'd done was kiss her, but something about his attitude had gotten under her skin.

"Hey," he said, setting down his fork and turning to face her. "I meant it as a compliment, not to get you all fired up."

She went back to her breakfast, ignoring him.

"And I haven't exactly had the chance to meet a whole lot of ladies since I've been back. First I moved back home, then when I finally took over this place, I was spending more hours in the office than anywhere else. I haven't had time for socializing, other than when I've had to for work."

"You mentioned you were in the army," she said, calmed down and not so ready to jump down his throat. She'd seriously overreacted before.

"In another lifetime, yeah," he said, but he looked away as if he wasn't at all interested in talking about that other life. "Anyway, we're supposed to be talking about you. Tell me what happened. Why aren't you dancing now?"

Blake was intrigued. He'd bedded her already, and most of the time that was when his interest stopped, but she was something else. Even before he'd seen the blog post about them leaving the benefit together, which his sister had been so kind as to forward to him with a message that this one sounded a whole lot more promising than the airheads he'd been photographed with other times.

Blake kept eating his waffles, not wanting to stare at her and make her uncomfortable. He believed her that this wasn't her usual scene—she'd looked like a deer in headlights when he'd come back into the bedroom after hearing that she'd woken. His first instinct had been to dive straight back under the covers, until he'd seen her face and changed his mind. He still wanted her—he just wasn't going to be so forward.

Having a late breakfast with her and relaxing for once was making it clear he'd been way too focused on work the last few months. He'd become so determined not to buckle under the pressure and settle down, just because it would be good for business, but he was starting to realize he'd been missing out.

Saffron's red hair looked darker in the morning. Maybe it was the lack of bright lights, but it still looked incredible. The richest color against skin the lightest, barely there shade of gold, and dark brown eyes that just kept on drawing him in. He cleared his throat and set down his fork.

"Come on, what happened? Maybe I can help?" He doubted it, but he wanted to hear the story, and if she needed help finding work or someone to assist her with whatever injury she had, he did have helpful contacts.

His phone buzzed and he quickly glanced at it, not wanting to be rude by picking it up. He could read just enough of the text to see it was from his assistant and that the investor he'd been trying to impress had seen the paparazzi story. *Great.* Just when he'd been making some headway, now he was going to be labeled the rich playboy again.

"Nobody can help me," she said in a low voice. "Most dancers get injured and that's it, they're injured. Me, I'm out. Which means my career is over, because soon I'll have to go home with my tail between my legs, the washed-up former ballerina. I don't have enough money to stay here without working, and my physical therapy and specialist bills are crazy."

Blake frowned, forgetting the text and focusing on Saffron. "There's no other way for you to stay here?"

Saffron picked at her food, taking a mouthful that he was sure was a delaying tactic. When she finally looked up at him, her eyes were swimming. Big brown pools of hurt, bathed in unshed tears.

"I had a dream of dancing with the best ballet companies in the world, right from when I was a kid. I used to practice so hard, train my heart out and eventually it paid off." He listened as she blew out a big breath, sending a few tendrils of shorter hair around her face up into the air. "My hours of practicing got me noticed at the Lexington Ballet School in Kentucky, and eventually it turned into a dance scholarship with the New York Ballet Company. I started training there, danced my heart out and eventually went on to be an apprentice by the time I was eighteen."

"Wait, you moved to New York on your own *before* you were even eighteen? How old were you when you got the scholarship?" He knew plenty of models and other creative types started their careers early, but he'd never really thought about teenagers making such a big leap on their own. "Your parents didn't come, too?"

She shook her head. "Nope. Just me. I stayed with a relative for the first few months, then I moved into an apartment with some other dancers. I was only seventeen when I officially went out on my own, but I was so determined and focused on what I was doing that my parents didn't have any other choice. I would have resented them for the rest of my life if they hadn't let me come."

He got that. They'd let her follow her dream, and he admired any parent who encouraged their kids. "And then what? You make it sound like your career has already ended, like there isn't any hope." Blake hated hearing her talk as if it was over. She was doing what she wanted to be doing, and nobody was trying to hold her back, stifle her dreams.

"I tore three ligaments in my leg one night when I was dancing *Swan Lake*. I was finally in the role I wanted, as the lead, and I didn't even dance for an entire season at the top before my accident." She was looking away now, couldn't seem to meet his gaze. Blake wanted to reach for her, but he didn't, *couldn't*. The pain of what he'd lost and left behind was too raw for him, and he was barely coping with it on his own without having to help someone else.

"You could recover from that," he said gently, careful to choose the right words.

"No, I won't. I have a form of arthritis that I've battled for years. It first showed when I was stressed over a big performance, and in the past my doctors have been able to manage it. But from what I've been told, we're past that point now. That's why I'm out, why they wouldn't just let me stay on leave due to injury. They don't ever expect me to make a full recovery."

Blake steeled his jaw, hating that someone had had the nerve to put a damper on her dreams. On anyone's dreams. As far as he was concerned, the fight was worth it until the very last.

"You need to see more specialists, research more treatment, get your body strong again," he told her, wishing his voice didn't sound so raspy and harsh. "You can't take no for an answer when you're so close to living that dream."

Her eyes were angry, glaring when she met his gaze. "Don't you think I've done everything? As much as I could?"

He held up both his hands. "Sorry, I didn't mean to jump down your throat like that. I just…"

"I don't need to be told what to do," she said angrily, still holding his stare. "The only thing that will save me now is winning the lottery or a miracle. Money is the only way I can stay a part of this world, to keep searching for help, trying to keep training. Either money or a new treatment to help me get back on stage." She slumped forward, looked defeated. "Instead I'll be back in Hicksville, the girl who had so much potential and still ended up a nobody."

Blake bunched his fists, wished there was something he could do. He didn't know why her situation made him so angry, but it did.

Just then his phone buzzed and he glanced at it quickly. He read the screen, cursed his sister for wanting to be so involved in his love life.

So? Spill! Is she really a ballerina? She looked gorgeous. Keep this one!

Blake didn't bother replying, not about to engage with his younger sister over anything personal. And then he looked up and found Saffron watching him, her full lips parted, dark eyes trained on his.

She needed a way to stay in New York. He needed a wife.

He pushed his sister from his mind and pulled his bar stool closer to Saffron's, thinking that she was the most intriguing, beautiful woman he'd met in a long time. He didn't want to be married to anyone, but the truth was, he needed to be. That text just before was a slap-in-the-face kind of reminder. He was at the helm of a family business that was worth tens of millions of dollars, and he needed to maintain the right image. They were negotiating for a huge contract, one worth millions over the next two years alone, not to mention the investors he was trying to bring on board to grow the business. But his biggest potential investor had made it beyond clear that he was worried about Blake's playboy status, didn't like the fact that he wasn't settled down and married. They were rich men with strong family values, the kind his own father had always managed to impress. Being married could be the key to finalizing those deals, and no matter how much he'd tried to pretend otherwise, it was true, which meant he had some serious damage control to do.

He reached for his coffee and drained it. Real marriage wasn't something he wanted, hadn't been on his agenda since the day his first love had walked away from him as though what they'd had meant nothing. He could still feel the cool sting of betrayal as if it was yesterday. But if he could package a marriage of convenience into something that could work for both him and Saffron? Now that was something he'd be willing to do.

CHAPTER THREE

BLAKE CONTINUED TO sip his coffee, watching Saffron. She was beautiful. She was talented and accomplished. She was interesting. If he had to pick a wife on paper, she was it.

"So come on, spill," she said, setting her knife and fork down, surprising him by the fact she'd actually finished her entire breakfast. "The more you tell me you don't want to talk about yourself, the more I want to know."

He shook his head. "No."

Saffron's laughter made him smile. "What do I have to do then? To make you tell me?"

Now it was Blake's laughter filling the space between them. "Marry me."

Her smile died faster than it had ignited, falling from her mouth. She stared back at him, eyebrows drawing slightly closer together. "I think I misheard you."

Blake smiled, knew he had to tell her his plan carefully, to sell the idea to her instead of having her run for the door and get a restraining order against him. She was probably thinking he was a nut job, some kind of stalker who was obsessed with her after one night together.

"Look," he said, spreading his hands wide as he watched her. "If you married someone like me, you would have access to the best medical treatments, and you could stay in New York without any worries."

She did a slow nod. "Funnily enough, I've been joking about that with my friends for weeks—that I need to find a wealthy husband. But I'm used to having a successful career and standing on my own two feet."

Blake shrugged. "What if we did it? If we got married so you could stay in New York and get back on your feet, so to speak? I could pay for any specialist treatment you need to get you dancing again."

Her gaze was uncertain, maybe even cool. He couldn't figure out exactly what she thought now that her smile had disappeared. "I know why it would be good for me, I just don't get why you'd want to do it. What's in it for you? Why would you want to help me?"

"Marriage to a beautiful ballerina?" he suggested.

"Blake, I'm serious. Why would you marry me unless there's something in it for you? A hidden catch?"

"Look, plenty of people marry for convenience. Gay men marry women all the time to hide their sexuality if they think it's going to help their career or please their family."

She sighed. "Well, I know you're not gay. Unless you put on the performance of your life last night, that is. And anyway, I know plenty of gay people, and it hasn't hurt their careers at all, to be honest."

"Well, you're a dancer. Corporate America isn't always so accepting, even if they pretend to be."

"Back to you," Saffron said, studying him intensely, her eyes roving over his face. "Tell me now, or I'm walking out that door."

Blake wasn't about to call her bluff. Just because she needed a boost in finances didn't mean she was automatically going to say yes to marrying a stranger.

"Running my father's company was never part of my plan," he told her. "Now I'm CEO of a company that I'm proud of, but not a natural fit for. It's not the role I want to be in, but there's also no way I'm about to let that company fall into the wrong hands. I need to keep growing it, and I'm working on two of the biggest deals in the company's history."

"I hear you, and I'm sorry you don't like what you do, but it doesn't explain why you need a wife. Why you need to marry *me*?"

Blake didn't want to tell her everything, didn't like talking about his past and what he'd lost to anyone, why he didn't want a real wife, to open himself up to someone again. Eventually he'd have to tell her, otherwise she'd end up blindsided and their marriage would be uncovered as a sham, but not right now. Not until he knew he could trust her.

"I'm sick of the whole tabloid thing, the paps following me because some stupid magazine announced that I was one of New York's most eligible men." They'd called him the Billion Dollar Bachelor, the headlines had screamed out that women should be fighting over the former soldier back in the city as a corporate CEO and he hated it. Hated the attention and being known for his family's money after doing everything in his power to prove his own worth, make his own way in the world. But most of all he hated that people he most needed to impress right now read the rubbish being written, viewed him as a playboy, were unsettled by the fact that he *wasn't* settled.

"My dad built up the company as a family business, and our clients like that, especially a large-scale investor I've been working on for months. I don't want them to start thinking the company isn't going to continue to succeed because some loser rich-kid playboy is at the helm, and if I can set the right image now, it won't matter if I'm not married in a few years' time because the deals will be done."

Saffron didn't say anything when he paused, just stared at him.

Blake laughed. "Plus I'd like to get my mother and two sisters off my back. They're driving me crazy, trying to set me up all the time." He stood, pushing his hands into his pockets, watching, waiting for a reaction. He probably shouldn't have added the joke about getting them off his back. "So what do you think?"

"What do I think?" she muttered. "I think you're crazy!"

"We can talk through the details later, but please just think about it."

"Wow," Saffron said, holding up her hand. "I need time to think, to process how absurd this is."

"It's not that absurd," he disagreed.

"This is only-in-the-movies absurd," she fired back. "I'm not saying no, but I can't say yes right now, either."

Blake nodded. "I need to head in to the office. Why don't you stay here a bit, take your time and meet me back here tonight if you decide to say yes. I can get the paperwork and everything sorted out pretty quick, and we can go choose a ring together tomorrow."

Saffron shook her head, smiling then bursting into laughter. "I can't believe you're actually serious, that I'm not just being punked right now."

"Sweetheart, I'm deadly serious."

Blake took a few steps forward, touched her chin gently and tipped her face up, his thumb against her smooth skin. He slowly lowered his head and dropped his lips over hers, plucking softly at her lips.

"So we'd actually be married?" she asked, breathless, when she pulled back, mouth still parted as if she was waiting for more.

"Yes," he said, thinking how cute she looked in his hoodie. "You can set the boundaries, but we need it to look real."

He bent and kissed her again, softly.

Saffron could hardly breathe. She'd been outside for at least ten minutes, but her lungs still felt as though they couldn't pull in enough air. Marry him? How could he have asked her to marry him? They'd spent one night together—but marriage? Did she need rescuing that bad?

She pushed through a crowd of people passing on the street to reach a bench seat, dropping the second she found one. Could she actually marry a man she didn't even know, just to stay in New York? Just to get her career back on track, if that was even possible? She wished she could laugh it off and tell him there was no way she'd accept his proposal, but the truth was that it was the perfect solution for her. If it was the only way to give her recovery one last, real shot… Saffron gulped and turned her attention to the people walking past. Tried to lift her thoughts from Blake and failed.

What she needed was a piece of paper and her laptop. She would do what she always did—make a list of all the pros and cons, just like when she'd been offered the scholarship to dance with the New York Ballet in the first place. When she was sixteen, the list had been heavy on the pros and low on the cons, the only drawbacks coming from her parents, who wanted her to stay and didn't understand how desperately she wanted it. This time her list might be more balanced.

Marriage had always seemed so sacred to her, so special, but… She held her breath then slowly blew it out. Dancing was all she had. It was her life. If getting that back, having the one thing in the world back that meant so much to her, meant having to get married, then she had to consider it. Dancing had been her salvation. Could Blake really help her get that back?

Her phone buzzed and she picked it up, seeing it was Claire. She'd been out of touch with most of her dancing friends for the past couple of months, finding it too hard to hear about ballet and what they were training, the pain like a knife to her heart. But Claire had been there for her, been different and she'd enjoyed being part of her arty world.

"Hey," Saffy said when she answered.

"You're not still there, are you?" Claire giggled. "I still can't believe you did it. You're usually such a prude!"

Saffy laughed. "I am not a prude! Just because you have loose morals."

Now it was Claire in fits of laughter. "I'm not loose, I just don't see the point in saying no to a good time. Obviously my amazing personality has rubbed off on you."

Saffron felt better already after talking to Claire. "He…" Saffy changed her mind, not wanting to tell her. Claire was pretty open-minded, but even she might think it was crazy to consider the proposal.

"What? Tell me what you were going to say! He was amazing, wasn't he? Tell me more!" her friend begged.

Saffy sighed, the weight of her decision hanging heavy. "He was amazing, incredible, but…" Her voice trailed off again. "He wants to meet again tonight."

"Awesome! He's seriously hot stuff. Not to mention he paid up big-time for my painting. I've already had phone calls from buyers asking about my commissions and existing work."

If there hadn't been the whole marriage thing to consider, she would have been more excited. Giddy over being with a man like Blake, a man who'd made her pulse race and her mind forget all about what she'd lost while she'd been with him. She'd have liked the idea of getting to know him better, *dating* him, not marrying him.

"Good, you deserve it. And he was lovely. I'm just not sure about everything."

Silence stretched out between them, just long enough for it to be noticeable. "You're thinking about having to go back home?"

"Yeah." Saffy wasn't lying; she just wasn't telling her everything. Besides, Claire would be the one person to know the truth if it did happen, that she'd only met Blake the night before. She trusted her not to say anything, to keep her secret, but she just wasn't ready to open up about it yet, not when she was still trying to process it herself.

"Do you have any more doctors to see? Any other specialists you could visit or anything?" Claire asked. "Can you afford to keep going for a bit longer?"

Saffy shook her head, even though she knew Claire couldn't see her. This was why she was considering the marriage—this was why she *had* to. "No," she murmured. "I've done everything. There's no one left to see, or at least no one I can afford now, and I'm like damaged goods on the dance scene. If I dance again, there's only one company I want to be with, and that's a firm no right now."

"Fight till the bitter end, Saffy. Don't go quitting until you have no other options left."

Saffron had no intention of giving up until the last; it had been her attitude all her life. But even she had to admit that when it was over, it was over.

"There's one last thing I have to consider," she told Claire. "One last option."

"Give it a go—you owe it to yourself."

"I'm going to go, I have a few jobs to get done," Saffy said, wanting to end the call so she could think some more. She started to walk, the familiar twinge in her knee bearable at a walk when she was wearing heels. Barefoot it was almost unnoticeable. It was when she tried to push herself harder or dance that it really hurt. "Enjoy the weekend."

"You, too. Give me a call tomorrow so I can hear all the juicy details from tonight."

Saffy said goodbye and kept walking, suddenly realizing how terrible she must look. She was wearing her blue satin dress, her hair was tangled, and her heels weren't exactly daytime wear. Thank goodness there had been no cameras flashing when she'd exited out the back of Blake's building, through the café. Her career being over was bad enough—the last thing she needed was for the public to see pictures of her looking like she was right now.

Marriage. No matter how hard she tried to clear her head, Blake's proposal was the only thing on her mind. And she was pretty certain that, like it or not, she was going to have to say yes.

Blake sat in his office, staring out the huge windows that bordered two sides. It was a stunning corner office—luxurious and extravagant—but it didn't feel like his. For two decades it had been his father's office, and he'd been in it numerous times, often when his father was trying to convince him that the company was where he should be. That it should be his dream, as if he should grow up to be a carbon copy of the man who'd raised him. But Blake had never wanted to be his father, had had dreams of his own, dreams that were still with him that he'd been forced to leave behind.

He stood and walked to the window, restless being inside and having to stare at paperwork and sign contracts. The city was alive below him, people milling everywhere, and he wished he could just disappear in the crowd and leave his responsibilities behind. But he'd made the decision to come back, and he wasn't a quitter.

"This is your life, son. You're my eldest, and I expect you to take over the business. To look after your family."

The words had echoed in his mind long before his father had died, but now they were never ending. Every time he wanted to walk away, they haunted him, kept him awake at night. He was the eldest, and he'd always had a sense of responsibility that his younger brother and sisters had never had. But it hadn't stopped his brother from wanting to run the company, to absorb everything their father had to share and teach.

Everything had been going to plan—Blake was doing what he loved, and his brother was shadowing their dad, learning the ropes, prepared to take over the company one day. Until everything had gone horribly wrong.

Blake clenched his teeth together and crossed the room, reaching for the whiskey his father had always kept in the office, filling one of the crystal tumblers he'd seen his father drink from so many times. He poured a small amount into the glass and downed it, liking the burn. *Needing* the burn.

The chill he'd felt when they'd died, when his mother

had phoned him and he'd heard the choke in her voice, knowing the helicopter had gone down. He'd gotten there as fast as he could, been with the rescue team on the ground, seen the wreckage with his own eyes. At that moment, he'd known he had no other choice—he had to step up and take over the business just like his father had always wanted him to do. He'd lost so many good people in his life, but losing his father had never been something he'd thought about until it had happened.

Blake set the glass down again and went back to his desk. There were things he couldn't change, memories that would be with him forever, but the only thing that mattered right now was doing the best, given what life had served him. And Saffron would go a long way to helping make his life easier, making sure he secured the deals and the financial backing he needed to take the company to the next level. He needed a wife at his side, and she was the perfect match to him, could be the perfect, capable woman at his side…because they could enter into the relationship with a contract that gave them both exactly what they wanted.

He checked his phone. He'd half expected her to text or phone him after thinking about it, but then he'd also seen the determined look in her eyes, known that she was a fighter from the moment he'd heard about how she'd risen to the top. A ballerina who'd defied all odds and risen through the ranks to become one of New York's most respected dancers. It wasn't an easy path, and he doubted she would like having to do something she didn't want to do.

It was easy for him because it was a win-win situation. He would have a wife, a beautiful woman by his side who intrigued him, and they'd be divorced within the year. He didn't want a family, didn't want children, and he certainly didn't want an *actual* wife. They were things he'd dreamed of a decade ago, before the only person in his life he'd ever completely opened up to and been himself with had ripped out his heart and torn it to shreds. He wasn't ever going to put himself in that position again, just like he would never deceive a woman into marrying him without clearly setting out his terms.

Blake smiled and sat back down in the plush leather chair. Usually Saturdays were his favorite day to work, when the office was quiet and no one was around to bother him. But today his mind was wandering, and it was a stunning redhead on his mind that he couldn't stop thinking about. Whoever said he couldn't mix a little pleasure with business?

Saffron stared at the list she'd made, chewing on the end of her pen. It was a pretty short list. She leaned back into the sofa. There was no other way. Blake had just given her the perfect way to stay in the city, but being at the beck and call of a man like him was…scary. She shut her eyes, smiled when she thought about the night they'd shared.

She was going to do it. Saffy laughed out loud, feeling kind of crazy. Maybe she'd drunk too much the night before and it was still in her system, or maybe she was actually crazy, but she had to do it. She stood and flexed, grimaced when she tried to push up onto her toes and flex her muscles. The pain was tolerable, barely there compared to the excruciating pain she'd experienced at the time, but it still told her that things weren't right. That without some kind of miracle, she wouldn't be dancing anytime soon. But it didn't mean she couldn't keep her body strong and exercise.

She pulled on her trainers and laced them up, carefully stretching out her muscles just like her physical therapist had showed her. Her body was everything to her, and she had always taken care to stretch and warm up slowly, but now she had to treat it with even more care than ever before. Saffron rose up onto her toes, watched herself in the full-length mirror she had propped against a door. She held her arms out, tucked one leg up, bit down hard on her bottom lip as she flexed, forced herself to take the weight on first her good leg and then her bad.

No more. She released her lip from her teeth, expecting to taste blood she'd been biting so hard. The pain was there, was just as bad, and that meant she had to stop even though she would have loved to have tried to push through it.

Instead she grabbed her iPhone and stuck her earbuds in, planning on walking for an hour. She'd rather be running or dancing, but right now it was either walking and swimming or nothing at all. If she pushed herself too hard before she was ready, she wouldn't have the chance to make the same mistake again.

She checked the time before pulling the door shut behind her. She could walk for an hour or so, grab a coffee, then shower and head to Blake's house. Money was tight, which was another pro on her list, because if she married him then she'd be living with him. If she didn't, it would look like the sham it was, and she knew he wanted to keep it real. Besides, he'd told her as much—that she wouldn't have to worry about finances.

Right away she could cut almost all of her expenses, and her back account was already screaming out in the red after the cash she'd spent on all sorts of alternative therapies in conjunction with the specialist's advice.

Saffron Goldsmith. It sure had a ring to it. She glanced at her finger. Tomorrow there could be a diamond sparkling there, a real ring, a ring that would tell everyone that she was engaged. She hadn't exactly been the type to dream of a wedding when she was a girl—she'd been too focused on her career—but it still seemed weird.

She breathed in the fresh air once she was outside and started walking, slow at first. In a few hours' time she was going to be saying yes to a man she hardly knew, which meant this could very well be her last little glimpse of freedom before she had another human being to answer to.

CHAPTER FOUR

SAFFRON SHUFFLED HER bag from hand to hand, hating that her palms were so sweaty. She usually got nervous only before a performance, and even then it always passed as soon as she stepped on stage. This was a weird kind of nervousness that she hadn't felt before.

She took a big breath and squared her shoulders before pushing the button to Blake's apartment. He didn't say anything through the intercom, but the door clicked and she opened it and let herself in, going up in the elevator. When the metal doors opened, she found him leaning on the doorjamb, eyes searching hers out.

"I see you've brought a bag," he said, not taking his eyes from hers.

She kept her chin up, didn't want to appear weak. She felt like a prey animal having to stand up to a predator, standing her ground and being brave even when all she really wanted to do was cower.

"I have," she said back.

"Well, then, come on in. *Fiancée*."

Saffy gulped and stepped forward, walking straight past Blake and into the apartment. The apartment she lived in was like a shoe box in comparison, small enough to fit inside his five times over. The sprawling spaces reminded her more of places back home, where space wasn't at a premium.

"We need to establish some ground rules," she said, deciding to start how she wanted things to be, not wanting him to think he could boss her around.

"I'm all ears." His smile made him even more handsome, eyes twinkling as he watched her.

She wasn't going to let him rattle her with his gorgeous face. Or his gorgeous body. Although the way his arms were folded across his chest as he stared at her made his shirt strain across his biceps. Even worse was how chilled out he seemed about the whole thing.

"I want everything in writing," she began, setting down her bag and taking a seat on the same bar stool she'd been perched on earlier in the day. "I need to give up the lease on my place and know that I can live here while we're married, for at least a year. I'll continue to pay for my own personal things, but you need to cover all my medical expenses, including any new specialists I find. I'm doing this only because I think there's a chance I could find someone to help me if I have the funds."

He raised an eyebrow, one side of his mouth kicked up at the sides. "Is that all? Or do you have a full list of ransom details?"

Saffy cracked a smile. "That's it."

He walked toward her, and a shiver ran down her spine. She had the distinct feeling that he was the one in charge, even though he'd just agreed to her terms.

"I agree," he said simply. "In fact, I already have a contract for you to sign."

She laughed. "Your lawyer did up an agreement for you on a Saturday?"

His shrug told her this wasn't out of the ordinary. "We have him on a pretty good retainer."

"So just like that, you agree?" she asked. Once again, it seemed too good to be true. For her, anyway. "To funding me and promising that this will go on for at least a year?"

"Sure. I'll even let you keep the diamond ring as a separation gift when we part ways." He didn't look worried about anything. "I need this *marriage* to exist for at least a year, too, to make sure my investors sign on the dotted line and to ensure it doesn't look like a sham. Once I have everything in place, it won't matter whether I'm married or not."

His smile was wolfish now, and she wasn't sure if he was joking or not. "You actually mean it about the diamond?"

"Yes. We can pick something tomorrow." She watched as he picked up a thick envelope from the coffee table. "This is some light reading for you—sign when you're ready."

She nodded. "Okay."

"I'm going to leave you to read it, give you a bit of space. Maybe a couple of hours for you to look over the paper, sign, and take a walk around the apartment without me being here. Feel free to consult with your own attorney if you want to, but you'll find that there's nothing in there not spelled out in plain English."

"Sure." It all seemed so weird, so formal, but she'd made up her mind and she was going to do it. There was no backing out now, not unless he had something sneaky in the contract that took her by surprise.

"We'll head out to dinner to celebrate," he said, passing her the envelope and reaching for her face, touching a stray tendril of hair and then running his thumb down her cheek.

She stared into his dark eyes, wishing she knew more about the mysterious man she was about to marry.

"My mother is going to love you," he said with a chuckle before stepping backward.

If only he loved her. She quickly pushed the thought away, checked herself. Blake was virtually a stranger—the last thing he'd feel was love for her! Maybe she was suffering from some sort of Cinderella complex, because it felt as if Blake was saving her, had ridden to her rescue and was offering her everything.

The everything part was true, but he was no Prince Charming. She was kidding herself if she saw him as anything other than a man who needed something and was prepared to do whatever he had to in order to make that happen.

"Your mother'd better love me," she finally managed in reply.

"Did I mention I also have two interfering sisters?" he asked as he shrugged into a jacket.

Saffy groaned. "Don't say anything else, or you might find the envelope unopened and me long gone." If only she had the power to do that, wasn't trapped in a corner with no other options. She'd still be interested in getting to know him better, but she sure wouldn't be jumping headfirst into marriage.

Blake just grinned and held up a hand. "See you soon. Anything you don't eat?"

She shook her head. "Not really."

"Good, I'll make us a reservation for seven. See you later on."

She watched him go, sat silently, until he had his hand on the door.

"Wait!" she called.

Blake turned, eyebrows raised in question.

"Why don't you stay? Then we can just talk through the whole thing." She didn't actually want to be left alone, didn't want to sit in silence trying to figure out legal jargon on her own.

Blake's smile made her heart skip a beat. "I thought you'd never ask." He shrugged off his jacket as fast as he'd put it on only moments earlier, dropping down onto the sofa, eyes still on hers. "You read, I'll answer questions."

She slowly ripped the envelope open, scanned a little of the first page before leaning on the bar and looking at Blake.

"So obviously there's a prenup," she said.

"Yep," he said. "Standard terms, including that if there were any children born during our marriage the child would be cared for." He laughed. "Obviously that's not in either of our plans, though, right?"

Saffy laughed straight back. "Have you ever seen a pregnant ballerina?" She definitely wouldn't be getting a penny from Blake, because there was no way she was getting pregnant, no way she *could* get pregnant.

"Which leads to the next clause, to ensure that every precaution is made to ensure no children *can* be conceived, something about blah-blah it not being part of either of our plans."

"Phew. Glad we got that sorted out," she said with a giggle, liking that she made Blake laugh again. His smile lit up his face, and it made her feel more relaxed. "Please tell me you have it in writing that I get to keep whatever rock you put on my finger?"

"Why, yes. The bride may keep the ring after separation or divorce. It'll be all yours once you've done your duty."

"Uh-huh," she said, scanning through a few more pages, seeing that everything he was saying was listed. And then she reached the part about the marriage being real, blushed as she looked up to find Blake watching her.

"We must live as a real husband and wife," she forced herself to say out loud.

"You're so cute when your face goes all pink," he said, rising and crossing the room.

She looked down, hating that she was so reactive when it came to him.

"It only stipulates that we have to live together at all times…that we remain faithful and don't speak to the media." He brushed past her, moving into the kitchen. "Beyond that, it's up to you. I just don't want anyone, from colleagues to housekeepers, not to believe that our marriage is real."

"So there's nothing in here you're trying to hide from me? Everything's as you say?" she asked, scanning though the pages again, pleased it wasn't a long document.

"I'm not trying to deceive you. It goes on to say that all your medical costs, including elective consultations and treatments, are covered. You have my word."

Saffy knew she needed to just sign it, that it was the best thing for her right now. So long as she didn't let herself get emotionally involved. She signed at the end, taking a pen from the kitchen counter that she could reach. Then there was a single document, just one page that fluttered out from beneath. From what she could see it was a separate contract.

This one was stamped confidential. She scanned it, realizing that this was the divorce contract. It was crazy—on the one hand she was signing a prenup, and on the other she was confirming a divorce was to take place when they both agreed it should, but in no longer than three years. She was to file for divorce, stating irreconcilable differences. Saffron hesitated, thinking of how long her own parents had been happily married, but she quickly pushed those thoughts away. This wasn't a real marriage. It was a convenient relationship for both of them, and they were both adults. There were no children involved, which meant that the only people that could be harmed by what they were doing were the two of them. The only thing she would have to be embarrassed about would be lying to her parents, because it wasn't exactly something she could keep from them. She'd never deceived them before about anything, had never lied to anyone she cared for, but this was her one chance to dance again and when it was all over she'd tell them the truth.

Saffy signed the second document, looking up and realizing how silent Blake had been.

"All done."

He exhaled loudly. "Guess it's my turn then." He leaned over her, his musky cologne making her wish she'd held her breath instead of inhaling. And then it was done.

"Take a look around. I'll make us a drink," he said with a wink.

"Mind if I take a shower?" She was dying to stand under hot water, needing some time to think.

"It's your home now. You can do whatever you like."

Saffron gulped and left him in the kitchen, going first into Blake's bedroom, taking a look around the very masculine space. The bed was made—a dove-gray cover paired with white pillows and a smatter-ing of gray cushions against a black leather headboard. She'd already looked in his closet that morning and seen the bathroom, so instead of looking around more, she decided to just jump in the shower. Wash her hair and luxuriate in a bathroom that was bigger than her former bedroom, the floor-to-ceiling tiles reminding her of some of the lovely hotels she'd been fortunate to stay in when she'd been touring a few times. She went back out and got her suitcase, pleased to see that Blake was on the phone so she could just slip straight past him, putting her luggage in the middle of the bedroom.

Saffron stripped down, leaving her clothes in a puddle on the bathroom floor and turning the faucet on. The water was warm almost instantly, but she quickly walked out, naked, to retrieve her cosmetic bag that had her shampoo and conditioner in it. The shower was so good, the nozzle spraying so much water out and the steam feeling so good around her that she didn't want to get out. Instead she just shut her eyes and stood there, wishing she could stay there all day. Her hair was washed, the citrusy smell of her shampoo wafted around her, and all she had to do now was soap up her body...

"You need anything?"

Her eyes popped open and water blurred her gaze. Saffy quickly soaped herself and rinsed. Had he just walked in?

"Saffy? Do you still want that drink?" Blake's deep voice sent shivers down her spine, made her self-conscious with no clothes on.

"Just a sec!" she called back, hoping he'd stay in the bedroom and not actually walk on in.

Saffy turned the faucet off and jumped out, hurriedly reaching for a towel and rubbing it down her body then back up again. She was just about to dry her hair when his voice sounded out a whole lot closer.

"Hey. I wasn't sure if you'd heard me."

She wrapped the towel around herself and flung her hair back. Blake was standing in the doorway, looking straight in at her in the bathroom. Granted, she hadn't closed the door properly, but she hadn't expected him to walk in on her!

"Um, I just..." She stammered, knowing it was stupid being so body conscious, given the fact he'd seen her stripped bare less than twenty-four hours earlier, but she couldn't help it.

"Sorry, I didn't think you'd…" Blake was talking to her, but his eyes weren't on hers. They kept drifting down, and she held the towel a little tighter. "I can see this wasn't a good idea. I'll make you that drink."

"Uh, yeah, sure."

Blake was still watching her, but his eyes were trained on her face now. "This is weird, huh?"

She tucked the towel in at her breasts. "Um, yeah. Very weird."

Blake backed up. "I'll give you a minute to get, ah, dressed."

Saffy slipped to the floor in a puddle when he disappeared, her back against the glass of the shower. This was ridiculous! She was craving him, wanted him against her so she could kiss him all night, but at the same time she was a bundle of nerves about him even seeing her bare skin.

Maybe it was just because there was so much at stake now. Or maybe she just didn't want to admit that after being bored for so long after she'd had to quit dancing, she was finally feeling alive again and it scared her.

She picked herself up, dashed into the bedroom to get some clean underwear, and slipped on a big thick white terry cloth robe that she'd seen earlier in Blake's closet. She tied it around herself, liking how snuggly it was. It also covered up her body, which she thought might be a good idea in case Blake came back in. Saffy towel dried her hair, deciding to put on her makeup first and rub some moisturizer into her legs since she wanted to wear a dress out for dinner.

They weren't even married yet, and already she felt as if she'd lost control.

Blake sat on the sofa then jumped up and paced back toward the kitchen. He wasn't used to being so…rattled. Seeing Saffron in his bathroom, knowing exactly what was under the towel she'd had clasped to her slick wet body… He groaned. Maybe the marriage contract had been a bad idea. *A very bad idea.* She was supposed to make his life easier, and instead she was stopping him from thinking about anything else.

He glanced at the paperwork on the counter and then looked back toward his bedroom. It was all signed, which meant all that was left was for him to actually go down on bended knee for real so they had a story to tell everyone about their engagement.

Blake opened a bottle of wine, needing to take his mind off Saffron. There was something easy about what they'd agreed to, but for a man who'd sworn off marriage and family years ago, it was unsettling, too. He'd lived alone all his life unless he'd been working, when he'd been bunked down with his unit, and until Saffy he hadn't even brought a woman back to his apartment. And now he'd gone and broken all his rules, let someone get close to him, even though this time around he was in control of the situation. He was never going to be made a fool of again, never wanted to voluntarily feel hurt like he'd felt in the past, but so long as they both stuck to the rules…

"Dollar for them?"

Blake looked up, pulled from his thoughts. She was standing forlorn in the middle of the room, staring at him. Her hair was still damp, hanging loose and tumbling down over her shoulders, and she was wrapped in his robe. A robe he hardly ever wore, but his nonetheless. It was the second time he'd seen her in his clothes, and he was starting to more than like it.

"Nothing," he said, turning his body to face her. "Nothing important, anyway."

He watched as she shifted, looked uncomfortable. Blake had a feeling he wasn't going to like what she had to say.

"Is everything okay?"

She sighed loud enough for him to hear. "I don't know about you, but this whole thing just seems…"

"Unusual?" he suggested.

"Kind of uncomfortable," she said. "I don't know, I just don't know how to act around you. Last night I was me, or at least a version of me. But now…"

Saffron didn't seem to be able to finish her sentences, as though she was overly nervous. He stood but decided not to walk over to her, to keep some space between them instead of pushing her. The last thing he wanted to do was scare her off now.

"How about you finish getting ready for dinner," Blake said gently, trying his hardest to say the right thing. He had two sisters, so being around women and knowing what to say should be second nature to him, only for some reason it wasn't helping him right now. "Maybe we can take a step back, forget about the contract for a bit. We can pretend this is real if we like. Just actually date and try to ignore the marriage part to make it easier."

He had to fight a grin when her saw her lips kick up into a small smile.

"You really think we can go back? Trick ourselves that this is real?"

Not for a minute, because the only way he would ever propose to a woman was in a situation like this. "Sure we can," he said, trying to sound optimistic. "And if we can't do that, then there's no reason we can't be friends, enjoy the next year or so together." He knew that was a lie, too. Because there were plenty of ways they could enjoy being together, but strictly as friends wasn't what he had in mind right now or probably ever would with her.

Saffron turned and disappeared back into the bedroom, and within minutes he heard her hair dryer going. The beautiful ballerina would no doubt emerge a knockout, just like she'd looked last night.

He could be plenty of things to Saffron without having to open up, though. He had no interest in baring his soul to another human being, or reliving any of his past and opening up about anything. If he was in a real relationship, those things would be nonnegotiable, but with Saffron he could choose how much to divulge, how much of his true self to give. Because no matter what they pretended to the contrary, what they had was a contract. He'd fallen in love before, had his heart broken by someone he'd trusted more than anyone else. Fool him once, but never twice…

Blake took a sip of his wine and stared at the documents sitting in front of him.

It was done. He was officially about to become a married man.

Blake pulled his phone from his pocket and dialed his mother. He wanted to get it over and done with now, and he only had to phone one of the women in his family, because news spread like wildfire between his mom and sisters.

"Hello, darling."

"Mom," he said, clearing his throat. He could still hear Saffron's hair dryer, so he launched into what he had to say. "I know you've seen the pictures from this morning."

"Of course I've seen them. I'm just disappointed you've kept such an interesting woman hidden away from us."

If Saffron was really his fiancée-to-be, he would definitely be keeping her hidden from his family! "Mom, I should have told you, but we've just been lying low, getting to know each other without…"

"You don't have to explain yourself, sweetheart. I'm just happy that you're seeing such a fantastic young woman!"

"The girls have been googling her and showing you the results, haven't they." Blake had no doubt that they'd be all over the internet. There was no way his mother was that tuned in on her own; he'd bet they'd all been gossiping and flicking through web pages together.

"Of course!"

"Mom, I hope you're sitting down, because I have news."

"Blake! What is it?"

"I've asked Saffron to marry me."

"Girls!" His mother's screech forced him to pull the phone from his ear.

"I have to go, Mom. We're going out to dinner to celebrate, and I wanted to share the good news with you before anyone else found out."

"Could we join you? Meet this woman who's going to be my daughter-in-law?"

Blake could hear the excitement in his mother's voice, felt a pang of guilt for deceiving her. His mother got on his nerves at the best of times when it came to his personal life, and his sisters drove him crazy sometimes, but he loved them as fiercely as was humanly possible and lying to them made him feel worse than he'd expected.

"Let me take Saffron out tonight, just the two of us. I promised her something special to celebrate," Blake said. "But we'll see you soon, okay? I won't keep her hidden away forever."

He wondered if his mother would even take the bait, if she'd be instantly suspicious, but then she was used to him keeping his personal life private. And as far as he knew, she'd been shielded from what his dad had done, had never been exposed to the truth of the only serious relationship he'd ever had before. Never known how much pain her eldest son had been in.

When he finally got her off the phone and managed to end the call, he glanced up to see that Saffron was sitting on the sofa. He'd been so engrossed in talking with his mom, staring out the window as day became night, that he hadn't even heard the hair dryer switch off.

"You heard all that?" he asked.

Saffron shrugged, still flipping through a magazine. "Mmm, some of it." She looked up. "Do you feel kind of guilty?"

He nodded. "Yes, but it's for the best."

"I'm going to have to put on the performance of my life for your mother, aren't I?"

Blake didn't want to scare her. "Look, she'll be so excited to meet you that she'll probably do all the talking. The real performance will be when I have you by my side at business functions. That's why I'm marrying you."

She didn't look worried about it.

Blake unbuttoned his shirt and stretched out. "Give me a minute to take a shower."

He could feel her eyes on him as he walked, knew she was watching him. His problem was that he didn't know how to behave, how to act. He wanted to forget everything and just... He steeled his jaw. Sex should be the last thing on his mind. He wasn't doing this for sex—he could get that without being married—but looking at Saffron made him think of one thing and one thing only.

He left her on the sofa and stripped, showering then tucking his towel around his waist when he was finished. He went back into the bedroom adjoining the bath and pulled out a fresh shirt. He dressed quickly, ran his fingers through his hair and put some product in.

When he went back out, Saffron was still sitting on the sofa where he'd left her.

"Ready?" he asked, voice sounding gruff to his own ears.

She stood. "Yep, ready."

He walked ahead, opened the door and stood back for her to follow. Her dress was short, cute and covered in sequins. It showed off her toned, slim legs, and there was plenty of skin for him to admire up top, too. Her top was loose but with a low front, hair flowing down her back. It was the hair that got him more than the skin, though. Because when he'd first woken after their night together, it had been her hair touching his skin, falling over his chest. Her hair that he'd stroked.

"Where are we going?" she asked.

Blake cleared his throat. He was lucky she wasn't a mind reader. "Somewhere close. We can walk."

She shrugged her leather jacket on and they walked side by side, lights twinkling and showing the way along the road.

"I booked us in for Japanese. I'm thinking sushi, sashimi and teppanyaki."

Her smile was so innocent he wanted to reach for her and tug her closer. Maybe that was why he'd been drawn to her in the first place, not just because she was beautiful, but because there was something vulnerable about her. Something so unlike most of the women he met, a fragility that was tempered by how successful she'd been in her career.

"Are we sitting at the teppan table?" Saffron asked, her grin infectious. She was more excited child than grown seductress for a moment.

"We sure are. I thought you might like watching the food cooked in front of us."

She laughed. "You mean you thought it would be a good distraction when we ran out of things to talk about."

Blake held up his hands. "Guilty."

They walked in silence a bit longer.

"This is the weirdest one-night stand I've ever had," Blake confessed. "It's kind of awkward, in a we-wouldn't-usually-see-each-other-again kind of way. It's like extending the morning-after part."

Her laughter was gone but her eyes were still twinkling with humor. "I wasn't lying when I said I hadn't had a one-night stand before. So the whole awkward-morning-after thing is all new to me."

"Well, let me tell you it's normally over really fast and then you forget about it." He chuckled. "Although if I'm honest, you might have taken a little longer to forget about."

"So no serious girlfriends? No ex-wives I should know about?"

The last thing Blake wanted to do was talk about his ex. With anyone. "Let's just say that my mother never thought I'd settle down. I've always made that pretty clear."

"Right," she said as he guided her into a restaurant. It was only a few blocks away, so the walk had been brief. "So you've preferred to be the party bachelor boy all your life?"

He kept his anger in check. The last thing he wanted was for her to think the same way about him that everyone else seemed to in this city. "I was too busy with my career to be the party boy, even though everyone seems to forget how long I was away serving."

Saffron seemed confused when she looked up at him. "I'm getting the feeling that there's someone who broke your heart. Someone you really don't want to talk about."

"So let's not talk about it," Blake ground out. It wasn't as if he had a problem talking about the dates he'd had or the women he'd been with—it was just one particular woman who still made him want to slam his fist into a wall. It wasn't because he still had feelings for her; it was the way she'd hurt him, the way his father had been able to hurt him so easily through her. "I'm starving. You?"

He listened to Saffron sigh, knew the sound and that it meant the conversation wasn't over. His sisters made the same noise all the time. But to her credit she didn't bring it up again.

Saffron stayed silent as they were taken to their table, sitting down and starting to toy with the menu. Blake couldn't stand it.

"Look, I didn't mean to shut you down like that, but there are just some things I don't want to talk about."

"Me, too, but we kind of need to know everything about each other."

"What do you want me to say?" he muttered, keeping his voice low so they weren't overheard. "That I was in love once and she ripped my heart out and tore it to pieces?"

Saffron blinked at him, but the expression on her face hardly changed. "You know what? I think this whole thing was a bad idea."

She stood and pushed back her chair, reaching for her purse.

"Saffron, wait." He jumped up and reached for her, one hand over her arm. "I'm sorry." What was he doing flying off the handle like that?

Her eyes were swimming with what he guessed was hurt or maybe just frustration. "This is crazy. I can't be this desperate," she murmured.

"I'm an idiot, and this isn't crazy. It's…" He shrugged. "Convenient. And it's going to work out just fine for both of us."

She looked unsure still, and he ran his hand down her arm until he could stroke her palm and then link fingers with her. He seriously needed to work on his bedside manner.

"Please. Just give me a chance. I promise I'll be better behaved."

Saffron slowly sat down again. Blake would bet there were eyes watching them, but he didn't care. He quickly ordered them champagne, then turned his full attention to Saffron. He sucked back a breath and forced himself to say the words.

"I was in love once, you were right. With a woman I wanted to spend the rest of my life with," he admitted, knowing that if he didn't do something, he was going to end up losing the woman he needed right now. Talking about his past wasn't something Blake made a habit of, and for ten years he hadn't shared what had happened with another soul. He cleared his throat. "Her name was Bianca, and we'd been together for three years. We met in school, and we were joined at the hip from that day on. I thought it was true love, or as true love as it can be when you're barely eighteen and haven't had a load of experience. I would have done anything for her, she was the love of my life."

Saffron's eyes were wide as she listened. "What happened to her?"

"Well," Blake said, nodding his thanks when their champagne arrived and reaching for the glass stem to worry between his forefinger and thumb, "we were off to college and planning our future, and I proposed to her. She said yes, we had crazy good sex, like we always did, and barely three weeks later she disappeared."

"What do you mean, disappeared?"

Blake held up his glass to clink against hers, taking a long sip. He wasn't big on bubbles, but they were supposed to be celebrating their engagement, and Saffron had seemed to enjoy the Veuve Clicquot the night before.

"She broke my heart," he said simply, still feeling the sting of betrayal. Not so much from her as from his father. "I searched for her. My father looked on, and eventually he admitted that he'd offered her money to leave. To not go through with the engagement."

"Your dad did that to you? You must have hated her for taking it!"

"I hated them both," Blake said honestly. "I already disliked my father, knew the moment I confronted him that it had been his doing. He never thought she was good enough for me—her family was not highly regarded or wealthy enough. But she was my girlfriend, the most important person in my life, the one person I was myself with and loved unconditionally." Blake leaned back. "My dad told me he'd known all along she was using me for our money, and he said all he'd done was prove he was right, that he hadn't actually done anything wrong. His theory was that she'd be knocked up within months just to make sure she had me trapped, well and good." He grunted. "Turns out the old man was right after all, although it didn't make me hate him any less. It was a lesson in love for me, and right then and there I decided it was going to be my last."

Saffron stroked his hand, her arm covering the space between them as she touched him. "Do you still love her?"

Blake laughed, but even to him it sounded cruel, dark. "No, sweetheart, I don't still love her. It was a decade ago now, and all it did was show me that the only person in life I could trust was myself."

"Do you still believe that?" she asked, leaving her hand on his as she sipped her champagne. "After all this time?"

He shifted so their connection was lost, disturbed by how easy their touch was. "I trusted my men when

I was serving and the pilot sitting to my left, but I've never trusted another woman since."

She nodded, as if she understood, but he doubted she could. "I've only had one proper relationship."

"Hard to believe," he joked. "I could imagine you having suitors lined up for you backstage."

Her smile was cute, almost bashful. "It wasn't for lack of interest, but I just haven't had time. Work meant everything to me, right from when I was at high school, so it just never happened. Until I met Raf, a dancer I was paired with…"

Blake lifted his glass and she did the same. He waited for her to continue, not wanting to push. He knew how hard opening up was; he was still wondering what he'd just done by telling her about his past. But if they were going to make this work, make the next twelve months bearable, it had to be done.

"I fell hard for him, thought what we had was special. But he was sleeping with every other dancer behind my back. I felt stupid and ashamed, and when I ended it, he made me feel like I was the problem, not him." She shrugged, but the casual action didn't match the emotion he could see on her face, in her eyes. "I decided then and there I was better on my own, and I haven't let myself even come close to being hurt ever since."

"Here's to keeping our hearts safe," Blake said, holding up his glass.

"I'll drink to that," she agreed.

"You see, we're both proof that what we're doing is for the best."

"Yeah, maybe," Saffron muttered.

Blake wasn't sure he liked the fact he'd been so open, but he'd told her now and it wasn't as if he could take it back.

"Let's order, and no more talking about exes," Saffron said.

Blake couldn't have put it better if he'd tried.

CHAPTER FIVE

"So here we are again."

Saffy shivered, even though the apartment was perfectly warm. She'd already discarded her leather jacket, so her arms were bare, but she felt exposed, as if she was naked. Blake's words were having an effect on her all over again; the only difference was that tonight she'd only had one glass of champagne, so she couldn't even blame the alcohol.

"Blake, can I ask you something?"

She watched as he threw his jacket down over the sofa and crossed the room, reaching for a bottle of whiskey.

"Did you know who I was when we met last night?"

He was frowning when he looked up. "No. I was bored, and you were the most interesting person in the room."

She had no other choice but to believe him. Saffy was about to say something else when he turned with two tumblers and moved toward her. "I want to make it very clear that you deserve someone amazing one day, a man who'll love you like every decent woman deserves to be loved. I'm not that guy to any woman, but I will treat you well while we're under contract."

Even though she'd known exactly what she'd signed up for, had her eyes wide-open, the truth of their agreement still stung when he said it like that. It hurt that she was good enough for sex but not a real relationship, even though she understood his reasons. She was being sensitive, but knowing that didn't make it any easier to deal with.

She took the glass he passed her. "So is this to celebrate our twenty-four-hour anniversary?" she asked.

Blake's smile made his already perfect face appear even more handsome. It softened his features, made her yearn to touch him and be in his arms again.

"Here's to us," he said, voice silky smooth. "I never break a contract, and I never back down on what I say. So I'll put good money on it that you'll be up and dancing again once you've had access to the best specialists money can buy."

She wished she could be as optimistic, but she knew firsthand that no matter how much money she had behind her, it wouldn't be easy. It gave her a better chance, but it didn't guarantee anything.

"And all I have to do is be the model wife, right?" She was only half joking, although she had no intention of giving a Stepford wife a run for her money.

"Don't lie to me, play the part when I need you to and we can coexist happily."

They stood facing each other, and Saffron held up her glass, clinking it to his and sipping when he did. The liquor was like silk in her mouth and fire in her throat, and when she swallowed her eyes burned. She blinked the tears away, not liking how amused Blake looked.

He laughed. "*More* than happily."

"I won't lie to you," she said honestly. "All I want to do is dance, and if you can give me that back, then I'll owe you everything." It was the pure, raw truth. There wasn't much she wouldn't do to get her dream back, and even though she was so close to losing hope, she would not stop fighting until the bitter end.

"Come here," he said gently.

Saffy hesitated, waited, wasn't sure if she wanted to give in to the way she was feeling just yet. Until Blake reached for her. His fingers closed over her arm, then worked their way up, each movement sending shivers through her body that she couldn't control. Her mouth parted as he slid his body forward, moved into her space, his body just grazing hers.

"I don't want to presume anything. I mean, anything we do for real has to be your choice."

Saffy stared up at him, eventually nodded. "Uh-huh," she whispered back. She liked that he wasn't pushing her, that the ball was in her court.

"It's your choice," Blake said softly, his eyes full of concern. "I have a perfectly nice spare bedroom with its own bathroom that I haven't even showed you yet, or you could just move into my room with me. We'd need to keep most of your things in my room, though, because I don't want my housekeeper being suspicious, or anyone else who might come over."

Saffron gulped, her eyes fixed on his mouth, carefully pressing her lips to his when he kissed her again, slipping her free arm around his neck to draw him even closer. He was magnetic and handsome and sexy…and technically he was hers. And she did want to be in his room. Besides, her excuse could be that she didn't think the housekeeper would buy their marriage as real if the sheets in the spare room were always rumpled.

When Blake finally pulled back it was to down the rest of his whiskey and discard his glass, placing it on the coffee table and turning back to her with a smile that made her think of only one thing. For a girl who was always so focused and made the right decisions, she was ready to make a bad one all over again very quickly.

"What do you say, fiancée?" he asked.

Saffron bravely sipped her drink, the burn just as bad this time as the first. "I say I haven't had much to make me smile these last few months. Why not?"

Blake took her hand and led her to his room. They stopped only for him to flick off the lights, bathing the apartment in darkness. The only light was from the bedside lamps in his room.

What she was doing was so out of character, but for some crazy reason it felt all kinds of right. Thankfully the awkwardness of earlier had faded a little.

When they reached the bedroom, Blake stood in front of her, kissing her again before gently slipping the strap on her dress down and covering her bare shoulder with his mouth.

If only it was real. She couldn't help her thoughts, even as she tried to push them away. Part of it was real, surely, but the other part…he might not want to date her, or marry her, but his hands on her body and the look in his eyes told her that his desire for her was definitely real.

"Blake, I…" Saffron groaned, not wanting to ruin the moment but needing to.

"What is it?"

"I just, I need you to know why I said yes."

"Right now?" he asked, eyebrows raised.

She nodded, reaching for his hand. Suddenly she needed to tell him, had to get it off her chest so he understood who she was.

"Talk to me," Blake said, pulling her over to sit beside him.

Saffy sighed. "When I was younger, I had an operation for cervical cancer. I've known since I was nineteen that I couldn't have children, so I want you to know that's something you don't need to worry about with me." It wasn't something she usually shared, except with other women to encourage them to have regular checkups, but she wanted Blake to know. She knew how lucky she was to be alive, and it had been the only other time in her life that she'd had a break from dancing. Although that had been a very short one, and it hadn't had any impact on her career, as she'd simply been declared injured for a month.

"I'd always imagined my future with kids in it, once I'd fulfilled my career ambitions, but since that happened I've focused on dancing being my future. I need to dance, because it's the only part of my future I feel I can have any control over."

"I get it," he said. "I'm sorry for what you went through."

"Thanks," she whispered, dropping her head to his shoulder.

"So you can't ever get pregnant, or it's unlikely?"

"Can't ever," she said. "So you've got no worries with me. Besides, I couldn't ever dance the hours I need to and be a mom, so it's not that big a deal to me anymore." Saffron could joke about it now, but at the time she'd mourned the children she would never have, and even joking about it still stung deep down. She'd been too young at the time to want to be a mother then and there, but when the possibility was taken away it had still cut deep, because it had changed the future she'd imagined for herself. But then she'd simply thrown herself back into ballet and tried never to think about it again.

"Come here," Blake murmured in a low tone that sent a delicious shiver down her spine. He pulled her closer, facing her now.

She loved the gruff way he spoke to her, tugging her hard against him.

"Kiss me again," Saffron whispered, forcing herself to be bolder, to ask for what she wanted. She wanted to forget about everything she'd just told him now she'd gotten it off her chest.

Blake didn't disappoint. His lips crushed her, hands skimming her body as she looped her arms around his neck. As far as forgetting all her troubles, this was exactly what she needed. Short-term, fun, mind-blowing… the perfect interlude while she focused on her body and got back her strength.

As she used her toes to push herself forward, climb

up closer to him, she couldn't help the grin that took over her mouth.

"What?" Blake muttered.

"It didn't hurt," she whispered back, flexing her toes and her legs again.

"What? My kissing you?"

"My leg, stupid." Saffy didn't want to talk about it, but her lack of pain when she'd put that kind of pressure on her pointed toes had sent another kind of thrill through her.

Saffron woke and reached out in the bed. She didn't connect with anything. She sat up and searched in the dark for Blake, but the only thing she saw was a sliver of light coming through the door from the living room.

She stretched and got up, still tired but feeling restless. It was weird waking up in Blake's apartment, feeling like a visitor yet knowing she was here to stay. She pulled on the shirt he'd discarded earlier, wrapping it around herself and padding across the thick carpet. The light that she'd seen was a lamp in the far corner of the living room. The light was bathing part of the apartment in a soft light, and she could see the back of Blake's head. She guessed he might be working, unable to sleep and putting his time to good use, but when she reached him, bending down to run her hands down his bare chest from behind, she saw he was staring at a photograph.

"Oh," she stammered.

Blake jumped, dropping the photo.

"I'm sorry. I thought you'd be working, or reading a book or something. I just…"

Saffy didn't know what to say. She looked away as he brushed his knuckles against his eyes, knew that she'd been right in thinking she'd seen tears glinting there. She'd interrupted what was definitely supposed to be a private moment.

"Are you okay?" she asked.

"No," he ground out, sitting deeper into the buttoned leather armchair again and wearing only his boxers.

"Was that…?" She had been about to ask if it was his dad before his blank look silenced her.

"Go back to bed," he said.

Saffron watched him for a moment, thought about pushing the point, then did as he said. He might appear carefree, as though he was in control of everything in his life, but Blake had demons. She'd just seen them firsthand, sitting there in the dark alone, and she knew there was more to her husband-to-be than met the eye. He was acting the part of the happy bachelor, but she didn't believe it for a second.

And he wasn't alone. Tears pricked her eyes as she closed the bedroom door behind her and flopped back onto the bed, pulling the covers up and wishing it were her room and she wouldn't have to face him again. There was so much she had locked away, hidden so deep within herself that she would never open up to anyone. Only she was better at hiding it than Blake, because she'd just glimpsed his soul and his hurt looked a lot closer to the surface than she would ever let hers be.

She pulled a pillow closer, hugged it tight and buried her face into it. If only she could dance again, then everything would be okay. And she wouldn't have to stay here if things turned weird and she wanted out.

Blake felt terrible. He wanted to roar like a lion, yell about the injustices in the world and smash something. Slam his fist into a wall. But instead he stayed silent, lived with the guilt that was weighing on him like a ton of bricks, pushing down so hard on him that he could hardly breathe. He wasn't the angry type, which was why he was beating himself up so much right now.

It always happened at night. He'd go to sleep, fall into a deep slumber, then wake in the darkness, a tangle of sheets and sweat. If it wasn't his father, the helicopter wreckage, doubling over when he saw his brother's mangled body, it was the carnage he'd seen when serving. And that's why it affected him so badly. When he'd been away, he'd been able to compartmentalize the horrors, put his memories into a little box that he'd mostly managed to keep a lid on. But seeing his father and brother dead, like casualties of war among the pieces of metal covering the grass and strewn through trees, had changed everything. Because now images of war, memories he'd once buried, were merging with fresher ones, morphing into visions that often took hours to push away, if he could at all.

Blake steeled his jaw, glanced over at the whiskey bottle but refused to get up and reach for it. He'd gone to sleep with a beautiful woman in his arms, felt at peace, but when he'd woken, his demons had returned stronger than ever.

He shouldn't have shut her down like that, but then he shouldn't have done a lot of things. Maybe everything was just catching up with him. Maybe he should have found new investors, cashed in the business. He could have left his family in a great financial position, provided more for his mother and sisters than they'd ever need, but he was too loyal, too proud or maybe just too stubborn to give up what his family had built.

He shut his eyes, leaned back. His father had finally managed to turn him into the puppet he'd always wanted him to be, controlling him from the grave. All the years he'd fought with him, hated him, stood up to him, and now he just wished he was back. Then everything could go back to normal. That he could have his brother alive and kicking again. Because that was his biggest regret, falling out with the one person who'd have had his back no matter what, but whom he'd been too pigheaded to apologize to. Just another thing he'd never forgive himself for.

Blake doubted he'd find it easy to get back to sleep, and he also doubted Saffron would want him crawling in beside her. And what would he say to her? How could he even start to explain the way he felt? The things that haunted him were not things he wanted to burden anyone else with. Besides, they'd known each other less than two entire days. He wasn't about to crack his heart open and pour out all his feelings to her. Or to any woman. He'd already told her enough when he'd confessed about his ex.

Trouble was, he liked Saffron. And he hated the way he'd spoken to her. Because behaving like that only made him like his father, and he'd rather jump off a bridge than turn into even a shadow of his dad.

He picked up the photo of his father and brother he'd been holding, stared into his brother's eyes one last time, remembering his smile, how passionate he'd been about helicopters and taking over their dad's corner office one day. How good he'd been at schmoozing clients and smoothing over problems. Problems that peeved Blake, first world issues that drove him nuts. After what he'd seen, the things he'd had to do to protect his country, to serve, they weren't real problems in his eyes. Their clients, who were worth millions, hired and leased Goldsmith's helicopters and private planes. They'd made his family a whole lot of money, and his father had been well-known among New York's elite—*America's* elite. But that man, that smiling face that everyone else saw, wasn't the true man. Which might have been half the reason Blake had never been able to smile himself unless he truly meant it.

He tucked the photo into a book and switched off the lamp, staring out the window for a while. New York was the city that never slept, and he was starting to be the guy who never slept. The fatigue was killing him, but somehow a few strong coffees always seemed to give him enough energy to get through the following day. *Just.*

Saffron had a sick feeling in her stomach when she woke. She kept her eyes shut, this time hoping that Blake wouldn't be there when she slowly slid her fingers across the sheets. She peeked out, breathing a sigh of relief when she found she was alone. Again.

She got up, walked into the bathroom and retrieved the robe she'd left in there, tucking herself up in it. Then she summoned all the bravery she could and walked out, expecting to find Blake asleep on the sofa. Instead, she discovered him standing in the kitchen, bare chested and staring intently at something.

"Morning," she called out, surprised by how normal her voice sounded when she was a bundle of nerves.

Blake was frowning when he looked up, but his face quickly transformed into a smile when he saw her. "Morning."

She wasn't sure what else to say, whether they were just going to pretend nothing had happened or whether she should bring it up.

"I'm trying to make you breakfast," he said. "And for a guy who's used to ordering in, it's not as easy as it sounds."

She relaxed a little. "What are you making over there?"

His smile encouraged her to go a little closer. "Waffles again. I was given this fancy maker and I've never used it, so here goes."

Saffron laughed. "First of all, you don't need to keep feeding me. I'll never be a ballerina again if I keep eating with you." She was going to lean over the counter but decided to go around instead. "Second, you just whisk up the batter and pour it in. It ain't rocket science."

"You've making me feel like an idiot," he said with a chuckle. "I can fly a helicopter, but I can't use a whisk."

"You can?"

He gave her a quick sideways glance. "Yeah. It's what I've been doing most of my life."

Saffron tried to hide her surprise. Instead she leaned over and checked out the batter. "You're doing okay, just keep whisking until the lumps are out and give it a go."

Blake turned his attention to her, and she found it hard to read his expression.

"I'm not good at apologies, but I shouldn't have been such an idiot last night."

She appreciated he was trying to say he was sorry. "It's fine. I didn't mean to sneak up on you. I had no idea…"

He shook his head. "Let's just forget it. Okay?"

She nodded. "Okay."

There was something so magnetic about him, a feeling that pooled in her belly whenever she was with him. And seeing him standing in his jeans, bare chested with all his sinewy muscles on display, only reminded her all over again of how much fun she'd had in his bed. Even if she was still cautious after the way he'd reacted.

It was as though they were playing some silly cat-and-mouse game, only she didn't quite have a grasp of the rules yet.

She decided to make coffee instead of ogling his gorgeous body. "Coffee?" she asked, realizing she had no idea how he liked it.

"Love one. Black with one sugar."

Saffy busied herself, keeping her back turned even though she was still crazy aware of him. She got that he had issues, and she'd been so hurt last night, but they hardly knew each other and they were suddenly living together. It was never going to be easy.

"Here we go," she said, spinning around and just about slamming into him. She hadn't been expecting him to be just standing there.

"Thanks." He held out a hand to steady her, smiled down at her with his dreamy dark eyes. She really needed to get back to work! It wasn't like her to be so taken with a man, and she was blaming it on not having anything else to think about.

Blake didn't pull away immediately, and she held her breath, gazing back at him. She was also starting to blame not getting this sort of thing out of her system on when she was younger. The excitement of what they were doing felt forbidden because it was so different from her usual behavior.

She smelled something that didn't seem quite right. "I think your waffle is burning."

Blake spun around, sloshing his coffee and making her laugh. "All I had to do was wait for the green light to come on. Who could burn a freaking waffle?"

Saffy perched on the bar stool so she could watch him. "Just throw it out. The next one will be perfect."

He muttered something and did what she'd suggested. Her stomach rumbled as he poured more batter in.

"So what would a normal Sunday look like for you?" she asked.

"Honestly?" he said, hands flat on the counter as he leaned forward. "I'd probably be eating breakfast that

I'd ordered from downstairs, then I'd be heading in to the office for a bit. Maybe going to the gym. You?"

She watched as he removed the first waffle and put it on a plate. He pushed it along the counter and passed her the maple syrup.

"If I was dancing, I'd be there around ten. My breakfast would probably be a protein shake instead of something like this, because I'd be being a lot more careful with my weight!"

"So you always worked on a Sunday?" he asked.

She cut into the waffle, slicing the first heart-shaped piece apart. "We only had Mondays off, and even then I'd be doing something work related. Although I always tried to get a massage in the afternoon." A wave of nostalgia hit her, just like it always did when she talked about dancing. "Every other day of the week I'd be in the studio by ten, and I'd be dancing or doing dancing-related things until around seven each night, unless we were performing, and then it'd be closer to eleven."

Blake whistled. "I had no idea the hours were so long."

She grimaced. "It's a killer, especially when you first start, but I love it. I would do it until I was sixty if I could."

"So tell me what happened," he said, voice suddenly a whole lot gentler. "I can see how much it hurts for you to talk about."

"I want to talk about that as much as you want to open up to me," Saffy said honestly.

Blake flipped out another waffle, stayed silent, although it wasn't awkward this time. She ate a few mouthfuls of her waffle, loving the drizzle of maple syrup.

"This is great," she praised him.

He smiled and passed her another, even though she stuck her hand out to protest.

"No more!" she managed when she'd finished her mouthful.

Blake just grinned and kept cooking.

"We were performing *Swan Lake*, and I was the lead. It had been amazing, night after night of great reviews," Saffron told him, suddenly needing to get it all out, to just tell him and get it over with instead of keeping it all bottled up inside. "I've had a lot of problems with a form of arthritis since I was young, and I was probably pushing myself too hard. That night I ripped three ligaments in my leg, which was bad enough without the crippling arthritis in my knee."

Blake looked up at her but didn't say anything, and she didn't want him to. There was nothing he could say that would make it any better.

"When I was in the army, I flew helicopters every day, doing what I loved," he said in a quiet voice, not making eye contact, just staring at the waffle machine. "I'd butted heads with my dad for years, but I wasn't going to back down on doing what I was passionate about. I wanted to make a difference, and I wanted to do something that made me feel great. The types of helicopters I was flying, dropping Navy SEALs into remote locations, being part of the most incredible teams…" He paused. "It was the best job in the world."

Saffron forced herself to keep eating, knowing how

hard it was to share when every word felt so raw. Maybe that was why she was so drawn to Blake, because even though they were so different, they'd both lost what they loved. It wasn't a person they'd lost, but the pain was so real, so true, that Saffy felt every day as if her heart had been ripped out. She got it.

"Last night, you saw me looking at a photo of my dad." She listened to him take a deep, shaky breath. "And my brother."

"You lost them, didn't you?" she asked quietly.

He nodded. "Yeah, I did. And as much as I miss my brother, so bad, I feel like it was just one more way for my dad to force me into what he always wanted me to do. Another way for him to control me. I know it sounds stupid, but in the middle of the night that's all I can think about."

Saffron wanted to reach for him, but she didn't know if it was the right thing to do or not. When he joined her at the counter and poured syrup over his waffles, she turned to face him, coffee cup in hand.

"We just have to cope as best we can, right?" she said. "It's so hard to make a career from doing what you love, and when that gets taken away…"

"It's heartbreaking," he muttered. "But yeah, you've just got to grit your teeth and keep on going. What other choice do we have?"

They sat side by side and finished their breakfast, and Saffron rose to rinse the plates and put them in a dishwasher.

"What do you say we go ring shopping?" Blake asked, taking her by surprise.

She tried to hide her grin. Ring shopping sounded like a lot more fun than her usual Sunday afternoon, and she liked the idea of getting out of the apartment. "Give me an hour. A girl's got to look good for that kind of outing."

"You always look good."

Saffy paused, heard what Blake had muttered. She was going to say something, but her brain was blank. Instead she closed the dishwasher door and headed for the bathroom. When she got there, she did what she always did in the mornings, lifting her right leg high and placing it on the edge of the bathroom cabinetry to stretch out her muscles. The granite in Blake's bathroom was cold against her skin, but it felt nice and she let her body fall down, the burn of her muscles making her feel alive. She lifted up then down again before repeating the stretch on the other side, the movement as natural to her as brushing her teeth.

Once she was finished she stared back at her reflection, checked her posture. She would always be a dancer. Every fiber in her body told her it wasn't over yet, and this morning her determination to listen to that feeling was back tenfold.

CHAPTER SIX

"WHAT DO YOU THINK?" Blake asked as they walked through the door of the antique jeweler his mother had always favored.

Saffron's eyes seemed to twinkle when she looked up at him, holding his hand. He'd linked their fingers as they'd headed through the door, conscious of how they appeared together, and somehow it felt right. He was oddly comfortable around Saffron most of the time, more himself than he probably was around even his family. Maybe because he'd laid it all out on the line with her, been honest from the get-go because of the kind of relationship they were in.

"I was expecting Tiffany's," she said.

"We can go there if you want."

"No," she said, letting go of his hand to peer into a display cabinet. "I didn't say I didn't like it—it's amazing. Besides, beggars can't be choosers, right?"

He laughed and watched as she wandered around, smiling to the assistant when she came over.

"Can I help you?"

"Yes," Blake said. "I'm looking for something for my fiancée here. Something elegant."

They started to look, with the assistant showing them a few engagement rings.

"Sir, is there any price range I need to be mindful of?" she asked in a hushed tone.

Blake smiled, reaching out for Saffron. "No. Whatever she wants."

Saffron shot him a look, and he just raised an eyebrow and smiled back at her. He was enjoying the charade more than he'd expected to.

"How about this one?" Saffron asked, pointing to a solitaire diamond surrounded by smaller ones, with baguette diamonds on each side forming the band.

The ring was beautiful and no doubt expensive, but he admired the fact she hadn't just chosen the largest, since he'd already told her she could keep it when their charade was over.

"Try it on," he instructed.

When the assistant passed it over, he quickly grabbed it, changing his mind. "Let me," he said.

Saffron turned to face him, and he smiled as he dropped to one knee in the store. "Saffron, will you marry me?" he asked, wanting to see her smile, knowing it would make her happy even though they weren't marrying for real.

They had talked about marriage, about what they were doing, but he hadn't actually proposed to her. Until now.

She held out her hand, letting him slip the ring on. "Yes," she whispered, laughing at him.

The shop assistant clapped as Blake rose and dropped a gentle kiss to her lips, liking how soft and warm her mouth was against his. It wasn't as though kissing her was a hardship.

"We'll take it," he said when he finally pulled away, reminding himself that it wasn't real, no matter how good Saffron felt against him.

The lines between fact and fiction were blurring between them, or maybe they'd always been blurred. The attraction between them was real; he just had to remember that it couldn't become—*wouldn't* become—anything more. It wasn't part of his plan, the future he imagined for himself, and there was no way he'd ever want a wife or a family. The example his father had set for him was testament to that. Besides, there would never be a woman he could trust enough with his heart or his money, and if he couldn't truly be himself without trying to protect himself and his family's fortune, then he'd never marry for real.

Once they'd paid for the ring, they left the shop with it on her finger.

"Well, that wasn't too hard," he said as they walked hand in hand down the sidewalk.

"It's beautiful," she said.

"And it's yours," he replied.

Saffron laughed as she leaned into him, still holding his hand. "It feels weird. I'm so girly and excited over the bling, but then this whole thing isn't real. I feel like I'm living someone else's life."

"Ditto," he said. Only he'd felt like that well before Saffron had come along. Every day he felt as if he was playing a role, one that had been destined for his brother, and he hated it. Every single day, he hated it.

"When we get back, I'll give you my planner to take a flick through. Anything marked social you'll need to attend with me, and I'll let you know in advance of any client dinners if I want you to join me."

Saffron looked up from admiring her ring. "Good. And I'll let you know how I do searching for specialists and treatments. There's an acupuncturist who works with celebrities I'd love to get in with, so I might need you to make the appointment!"

"I'll issue you a credit card tomorrow," Blake said, unworried, thinking through the logistics of everything. "That way you can pay for any medical expenses. Sound okay?"

She grasped his hand even tighter, but Blake didn't mind. "You've given me hope again, Blake. Just keep me in New York and I'll be the best wife you could have wished for."

He didn't doubt it.

"Oh, did I mention I want you to quit your job?" He'd forgotten all about telling her, but the last thing he wanted was for her to go back to pouring coffee. She could be a resting ballerina, holed up in his apartment or doing whatever she wanted, but he didn't want her tied to a job that she didn't even care about. If she was his wife, he would keep her and make sure she was available whenever he needed her. Besides, no one would believe in their marriage if he let Saffron work for minimum wage.

"You're serious?" Saffron asked, giving him a look that made him realize she actually thought he was joking.

"Deadly," he replied. "No one would believe you were my wife if I let you slave away nine to five."

He saw a hesitant look pass over her face that made him wonder if she didn't like the idea of him keeping her. "Okay," she said. "I guess if you were my husband that's what you'd want."

Blake nodded, but her words jolted him. It was weird hearing her say the *husband* word, especially when in his mind he could still see his mother sobbing over something his father had done when he was only a child. They weren't blurry memories like so many of his childhood recollections, but a perfect snapshot of his mom crying that the man she'd married didn't deserve to be called her *husband*, the man who slammed the door and left her to cry.

He pushed the thoughts away and smiled down at the gorgeous redhead at his side. All the more reason to have a contract, to be clear up front about what he wanted.

Blake wasn't fit to be a real husband, didn't want that life. But he did want to be the one to step his family business into the future, wanted to make his family proud. Because if he wasn't so honorable, he'd have left and never looked back after the funeral, returning to the life he loved. Selfishly leaving everything behind to pursue his dreams, away from his family name and far away from New York. But that was the past now, and it wasn't something he could get back. *Ever.*

Oddly, he felt happier with Saffron at his side than he had for a long while. Or maybe it was just the promise of having her in his bed every night, and the fact he'd been honest with her about who he truly was.

"So this is the woman who got you all tied up in knots?" An elegant older woman with her hair pulled off her face stepped forward to collect Saffron's hand. Her palm was warm, and even though she screamed old New York money, her smile was genuine.

"Mom, I'd like you to meet Saffron," Blake said, coming to her rescue and slinging an arm around her so he could pull her back.

"It's great to meet you," Saffron said, training a smile. "I've heard so much about you."

His mother's smile was wry, and it reminded Saffron of Blake. "I can't say the same about you. My son has been very tight-lipped about the beautiful woman he's all set to marry."

"Nothing fancy," Blake cautioned, taking Saffy's hand and pulling her toward him. She sat down on the sofa beside him, careful to curl up close, keeping a hand on his thigh. "Just a simple wedding."

He glanced down at her, and she retreated with her hand. The heat in his gaze was making her uncomfortable. This might be fake, but their chemistry wasn't, which was why she wasn't finding it that hard to pretend.

"When you say nothing fancy…?" his mother asked.

"I mean we're heading down to the registry office and signing the paperwork. No big ceremony, no fuss. You can wait until the girls get married for a big wedding, because I want this completely under the radar."

His mother pursed her lips, but Saffron could see she didn't want to argue with him, or maybe she knew from experience that there was just no point.

"Saffron, I don't want to offend you, but I must bring up the delicate subject of a prenuptial agreement."

Blake laughed and Saffron leaned into him. She'd been prepared for this, would have thought it odd if any mother with their kind of fortune hadn't raised an eyebrow at how quickly they were getting married.

"Please, Mrs. Goldsmith, that's not something you have to worry about. I have no intention of taking anything from your son or your family, and we've already organized the paperwork." Saffron chuckled. "But don't think for a moment I'm going to let your son run my life. I intend on having my career back on track very quickly. As soon as I've given my body a chance to rest and recover, I'll be back with the New York Ballet Company."

His mother smiled and looked to Blake. "I like her."

Blake dropped a kiss into her hair. It was just a casual, sweet gesture, but the gentleness of his touch took her by surprise.

"She's the one."

Saffron felt guilty sitting there, smiling away and pretending to dote on this woman's son. She seemed like a nice person, and lying wasn't something that came naturally to her, even if she was putting on a good show of doing exactly that right now. She wondered what it would be like if this were real, if she were actually being welcomed into the family. Saffron could see that she'd enjoy Blake's mother's company, which only made her guilt pangs stronger.

"You do realize the tabloids will stop hounding you. Not to mention it'll be good for business," his mother mused, shrugging into her coat and collecting her purse as they watched. "We should hold an engagement party for our clients, let them see what a family man you're becoming. What do you think?"

Blake stood, and she kept hold of him as she rose, too. "I think that sounds like a great idea. How about you organize it?"

His mother's smile was wide. "Excellent."

"Actually, maybe we should just start an annual party for our guests, and we can announce our marriage at this inaugural one to keep it low-key." He knew whom he wanted to impress, but it wouldn't do any harm to invite all their important clients.

Saffron nodded, listening and playing the part of attentive fiancée. She was used to playing a role as a dancer, to being in character, which was probably why this seemed easy. Or maybe Blake was just easy to be around. If she'd had to pick the kind of man she'd want to marry one day, it could have been him. *Maybe.* Although from what he'd said, he had no intention of ever marrying for real, never wanted to settle down.

And that was fine by her. Once she was dancing again, she'd have no time for a husband anyway. Blake would be a distant memory, and hopefully a pleasant one.

"Please tell me you'll invite me to the ceremony," his mother said as they walked out her door.

"Maybe," Blake answered. "Let's see if Saffron survives meeting my sisters first. She might run for the hills before I get her to sign on the dotted line."

Blake laughed and she forced a chuckle. If only his mother knew that she'd already well and truly signed on the dotted line. She was bound to marry Blake, which meant they were as good as husband and wife already. Besides, they'd already decided that they were going to get married in secret as soon as the license came through.

CHAPTER SEVEN

SAFFRON WAS SMILING, and even though her happiness wasn't forced, she wasn't finding it easy to look happy. What was she doing? Blake was treating her like his actual wife, and aside from when he woke up in hot sweats during the night and didn't want to talk about it, everything seemed…good. *Real.* Not that she was under any illusions, but still, it was weird.

"Come on, let's go," Blake said, kissing her on the lips and holding their joined hands in the air. "You were great tonight."

"You sound like my choreographer," she said with a laugh, still smiling as the crowd watched them. She was well used to being the center of attention, and far from feeling unusual having her every move watched just because she was on a man's arm, she was getting a kick out of it. Usually she basked in the attention, full of pride that so many people were enjoying her creative outlet, a performance she'd put hours of her time, not to mention sweat and sometimes blood, into. This time she felt like an actress, and for some reason it didn't feel any less satisfying. "Or maybe my cheerleader."

"You're brilliant, has anyone ever told you that?"

Blake swept her into his arms and out of the room. She was starting to get the feeling that he was enjoying the performance as much as she'd enjoyed putting it on.

Saffron didn't want their conversation to turn around to her dancing, so she let it go and didn't answer. They headed straight outside and into the waiting town car.

"I think they bought it," she said.

Blake leaned over and kissed her, his lips familiar to her now yet still making her body tingle. It would have been a much easier arrangement if they hadn't started out by being intimate, although given the way her body reacted to him, she was starting to wonder if they could ever have been platonic.

"I have some key accounts that have always referred to my dad every time we met, gone on about the roots of the company being a family business and questioning my commitment, or at least that's what it's seemed like," Blake said, settling back into the leather seat. "I don't know if a rival was trying to get to them and spinning rubbish, or if it was just the reputation they thought I had, but things felt fragile there for a little while. Marrying you has made all that go away, and after tonight, man. You seriously wowed my big investor. I definitely believe you can be my little star for the next while."

"So it's been worth it for you already?" Saffron asked.

He grinned. "Yes. You?"

"You've given me access to medical professionals I'd never have been able to afford to consult with," she said honestly. "And I'm still here. I still have a shot.

So yeah." Saffron laughed. "Marrying you hasn't been half-bad!"

The car ride was only short, and soon they were heading up to their apartment. It already felt like home for Saffron after two short weeks, or as home as anything ever felt to her. She wasn't used to spending a lot of time wherever she lived, and she'd been living out of a suitcase on and off for years. But she had some photos up, Blake had given up half his wardrobe space to her and her perfume lingered when she walked into their room.

"I'm just going to respond to some work emails. I'll be in bed soon."

Saffy undressed and put on a nightie, then padded into the bathroom to take her makeup off. She never took the luxurious space for granted, with its floor-to-ceiling tiles and beautiful fittings, and the oversize fluffy towels were her idea of heaven. Especially since he had the housekeeper come in twice a week, so she didn't even have to lift a finger to keep them that way.

The apartment was silent except for the low hum of the television—she was used to Blake having it on whenever he sat up and worked late, which was most nights. She lowered herself to the ground, relaxed into the splits and dropped her body down low, covering first one leg and then the other. Once she was done stretching, she stood and raised up, on tiptoe, smiling to herself as she leaned to each side, reached up high, before doing a little turn. The acupuncture had definitely helped, and even though she could have kept going until she collapsed, she was going to follow her new specialist's orders and only stretch her muscles like that for five minutes each evening and morning.

Still smiling, she curled up beneath the covers and flicked through a magazine before turning off the bedside lamp and closing her eyes. She was going to wait up for him, but they'd had late night after late night and…

Saffron woke up with a fright, sitting bolt upright, heart racing.

"No!"

She blinked in the darkness, eyes slowly adjusting, realizing that it was Blake who'd woken her. She instinctively pulled back, putting some space between them.

"Blake," she said, loudly, forcing her voice. "Blake!"

He groaned but didn't wake, pulled the sheets tighter around himself, thrashing out.

"Blake!"

His eyes opened, a flash of brightness that scared her for a moment until they locked on her. He sat up, disheveled and disoriented looking.

"Saffy?" His voice was hoarse as he pushed the covers down.

"You were dreaming. Are you okay?" she asked, hesitant. She didn't want to push him—they had a good thing going, and that didn't involve asking too many personal questions, going too deep, unless they had to.

"Same thing every time." Blake sighed. "Every single time."

Saffron tucked her knees up to her chin. "Your dad?" she asked.

Blake flicked his bedside lamp on. "Yeah. Always

him. Always a weird, I don't know, collage of memories, I guess. Just a jumble of things all mashed together."

"Do you still wish you were serving?" she asked. It was a question that had been on her lips all week, wanting to ask but not knowing if he'd want to talk to her. "That you could go back, even though you have these dreams?"

"Yeah," he said, running his fingers through his hair, shutting his eyes as he leaned back into the headboard. "Or maybe I don't. I don't know. All I know is that I miss flying, miss having my own identity that isn't tied to my family. As hard as it was, I still miss it, want it."

"I'm not sure what would be harder—having a dream and never turning it into reality, or the feeling of having that dream snatched away when you've already tasted the reality of it." Saffron reached for Blake, her fingers crawling the space between them until they connected with his. At least they knew what it felt like, understood what the other had been through on a level that no one else could.

"Having it taken away," he replied, squeezing her fingers back. "Definitely having it taken away."

"Or maybe we wouldn't have the same fire burning in us if we hadn't tasted that reality, that dream," she whispered. "Maybe we're still the lucky ones, we just can't see it."

"Maybe." He groaned, and she wasn't sure if it was from pain or the subject matter.

"Tell me what it was like, what you loved about it," she asked, suddenly wide-awake, not wanting to go back to sleep if he wanted to open up to her, to talk.

"One day," he said. "One day I'll tell you all about it. About the kick I got every time I put a Black Hawk up in the air or took a unit to safety in a Chinook. But not right now. I need some rest."

She knew he had issues, that whatever was troubling him needed to be dealt with, but as he kept reminding her, it wasn't her problem. She wasn't his real wife. She was more like a live-in mistress with extra benefits.

His problems were his. Her problems were hers. A year or two of fun. A year or two of great sex and parties. One year or maybe more to get her career back on track and have fun while she tried to find her way back to the top. It sure beat going home to serve coffee for the rest of her life at a diner and wishing for what she didn't have. At least this way, what she'd lost still felt as if it was within arm's reach. What she craved so badly was still a possibility instead of simply a memory of what could have been.

CHAPTER EIGHT

Three months later

SAFFRON SMILED UP at Blake, expertly running her fingers down his dinner jacket–clad arm. It wasn't hard to pretend she adored him, but the weird thing was reminding herself all the time that it wasn't *real*. They slept in the same bed, they went to parties and functions, and they put on a perfect show of being a real couple. Which they kind of were. Pity he was so darn irresistible.

A waiter passed and she took a glass of champagne. She held it for a while, listening to Blake talk business, before raising the glass to her lips. She went to sip but then recoiled as the bubbles hit her tongue.

"Excuse me," she said, stepping away from Blake quickly and scanning for the restroom. Bile rose in her throat, and she forced it down.

"Are you okay?" Blake's dark brown eyes met hers, concern etched on his face. So far she'd never let him down once, but this time she needed to bolt. Fast.

Saffy just nodded and hurried as fast as her high

heels would let her. Thankfully her leg was feeling great and she hadn't had any problems with her knee, so she was able to move fast. Otherwise she'd have been vomiting in the nearest corner!

She left her glass on a ledge in the bathroom and only just made it to a stall, holding her hair back as she threw up into the toilet. Her body felt burning hot then chilled, sweat beading across her forehead before her skin turned cold. What on earth had she eaten? Or had she caught the stomach flu?

"You okay in there, sweetheart?" A kind voice sounded out.

Saffron hadn't even noticed anyone else. She'd been so desperate not to be sick out in the open that she'd just hurried straight on through. "Um, I think so," she managed to say back, trying to hold down everything else in her stomach, if there was even anything else left.

"You don't sound drunk, and you didn't look drunk, so either you've eaten something bad or you've got a little one on the way. Am I right?"

Saffron laughed. "Has to be bad food." Another wave of nausea hit, and she leaned forward again, trying hard to hold it down and failing.

The woman sounded closer this time when she spoke. "You're sure it's not a baby?"

Saffron sighed and leaned against the wall of the stall. Usually she was grossed out by any kind of public toilet, but the cool felt nice against her body when she pushed back, and it was a pretty posh tiled bathroom with fancy lights and wallpaper. She hoped it was clean. Besides, she didn't have any other choice.

"Can't be a baby," she replied with a sigh. "Not for me." Saffron finally opened the door and came face to a face with a nice-looking lady dressed in a beautiful taffeta gown. Her gray hair was pulled up into an elegant do.

"I was sick as a dog when I had my boys. Thin as a whippet so nobody knew I was pregnant, and I threw up for months."

Saffron appreciated her concern, and it was nice to have someone to take her mind off how ill she felt. The nausea had passed now, only returning when she thought about the champagne she'd almost drunk. She usually had a cast-iron stomach, so it seemed strange.

"Saffy, you in here?" Blake's deep voice boomed through the restroom.

She cleared her throat. "Just a sec."

"I'll tell your man you're not well. You take your time."

Saffy pulled herself together, taking a mint from her purse and then walking over to the mirrors to check her face. She looked pale and gaunt, but the sick feeling had passed. After washing her hands, she went to find Blake.

"What's wrong?"

His eyes were searching her face, and she had to look away. The hardest part about being with Blake was trying not to fall in love with the man. They'd felt like a real team when she'd been at his side, meeting his new investor and his wife; when Blake had secured the investment, she'd fist pumped and squealed as if it was her deal that had come together!

"I started feeling all weird, sweats and nausea. I think I ate something bad."

He frowned and put his arm around her as they walked back out. "Let's head home."

"No, you stay," she insisted, looking away when a waiter passed. She couldn't stand the thought of alcohol or food. "Schmooze your clients, do your work and let me go. You don't need me here—they've already seen you're a doting husband if that's what you're worried about."

She'd meant to sound positive, but instead it had come out all wrong.

"Just because this isn't, ah—" he cleared his throat, frowning again "—doesn't mean I don't care about you."

Saffy squeezed his hand. "I know. I just meant that I've already fulfilled my purpose." She felt sick again and held his hand tight, waiting for it to pass. "I really have to go."

Blake let go of her hand and pulled out his phone. "Make your way out. I'll call the driver now and have him waiting for you."

Saffron smiled her thanks and hurried through the throng of people toward the exit. She kept her head down, not wanting to make eye contact and have to talk to anyone. She just wanted to undress and crawl into bed.

As promised the car was there within minutes of her walking outside, although she would have been happy to stand and gulp in the cold air for longer. She got in the vehicle and slumped on the backseat. As they headed for home she stared out the window, her hand resting on her stomach in an effort to calm it. It wasn't working, but she kept it there anyway.

Pregnant. She smiled despite how shaky she felt. There was no way she could be pregnant. The specialist had made it so clear to her, and she'd looked into freezing her eggs before having it done, but the success rates of thawing those frozen eggs hadn't seemed worth it to her, not when she'd been so short of money.

Pregnant. Was there even a slim chance? She'd only been with Blake that one time without protection, and if her chances of getting pregnant were statistically zero, surely it couldn't have happened...

"Pull over, please!" she cried as they passed a convenience store.

The driver did as she asked, pulling over farther up the block when it was safe and there was space to park.

"I'll only be a minute," she said, jumping out and rushing back. She entered the store and found the section with women's things, reaching for the first pregnancy test she could find. There were two types, so she grabbed the other one as well, hands shaking so hard she had to concentrate on getting her card out to pay.

"Thanks," she mumbled as she took her things and raced back to the car. It was only a short drive, but it seemed to take forever. When they pulled up outside she raced in, forgetting how ill she'd been. Saffy headed for the bathroom, not bothering to turn any lights on except the one she needed to. The rest of the apartment was dark, except for a couple of lamps, but she didn't care. All she wanted was to do the test so she could be sure that there was absolutely no chance of her being pregnant.

Saffy hovered above the toilet and held the stick out, counting to three before retrieving it. She put the cap back on it and placed it on the counter, staring at the tiny screen that would show one line if she wasn't pregnant. That line showed, strongly, and as she held her breath another faint line appeared, slowly but surely. *Two blue lines.* Nausea washed over her again, but this time she was sure it was from nerves. She couldn't be pregnant!

She paced around the bathroom for a few minutes then ripped open the wrapper on the other test. This one was more expensive, so she was sure it would be more accurate.

She'd only just been, but she forced herself to go again, to do just enough so that the test would work. And then she played the waiting game again, staring at the slightly bigger screen.

Pregnant. Just one word. One simple word.

And it changed everything.

CHAPTER NINE

SAFFRON CLUTCHED HER bag tight and walked back out onto the street. The day was warm and the sun was hot on her bare arms, but she hardly noticed. She just wanted to get to the studio where she'd been training.

Pregnant. She'd known the two home tests the night before couldn't be wrong, but still. After so many years of believing she could never be a mom, it was almost impossible to comprehend. And what was she going to tell Blake? Saffy groaned and held her bag tighter, scared of what was happening inside her, how much everything was changing.

She felt a vibration against her and realized it was her phone. She pulled it out, glancing at the screen and expecting it to be Blake, not ready to talk to him yet. But it was a number she didn't recognize.

She inhaled and stopped walking. "Hello, Saffron speaking."

"Saffron, it's Benjamin. From NYC Ballet."

Her heart just about stopped beating. "Oh, hi," she stammered.

"I wanted to know how you are. Whether you've had any success with your recovery?"

Saffy flexed her foot, something she always did whenever she thought about her injury or someone asked her about it. She couldn't help but smile when she did it without pain. "I'm doing really well. I've seen some great physical therapists, an acupuncturist and a specialist doctor, and I think I'm ready to ease back into dancing again."

It was a half lie, because the amazing people she'd been seeing had all told her to simply start exercising more, to slowly start dancing ten or so minutes a day after running through a series of stretches and strapping her leg. To try taking a few dance classes but not specifically ballet, and they'd been making her consume all types of natural wonder products in conjunction with the medicines the doctor had prescribed. The specialist had been incredibly helpful, referring her to the almost-impossible-to-get-in-with therapist in the first place. She'd already enrolled in modern dance, just to start using her muscles, but only ballet was going to fill the void she felt every day.

"That's fabulous news, darling," Benjamin said. "We all thought you might have gotten married and forgotten about us."

"Never," Saffron murmured. "Dance will always be the most important thing in my life."

He laughed. "Just don't let your new husband hear you talk like that!"

Saffron felt as though she was walking on ice, just teetering and waiting. Why had he phoned her? She was too scared to ask. There had to be a reason for a call to just come out of the blue after so long with no contact.

"Darling, the purpose of my call is to see if we can book you. It's not for another four months, but it's you we need." He cleared his throat. "Can you be ready by then? Are you planning on making a comeback?"

Saffy went burning hot then freezing cold, as if her body was going into shock. Four months? Her hand went instinctively to her stomach. In four months she was going to have a bump. A *very* big bump. If she had this baby, there was no way she'd be able to dance then, no matter how well her leg was holding out.

"Why me?" she asked.

"It's for Pierre. He's retiring from the company, and he's requested you as the dancer for his final show. It's just a one-off performance for him, to thank him for all the years he's put into our choreography, but it's you and only you he wants."

Saffron gulped. Pierre was the reason she'd been the lead in *Swan Lake*. Pierre had given her that big break, had believed in her and what her future could hold. Pierre was the key to her getting back on stage, because only he would request her and not take no for an answer.

"Can I have some time to think about it?" Saffron said, stalling, not ready to say no when she didn't even know what she was going to do, what the next few months of her life would even look like. "I'll need to talk to my physical therapist and specialist, make sure they don't think it's too soon. I don't want to risk injury again." She shook her head, wondering where the words were coming from. She wasn't even over her old injury yet!

"We love you here, Saffron," he said. "Take the week

to think about it and let me know. If you do this, you'll be officially invited back to join the company. You were one of Pierre's best principal dancers, darling. We want you back home where you belong, and I just don't believe you're done yet."

Tears welled in Saffy's eyes. It was the phone call she'd been dreaming of, her big chance. But even without the baby, she had no idea whether she'd ever be strong enough to be a principal again, not until she started training and saw firsthand if her leg tolerated the punishing hours.

"I'd do anything to be back. Trust me," she said, voice as shaky as her hands as she gripped her phone.

When she hung up, all she felt was emptiness. What she'd wanted was so close she could almost taste it, almost within her grasp. But then once upon a time, being a mother had seemed important, when the idea of being a parent had been taken from her. She'd been horrified at the time that she would never have children, something she'd slowly forgotten about the more she'd progressed in her career. But now... She slid her hand back down over her belly, the action seemingly normal now. She was suddenly protective of the little being growing inside her, even though she wasn't sure how she felt about the whole thing. *She was pregnant.*

She reached the studio and entered, pleased there was only one other dancer there running through a routine. She stripped down to her leotard and tights, carefully putting on her ballet shoes and looking down at her legs. She warmed up by stretching out slowly, trying not to think, trying to just focus on what she was about to do, on dance. She lifted a leg carefully into the air, stretched up, rose up then down, using the barre, feeling her muscles as they pulled then released. When she had both feet back on the ground, she stretched some more before leaving the barre to dance a quick routine, to cross the room once, dancing like she used to, dancing in a way that used to come as naturally as breathing to her.

And it still did. Breathless but not in pain, Saffy stopped, knew she had to. If she had it her way she would dance all day, but she wasn't ready. Not physically.

After warming down, stretching some more, she slipped her yoga pants back on and then her sweater, collecting her bag and heading back out the door. Saffy set off at a walk, heading for the apartment, needing to face reality. Either she told Blake and he would deal with it, let her make her own decision about what to do, or she never let him find out. He didn't want to be a dad—he'd made that clear when they'd signed the marriage contract—and she'd told him outright that her getting pregnant was impossible. He'd just think she was a liar, that she'd purposely deceived him, set out to fool him. This didn't have to be his problem; it was something she could deal with on her own. If she wanted this baby, she could do it. Trouble was, she'd signed a marriage contract, and she knew Blake only had one of the deals together that he'd needed her for, and she doubted he'd want to let her out of the contract so easily. Not until he had what he needed from their arrangement.

She let herself in and went straight for the kitchen,

pouring a big glass of water and drinking it down. Then she peeled a banana and sat in silence, eating.

"Saffy?"

She jumped, choking on her mouthful. What was Blake doing home?

"Blake?" Saffy walked toward the bedroom. "Where are you?"

"In bed. I'm sick," he said.

She peeked in. "I had no idea you were here."

"I think I've got the stomach flu that you had," Blake said, groaning. "Where have you been?"

It was an innocent question, but it felt like an interrogation all of a sudden. Because for once she'd been somewhere she shouldn't have. "Um, just the doctor," she told him, going closer and sitting down on the bed beside him, reaching for his hand. It was warm, his skin comforting against hers. "I've been thinking about going back to the studio some more, actually pushing my leg a little to see how I do, see if I'm ready to go back."

His smile was kind, and he let go of her hand to prop himself up on the pillows. They'd developed a relationship that went way beyond a simple contract, an easiness that she would miss. Blake was complicated yet beautiful, a man who was straight up about what he wanted, but one who was hiding a power load of pain. He'd shared so little with her about how he truly felt, had just scratched the surface and told her the bare bones of his past, but she knew how much he hurt, how hard it was for him to trust. And now she had to figure out how to tell him what had happened, make him believe that she hadn't deceived him.

"What happened?" he asked, staring into her eyes like he always did and making her feel as if she was the only person in the room, as though what they had was genuine. As real as it felt sometimes.

Heat started to rise up her body, flooding her cheeks. This time she had to lie. "I had a phone call. An opportunity."

"To dance again?" he asked.

Saffy nodded. "Yes. In four months' time, if I'm up to it."

"That's great news," Blake said with a smile. "I'd offer to celebrate with you, but…"

She held up her hand and rose. "I'll let you rest."

Saffron was relieved to walk away and not have to talk more, because she had a lot of thinking to do. More than that, she needed to make a decision. The doctor had been very diplomatic in explaining all her options, but the thought of anything other than protecting the growing baby inside her made her want to be physically sick. But what if this was her one and only chance to dance again? What if this was the last time in her life she'd be offered an opportunity like this? What if…

Saffy bit down hard on her lip. *Be a mother.* She collapsed onto the sofa, finding it hard to breathe. *Or be a dancer.*

She dug her nails into the cushion beside her. *Run away from Blake and never look back.*

Right now, it was sounding like the best option. Or maybe it was feeling like her only option. She couldn't give up this baby, which meant she couldn't be a dancer, not now, maybe not ever, because Pierre would be gone and then she'd have to try to impress a new choreographer who didn't know or love her. Besides, the two didn't go hand in hand, not with the hours she'd have to dedicate to dancing again *if* her body ever let her. And there was no way she could dance that punishing routine at all during pregnancy, not a chance.

Blake checked his watch and frowned at the time. It was unusual for Saffron to be so late. He was going to wait another five minutes but changed his mind, leaving a tip on the table and simply walking out. He wasn't that hungry anyway, and he wanted to make sure she was okay.

He dialed her number and it went straight to voice mail. Again.

Blake left a message this time. "Hey Saffy, it's me. We had a dinner reservation at seven—did you forget? I'm on the way home now. We can always order something in. Call me."

It didn't take him long to make it back, and when he let himself in, something felt wrong.

"Saffy?" he called. When she didn't answer he headed straight for the bedroom. Maybe she was in the shower. "Saffron?"

And then he stopped. There was no five-book-high pile on her bedside table, no perfume bottles or jewelry scattered on the buffet beneath the big mirror. He walked faster into the bathroom. No makeup, no hairspray, no deliciously citrus smell.

Blake stopped dead in front of the closet, not hesitating to yank the doors open and stare inside. The empty space hit him like a fist to his gut. What was going on?

Saffy was gone. She was gone as though she'd never existed in the first place, as if she'd been a figment of his imagination.

Just like Bianca. Just like the day he'd found their little apartment empty all those years ago.

He walked backward until his legs touched the bed, and he dropped down on to it, not noticing the cream envelope until he was sitting. He slipped his finger beneath the seal and plucked out the single piece of paper inside, unfolding it and instantly recognizing Saffron's handwriting.

Blake,
I left like this because I didn't want to look you in the eye and tell you the truth myself. The last few months might have been an arrangement, but I feel closer to you than I ever really have to any other person before. And that's why I didn't want to see the distrust in your eyes when you found out that I was pregnant. You deserved to know, but you don't owe me anything. This baby suddenly means the world to me, and I'll do everything I can to make this little person be loved. I'm sorry I left when I was supposed to stay with you as your wife for longer, but staying would have only made things more complicated. You made it clear that you never wanted a family, or a real wife, and the last thing I want to do is trap you into something else you don't want.

I've kept the ring only because you told me it was mine, and it'll help tide me over until I can work again.

I'm sorry things had to end this way, and I want you to know that you'll always hold a special place in my heart. Don't try to find me, just let me go.
Saffron

What the... Blake screwed up the letter into a tight ball and threw it across the room. She was *pregnant*?

He rose and stormed into the kitchen, wrapping his hand around a bottle of whiskey and pouring a big splash into a glass. He knocked it straight back.

Pregnant? How? They'd always used protection. Besides, she'd told him she couldn't have children, that it wasn't possible, that...*one night*. There had been that one night, months ago. Before the contract. Before he'd proposed. Before they'd gotten married.

Maybe this had been her plan all along, to lure him in and have a child, just like countless women had done to rich men in the past. Maybe she'd played him right from that first night. Maybe she was no better than the first woman who'd scorned him.

Damn it! They'd had an agreement, a contract, and he'd be darned if he was going to let her walk out on that and have a baby. A baby that he'd have no choice but to support, to see, to know. A baby he didn't want. A baby that shouldn't even exist. The one thing in life he'd been certain about for the past decade was that he didn't want a woman in his life and he didn't want a family. Ever. The one and only time he'd slipped up, put his trust in someone else… Blake poured himself another nip, swallowing it down fast before pushing the glass away. He'd had enough, needed to keep his head, to stay in control.

Saffron might be able to run, but he wasn't going to let her hide. Not with his baby on board. Not now, and not ever.

He sat in silence, in the dark. She was supposed to be dancing again, or had that been a lie? She was supposed to be in contention for a role that she'd seemed excited about. Or was that just a ruse to throw him off track, not make him suspicious?

Blake picked up his phone and scrolled through some numbers until he found the contact from the art auction. It was late but he didn't care—he'd make a donation large enough to make it count. If he found her friend Claire, he'd find Saffron. And if that didn't work, then he'd start at NYC Ballet. He'd contact the airlines, stop her from flying, do whatever it took. She wasn't leaving him—not with his baby.

CHAPTER TEN

SAFFRON HAD NEVER felt so guilty in her life. The pain was shooting through her chest, making it hard to breathe. But the problem was that guilt wasn't the only thing she was feeling.

Her heart was broken. Saffy gripped her water glass tighter, staring at the slice of lemon floating as she sat at the bar in the hotel. Just like every time she started to doubt herself, she touched her stomach, ran her palm lightly across it, just enough so that she hoped the baby could feel.

She checked the time and stood up, ready to take her taxi to Newark airport. It had been a long night, lying awake, wondering if she was doing the right thing, but she'd made up her mind and it was time to go. Maysville, Kentucky, wasn't New York, but it was an amazing place to raise a child and she had her family there. She could start a dance studio one day, nurture young talent, incorporate what she loved with being a mother. Or at least that was what she was telling herself to deal with the move.

"You're my little blessing," she murmured as she

walked, one hand carrying her bag, the other on her belly still.

She wasn't supposed to have a baby, and the fact that she'd gotten pregnant was a miracle. A miracle that she had no intention of turning her back on. Dancing had been her everything, until her body let her down. Now her body was doing what it was never supposed to do. It might have been a shock, but she could sure see the irony of it.

Saffron spoke to the concierge as she passed through the lobby and was directed to her taxi, getting in and letting them take care of her luggage. She didn't have a lot, just two suitcases. It seemed ironic that after so many years living in New York, she had so little to take home with her. But her mom would be there to welcome her with open arms, even though they hadn't seen each other in a long time. They were like that—could just pick up where they'd left off. Same with her dad. They knew she loved them and vice versa; she'd just spent so many years doing her own thing that they weren't the best at staying in touch.

She rested her head against the window, the cool glass refreshing against her hot skin. The city whizzed past once they'd gotten through the worst of the traffic, and when they finally reached the airport, she almost couldn't open her door. Leaving New York had never been part of her ten-year plan.

"Ma'am," the driver said, looking back over his shoulder.

Saffy smiled and forced a shaky hand up, opened the door and got out. He was nice enough to help her out with her bags, and she paid him the fare plus a decent tip. Then she went in, checked in for her flight and kept only her carry-on bag in her hand. She knew there would be a long wait ahead of her to get through security, so she went to get a coffee first. When she was finally in line, her hands began to shake, and she clutched the takeout cup tighter even though it was starting to burn her palm.

The line moved slowly, and the anxiety she'd started to feel in the taxi compounded so fast she could hardly breathe. What was she doing? How could she leave New York? She should be dancing for Pierre, she should be back as a principal, her leg was better… Saffy took a slow, steady sip of coffee in an attempt to calm herself.

She was having a baby, and that was the most important thing in the world. She was going to be a mother. She was going to have a gorgeous little child to hold in her arms and love. She could go back to ballet.

Couldn't she?

"Saffron!"

Saffy almost dropped the cup. What the…was she hearing things?

"Saffron!"

Saffy turned slowly, sure she was imagining the deep, commanding voice calling out her name above the din of the airport, the noise and bustle of the busy terminal. She was going crazy, actually crazy.

Blake? *Oh my god*, it *was* Blake! Her heart started to pound. Should she push to the front of the line? Get through security and away from him, beg to be let through? She knew that was stupid—Blake was worth a small fortune, and he'd just buy a ticket no matter what the price so he could follow her.

Saffron held her head high, not losing her place in the line as she defiantly met his gaze despite wanting to cower as he glared. She'd done her best to run away and not have to deal with him, to face a confrontation, but he'd found her and she couldn't back down. It had been cowardly of her to leave him a note, but it had seemed like the only way to break free from him.

"You're not getting on that plane."

Saffy gulped. She guessed they weren't exchanging pleasantries. "I'm going home, Blake, and you can't stop me."

His gaze was cool. Unrecognizable. "Oh, yes, I can. You're not abducting my child, Saffron. Not now, not ever."

She didn't know what to say. It was his child, but she'd expected him to want her to abort, to...maybe he still did, and he was just trying to take charge any way he could.

"I'm keeping this baby, Blake," she said, hand to her stomach, not caring who heard.

"You're coming with me. Now," Blake said, reaching for her, hand closing around her arm and holding tight.

"My luggage is already checked and my flight leaves in two hours."

"Saffron, you're not getting on that plane." Blake might have been angry before, but now he was furious.

"Let go of me," she hissed, tears welling in her eyes, her resolve fading fast, no longer feeling brave. "You can't just make me."

He didn't look like a man about to take no for an answer. "Sweetheart, we're leaving this airport together whether you like it or not."

She gasped when he pulled her, not letting go. She thought about screaming for security, yelling for help, but the people waiting behind her just looked away, not caring for someone else's problems. Saffron let herself be pulled, wished she was stronger or more determined, but the fight was gone. Extinguished as if it had never existed. Blake would have found her no matter where she was—she'd been kidding herself to think she could run and that he'd forget all about her.

"You can let go of me now," she huffed, pulling back and forcing him to slow down. Blake was impatient, but he did slow, his fingers not gripping her quite so tightly. "And in case you care, you're hurting me."

Blake let go completely then, his hand falling to her back instead, pointing her toward the exit. "Just come with me."

"What about my things?"

"I don't care about your things right now!"

She stopped walking, glared at him. "We're getting my luggage or you can go to hell."

He stared at her for a long moment before marching her back over toward a counter, keeping hold of her as he spoke to someone, flashing a card that she guessed showed he was a priority flyer or something.

"I'm having your things sent. Come on."

Saffron chose to believe him, and within minutes they were seated in a sleek black car, the driver taking off the moment they were buckled in.

"You can't just take me hostage," she managed, forcing the words out as they choked in her throat.

"For the next six months or however long I need to, that's exactly what I intend on doing."

She turned to face him, stared into the eyes that belonged to a stranger right now. Not the handsome, beautiful man she'd slowly fallen for since the night she'd met him. The man she'd been so scared of getting close to, of letting see how broken she was, only to find out that he was broken in just as many ways. Except right now she saw no breaks, not even a crack, just a man calmly and almost silently controlled. This was the first time she'd glimpsed what she presumed was soldier Blake—calm, cool and in control. There was a coolness that was just...*empty*.

"So you want me to have the baby?"

He looked away. "Yes. You can leave as soon as it's born if you like."

"I will not!"

He stared at her, but she wasn't backing down. Not when it came to her baby, and she sure wasn't going to be separated from her child, no matter how much money he had to throw around!

"You used me for my money," he muttered. "You got pregnant, fooled me with your stories of your career aspirations, made me believe that you couldn't ever have a baby. Fool me once, Saffron, shame on you. Fool me twice, and you'll wish you hadn't. I just can't believe I let you close, believed that you were different."

She gulped. "Blake, I'm not going to give you my baby. That's ludicrous!"

"What, you'd prefer just to take my money and raise it alone?" He glared at her. "Not going to happen. You've already done more than enough of that. We're talking about a child here."

"I didn't do this for your money, Blake! You want to investigate me, then go for it. Contact my oncologist, I still have his number in my phone. See my notes, figure out for yourself what a miracle this is that I'm even carrying a child right now," Saffron snapped at him, her confidence seeping back, not about to let him push her around, not now. "No one, not even you, Blake, can act like I haven't worked my butt off for what I've achieved. And that was supposed to be my life, my everything." She fought the tears, wanted to stay strong. "I haven't lied to you, I haven't tricked you, I haven't done anything other than try to deal with this baby on my own so you didn't have to. You've made it more than clear that you don't want a family, and I'm going to make sure my baby feels loved."

He was still just staring at her. "Are you finished?"

She turned away, not about to get into a staring competition. "You can think what you want about me, Blake. But you're wrong."

They didn't speak for the rest of the journey. Saffron wanted so desperately to cry, to just give up, but she couldn't. For the first time since she'd set her mind on being a professional dancer, she had a burning desire within her that no one could dampen. She was going to protect her baby, and no one was going to stand in the way of her being an amazing mom. She might not have wanted to get pregnant; she might not be sure how on earth she was going to do it or what the future held. Except that she had a little baby on the way who needed her more than anything else. Everybody needed a person, and she was her baby's person.

She only wished she had a person herself, someone to look out for her and love her unconditionally.

CHAPTER ELEVEN

SAFFRON HAD HIDDEN in the spare room for as long as she could, but it was starting to feel like being left in isolation in the most desolate of prison wards. Besides, if she stayed hidden any longer, she'd probably die of starvation. The little person growing inside her was demanding food all the time—she could hardly keep up.

"Morning," Saffron said as she forced herself to walk through the living space.

Blake looked up from where he was sitting at the dining table, his laptop in front of him and paperwork sprawled. He didn't say a word, just gave her an emotionless kind of stare.

She opened the fridge with a shaky hand, summoning all her strength, not about to let him bully her. She at least wanted to look strong and in control when he was watching her.

"You can't keep me here like a prisoner," she said, continuing what she was doing so she didn't have to look at him.

He ignored her. She hated the silent treatment, would rather he just yell at her and be done with it.

Saffron felt her body temperature rising, just a slow pooling of heat that started deep in her belly and rose slowly up until it flooded her face. She took a deep breath, trying not to explode.

"How dare you," she whispered, forcing her voice as loud as she could make it. "How dare you treat me like some sort of possession, as if you can tell me what to do?"

"You're not leaving, Saffron. That's all there is to it."

"You jerk," she cursed, fingers digging into the counter for support, not scared to stare at him now.

He finally showed something, let her see a flash of anger as he glared at her. "You signed the contract, remember? You were only too happy to live that life, to take my money, hang off my arm and play the doting wife." He sighed loudly. "And let's not forget about that diamond that used to live on your finger."

She swallowed, refusing to cry, to let him see that he'd hurt her. Who was this man? Where was the man she'd fallen for? Who for a moment in time she thought might have felt the same way she did. How had he disappeared so quickly?

"You told me the ring was mine," she choked out.

"And you told me that you didn't need it," he said, voice cold. "Or have you forgotten that already?"

She took her left hand off the counter, her thumb rubbing over the spot where the diamond had once sat. For months, it had been in permanent residence there, fooling her into a sense of…what? Love? She'd never once thought that he'd actually loved her, but she sure had thought she meant something to him. That it hadn't all been make-believe to him. She'd thought they'd leave their fake relationship as friends, maybe even lovers still.

"You know what? You need to leave, give me some space." She was feeling exhausted, didn't have the will or want to fight with Blake.

"And let you just walk out the door? Not a chance."

Hands on hips, she faced him. "I'm not going to run off, Blake, not now that you know. But I do need you to treat me like an actual person instead of some sort of convict."

He pushed back in his seat, eyes on her. "You expect me to believe that you won't run as soon as I turn my back?"

She glared at him. "I'm not going to run." Saffron shrugged. "You know what? Take my wallet so I don't have any money or identification. Is that enough to convince you I won't run?"

Saffron walked out, moving as fast as she could. She only just made it, not even having time to slam the bathroom door shut before she was doubled over the toilet, throwing up so violently she ended up slumped on the floor after. She wriggled down, put her cheek to the cool tiles on the floor.

"Saffron, are you okay?" Blake's deep voice echoed out from the bedroom.

He could probably see her, but she didn't care, didn't have the strength to rise or even look up. The pregnancy was taking everything from her, draining her, making her so ill she could hardly stand it, and the added stress with Blake wasn't helping.

"Go away," she muttered.

There was no other noise, no other words, and she shut her eyes, wishing for sleep but knowing that what she really needed right now was food. Something small and plain to settle her stomach, to give her the strength to face the day. To face Blake.

A door banged shut and still she didn't move, just lay there, wishing things were different, wishing he hadn't found her. Or maybe she should have just faced him, been honest in the first place.

She'd seen the laughter in their eyes, the way they'd enjoyed her pain. She'd been in love, and he'd been sleeping with more women than she could count.

Don't cry. She'd chanted those two words all day, every day. The other dancers were like hyenas, smelling out tears like a predator smelled blood, and she wouldn't give them the satisfaction. They hated her because she was too young, because she'd gotten the lead role too fast, but she didn't care.

"Sticks and stones," she'd muttered, holding her head high, pretending she just didn't care.

But the truth was that Raf's infidelity had almost killed her, because it had drained her of every bit of energy, every bit of confidence she'd had. But she'd survived it, and then she'd never trusted another man again, surrounded herself with a careful little group of friends she could count on.

Blake wasn't going to be the end of her. Blake wasn't going to take anything from her. Blake wasn't going to have the chance to make her feel the way Raf had back then, because she wouldn't let him.

The door banged again, and she forced herself to rise, one foot after another. She splashed water on her face, stared at her reflection in the mirror before braving the living room again. All she needed was something to eat, and she could go hide in bed again, take a long, never-ending shower.

"I put some things on the counter for you," Blake said, zipping his laptop into its Louis Vuitton case as she walked out. "Decaf coffee, a croissant and a bagel. I figured you'd want something."

Saffron could barely hide her surprise. "Thanks."

"Don't even think about leaving," he said, giving her a hard-to-read look. "Just don't."

And with that he was gone, disappearing into his bedroom for a moment before heading out the door.

The apartment was silent, the only noise the barely there hum of the city outside. Saffron took a look inside the bags, the smell sweet but her stomach tender still. She plucked at a piece of croissant, the delicate pastry still warm and tasting like heaven as it dissolved in her mouth.

She hated him. And she loved him.

How could he be so cool one moment then so thoughtful the next? Or maybe he just felt sorry for her. Or maybe she'd honest to God hurt him so bad he couldn't forgive her. For the sake of their unborn child, she sure hoped not.

Blake stayed at work longer than he should have, but it was easier than going home. His assistant had long since packed up and turned everything off except the two matching lamps in his office that were bathing the room in light.

He'd so far fielded calls from his mother wanting them to go out to dinner with her and postponed a business meeting that was supposed to take him out of town, and he was already exhausted with the lies. His life had once been so simple, so easy. He'd worked alongside men he could trust with his life. He'd flown Apaches and extracted teams from live danger areas. His life had been a mixture of adrenaline and fun and passion. And now he was living a life he'd never imagined, a life he'd thought he'd left behind for good. And having to lie about his fake wife who'd thrown him a curveball. He'd been stupid to think a relationship could be anything other than personal, to think he could have lived with a woman like Saffron without getting close, giving part of himself that he'd sworn never to give again. She'd hurt him just when he'd thought he couldn't be hurt by anyone ever again.

Blake poured himself a small shot of whiskey and downed it, wishing the burn of liquor did more for him rather than just temporarily stun his senses. Marrying Saffron was supposed to have made his life easier, supposed to have helped him, given him some breathing space workwise, solved his problems. After a short reprieve, now all it had done was make what was already an existence he didn't want, worse.

What he needed was to fly again, to get up into the sky and see the clouds and feel weightless. To be the rebel he wanted to be, rather than the perfect son forced to conform. His family meant so much to him;

he wanted to care for them and provide for them, but to do that he'd sacrificed his soul. Made a deal with the devil that was his father.

Blake collected his coat and flicked off the lamps. On his way home he collected takeout, choosing Italian since he knew Saffron liked it. He had no idea how he felt about her, what he wanted from her. All he knew was that she was carrying his baby, and that meant he couldn't just kick her to the curb. And he didn't want to.

Saffron had driven him crazy, made him believe in people again, and then she'd gone and betrayed him. Just like Bianca had. Just like his father had.

He steeled his jaw and let himself up to the apartment. At first it took a minute for his eyes to adjust; the lights were on low with lamps illuminating the room. Music played softly from somewhere.

Blake was about to flick the main lights back on, had his hand raised, when he saw her. Saffron had her back to him, arms raised above her head as she stretched then leaped, reaching up, doing something that looked impossible to him on pointed toes before spinning.

He was transfixed, couldn't take his eyes off her.

She dropped forward at the waist, seemed to fall effortlessly down before sweeping back up again and moving side to side. Blake never moved, didn't alert her to the fact he was standing there gaping at her. Because he'd never seen her dance before, and now all he wanted was to watch.

And then she spun in an incredible circle, and he knew he'd been spotted.

"Blake!"

She was breathing heavily, staring at him, eyes wide. It was obvious she'd had no idea he'd been standing there.

"I, ah—" He cleared his throat. "I have dinner. You looked great."

Saffron shrugged, and he noticed how her hand fled protectively to her stomach and stayed there.

"I can't move like I used to, but at least I'm not collapsing into a heap anymore."

Blake set down the food on the table and went to get some utensils and plates.

"You're still wanting to dance?" he asked, wishing he hadn't just asked outright the second the words came out of his mouth. It wasn't exactly something she could just decide to go back to with her stomach rapidly expanding.

"As opposed to having this baby?" she asked, hands on hips.

He hadn't expected her to be so defensive, so protective. She was already like a mama bear, and he admired it, even if he didn't trust her. He liked the flicker of a flame within her, was why he'd been so drawn to her from the beginning.

"You obviously want it," he said, cringing again. For a guy who didn't want to say the wrong thing, he was doing a darn fine job of it. "I just…" He didn't bother trying to finish his sentence or dig himself an even bigger hole.

Saffron blew out a breath, stretching her long limbs out. Her legs were slim but muscled in the way only a dancer's could be, and he dragged his eyes from her.

She was beautiful—that was a given even if he didn't like her anymore. Even if he didn't trust her, didn't want her in his bed, didn't… Who was he kidding? He still wanted her in his bed, only he wanted to yell at her and get everything that was weighing him down off his chest first.

"Yes, I want this baby, Blake. It's the only thing in this world I'm certain about right now." She sat down at the table, opening a container and looking in as he watched. "That and the fact that I'm guaranteed to be doubled over that toilet again at least once before morning, because what I seem to have is all-day sickness. The whole *morning* sickness thing is a lie."

Blake didn't know what to say to her, so he just sat, opening another container and waiting for her to have her first choice. She picked spaghetti Bolognese and he chose the linguine, twirling it around his fork as soon as he'd served himself, beyond hungry. Besides, eating meant he didn't have to make conversation and that he could keep his anger in check. Ever since he'd read Saffron's note it had been bubbling, always on the point of boiling over, and being around her only made it worse. He always stayed in control, was used to remaining calm in the worst situations when he'd been a soldier, but nothing had prepared him for dealing with Saffron.

"Are you worse in the mornings?" Blake asked, setting down his fork.

She looked up at him. "So long as I eat early enough I usually make it through the day. Why?"

He wasn't sure it was the best suggestion, but he was drowning here. With Saffron, without flying, with his

mind such a jumble of thoughts he couldn't piece together, he was seriously starting to lose it.

"I want to take you somewhere."

She had a look on her face that told him she no longer trusted his suggestions. "What kind of somewhere?"

"Flying," he told her. "I know we've had a rough—
well, whatever we've had has been difficult. But I want
you to come flying with me tomorrow. In a helicopter."

If she was shocked she didn't show it. "Fine."

Blake was happy to leave it at that while it felt like
a win.

"Have you told anyone?" he asked.

"About the baby?" Saffron was watching him, a fork-
ful of spaghetti hovering in her hand.

When he nodded, she took a visibly big breath. "No.
Up until you found out, it was just me and the doctor."

He was pleased to hear that she'd at least seen a doctor, that it wasn't just a home test. Although from how
sick she'd been, it wasn't likely to be a mistake. And seeing her dancing, the way she'd touched her stomach…
despite the fact that she still looked the same physically,
she had looked so instinctively pregnant that he knew
without a doubt it was true.

"Saffron, this is a difficult question, but…" He
pushed back in his seat, knowing she was going to explode, that he would ruin the sense of calm they were
finally experiencing. "You're certain it's mine?"

He'd expected anger, but he hadn't expected the tor-
rent of fury that hit him like a power wave.

"Are you kidding me?" Her words were so low, so
quiet, but they hit a mighty punch. She rose, palms flat

to the table, leaning forward as she stood, staring him down. "How dare you ask me that?"

When he rose her eyes flashed with such a powerful anger that he should have known to back down rather than try to placate her. Blake reached for her, wanting to tell her that he'd needed to ask, to hear her say it, but the moment he approached her—

"Saffron!" He cursed as her palm made contact with his cheek. It took all his strength not to react, to steel his jaw. But he did grab her wrist; he wasn't about to let her get a swing in again.

"Don't you ever ask me that question again, Blake. Never." She yanked her arm, hard enough to make him release it, her glare like venom.

"It was a fair question," he muttered, annoyed now.

"For an idiot," she snapped.

"Come on, Saffron!" Blake laughed bitterly. "It was a legitimate question! You're asking me to be a father, to parent a child that you know is yours, and I have no idea if…"

"Stop right there," she yelled back. "I never asked you to be a father, Blake. I wanted to give you an out, to raise this child on my own without anything from you, because I knew you didn't want a baby. I wanted to give my child all the love in the world, and I didn't want to back you into a corner, to force you to be someone you didn't want to be."

He sucked in a big lungful of air, calmed down, lowered his voice. "Why? Why give me an out? Why not make me step up? Make me at least reach into my pocket? Isn't that what you wanted?" He shook his head.

"Or was that diamond ring enough money for you?" Blake knew it had been a low blow, but she'd pushed him over the edge and he wanted to hurt her the way she'd hurt him. The pain she'd caused him was real, had pushed him into behaving like someone he wasn't. He knew he was being an idiot, but he couldn't help it.

Saffron had tears swimming in her eyes now, but she didn't back down. Looked so stoic, refusing to show any weakness in front of him, and he had to admire her for that.

"You want the ring back?" she asked, staring at him as she reached into her pocket. "Here it is, Blake. Have it."

She threw it at him and it landed at his feet. He never picked it up, just looked back at her.

"You didn't sell it?"

Saffron laughed, but it was a sad, morose sound. "Maybe it meant more to me than you realized."

She left him in the room alone, with a solitaire in front of his booted feet and a table full of half-eaten Italian.

Blake fisted his hands, clenched his jaw tight and refused to react. He wasn't about to trash his apartment just because he could no longer keep his anger in check.

He bent to collect the ring and stared down at it, remembered the laughter and happiness of that day. Even though it had been a contractual agreement, not love, they'd still had fun. And Blake knew that the way he felt about Saffron wasn't...

He slipped the ring in his back pocket and sat back down at the table.

Betrayal wasn't something he was used to feeling, but he knew there was only one reason it had hit him so hard. Because he felt differently about Saffron. Because he cared about her. Because the feelings he had for her weren't anything to do with a business arrangement.

And that's why what she'd done had hurt so badly.

CHAPTER TWELVE

BLAKE HAD HALF expected Saffron to stay in her room all morning, but when he stepped out of the shower, he heard music playing and knew she was already up. He dressed and headed out, checking his watch for the time. It was a perfect, clear day, and he wanted to get up in the air as soon as they could to make the most of having the chopper for the day. It wasn't often they had one grounded unless it was waiting for maintenance, and he'd instructed his team to keep this one that way even if an urgent booking came through.

"Good morning," he called out.

Saffron was fiddling with her iPod and the music died. She was wearing the same outfit he'd found her in when he'd arrived home the night before, tight black leggings and a skintight top. He wanted to glance at her stomach, see if he could glimpse a hint of roundness there, but she gave him a frosty stare and he changed his mind.

"Are we still going up?"

Blake nodded. Living with Saffron and having so much dislike and distrust between them was like being back in his family home when his mom had been giving his dad the silent treatment. Blake had never asked, but he was certain his father had been unfaithful, knew deep down that was the reason behind why the light in his mother's eyes had slowly faded during his teenage years.

"I don't want it to be like this between us," Blake said.

"Says the man holding me hostage and treating me like a criminal," Saffron said, walking away from him.

He didn't bother answering, let her go and listened to the shower when she turned it on. A quick glance around told him she'd already had breakfast, or at least something to eat. Blake thought about ordering up something for himself but changed his mind. He'd collect some food and coffee on their way past to take up for the day.

Spending the day out with Saffron might not have been his best idea, but they were stuck together regardless of what he wanted, and he was ready to man up and deal with it. Even if catching feral cats sounded a whole lot easier than dealing with Saffron right now.

Saffron forced a smile as she stared at the helicopter in front of her. As a dancer, she was used to plastering on a smile and making herself look happy even when she wasn't. And if she was going to survive Blake, she needed to start thinking positively and acting as if she was happy—maybe one day she'd trick her own brain. She had no idea how long she was going to be stuck with him if he became intent on staying in control where their baby was concerned.

"All set?" Blake asked.

She thought about all the times they'd pretended together—that they were a happy couple, that everything was great between them. Saffron knew why that had worked, though, why it had seemed so natural and easy. She'd loved his company, liked the man he was and everything he believed in. And because they'd both entered into their arrangement with eyes wide-open, everything had seemed transparent.

"Let's do this."

She'd never been up in a helicopter, and her legs were a little wobbly at the thought of being so high in the air. Up front. With Blake as her pilot. Saffron gulped.

"You okay?"

She nodded. "Uh-huh."

"For what it's worth, I'm sorry about last night."

She brushed his apology off, not wanting to engage. The last thing she wanted was to argue with him before they went up in the air, and she wasn't ready to forgive him yet, wasn't sure when she'd ever be.

She followed his lead, keeping her head ducked down even though the rotors were still stationary. She'd been reading up about helicopter safety on her iPhone overnight, so she was fully briefed and didn't have to keep asking Blake questions.

Once they were seated, he leaned over her and helped to buckle her in. She held her breath, glanced away, but when she looked back he was still fumbling, his hand grazing her stomach.

"Sorry," he mumbled.

Saffron instinctively sat back, pulled away from him. "It's fine." Once, she'd loved any excuse to touch him and liked whenever he'd touched her. She still *wanted* to want it, but she doubted it could ever be like that again.

"I've done that a hundred times for other passengers. This is crazy." He finally snapped her safely in and sat back, doing his own safety restraints.

Saffron sat back and listened to the helicopter fire into life. He passed her a headset to wear, and when they were finally rising into the air, she clutched her seat as the ground receded below.

"How you doing, rookie?" he asked, grinning across at her.

Saffron forgot all about the ground disappearing below them when Blake flashed her his big smile. She hadn't seen a smile light up his face like that since before they'd gone out to their last cocktail party, the night she'd ended up in the restroom and found out she was pregnant.

His burst of happiness hit her like a jolt, reminding her of why she'd liked him so much, why she'd wanted to stay with him and why she'd been so afraid of hurting him. Of breaking his trust.

As he expertly maneuvered the chopper, she stared at him, unable to tear her eyes away. He was happy. Genuinely, one hundred percent happy. And it showed her a different side to him.

"You're different when you're flying," she said, still watching him.

He looked at her. "How's that?"

"Everything about you," she told him. "Even when you're just sitting, there's a bit of a smile hovering, there's a lightness in your eyes. You're just…" Saffron frowned. "Different. I can't explain it."

He was looking straight ahead now, and she admired his strong, chiseled jaw, the handsome side profile. She might not like the way he'd treated her, but deep down she got it, understood why he was so hurt by what she'd done. She only wished he'd trusted her enough after spending three months with her as his wife, instead of labeling her a gold digger without at least giving her a chance to explain properly.

"That's because this is the first time you've seen the real me," Blake said, not moving a muscle, staring straight ahead.

Saffron turned away, stared out the window, where everything started to blur a little as they moved fast through the sky. She'd been nervous about going up, but now the helicopter ride was the last thing on her mind.

"Why did you give it up?" she asked. "How could you give what you love up like that? You had a choice, didn't you?"

Blake never answered her, and she never asked again.

They'd been up in the air for what felt like forever, but Saffy still hadn't had enough time to think. She doubted she ever would, not when it came to Blake. Something about him made her crazy, made her feel things she was scared of and had thought would never happen to her.

"Descending," Blake said, loud and clear through the headset.

He hadn't spoken a word to her since just after take-off, and Saffron felt a weird kind of divide between them. There was so much she wanted to ask him, wanted to say. Only nothing felt right when she sounded it out in her head first.

They landed in a field, a ranch from what she could see, and Saffron stayed quiet as Blake did his thing. When he slipped his headset off, she did the same, watching as he exited the helicopter and then opened her door and held up his hand to help her out.

Saffron took it, letting him guide her down. She stretched, taking a look around.

"Let's go," Blake said.

"Where?"

"For a walk over there." He pointed. "We can have lunch under that tree."

Saffron didn't question him, just followed, staying a step or two behind him and looking at their surroundings.

"Where are we?" she asked when he stopped under a pretty oak tree, its branches waving down low and shielding them from the intense sunshine.

"My family used to own this ranch," Blake said. "It was somewhere we came over the summer or just for a weekend getaway. My best childhood memories were spent here."

Saffron listened as she continued to look around. She touched the trunk of the tree, ran her fingers across its gnarled bark. There were indentations in it, markings that she couldn't quite figure out.

"That's me," Blake said, standing close behind her.

She could feel his breath, the warmth of his big body as it cast a deeper shadow over her, making her own body hum even though she tried so darn hard to fight it.

"You?" she managed.

"Yeah." He leaned past her, his arm skimming hers as he traced his fingers across the same spot hers had just trailed over. "I etched my name in here a few times. I used to ride out here on a cute little pony who was always happy to go as fast as I wanted, and when I got older, I landed my first solo here."

Saffron was aware of everything, could feel his body even though he was no longer touching her, her breath loud in her own ears, heart thumping. There was nothing she could do to stop the way she reacted to him.

"My dad saw how much I loved it here, knew how much pleasure I got from flying out here, practicing everything I learned."

"He didn't want that?"

Blake made a grunting noise, and she knew he was stepping away. It gave her breathing space, but she liked having him near, wanted him to stay closer.

"It was around the time we'd started to butt heads a lot. All the time," Blake said. Saffron turned and saw him hit the ground, his big frame sprawled out. He had one leg out straight, the other bent, resting on one arm as the other plucked at a strand of grass. "I started to talk about what I wanted to do with my life, and that didn't tally up with what he wanted. He went from loving my interest in helicopters to despising it, because every time I went up in the air it made me more determined to carve my own path."

Saffron sat down, leaning against the trunk she'd been studying. "I'm sorry."

He laughed and raised an eyebrow. "What for?"

"I'm sorry that you had a dad who couldn't support your dreams. That he had a hold on you that you still haven't been able to shake."

Blake's stare hardened. "I lost that hold, Saffron. I lost it for years, but in the end it was a hidden choke hold that I'd never truly escaped. It started back then, tightened when he paid Bianca off to leave me and then again when he died."

"You need more of this. To remind yourself of what you love."

If she'd been his wife, his real wife, it would be what she'd insist on.

"Anyway, why am I telling you all that stuff?"

She wasn't buying his laugh, knew it was no joke to him. "Because you wanted me to see the real you," Saffron said quietly. "You wanted to show me who you really are."

"You sound so sure about that." Blake opened a bag and pulled out a couple of Cokes, holding one out for her.

"Can I ask you something?" Saffron said, her heart starting its rapid beat again, near thudding from her chest.

"Shoot."

"Did you ever feel anything for me? I mean, anything real?"

Blake had the Coke halfway to his mouth, but he slowly lowered it. "Did you?"

"I asked you first," she insisted, wishing she hadn't asked him but needing, *craving*, the answer.

"You mean did I want you in my bed? Did I want you at my side, on my arm?"

She sucked in a breath. "I know you wanted me in your bed—that's the only thing I'm sure about. But…" Saffron paused. "Was the way we looked at each other real? The way we…"

This time when her voice trailed off she didn't bother to finish her sentence. What was she trying to say?

"Whatever we had was just part of a deal," Blake said matter-of-factly. "Was I attracted to you? Of course. Any hot-blooded man would have been. But we didn't have anything more than sex and a contract."

Saffron had tears burning in her eyes like acid, making her want to scream in pain. But she stayed silent, swallowed them down. She'd thought the feeling had been reciprocated, that he'd felt something real for her, like she had for him, but she'd been wrong.

"Why, did you expect something else?" he asked.

Saffron bravely shook her head. "No. I was just curious." Sobs racked her body, jarred her ribs and her shoulders and every other part of her. But she kept her chin up, sucked back silent gasps to stop herself from giving in, from letting him see how much he could hurt her. *Just like dancing*, she told herself. Crying over real pain, over a real injury, was one thing, but that was the only thing any dancer would ever shed a tear over.

"Do you have anything to eat in there?" she asked instead, desperate to change the subject.

Blake nodded. "Sure. You hungry?"

Saffron nodded. She'd rather eat than talk any more.

Blake had shown her his true colors, how happy he could be in the air, what made his heart sing. Only she'd expected, *hoped*, that there would be more. That he'd say something else, tell her that he felt something, *anything*, for her.

Because even though he'd hurt her and she'd tried to run back home, what she felt for Blake was real. It always had been. She'd slowly started to fall in love with him, a man so beautiful yet damaged by a father and an ex-lover who had done him more harm than good, and a career that he'd loved yet one that had shattered parts of him emotionally, as well.

But that man wasn't hers to take, wasn't hers to love. She was having his baby, and that was it. He didn't love her back—maybe he didn't even care for her beyond what she meant to him on paper.

And that hurt so bad it made her injury seem like a cakewalk.

She touched her hand to her stomach, something she was doing instinctively all the time now. If it wasn't for the baby, she'd be long gone now, and Blake would be a distant memory. *Or would he?*

Maybe without the baby everything would have stayed the same. They'd still be living in their little faux bubble of a marriage.

"Sandwich?" Blake asked, leaning forward and passing it over.

"Sure," she murmured, not bothering to ask what was in it. She didn't care.

"You sure you're okay? You're feeling all right?" Blake asked.

Saffron forced a smile. "I'm fine. Thanks for bringing me here."

"You're the first person I've ever flown out here," he said, taking another sandwich out and holding it in his hands, watching her.

"I thought…" She didn't know what she'd thought. Did that mean something—was it supposed to mean something?

"I want our baby to start flying young," Blake said, surprising her with his smile. "It's all I ever wanted, and if I'm going to share it with anyone, who better than my child?"

Of course. It was the baby. That was the only reason he'd brought her. She'd been fooling herself that maybe he wanted to talk to her, to get away from the city with her for a reason, but now it was all about the baby.

So much for him not wanting to be a dad.

"We need to figure this out, how it's going to work," Saffron said, not seeing any point in putting it off. "You don't have to do this, playing the dad role. It was my choice to keep the baby, and I'm okay with that."

The happy lilt of Blake's mouth disappeared, replaced with a much tighter line. "Oh, yeah? So I could just write a card on birthdays or maybe just Christmas?"

Saffron refused to take the bait, didn't want to end up arguing with him when she had no chance of winning.

"What I'm trying to say is that I want custody. I don't want to fight about it, but a child needs to be with its mom," she said, bravely meeting his gaze head-on and refusing to shrink away from him. "You'll always be welcome, I'm not trying to tell you to stay away, I'm just saying that…"

"Oh, I hear what you're saying," Blake muttered. "You're laying it on pretty thick."

"Blake! You don't even want this child! You don't want to be a dad!" Saffron didn't know how to keep her cool, what to say. He was driving her crazy. "We're not a real couple. There is no way for this to work."

Blake stood and stared down at her, his shadow imposing. "I wasn't under any illusion there."

He stormed off, and she didn't bother calling out. She wasn't about to follow him, either. Instead she sat there, picking at her sandwich even though the last thing she felt like was eating.

How had her life turned out like this? She was sitting here all high and mighty about how much she wanted this baby, and she did, but she wasn't *actually* ready to be a mother. All she wanted was to be back on stage, back dancing. Saying yes to performing at Pierre's retirement party. And instead she was growing a big round belly and thinking about names and genders and how on earth she was going to provide for the little future love of her life.

Saffron bit hard on her lower lip. Everything was a mess. She didn't want Blake and his money, but if he didn't let her go back home, then she'd have no other choice but to take whatever he offered. But if he even for a second wanted to take her child from her, take control… She pushed the thoughts away. It wouldn't come to that, because she wouldn't let it.

Suddenly Blake was storming back in her direction, his face like thunder. As she watched, he gathered everything up and marched it back to the helicopter. Saffron stood and reluctantly followed—it wasn't as if she had an alternate ride home.

"We're going," he said.

She shook her head. "Why can't we stay? I think you should blow off some steam before…"

He spun around, only a few feet from her, his hands clenched at his sides, his anger palpable.

"You know why I brought you here?" he asked.

Saffron stayed still, stared at the bulge in his neck where a vein was about to pop out from under his skin.

"I thought we could start fresh, put the past behind us. I brought you here because this place means something to me, and I wanted to show it to you." He ran a hand through his hair, anger still radiating from every part of him. "I wanted to see if you actually cared about me, whether we could at least agree on something to do with this child, *our* child."

"I do care about you, Blake," she said softly, telling him the truth. "You're the one who just acted like what we had meant nothing, that it wasn't real."

"Yeah? You care about *me*?" He laughed, but it sounded forced. "Well, you've got a real strange way of showing it."

"Blake…" she started. He'd just been the one saying there was nothing real between them, yet now suddenly everything was her fault!

"Get in the helicopter, Saffron," he demanded as

he spun back around. "Or find your own way back to the city."

She wanted to believe that he wouldn't actually leave her behind, but given his mood, she wasn't sure about anything right now.

"I'm sorry," she said as she followed him.

"Yeah, me, too," he muttered back.

Saffron took his hand to guide her into her seat, but she never looked at him when he settled beside her and started to flick switches, the engine humming into life. Things had gone from worse to bad to worse again, and there was nothing she could do to change it.

CHAPTER THIRTEEN

THEY'D BEEN SILENT since the ranch. Saffron had goose pimples rippling across her skin whenever she looked at him, but still they never uttered a word. They'd landed, he'd helped her out, driven her home, and now he was about to head out the door for takeout. She knew this because he'd phoned and ordered Thai, and she'd been sitting in the same room as him, snuggled under a mohair blanket while he'd been positioned at the dining table furiously banging away at his keyboard. She was half expecting him to need a new machine in the morning the way he'd been treating it.

"I'll be back soon," Blake said.

When she looked up, he was standing near the door, his eyes still shining with anger. Or at least she was guessing that's what it was.

"Okay." Saffron forced a smile, but he was still staring at her and his gaze was unnerving.

"That's it. That's all you've got to say to me?" His voice was so low, so quiet it was lethal.

Saffron gulped, wished she knew the right thing to say. But the truth was that she'd tried to run from a man with trust issues, and she had no idea what to say to make that situation better.

"I'm sorry. I'm sorry for what I did, Blake, I am," Saffron said, forcing the words out. "But I'm not sorry for what happened, because it's nothing short of a miracle, no matter how scary it is."

He went to turn and she breathed a sigh of relief, but he hadn't moved his body halfway to the door when he was staring at her again. He didn't say anything, just stared, but she could feel the unsaid words hanging between them, knew he was bottling a whole heap of something inside.

"Why can't you just accept that what happened was an innocent mistake? That I never…" She didn't bother finishing. They'd been through all this—there were only so many times she could apologize for what she'd done.

"You want to know why?"

Blake's words sent shivers through her. She was scared of the way he felt, of what he made her feel. The way she felt about him, despite everything.

"Why?" she whispered as he spun around to face her. She'd asked; it wasn't as though she could walk away from him now.

"Because I loved you." He hurled the words at her, and she instantly felt their sting. "I lied before, okay? I fell for you because I thought you were different. I was stupid enough to think that what we had meant more than…"

"Some stupid contract?" she said for him, finding her voice. "I didn't hear you ever offering to rip that up. Not once, during all the times we connected, when I felt like we were something more, did you *ever* make out like you wanted to make what we had real."

It was unfair—she'd agreed to their marriage bargain right from the start to help her stay in New York, but he was hurting her and it was all she had. Because she *had* felt the same, had thought she was falling for him, that something between them was real. That it wasn't all just about their stupid agreement.

"Why didn't you tell me," she finally said when he never spoke. "Why didn't you say something, *anything*? Why couldn't you have just done something to show me?"

"What difference would it have made?" Blake asked, his tone cold, blunt. "What would it have changed between us?"

It would have changed everything. Saffron squared her shoulders. "It would have made a difference," she said, knowing in her heart that it would have. That if she'd just known for sure that he felt about her the same way she was feeling about him…

"What, you would have felt bad about using me? About lying to me?" He laughed. "Would it have changed how guilty you're feeling right now?"

"No," she said simply, tears threatening to spill even though she was trying so hard to fight them. "Because then I would have known that my own feelings were real, that you didn't just think of me like…"

"Like what, Saffron?" he bellowed. "I've treated you with nothing but respect and kindness! I treated you like my real wife, didn't I?"

"I was in love with you, too!" she sobbed. "How could you not have realized how I felt? How could you have been so blind?" Saffron turned away then, couldn't look at him any longer. She was still in love with him, despite everything, and it broke her heart to argue the way they were. "All you had to do was say something, Blake. Instead you hid behind your daddy issues, kept acting like you could never be the man you were so good at pretending to be with me." She shook her head. "You kept saying you couldn't settle down, couldn't ever be a real husband, but in the almost four months I spent with you, I saw a man who could have had whatever he wanted. A man who could have been a darn good *real* husband if he'd wanted to be. You didn't exactly make it look hard."

He stared at her, but she was on a roll now, couldn't stop.

"You're hiding behind your past, not letting yourself live, because you're too scared of change, of what might happen, of being hurt and exposing yourself to that kind of real love. I'm not judging you—heaven knows I'm no different—but things have changed, Blake. Things changed between us long before I took a positive pregnancy test."

"Just go," he finally said, his voice hoarse, unrecognizable. "If you want to go back home to raise our baby that bad, just go."

She hated the emptiness to his tone, the hollowness. It was the same way she felt inside, like a soft toy with all the stuffing knocked from her. "After all that effort to keep me, now you're going to just give up without a fight?" Saffy knew she was being antagonistic, but it was true.

"What do you want from me, Saffron?" he whispered, eyes level with her own.

"I want you to want me, Blake!" she told him, voice shaking. "I want you to fight for me. Show me that I'm not just some asset to you."

"You want me to fight for you?" he muttered, marching toward her, stopping barely an inch away, towering over her, his body almost brushing hers, his gaze fierce. "Consider me in the ring then."

Just as she was about to reply, about to stand her ground, Blake's hand cupped the back of her head, the other snaking around her waist. He pulled her forward, dropped his mouth over hers and kissed her as if it was the final kiss of their lives.

"Stop," she protested, hands to his chest, halfheartedly pushing him away.

Blake didn't let up, kept kissing her. "This is me fighting," he said against her lips. "You want to go, you pull back."

Saffron tried—she wanted to push him away completely. She wanted to forget about him and get on with her life without him, but she couldn't. Because from the moment they'd met, something had ignited between them that she hadn't wanted to admit, and that spark was far from being extinguished. And he'd just told her that he'd loved her. Admitted that what she'd felt between them had been real.

"We can't do this," she whispered, finally parting her mouth from his, dropping her head to his chest, letting him cradle her as she absorbed the warmth from his body.

"You're my wife," he murmured, lips to the top of her head, soft against her hair. "We can do anything we like."

Saffron wanted to give in, wanted to believe him, but… "I can't. We can't." She shook her head, palms to his chest again, forcing some distance between them, needing to look up at him. "We need to talk. Actually talk. Not yell at each other, or make assumptions. I need to talk, and you need to listen. We can't just bury our heads in the sand. Not this time, Blake."

Blake took Saffron's hand and led her to the sofa, sitting down and waiting for her to do the same. He felt as if he'd just stepped off a roller coaster; his body was exhausted and his mind was a jumble. The past few days hadn't exactly been easy, had drained everything from him. And now he had to dig deep and not push his feelings away like he'd been doing for most of his adult life.

"So let's talk."

Her smile was shy as he watched her, and he sat back, glanced away, hoping to make her feel more comfortable. All he'd done since he'd hauled her back from the airport was to tell her what he thought, bully her, throw his weight around. And that wasn't him, wasn't the man he wanted to be. It was the man his father had been. The kind of cold, unfeeling, calculating man his father had shown himself to be time and time again.

Which was exactly why he'd never wanted to be in

this position, to be a dad or a husband. Blake pushed the thoughts away, focused on Saffron. Whether he wanted to be a dad or not was irrelevant now, because he was going to become one regardless. What she'd said had hit home, was true even though he didn't want to admit it. He had been hiding behind his past, living his life with a raft of excuses about what he couldn't do. And that needed to end now. If he wanted to step up and be a parent, not lose the woman who'd finally made him feel, then he needed to be a man.

"I never lied to you, Blake, and we can't move forward unless you believe that."

He nodded. "If I wasn't starting to believe that, we wouldn't be having this conversation." Blake wanted to blame her, but she didn't deserve it.

He watched as she blinked, staring down at her hands. There should be a ring on her finger, a ring to show every other man in the world that she was taken. Their relationship might have been fake to start with, but he was only kidding himself that he didn't want her as his, and he wanted it clear to every man alive that she wasn't available. Suddenly the fact that there wasn't a ring sitting against her skin made him furious.

"I'm scared of being a mom, of holding this baby when it's born and trying to figure out what to do with it, but for the first time I can remember, I want something as bad as I want to dance." She sighed. "And that scares me as much as it excites me."

Blake reached for her hand, squeezed it when he saw a trickle of tears make their way down her cheeks. If she'd wanted to show him what an idiot he'd been, she was doing a fine job. There was no way he could feel worse about his behavior if he tried.

"I'm sorry," he said, clearing his throat, wanting to do better, knowing it might be his only chance after what he'd said. "I'm sorry, Saffron. If I could take back half the things I've said to you, I would."

She nodded, eyes shut as she took a big, shuddery breath. "I want to dance so bad, but I also want this baby, Blake," she said. "I can't explain it, but it's so powerful, so instinctive."

Blake brushed the tears away with his knuckles when she opened her eyes, gentle as he touched her skin. He got how hard it was to open up and be honest, and she looked as though it was hurting her real bad to say how she felt.

"I've been an idiot," he said, finally getting the words off his chest. "I don't exactly find it easy to trust, but you didn't deserve the way I treated you. You deserve an apology."

"You're right," she said, "but I should have told you instead of running away. I made myself look guilty of the crime—you just put the pieces together. And you're not the only one who's said things they regret."

"Why?" he asked. "I still don't understand why you decided to run. I'm not going to lose the plot about it again, but you need to explain it. I need to be on the same page as you, Saffron. Why did you run?"

Her eyes filled with fresh tears as he stared into them, but this time he didn't brush them away, didn't try to comfort her. This time he just needed to listen, and she looked as if she was ready to talk.

"I was terrified you wouldn't want the baby," she whispered, no longer meeting his gaze. "That you wouldn't want anything to do with our child, and I didn't want this baby to feel unwanted."

"What?" He held her hand tighter, fought the anger as it started to bubble within him again. Blake waited a second, not wanting to overreact, needing to calm down before he spoke. He'd wanted her to be honest, and she was, which meant he couldn't judge her for her thoughts. But still, keeping a lid on the way he was feeling wasn't easy.

"I know how strongly you feel about not having a family. How determined you were *not* to be a father, to not ever be put in that position. Not to let your heart be broken by a woman, too."

He took a slow breath, not wanting to snap her head off. "I would never, ever not want my child to be born. And I'd never make a child feel unwanted. Not my own flesh and blood. *Never.*"

"But…"

"I'm terrified of the idea of being a dad, knowing that there is a baby coming into this world with half my DNA," Blake continued, needing to get it all off his chest before it strangled him. "I don't want to be a dad because I had a terrible example from my own father, and I don't want to become that kind of man. To have a child of mine feel such hatred toward me that the moment he finds out his own father has died he feels a sense of relief."

Blake stood, turned away, gulped away an emotion

that he'd never let out before. Something he always extinguished long before it threatened to surface.

"Blake?"

Saffron's hand was on his back, her touch light, her voice kind. But he didn't want her to see him lose it like this, break down when he was usually so strong, so incapable of anything getting under his skin.

"Just give me a sec," he muttered.

"You can't help the way you feel," Saffron whispered, her hand snaking around his waist, slowly, turning him toward her. "Whatever you felt when he died, it's okay. You can't keep all that bottled inside."

Blake shut his eyes, squeezed the tears away. He was not going to cry, not in front of Saffron. Not ever. Tears over anything other than an atrocity weren't for men who'd seen terrifying things, seen what he'd seen when he was serving. There was no way he was shedding tears, not now, not ever. Not over some stupid feelings he'd had for his father.

He opened his eyes and stared into dark eyes that seemed to see straight into his soul. Blake opened his mouth, wanted to tell her she was wrong, but instead a wave of guilt, of emotion and sadness and regret, hit him like a tidal wave. A gulp of tears burst out, the emotion flooring him, his knees buckling as everything he'd held back came pouring from him.

"Shh," he heard Saffron murmur as she held him, cradling his head to her stomach as he stayed on his knees, felled like an oak tree slain at the heart of its trunk in front of her. "Shh."

Her hands were warm, her touch so gentle, but Blake

couldn't stop, the sobs racking his body as the pain slowly washed over him. He didn't try to speak, couldn't get anything out except the grief he'd held so tight for so long.

"Tell me," she said. "Get it all out. You need to share it with someone. Just say the words."

Blake steadied his breathing, felt the rise and fall of Saffron's stomach against his cheek. He had no idea what had come over him, but he couldn't believe what he'd just done. And then he shut his eyes again, tears no longer engulfing him.

His baby was in there. Saffron had been holding him, comforting him, and he hadn't even realized how close he'd been to his little unborn child. It gave Blake the strength to rise and face her again, this woman who'd turned his life upside down and made him feel things, move forward instead of just treading water. If he was going to be a dad, he needed to be honest with himself. And with Saffron.

"I hated him," Blake finally said, keeping hold of her hand and drawing her back onto the sofa with him, keeping her in his arms so he could cradle her warm body against his. "I saw so much while I was serving, realized I was actually living the life I was supposed to live, making a difference in the world and flying the machines that made me feel so amazing. The only stumbling block in my life was my father. And the woman who'd hurt me, made me feel stupid and vulnerable in a way that only my dad had been able to do before."

"Did he ever accept what you did?" she asked, head

to his chest. "Ever give you praise for the career you'd made for yourself?"

Blake didn't want to look at her, just wanted to touch, to feel her there with him. It made it easier for him to say the words he'd only ever said in his head before.

"I grew up around helicopters and planes, and I loved it. I guess that's why Dad thought I was a natural fit for the company, or maybe it was just because I was his firstborn that he felt that way. Before I started to fly myself, at the ranch, I was trailing around after him at the hangars, checking out our stock and soaking up every word he or anyone else in the know said about them. It probably never crossed his mind that I wouldn't do what he wanted me to do."

"But you loved actually flying more than the company, right?"

Blake dropped a kiss into her hair, craving her, suddenly needing to stay connected after so long spent trying to push her away.

"I was addicted to flying from my first flight, and I was a natural in a helicopter, just like I told you today. After he sent my fiancée running for the hills with a pocket full of cash, I knew I had to get away. I hated him so much, and I found my place in the world. I had an amazing job in an industry that needed me, I got to fly every day and I had a new family with my army buddies."

Blake paused, thought back to how he'd felt the day his dad had passed. "He never supported my dreams or wanted to hear anything about my life, not unless I went to work for him. He didn't want to hear about the lives I'd saved, the men I'd flown into dangerous situations to help protect our country that he claimed to love so much. And he sure didn't want to hear about how bad it affected me, that half the time I couldn't sleep for weeks after I returned from a tour."

"You can't help that you hated him, Blake. We feel what we feel, and there's nothing we can do about it," she said.

"Things just got worse and worse, until I couldn't even stand being in the same room as him. Not even at Thanksgiving or Christmas, and I know it broke my mom's heart, which was something I never wanted to do."

Saffron was stroking his shoulder, her face to his chest as she listened to him.

"I have nightmares about what I saw when I was serving, dreams that will haunt me forever, but I'm the type of person who's okay with that because I want to know the realities of our world. I don't want to live in a bubble where rich people have everything and don't care about the world or real people or the next generation." He blew out a breath, amazed how fast the words were falling from his mouth now that he'd started talking, how desperate he suddenly was to share them. "When I heard his helicopter had gone down, that he was presumed dead, it was like a lead weight had been lifted from my chest, a weight I hadn't even known was there. It was a feeling I'll never forget for as long as I live."

Blake stayed silent for a moment, regretted the thoughts he was having, hated the pain he felt at what came next.

"And then I found out that my brother had been flying with him. That it wasn't just my dad, but my brother, too," he murmured. "In that one second, I wished so bad that it was all a mistake, felt so guilty that I'd been relieved about Dad disappearing off the face of the planet."

"You were close to your brother?"

Blake nodded. "My brother was my best friend growing up. We were so different and we fought like crazy sometimes, but I loved him. I'd do anything to have him back, would have traded anything and everything to change places with him and be on the chopper that day. I still would."

"You can't think like that," Saffron said, pushing back and looking up at him. "That's one thing you just can't let yourself think."

"Yeah, I can," he grumbled. "He was with my dad that day for work. If I hadn't been so pigheaded about making my own way in the world, it would have been me with him flying out to meet a new corporate client, not my brother. It would have been me missing, and he'd still be here."

Saffron didn't say anything, just kept stroking his shoulder, her fingers running lightly across his T-shirt.

"It should have been me," he whispered.

"But it wasn't, and I'm glad," Saffron said, her voice soft yet fierce at the same time. "Because then I would never have met you, and we wouldn't have a little baby on the way. This little baby that is an absolute miracle."

Blake touched her stomach, laid his hand flat there, the first time he'd done it, and it calmed him. Made him feel a crazy mix of emotions, protective over the tiny being he'd helped to create that was cradled in her belly.

"I'm scared," he admitted.

"Me, too," she whispered back. "But you're not your father, and I'll never let you turn into him. This baby is going to be whatever he or she wants to be. All we have to do is love and nurture and care for this little person. It's all he or she will need."

"You sound so sure." Blake looked down at her, realizing how stupid he'd been to have almost let her go. She'd been so close to just slipping from his life.

"Being in love and loving is the only thing I am sure about right now."

And just like that, it was Saffron with tears in her eyes and him wanting to be strong for her, and everything else fell away except the woman in his arms.

CHAPTER FOURTEEN

"So what are we going to do?" Saffron asked, closing her eyes and enjoying the sensation of Blake strumming his fingertip across her skin. She snuggled in closer to him, the sheets covering their lower halves, their uppers bare.

"Not much more of that," Blake said with a chuckle. "It can't be good for the baby."

She laughed. "It's fine for the baby. I checked with the doctor."

"I'm glad to hear you had your priorities straight when you were asking questions about our unborn child!" Blake flicked her, his touch no longer so soft and lingering.

Saffron pushed up on her elbows, looking down on Blake. "I'm serious. What *are* we going to do?"

"We're going to get married. For real this time," Blake said, pushing up and pressing a kiss to her lips, his smile serene, a peacefulness on his face that she hadn't seen before. "No registry office this time around."

She giggled when he tickled her. "I can't exactly wear white. I think the tummy will give away my virtue, or lack of."

Blake pulled her closer, rolling them over until she was pinned beneath him, his arms imprisoning her on each side.

"I can't promise that I'm going to be a good dad, but I'm going to try my hardest," Blake said, staring into her eyes. "I don't want to be my father. I don't want to ever be that kind of man, but I want this baby." She smiled, seeing the emotion on his face, the tears welling in his eyes that mirrored hers. "And I want you."

She slipped her arms out and slung them around his neck, needing to hold him, to pull him closer. "I love you, Blake," she whispered.

He dropped a soft, gentle kiss to her lips. "I love you, too."

Saffron smiled so hard, she couldn't have wiped it from her mouth if she'd tried. "I didn't think I'd ever hear you say that. Not to me, not to anyone."

He held her tighter, sighing against her skin. "Me neither, sweetheart. But then I never expected to come across a woman like you. The gloves are off, Saffron. I'm all yours."

"All mine," she murmured as he planted a full kiss to her lips. "And don't you forget it."

EPILOGUE

BLAKE COULDN'T TAKE his eyes off Saffron. *His wife.*
His cheeks were sore from smiling so hard, watching
as she somehow floated across the stage, twirling and
leaping and…he had no idea what any of the moves
she was doing were, but whatever it was, she looked
incredible. Seeing her like this reminded him again of
what he'd been so close to losing, how stubborn he'd
been about the only woman who'd ever managed to see
the real him.

"Mama."

He glanced down at the little girl sitting in his lap,
clapping her pudgy little hands at least every other minute. She'd wriggled to start with, but from the moment
her mom had graced the stage, she'd been transfixed,
quiet as a mouse as she sat on his knee in the front row.

"Yes, Mama," Blake whispered back to her. "Isn't
she amazing?"

"Mama," Isabella said again, clapping and tipping
her head back so she was resting against him as she
looked up.

Blake focused on Saffron again as she did something else incredible before stopping, her feet no longer moving, her pose perfect as the lights slowly went out. Within minutes the lights were rising again, flooding the theater at the same time that Saffron stood in the center of the stage, the crowd bursting into applause. Then she was joined by the other dancers, but Blake only had eyes for his wife, unable to drag his gaze away for even a second.

He couldn't believe how much she'd changed him, how different he felt from the man he'd been only a few years ago. He held Isabella tight, loving every second of having his little daughter close. She was the best thing that had ever happened to him, even if he was fiercely protective of her, so in love with her that it hurt sometimes.

"Go see Mama," Isabella demanded, wriggling so hard he could barely keep hold of her.

"Come on, let's go then," Blake said, scooping her up in one arm and holding her against his chest. She tapped his head.

"Sho-sho," she said, smiling up at him. Blake never had a chance of saying no to her, not when she looked the spitting image of her mother with her beautiful dark eyes, deepest red hair and angelic smile.

He lifted her up onto his shoulders, which was what she'd been asking for in her own little language, chuckling to himself about the fact he had a tutu all ruffled around the back of his neck. She was just like her mom when it came to ballet, too, and very opinionated about what she liked to wear. Tonight she'd wanted to look like a real ballerina, but she wasn't a pink girl, so it was a dark blue outfit with a tutu and matching shoes covered in bling and she looked impossibly cute.

"Mama!" Isabella squealed when she spotted her mother.

"Hey!" Saffron came running, her face alive as it always was when she was on a high after a performance. Blake hadn't seen her dance live in a show until Isabella was a year old, and now he hated to miss seeing her on stage. Although his daughter was very opinionated about being left home with a sitter, preferring to snuggle up in their bed.

"You were amazing," Blake said, pulling her tight into his arms for a quick kiss before he was pushed out of the way by his daughter, who now only had eyes for her mother.

"Hey, beautiful! Did you enjoy it?" Saffron asked her.

Isabella tucked her face against her mom's chest for a moment before pushing back and touching her mom's cheeks and then patting her hair. Saffron's hair was almost always down when she was home, but when she was performing, it was always pulled up tighter off her face and Isabella seemed transfixed with it.

"You know, if we were normal people, we'd have her with a sitter so we could go out for a late dinner," Blake said, laughing because he knew exactly what kind of reaction he was going to get from his wife.

"Wash your mouth out!" Saffron scolded, pulling Isabella's head tight to her chest and covering one of her ears. It was a constant joke between them, and even though Blake suggested it regularly, they both preferred to take Isabella out with them whenever they could. Especially now that Saffron was back dancing and he was so busy with the company during the day—they juggled as best they could, but after hours they liked to be a tight family unit. Unless his mother begged to have her granddaughter to stay, which usually resulted in a little girl packing her suitcase immediately and demanding to go.

"How about a quick ice cream on the way home instead?" Blake asked, reaching for his daughter and pulling her off Saffron.

"Yay!" Isabella squealed.

Saffron nodded. "Sounds good. Just let me change and say goodbye to everyone."

Blake waited for his wife, chuckling to himself how much his life had changed. Meeting Saffron had changed everything, made him realize how lucky he was in so many ways.

"You know, I took your mommy out for ice cream when I first met her."

"Mommy love ice cream," Isabella said, patting his arm, her beautiful dark eyes looking tired. Not that his daughter would admit to being sleepy for a second, though.

"Mommy was so beautiful then she took my breath away, and she still does," Blake replied without a hint of a lie. "I was a fool once, but when I found out you were in Mommy's tummy, I stopped being so stupid. I asked her to marry me."

"Tell me, story, Daddy."

"What story?" Saffron asked, slipping her arms around him from behind.

Blake grabbed her with his free hand, snaking it around her and pulling her close.

"I'm just telling Bella about when we were first together. Every time we're alone and you're dancing, I tell her how I fell in love with you when she was just a little button in your tummy."

"Oh, really?" Saffron said with a laugh, one eyebrow arched.

Blake laughed and dropped a lingering kiss to her lips when she tilted her head back to stare up at him.

"Really," he replied.

They left the building snuggled up tight, his daughter still in his arms and his wife tucked to his side. They'd never once told another soul the truth about their marriage, how they'd met and the marriage contract they'd once signed. Saffron had even managed to convince her friend Claire that they'd been secretly dating before their fake marriage. Only Blake's lawyer knew the truth, and he paid him enough not to breach attorney-client privilege.

"Our little secret, huh?" Saffron whispered in his ear.

Blake grinned and held her tighter. "Yes, Mrs. Goldsmith," he teased.

He had it all, and nothing would ever be more important to him than caring for his family, fiercely protecting them and doing everything in his power to be everything his father hadn't been.

He'd spent all his life terrified of becoming that man, and in the end nothing could be further from the truth. From the moment he'd accepted how much he loved

Saffron, to seeing his newborn daughter in his arms, he'd known there was no way he could turn into him. Not for a second.

"I love you," she murmured, head to his shoulder.

"I love 'cream," Isabella mumbled in a sleepy voice.

Blake grinned. "And I love Mama *and* ice cream."

They walked out the back exit to avoid any lingering fans, heading for their favorite ice cream parlor. The night air was cool, and he tucked Isabella closer against his chest and Saffron even snugger under his arm, loving the warmth of them.

"Surprise!"

Saffron laughed as her husband stopped midstride, eyes wide as he stared around the room. She ran over to him, throwing her arms around him. He gave her a glare that turned to a sigh and then a smile.

"You fooled me," he muttered.

She shrugged. "Yep, I did."

Saffron had told him it was a simple birthday celebration, just the three of them having dinner with his mother, and instead she'd filled their home with everyone he cared about, including some of his friends and former colleagues that she knew he'd been sorely missing.

"You're crazy," Blake said, holding her tight and kissing her hair.

"It's not only me who gets to live my dream."

He raised an eyebrow and she bit down on her lower lip, watching as his old buddies engulfed him, slapping backs and giving friendly hugs. She'd seen the pain he'd been in at giving that life up, and he'd made her dreams a reality by helping her every step of the way. Not to mention getting a whole lot of flak for re-scheduling his days when she was performing to be a stay-at-home dad. It was a role he loved, but she knew it wasn't exactly easy for a company CEO to take time off when all his peers had nannies.

"Saffron, you've got some explaining to do," Blake called out, pushing his friends away and holding out a hand to her, tugging her over.

She couldn't hide her smile, knowing what he was about to say.

"What kind of wife organizes a boys' helicopter weekend for her husband?"

Saffron winked at him, something he often did to her, and it made him chuckle.

"You might not be able to fly for the military again, but it doesn't mean you can't fly with at least some of your old team," she said, standing on tiptoes to kiss him, wanting him to have an amazing birthday. "It's only camping, but I figured it was the closest to replicating what you used to love. There's no use owning a fleet of planes and helicopters if you can't use them, right?"

His smile was impossibly charming, his eyes dancing as he gazed down at her. "You know what I do love right now?"

She tipped her head back. "What would that be?"

Blake swept her up in his arms, lifting her high-heeled feet off the ground and kissing her in front of everyone. His friends clapped and catcalled, but Saffron didn't care that they were putting on a show for them.

"You."

"Just so happens," she said, nipping his bottom lip when he tried to kiss her again, "that I feel the exact same way."

* * * * *

No*, Mia thought. *No, no, no.

He was here in Sugar Falls? And he was her doctor? How had this happened?

"It's you" was all he said. She stood there, stiff and numb, drinking in the sight of him but at a complete loss of what to say without looking foolish.

"You live here in Sugar Falls?" he asked when she remained silent. His eyes hadn't blinked and hadn't stopped their constant perusal of her. "And we're meeting like this? How could this have happened?"

His words mirrored her own thought process so exactly that the nervous giggle she'd been trying to swallow almost bubbled out. But then he smiled as though Santa had just delivered a long-sought-after Christmas gift to him, and a familiar cold panic spread through her. Mia reached for the file, the one containing all her personal information, including the fact that she was now carrying this stranger's child, and tried to yank it from his hands.

The hands that had so skillfully brought her body to life just two months ago.

* * *

Sugar Falls, Idaho:
Your destination for true love!

FROM DARE TO DUE DATE

BY
CHRISTY JEFFRIES

First Published in Great Britain 2016
By Mills & Boon, an imprint of HarperCollins*Publishers*
1 London Bridge Street, London, SE1 9GF

© 2016 Christy Jeffries

ISBN: 978-0-263-91970-7

23-0316

Our policy is to use papers that are natural, renewable and recyclable products and made from wood grown in sustainable forests.The logging and manufacturing processes conform to the legal environmental regulations of the country of origin.

Printed and bound in Spain
by CPI, Barcelona

Christy Jeffries received her Juris Doctor from California Western School of Law. But drafting court documents and working in law enforcement was merely an apprenticeship for her current career in the dynamic field of mummyhood and romance writing. She lives in Southern California with her patient husband, two energetic sons and one sassy grandmother. Follow her online at www.christyjeffries.com.

To my handsome, hardworking and tolerant husband. When I finally figured out what I was looking for, you ended up being there all along. I was beyond lucky when you called me back.

You are my heart.

Chapter One

The melting ice cubes in Mia Palinski's vodka and tonic were symbolic of the way her future was dissolving before her eyes.

She'd just turned thirty, yet no matter how many times she'd told herself that it was time to come to terms with her new life, she still couldn't shake the lingering wish that tonight it should've been her up on the stage of the Egyptian Theatre, pirouetting across the dance floor.

Watching the piano player on the opposite end of the bar, she wondered if the balding man once had bigger aspirations than playing old standards in the lounge of some swanky hotel in downtown Boise. Most performers did. At least she could take comfort in the thought that she wasn't the only one not living her dream.

And while she didn't begrudge her darling students

their chance to shine in their roles as the fairy-tale wedding guests in the Idaho Youth Performing Arts' rendition of Tchaikovsky's *Sleeping Beauty*, Mia would have been more comfortable if she hadn't been stuck backstage with Mrs. Rosellino, who thought her six-year-old daughter was going to be the next Martha Graham.

Along with most of the other dance instructors who had students performing in tonight's ballet, Mia referred to the delusional stage moms as idealists. Because unless sweet Madison Rosellino miraculously developed a decent amount of rhythm and learned to keep her finger out of her nose during performances, the sweet and quiet girl would probably never make it to Juilliard.

Her eye gave an involuntary twitch at the memory of her own mother, who was so similar to the Mrs. Rosellinos of the world. Mia took a sip of her now diluted drink, trying to wash away the reminder of the well-meaning but overbearing woman who had pushed her only child into competitive cheer rather than classical dance. Rhonda Palinski had wanted all eyes on Mia and had forcefully maneuvered her daughter onto the football fields, where the stages were bigger, the lights were brighter and the crowds were rowdier.

Her phone vibrated on the smooth-finished walnut bar beside her glass. She saw a group text message from her friends Maxine Cooper and Kylie Gregson. She loved them and knew they wanted an update on how the Labor Day performance had gone, but she couldn't bear to put on the brave face and pretend she wasn't hosting a pity party for one in an empty hotel bar. She grabbed a handful of fancy nuts out of a silver bowl. At least she gave in to her self-commiserations only in first-class establishments.

Mia loved and hated nights like tonight. She loved the music and she loved the dancing and she loved watching her young students and their contemporaries get to display the talents that they had worked so hard on during summer rehearsals. She truly didn't even mind the overbearing parents who expected their first-graders to be ballet prodigies and became annoyed when Mia didn't push the kids harder.

But the thing she hated was the fact that *she* could no longer be the one on stage dancing. Thinking such a miserable thought made her feel like a jealous old has-been, an emotion she despised even more.

She rubbed her sore knee through the black satin fabric of her slim-fitting pants, and then took another sip, willing the throbbing to go away. One of her pre-scribed pills might help with the physical pain, but nothing could diminish the emotional trauma of having her dancing career cut short by a golf club–wielding stalker who couldn't take no for an answer.

Nope. She wouldn't go there. It was one thing to wish things had worked out differently. It was quite another to sit here and relive the scariest moment of her life. She pushed her drink away and decided to go upstairs to her suite, order several desserts from room service and scroll through the pay-per-view channel looking for an interesting movie that could take her mind off what could have been.

Keeping a low profile meant she didn't get to travel the country as much as she once had as an NFL cheer-leader, so Mia normally took advantage of these quick forays into what her neighbors termed the "Big City" and made the most of the plush hotel accommodations.

She'd grown up as middle class as they came, with

most of her single mom's child support checks going toward cheer camps and extra lessons. And while Mia was careful with her income as the owner of the Snowflake Dance Academy in the small town of Sugar Falls, Idaho, she wasn't opposed to little splurges a couple of times a year—especially if they provided a quick, but safe, escape from the boring reality of her quiet existence.

And that was why she tried to ignore the text message that just flashed on her screen.

You're a great dance teacher. We're sure everything went perfectly. Don't go back to your room and sulk. Go out and live it up. We dare you!

Yep. Her best friends knew her, all right. Which meant they also knew she had no intention of accepting their ridiculous dare.

As she lifted a hand to signal the bartender to bring her check, a man walked into the lounge, his quick steps purposeful. Mia instinctively turned in the opposite direction, away from the stranger, and hoped that the guy was simply meeting someone in the nearly vacant bar. Ever since that incident with Nick Galveston, she had been careful not to draw any unwanted attention to herself and normally didn't hang out in cocktail lounges where traveling businessmen or lonely males might take any sort of interest in a young woman sitting alone at the bar.

She pulled her handbag closer to her. Why had she even stopped off here on her way back to her room? It wasn't as if she was a big drinker or looking for companionship. But after seeing the girl who played Aurora receive a huge bouquet of flowers right before the curtain closed and knowing that she would never experience that thrill again, Mia wanted something stronger than chocolate lava cake with peanut butter ganache to drown out her sorrows.

Unfortunately, the newcomer bypassed several of the empty tables and headed directly toward the small bar, near where she was sitting. He was handsome in that clean-cut all-American-boy way. However, in her experience, most men who looked like that were anything but pure and innocent.

She tried to keep her gaze averted, not wanting to risk making eye contact with him. But the large mirror across the room allowed her to take in his appearance. He wasn't overly large—just under six feet—and his suit was well tailored, but his silk designer tie was undone and hanging loosely around his neck. He didn't even look in her direction as he pulled out the leather upholstered bar stool a couple of feet away. His brown hair was close cropped and his face was set in a serious scowl. If he hadn't been dressed so well, she would've assumed he was in the military.

"I'll take a Glenlivet, neat, please," he said to the bartender. When the man still didn't acknowledge her in any way, she relaxed her shoulders and attempted a covert glance down at his shoes.

She was no expert, but her friend Kylie had just ordered those same handcrafted Italian leather shoes online for her new husband. So Mia knew they cost more than the monthly rent on her small dance studio. Nope. The guy definitely wasn't military because there was no way he would be able to afford to dress or drink that well on an enlisted man's salary.

Her ears picked up the tinny sound of Harry Chapin

singing about cats in cradles. The noise was in direct contrast to the piano and it took her a second to realize the song was a ringtone. His ringtone.

Whoa. This guy must have some serious daddy issues.

He fumbled, pulling his phone out of his pocket before silencing it and setting it on the bar. It immediately rang again and he whispered a curse before jabbing his finger at the screen. He had nice hands. Strong and capable-looking hands. Hands that would feel wonderful on…

"GP? Hello?" The hearty male voice coming out of the small speaker interrupted her wayward thoughts and caused the man next to her to practically jump off his leather stool in surprise. "Are you there, GP? Can you hear me?"

The skilled-looking fingers she'd just been lusting over must have pushed the wrong button, accepting rather than ignoring the call.

"Stupid damn phone," he said as he lifted the offending gadget off the bar and put it to his ear.

"No, Dad," he continued. "I don't want to talk about it anymore."

Mia took a sip of the drink she'd pushed away merely minutes ago, finding herself fascinated by the father-son drama unfolding right next to her. "You can't change my mind," she heard. Pause. "No, do not have them call me." Pause. "Listen, we will just have to agree to disagree. Have a safe flight home."

GP, or whatever his name was, looked as if he wanted to throw his now disconnected phone through the large window facing the quiet downtown street. The bartender brought the man's drink and Mia signaled for her own check. Damn it. She should've left when he was on his call. She didn't do angry confrontations.

"Sorry," he said, as he slipped his cell back into his sport coat pocket. "I hate people who take personal calls in public places."

He hadn't looked in her direction at all, so it took her a moment to realize he was speaking to her. She lifted her eyes to his and had to grip the bar's counter to steady herself when his hazel gaze met hers. A little pop exploded in her tummy and she suddenly felt like she was a fizzy bottle of champagne whose cork had just been released.

He was handsome. More than handsome. His clenched jaw was chiseled, yet serious, and his sad eyes didn't look the least apologetic. Nor did they seem very predatory.

Her eyes were drawn to his hands again and she noticed something funny about the way his suit jacket hit his wrists. She realized the man was wearing cuff-links—and expensive-looking ones at that. They were small gold-plated squares that had some type of an insignia embossed on them—an anchor maybe, but she couldn't tell for sure without getting too close.

And Mia knew better than to get too close.

Whoever this GP guy was, he seemed more upset with his father than intent on hitting on her. She kept her purse clenched tightly next to her side, but exhaled enough to loosen some of the tension in her body.

"Don't worry about it," she said, as the bartender set a small leather folder in front of her. "I was just getting ready to go anyway."

"Please, don't leave on my account. I didn't mean to disturb you. In fact—" he reached for her bill "—let me pay for your drink."

"No," she said a bit too loudly. "I'm not leaving."

He looked at the bill she had scooped up before he could grab it.

"I mean, I *was* leaving. But not because of you."

He smiled and his even white teeth softened his expression, making him appear more boyish, rather than hawkish. Swiftly, that fizzy sensation bubbled throughout her entire bloodstream. Wow. How strong had her vodka and tonic been? She would've stood up and ran out of the lounge, but she now couldn't trust her normally well-muscled legs to hold her petite frame.

Harry Chapin began singing from GP's pocket again. "Crap. I'm sorry, I have this new phone and I can't figure out how to turn it off."

He held up the ringing device with the contact name of "Dad" lighting up the screen. It was the same model as hers, and she was an expert at screening calls.

"Here," she said, taking it from him. "You just tap on this red dot and then, once the call goes to voice mail, you go to Settings…" He leaned in toward her and she could smell his musky citrus cologne. She didn't dare make eye contact with him again—not when they were this close. Instead, she stared intently at the screen as her fingers keyed in all the appropriate commands to effectively silence his phone.

"Then how do I turn it back on? You know, like next week when my dad calms down a little and finally accepts the fact that I want to live my own life and not follow in his footsteps?"

Yep, this guy definitely had daddy issues. But really, who was she to judge?

"Well, if he's anything like my mom—" she couldn't

stop the shudder that raised bumps on her bare arms "—I doubt it will only take a week."

"You don't know the half of it. But I *do* need this phone for work, so as tempting as it might be, I can't stay off the grid forever."

She nodded at his true statement. As much as Mia had tried to hide out these past couple of years, it was impossible to disappear completely. At least not without losing a part of herself. And if she lost any more of herself, she wondered what would be left.

"In that case, you can just block his number like this, but still get calls from everyone else." She tapped away at his screen. "Of course, this will only work until he catches on and tries calling from an unblocked number."

"Hmm. Sneaky. But my father's pretty resourceful, so I wouldn't put it past him."

"My mother learned to call me from my great-aunt Nonnie's rest home, knowing I couldn't *not* answer. I'm sure your dad will figure out a way eventually. I find it's best to just take the call, let them lecture you for exactly two and half minutes and then pretend you have a UPS delivery at the door that you need to sign for and disconnect the call."

The man who'd been called GP laughed loudly enough to draw the attention of the piano player and the bartender. If she thought his smile made her insides all bubbly, his laughter made her want to melt.

Seriously, what kind of person made jokes about wacky family members with someone she'd never even met? Apparently, the same person who was still sitting here grinning like a giddy schoolgirl at the good-looking man.

He slipped his phone back inside his inner jacket

pocket and when he did so, his hand rooted around before pulling out something else. He tossed a velvet-covered box on the bar and then looked up to the ceiling before running his hand over his forehead. The case looked like something that would hold jewelry—an engagement ring perhaps. The thought that this man was walking around with such an item, yet appeared to be so frustrated and let down, made her wonder what exactly had happened to him earlier this evening.

"That's a pretty swanky-looking box," Mia said.

"My father thought so when he gave them to me." The man opened the case to reveal a set of black onyx cuff links, the initials GPM embossed in gold over each one.

"They're very nice." Mia forced a polite smile, wondering why the man had such a wry look on his face.

"He said they're to remind me of who I am and where I came from." GP, whose last name must begin with an *M*, took another drink of his scotch. "The irony of the gift is that my father detests cuff links. In fact, he hates the way I dress altogether."

Mia leaned back so she could get a better look at his suit. As far as she could see, the man was dressed impeccably. Sure, maybe it was a little too tailored, a bit too metropolitan chic for Idaho standards. After all, this was Boise. Who wore such luxurious accessories in this part of the country?

Bolo ties, yes, but cuff links, no.

Maybe his father was some potato farmer who thought his son had gotten a little too fancy for his britches. Her own mother was the exact opposite. Every time she saw Mia, she chastised her for wearing her workout clothes around town and told her she had the potential of landing the coveted position of trophy wife, if only she'd put in some effort with her appearance.

"I take it your father isn't a suit man?"

"You could say that. Dad likes to describe himself as anti-establishment. He's what you'd call a free spirit and prefers to dress like he's just been eighty-sixed from a Beach Boys concert. Which never made sense to me, considering his education and what he does for a living. He calls me his rebel child."

"You don't look like much of a rebel," she said. He looked like an international businessman about to close a multibillion-dollar deal.

"I'll tell him you said so next time he calls." He gave the jewelry case a slight tap and it slid down the smooth bar a couple of inches. "So two and a half minutes, huh?"

He took another sip of the single malt scotch that was the exact shade of his eyes. Sheesh. Why did she have to look at those eyes of his again?

"Yep. I've got it down to a science. Anything less and they'll feel like they were short-changed and will only call back later. Anything more and it becomes the snowball effect, picking up speed and intensity and then there's no interrupting them once the full sermon gets going about all the sacrifices they made for you and how you're throwing away opportunities."

"I feel like I should be taking notes. Please, let me buy you a drink. You can tell me the top five best excuses for getting out of Thanksgiving family dinners."

She should've politely refused, grabbed her jacket and purse, and walked as quickly to the elevator bank as she could. But she thought of her own prospects for the holiday that was only a couple of months around the corner, and the hard, familiar lump of loneliness wedged in her throat. When was the last time she'd talked with a man who wasn't a well-known neighbor or hadn't been vetted by her two closest friends?

He must have sensed her vacillating because he shot her that boyish smile. "What are you having?"

Her nerve endings fizzled again and, before she could stop herself, she blurted out, "Champagne."

He looked doubtfully at the glass sitting in front of her—the one containing clear liquid and the remnants of a lime—and then raised his perfectly arched brown brows at her before asking the bartender to bring a bottle of Veuve Clicquot.

A whole bottle? What had she been thinking?

Maxine and Kylie would've told her she'd been thinking with her lady parts. Then they'd have high-fived her for double downing on their dare and told her it was about time she tested the waters of the romance pond. It had been so long, it wouldn't hurt to just dip her toe in.

Hopefully, she wasn't already in way over her head.

Garrett McCormick had been having the most frustrating evening of his life when he'd aimlessly wandered into the deserted lounge at the upper-class hotel. And that was saying something considering he'd been a battlefield surgeon in some of the hottest combat zones in the world. When he'd stormed out of the five-star restaurant down the street, leaving his argumentative and overbearing father at the table, he'd wanted a stiff drink and the kind of solitude he knew he couldn't get from the downtown college bar scene or from the officer's club near the Shadowview Military Hospital, where he was on staff.

He'd been so angry and so intent on downing something that would steady his nerves, he hadn't even noticed the petite raven-haired beauty sitting at the bar. If he had, his internal warning bells would've gone off and he'd have found another place to sit.

When his cell phone rang, he'd been startled and his embarrassment had forced him to take in his surroundings. What he'd told her was true—he hated people who were so self-important they answered their phones in public places, forcing strangers to have to listen to their private calls.

Yet, he wasn't sorry if his obnoxious telephone etiquette was the reason he now sat talking with her. She was wearing a strapless sequined top, and a black satin jacket hung off the back of her high leather chair. The shiny material matched her form-fitting black pants, making him think she was wearing some sort of feminine tuxedo. But softer. Sexier.

Considering it was almost eleven o'clock on a weeknight, she must've been at some fancy party before stopping into the hotel lounge for a nightcap. Either that or she was just all dressed up and on the hunt for some lonely traveling businessman.

He knew the types well. The gold diggers, the celebrity seekers, even the bored soccer moms who got their kicks by meeting random strangers at bars for one-night stands. But there was something about her shimmering blue eyes that made her look more like a scared rabbit than a prowling sex kitten. Besides, she was beautiful, but not in that surgically enhanced "tries too hard" way.

That was the first thing he shied away from when it came to women. His father was a plastic surgeon turned television producer who specialized in shows about surgical enhancements and makeovers. If there was one thing Garrett knew, it was artificial beauty. And he'd spent the past fifteen or so years of his life trying to get away from Med TV and the people who perpetuated that false and pretentious ideal.

He swallowed back his scotch just as the ice bucket and champagne showed up. The bartender set two glasses in front of them and, while Garrett had been intent on keeping company with only a bottle of Glenlivet Eighteen, his plans for tonight had suddenly taken a different turn.

"Here's to parents who don't know when to let go," he said as he tipped his champagne flute toward hers.

"Here's to a lot of people who don't know when to let go."

Garrett didn't know if her added comment was in reference to someone else she knew or if it was a premonition that they were both too uptight and needed to cut loose. He chose to focus on the latter because, after all, once he was discharged from the navy next week, he would be letting go of everything and starting his life all over again.

"So how far away did you have to move to get away from your parents?" he asked, wanting to get to know her better. She took a sip and tilted her head, as if pondering how much personal information she wanted to share with him. After all, they were two random people sitting in a bar. Who opened up to a complete stranger?

"My mom lives in Florida."

"Is that where you're from?"

"Not originally. We moved a lot when I was a kid. My mom was a bit of a flake when it came to herself, but as her only child, she was always seeking greater opportunities for me. She'd hear about some new dance troupe or a hyped-up instructor and she'd pack up all of my tights and leotards and off we'd go."

"So you're a dancer?"

"I was," she murmured before finishing off her glass. "What about you? Did you have to go far to get away from your parents?"

He took the hint that she didn't want to expand on what might be a personal subject and refilled her glass. "I moved away from home the day after my high school graduation, much to the chagrin of my dad and stepmothers."

"Stepmothers plural?"

"Well, Dad has gone through his share of wives. Not at the same time, mind you," he clarified when it looked as if she was going to choke on her champagne. "But most of them kept in touch with me, even if it was only for the length of time they received their alimony checks."

"My mom always hoped for an alimony check. But she and my father never got married so she had to make do with lowly child support. I never got it, you know?"

"The child support? She didn't use it for you?"

"No, she did. I meant that I never got that whole depending-on-a-man-for-money mentality. I guess, sure, men should pay for their kids and stuff, but I always thought it would just be easier to make a clean break from the loser and start fresh. Support yourself."

Wow, some guy must've really done a number on this lady. While it was refreshing to hear that there was a woman out there who wasn't looking to get rich off some unsuspecting meal ticket, Garrett couldn't help thinking of all the fake blondes back home who'd made it more than clear that they would love nothing more than to gain access to his large trust fund or the rolling cameras that constantly surrounded his family.

"I couldn't agree more," he said, raising his glass in an acknowledging salute. After all, cutting ties was exactly what he'd done when he'd left home at eighteen. He'd had access to everything his family's money could buy. But it came with the heavy cost of bowing down to his father's will and his father's lifestyle. "In fact, that's why my dad and I were arguing tonight. He doesn't understand why I want to support myself and make my own decisions—live my own life."

"My mother and I have had that same conversation multiple times. My girlfriend says that when I become a mom myself, I'll understand." Garrett made a mental note of the fact that she didn't have kids. She wasn't wearing a wedding ring, but that didn't mean much to some women. "She said to think how sad I'd be if my mom stayed out of my life because she didn't care about me at all. But you know what? I think I could live with that kind of sadness."

He nodded his head in earnest. "I've been told the same thing. Yet, most of the time it doesn't feel like caring. It feels like an ego trip. Like he doesn't necessarily want the best for me, he just wants my life to be a reflection of *his* accomplishments and his success."

"Yes!" she agreed and they clinked glasses again.

Here was someone who got it—who understood what his unorthodox childhood had been like. His head was lighter and his smile was freer. He must be feeling the effects of the scotch. Or the champagne. Or maybe a combo of both. "I don't think it matters what we tell our parents, though. It never seems to sink in."

"It probably never will," she said. "Ten years from now, you and I could meet up in this same bar and we'll be voicing the same complaints."

"Promise me that in ten years, we will," he said more seriously than he intended. But here was a kindred spirit. A woman who knew exactly where he was coming from.

"Oh, I don't know. That sounds a bit pathetic."

"Meeting up with me again?"

"No. That we'll still be so stuck in our issues that we'll need to travel back to Boise just to commiserate in our overbearing parents support group."

She was right. They did sound a little pathetic. And that was the last thing he wanted a charming and genuine woman to think about him. "So Boise isn't home for you?"

She darted her eyes to the left before reaching for the chilled bottle and refilling their glasses. "I'm in town for a ballet performance. I'm going home tomorrow."

That explained the fancy outfit—and allayed his fears that she was a local groupie or some suburban wife out looking for an anonymous fling.

God, she was beautiful. Her high cheekbones, her pale blue eyes, her creamy skin. She was turned facing him, her legs crossed with one of her kitten heels hooked into a lower rung of the bar stool.

"You have a gorgeous collarbone," he finally said, unable to look away from her.

"Did you say *collarbone*?"

"Yes." He reached out a finger, tracing the ridge between her neck and her shoulders. He heard her sharp intake of breath, but he was well and truly buzzed and unless she moved away or told him to stop, he planned to touch her smooth, velvety skin for as long as she'd let him. "I've always had a thing for clavicles."

Yep, he was definitely on his way to being intoxicated. Any more booze and he'd be calling things by their biological Latin terms.

She held herself completely still, but her tongue darted out and licked her full lips. "Why is that?"

"I just find them incredibly sexy. And real. It's one of the few parts on a woman's body that can't be surgically enhanced." He looked up into her eyes and saw her dilated pupils. Tonight, he didn't want to worry about his father, or the new practice he was opening next month. He just wanted to think about the incredible woman in front of him. His hand trailed down her arm and settled onto her waist, and still she didn't move away.

"I also find you incredibly sexy and real," he said right before dipping his head and placing his mouth on hers.

She made a slight sound that could have been a moan or a protest, but she didn't pull back. He tilted his head and opened his lips, coaxing her mouth to accept more of him. When she finally opened up, she welcomed his tongue wholeheartedly and responded by wrapping her bare arms around his shoulders.

He tasted the champagne on her tongue and wanted to drink her up. He wanted to feel all of her, but these damn bar stools were making things awkward. Without breaking contact, he rose to his feet, bringing their heads to the same height. He groaned when she allowed him to deepen the kiss, and he brought his other hand up to her waist to pull her closer.

A discreet cough, followed by the bartender's voice announcing last call, finally cut through the fog of passion that had overtaken him. He pulled back his head but didn't release his grip, wanting to maintain as much physical contact as he possibly could without drawing any more attention.

"I've never kissed anyone like that in a public place," she said, her voice much huskier than it had been earlier. The pink flush creeping up her cheeks could have been from embarrassment or could have been from desire. He was hoping it was the latter.

"Would you like to try it again in private place?"

"Like where?"

"Well… I could get a room…" What in the hell was he thinking? He didn't go around propositioning women in hotels. But it wasn't as if he could take her back to the officers' barracks. And he definitely wasn't ready to let her go.

His emotions were storming at top speed, and the alcohol he didn't normally consume wasn't helping him think straight. Yet for once in his life, he didn't want to think straight. He ran his fingers along the satiny waistband of her pants and wondered what kind of undergarments she could possibly be wearing underneath.

She looked around at the mostly empty bar and again lightly licked her lips, which had remained mere inches from his own. "I already have a room."

Garrett didn't bother to ask her for clarification. Pulling his wallet out of his pocket, he peeled out two one-hundred-dollar bills and threw them on the bar before grabbing the half-full bottle of champagne with one hand and reaching for her fingers with the other.

Chapter Two

The shrill ringing of the phone startled Garrett awake. He quickly reached out to answer it, fumbling with the receiver. "H'lo," he said when he finally got the right side to his ear.

"Who's this?" a woman's voice on the other end of the line demanded.

Opening his eyes, he squinted and looked around the dark hotel room. Old habits kicked in and he stayed silent until his hazy brain could register where he was and whom he was with. The memories from last night came flooding back and even though he sensed he was alone, he looked around, confirming his disappointment.

She was gone.

The caller must've been impatient because he heard the dial tone instead of more questions. He'd just hung up when the phone let out another shrill ring.

"Hello," he said, this time more clearly but with some added annoyance.

"You again?" the same person demanded. "Is this room eight oh four?"

"I have no idea," Garrett replied before thinking better of it. He sat up and flipped on the light switch by the bed, but it took a second for his eyes to adjust enough to focus on the numbers typed into the printed directory on the telephone. "Uh, yeah, it is. Can I help you?"

He heard mumbled voices on the other end, then the caller told a person in the background, "It's her room, but some guy answered."

Wait, did they know the woman from last night? "Excuse me. Hello? Do you know the woman who was staying in this room?"

"Oh, my gosh! Is there a problem?" The caller's voice became frantic. "Did something happen to her?"

Heck, he wasn't trying to scare anyone or cause an alarm. "What? No. I…uh…met her last night, but I didn't catch her name."

"If you don't know her name then why are you in her room?"

That was a damn good question. And one he didn't have an answer for.

"Is anyone there?" After a few seconds, the caller said, "Maybe we should call hotel security."

"No." Garrett stood up. "No need to call security. I think she left. She invited me up here and…" He let his voice trail off, not wanting to get the woman he'd slept with in trouble.

"No way. She would never invite some guy up to her hotel room."

Clearly, this person wasn't going to give him any answers and he couldn't very well defend himself without incriminating someone else. "Oh, did you say you were calling room eight oh four? Sorry, this is room four oh eight. Apparently, there's been a mix-up. Have a nice day."

He quickly slammed the receiver down and tried to think about what to do next. But his brain wasn't adapting as quickly as it used to when he'd get startled out of a deep slumber. Garrett had been a heavy sleeper ever since med school. When he was a resident at the Naval Medical Center in San Diego, he'd learned to crash whenever he got the chance. If there was an emergency, then an on-duty corpsman would be there to wake him up.

That must be why he'd never even heard the woman leave.

He stood in the hotel room, wearing nothing but a confused expression, looking at the tangled four-hundred-thread-count sheets and the empty bottle of champagne near the bed. He studied his bare torso in the mirror over the dresser and noticed the faint purple hue of a love bite on the left side of his neck. He ran a hand through his still-short military haircut, which made his already tender head ache even more. What could he possibly have been thinking to come back to a hotel room with a woman he'd just met?

Being raised with video cameras always hovering nearby, Garrett had learned to be especially cautious not to let anyone get too close to him for fear that they were after something bigger—like a shot at television stardom. Growing up under the harsh lights of studio sets back when his dad had been the star of his own television talk show, then later a producer of a string of other reality series, Garrett had suffered the spillover effects of being followed by the Hollywood paparazzi who constantly linked him to his dad's notoriety.

He was thirty-six years old and still had a difficult time discerning women who were genuinely interested in him from those who were on the hunt for their fifteen minutes of fame.

And judging by the way the beautiful woman had sneaked out this morning without a trace, it was obvious she hadn't been looking for much more than a good time. Or a notch in her D-list celebrity belt.

How could he have been so stupid?

Had his father set this up? Had she been sent by the show's assistants? Was the caller standing outside right now with a camera, hoping to catch them in the act? He hadn't watched any of his dad's shows in several years, but at dinner last night, his old man had confided that ratings were down and if they couldn't breathe some new life into the series, he could be facing cancellation.

God, he hoped this wasn't some sort of last-ditch publicity stunt.

No. He was pretty sure his gut reaction last night had been on target. The caller sounded surprised that the woman would take a man up to her room. So hopefully she had simply been a lonely traveler looking for a little excitement and companionship.

His official discharge from the military was right around the corner and he didn't want to worry about any risqué photos or incriminating evidence ruining his career.

Still. He'd hate for any news about him to leak to the press. He'd spent his whole adult life avoiding the cameras, and the only place he'd been able to feel comfortable in his own skin was in the navy. Garrett had purposely volunteered for the most remote assignments whenever possible just to escape the constant media attention that came from being Dr. Gerald McCormick's son.

He damn well wasn't going to blow his cover now, which was exactly what he'd told his father at dinner yesterday evening when they'd gotten into their heated argument about the career path he'd just taken.

Garrett sat down on the edge of the bed and looked at the abandoned luggage stand in the open closet. He remembered the woman had an open suitcase there last night. And she'd already had a key to this room when they'd come upstairs. He let out a breath and eased back onto the bed. So she had obviously been a registered hotel guest, and since even he had no idea that he'd end up at some hotel bar when he'd stormed out of the restaurant a few blocks away, then nobody would've had the foresight to set him up.

That was one crisis averted. There was also the fact that he'd been the one who'd approached her. Fragments of conversation were slowly coming back to him. She'd said she was a dancer—well, she'd definitely had the lithe and graceful body to prove it. She'd also mentioned not being from Boise. Maybe she was just some bored housewife who had to fly home before her husband and kids woke up.

Wait, she'd said she didn't have kids. He couldn't remember anything about a husband, but would she have been honest if she'd had one?

He pulled a pillow over his head, wishing he could bury his shame along with his guilt. He took a deep breath, hoping he wasn't the cause of some poor cuckold's broken heart. But inhaling was a big mistake because when he did, the lingering aroma of jasmine tickled his nose, reminding him of her intoxicating fragrance and of how he hadn't been able to get enough of her heady scent. Of how he'd smelled, kissed and tasted every square inch of the woman's perfect, flexible body last night.

Crap. *The woman?* He still didn't even know her name.

This wasn't like him. Lieutenant Commander Garrett McCormick was a trained battlefield surgeon and an orthopedic specialist. He was cool under pressure and never got rattled. He for sure never let his guard down and didn't do anything unbecoming an officer. So then why had he allowed some sad-eyed, incredibly stunning woman get to him? What had come over him?

He took one last sniff and then threw the pillow to the floor. *Lust,* he thought before standing up and striding toward the bathroom. That's what had gotten into him. Pure, old-fashioned lust combined with frustration at his old man and a need to establish his autonomy with a woman who'd actually taken the time to listen to him and could relate to having an overbearing and egotistical parent.

He wasn't his dad. He didn't sleep with every beautiful woman who fluttered her eyelashes at him. But Garrett deserved to have a little companionship in his life, didn't he?

He stepped into the shower and turned the water on as hot as he could stand it before trying to unscrew the cap off the miniscule shampoo bottle. He'd wash all trace of the woman from his body and then try to banish all indications of last night's events from his mind.

The problem was, he didn't think he could forget how perfect she'd felt in his arms. How warm and willing she'd been when he'd eased himself inside her. Or how her breath came in short gasps when she'd reached her peak and begged him not to stop.

Man. He needed to get over it. To get over *her*.

He dried off and wrapped the towel around his waist before going out into the room to look for his clothes. He spotted his smartphone on the bedside table, and his heart flipped over when he recalled her slim fingers running along his screen in the bar, showing him how to block his incoming calls.

Maybe she had programmed her telephone number in his list of contacts.

His pulse picked up speed as he scrolled through his phone, only to slow down until it was a disappointing lump in his throat. Nope, there was nothing but four missed calls from his father and one from his dad's assistant, Marty. Well, Dad and Marty would have to wait until hell froze over.

Control yourself, McCormick. He hated getting worked up like this. But he was angry with himself for falling for the beautiful woman in the first place and coming upstairs with her. And he was angry with her for disappearing into thin air.

He got dressed and took one last look around the room, maybe so that he could memorize this moment or maybe because he was searching for one last clue about the woman's identity. A knock sounded and his stomach flipped over.

Was that her? Had she come back after all? Or was it security?

He opened the heavy door and frowned when he saw

a tall, older lady in a maid's uniform. "Sorry." She spoke in halting English. "I thought you checked out already."

She picked up the clipboard hanging off her service cart, as though to make sure she hadn't made a mistake. Likely, she hadn't, and the woman who'd spent the evening with him had in fact checked out of the hotel. Garrett took a step closer, thinking he might be able to find out the woman's name by looking at the guest info sheet.

But the motion forced him to accidentally release the room door, and it whooshed closed with a heavy thunk. The sound caused the maid to look up at him sharply, and she pulled the clipboard to her gray uniform. She stared at him and he glanced at the locked knob and realized he couldn't get back in.

If he stood here much longer, this employee would also realize that he didn't have a key and he had no way to prove that he was a guest of the hotel. The walkie-talkie on her cart crackled to life and Garrett decided the last thing he needed was to have security made aware of his presence.

"Yes, my wife already checked us out," Garrett finally said, thankful he'd at least gotten dressed and that his wallet and keys were still in his pants pocket. "I'm supposed to meet her at the bar."

What in the world had made a confirmed bachelor like him refer to the woman from last night as his wife? Or mention that they were meeting at a bar. Who met at a bar at oh eight hundred?

The maid lifted an eyebrow at him and he couldn't blame her for being suspicious. Then again, this was a hotel and he was sure the employees had seen more scandalous behavior than his. But just to be on the safe side, he pulled out a twenty-dollar bill and handed it to her. "Here. We forgot to leave a tip for the turndown service last night," he mumbled before making his way to the elevator and down to the lobby.

The bar was deserted except for the lone bartender reading a newspaper and a busboy wiping down the tables from the night before. He flashed back to a memory of entering the lounge last night, hell-bent on drinking his anger away. The nerve of his dad trying to talk him into moving back to California to film a new show. Those cuff links had been the icing on the smug cake his father had served after dinner over a nice cold glass of familial guilt.

Garrett patted his coat pocket and pulled out the velvet case. He snapped it open, a visual reminder of what had brought him storming in here last night.

Then he frowned when he realized one of the cuff links was missing. Had he left it in the room? He looked back at the bank of elevators and wondered if it was worth the risk of having the maid call security on him. He remembered taking them out of his pocket last night as he and the woman had been drinking. But before they'd left, he clearly recalled her handing the box back to him. She must have known that he wasn't the kind of guy who would throw away something so personal and expensive, even if he didn't understand his father's purpose in presenting him with such a questionable gift.

He also remembered picking up both his jacket and the cuff link case off the elevator floor last night, then smiled at the memory of how those items had gotten there in the first place. He walked back over to the elevators and wasted several minutes looking into each one for the missing cuff link. But like the woman from last night, it was long gone.

So then what happened to it?

And what had happened to her?

The front desk was busy and Garrett quickly dismissed the thought of asking the clerk for a guest's information. The cleaning lady upstairs had eyeballed him as if he was a criminal. So what was he supposed to ask the college-age-looking kid behind the desk? *Excuse me, but can you tell me the name of the woman who was staying in room eight oh four? I spent the night with her, but I never thought to ask her myself.*

Please. Maybe if this was some no-tell motel, he could bribe the employee. But he doubted that a high-quality establishment, which had most likely already been put on notice by his mystery caller this morning, would be willing to bend the rules.

And did he really want it leaked to the press who was asking? He'd be lucky if he didn't appear on some sleazy tabloid show for this stunt.

His thoughts were circling around like the whirling blades of a Huey helicopter, and he couldn't decide on a course of action.

Or inaction for that matter. Maybe he'd just dodged a bullet. It wasn't as though he was in the market for a relationship anyway, so he really didn't need the extra chaos that this situation might cause. Especially during this transitional time in his life. It was best to get the woman and this whole experience out of his mind.

Leaving the hotel, he walked down the busy Boise street to where he'd left his car, doing a double take at any woman with long dark hair to see if it was her. His cell phone vibrated in his pocket and when he pulled it out, he saw Matt Cooper's name on the screen. A year ago, the chief of police for Sugar Falls had been one of

Garrett's more stubborn patients. But the former marine had also become a friend and had been instrumental in talking him into opening a specialized clinic in the small Idaho town.

Cooper had sold him on the concept that where there was a tourist trade that catered to extreme sports such as downhill skiing, river rafting and hiking, there was a need for orthopedic surgeons. It wasn't a hard sell since not only was the town unpretentious and as far removed from the limelight as Garrett could get, it also desperately needed a physician who could actually serve the local community for the better.

"What's happening, Coop?" Garrett said by way of greeting.

"I just got off the phone with Mayor Johnston and the city approved the zoning for converting that old lumber mill you bought into medical offices. My wife's friend has a brother who is doing some contracting and thinks he can have a crew start construction tomorrow."

"Is he any good?"

"As far as I can tell. But now that you're going to be living in a small town, it's best to realize that's how they do things here." Cooper was a transplant himself, first from Detroit and then the military, and during a previous conversation he'd confided that he was still adapting to the slower-paced life. "Everyone knows somebody who is related to someone else who can get things done for you. It took me a while to get used to it, but the system can be beneficial."

"Okay. Have him email me an estimate and a contract. As long as people up there know how to mind their own business, then I'll hire whoever they want."

Coop laughed. "Now, I didn't say they know how to

mind their own business. But the community as a whole is a tight-knit group, and if they like you well enough, they wouldn't sell you out to some big-city paparazzi. How did that talk with your old man go, by the way?"

Cooper was one of the few people who knew Garrett was related to the famous television producer. But that's because the guy would investigate the depth lines on a ship's anchor if he felt like it. And when he'd been hospitalized with two consecutive knee surgeries and nothing else to look forward to, the marine had been bored enough to investigate his surgeon.

"It went as expected. He wanted what he always wants, which is for me to return to California and start filming alongside him. I told him about my new plans. He said there's no reason for me to go into private practice in some—no offense—Podunk town where my patients will only be able to pay for my services in taxidermy animals and squirrel meat casserole."

"Ouch. Although, that's what I expected, too, before I actually visited Sugar Falls."

"Well, let's hope for everyone's sake that my dad and his entourage of cameras never decide to visit." Garrett thought about his former patient's family history and realized he might sound like a spoiled, ungrateful child. "Don't get me wrong, I love the man. But I should've known better than to meet him last night. If it weren't for that stupid dinner, I never would've gotten so pissed off and…"

What? He never would've walked to the hotel bar and experienced the most magical evening in his life?

Of course, he couldn't say any of that to Cooper. Even though the two men's relationship was moving into friendship territory, Garrett wasn't ready to confess to anyone that his unsinkable heart had nearly been caught in a rip current.

He climbed into his late-model truck and dropped his head to the leather-covered steering wheel. He was too embarrassed to say anything to anyone and didn't need a bored police chief to start asking too many questions.

Wait a second. Having Cooper asking questions on Garrett's behalf might be another thing altogether. The idea of having his friend assist him in finding the mystery lady was ridiculous, but that wouldn't stop him from exploring the possibility of it later. When he didn't already have eight hundred things to do before the big move.

"Anyway." Garrett started his engine. "Speaking of expectations, tell me more about some of these small-town neighbors I'm going to be meeting in Sugar Falls."

Chapter Three

Eight weeks later, while her two best friends sat in her living room for their regular Thursday night dinner together, Mia came out of the bathroom holding the small plastic stick in her hand.

"That was quick," Kylie Gregson said, looking down at the empty box. "It says that you needed to wait three minutes for the results."

"I know. But I didn't want to wait in there alone to find out. Here." Mia set the pregnancy test on a paper towel on the kitchen counter then rushed back to the couch and pulled her favorite throw blanket up to her chin. "It probably needs about two more minutes. I can't look. You guys tell me what it says."

Maxine Cooper walked over to the counter and looked at the stick. "Well, I don't think we need to wait that long. The second blue line is pretty clear already."

"What do two blue lines mean again?"

"It means positive," Kylie said, checking the instructions.

"Let's give it a little more time," Mia whispered. "Maybe the other blue line will go away." But she was a smart woman with a bachelor's degree in fine arts. She knew none of this was going away.

She was pregnant. Single and pregnant.

A flood of emotion overcame her and she didn't know how to feel at first. Even though she'd thought about this possibility well before she'd sent her friend around the corner to Lester's Pharmacy to pick up the test, she knew she wasn't upset.

She was terrified, but she'd dealt with scarier things in her life. She was in denial, but then, she'd lived as a shell of herself for the past few years, so the feeling wasn't too uncommon. She was ashamed, but there was something else pushing her guilt aside and giving her a glimpse at a happiness she hadn't experienced in a long time.

"Aw, sweetie," Kylie said. "I know this is overwhelming, but you're a strong woman. And you have us to help you."

"I know," she said, tears threatening to spill from her eyes. "I promised myself I would forget about that night in Boise. And it was almost getting easier until I realized my cycle had never been this late. I guess in my determination to forget everything, I didn't think about the consequences, either."

"Do you want to talk about your plans?" Maxine asked.

"I'm scared. Obviously. I don't know how I'll do it." As soon as she realized she was late, a fear set in. But so did another emotion—excitement. "Like a tiny part of me is kind of looking forward to having this baby. I know this sounds selfish because I hated growing up without a father and I always swore that if I had kids of my own I wouldn't make the same mistakes that my mom made with me. But I'm actually a little bit excited." She rubbed her knee, which was getting sorer with each passing day. "That bastard Nick took so much from me—and not just physically. I thought I'd never recover after he attacked me, that my life was ruined. Yet, the thought of having a baby—having someone who is only mine and who needs me—is unreal, but in a positive way. This pregnancy might make me feel like I have a purpose again."

Both of her friends looked at each other before turning back toward her. Then Kylie asked, "What about the baby's father?"

"What about him? It's not like I know him or would even know where to find him."

Maxine hesitated before saying, "Cooper has some connections with the Boise PD and he can talk to the hotel security, maybe ask some questions on the down low—"

"No," Mia interrupted. "What if the guy is married? Or a psychopath? I don't need him. *We* don't need him," she corrected, as she put her hands protectively over the not yet visible bump of her tummy.

Her friends looked at each other again and Maxine shrugged. "Nobody has to make any decisions right this second. How about you let everything sink in and then, if you change your mind, we'll help you find him."

Mia nodded, but knew she wouldn't ever change her mind. She was about to take control of her own life, of her own destiny, and she wasn't going to invite some strange man into her world to start calling the shots or vetoing her decisions—even if she knew where to find him.

The women turned their conversation to pregnancy symptoms and childbirth and their doubts about ancient Dr. Suarez, who was the town's only general practitioner and should have retired twenty years prior.

"I think I might look for an obstetrician in Boise," Mia said.

"Thank goodness I'm covered under Drew's insurance," said Kylie. She was married to a lieutenant commander in the navy and twenty weeks pregnant. "I only have to drive as far as Shadowview Hospital when it's my time to deliver. Don't you think going all the way to Boise might be a bit far?"

Mia flexed her knee, trying to stretch out the pain that had only increased over these past weeks. Her friend was right, but going to the town doctor would be tantamount to hanging a huge banner outside her dance studio announcing to the world that she was pregnant and unmarried. Some of her students' parents might think she wasn't a fit role model for their precious offspring. She also helped coach the high school cheerleading team and knew the PTA would surely call her morals into question. Sugar Falls was a small town, and her career didn't need that kind of negative publicity.

"What about that new medical center out at the old lumber mill?" Maxine asked.

"Oh, yeah." Kylie was nodding her head. "My brother, Kane, has been doing the construction on the building and said the first offices are unofficially opening next week."

"What kind of doctors will they have?" Mia was skeptical but any physician who was new to town would still be considered an outsider and wouldn't be so quick to divulge patient information to the rest of his cronies in the Kiwanis Club, as Doc Suarez was known to do.

"Cooper's surgeon from the base hospital is opening up an orthopedic clinic there now that he's out of the military. And I heard there was a new dentist moving in next month. But no OBs, as far as I know."

"Actually," Max added, "it would probably be a good idea to talk to Dr. McCormick about your knee, Mia."

"I know. It's been killing me lately. But now that I'm pregnant, I probably shouldn't have surgery or anything." Besides, a retired navy doctor sounded just as old and cantankerous as Dr. Suarez.

"That's true." Kylie patted her own stomach. "But trust me, when you start packing on the pounds, it's only going to get worse. Maybe he could give you a cortisone shot or something to get you through the next several months."

"Yep, the last thing you want is a bum knee when you have a newborn to take care of," Maxine said. "Trying to run the dance studio on top of everything else is going to be taxing on you."

These women knew Mia better than anyone. They were her former teammates on the Boise State cheer team and her lifesavers when she'd later fled Miami to start over in Sugar Falls. And now Mia was turning to them again.

Maxine was the owner of the Sugar Falls Cookie Company, the star attraction of the downtown Sugar Falls tourist industry and a famous bakery specializing in flavored cookies. She'd opened her shop when her eleven-year-old son had been a toddler and had first-hand experience on raising a child alone while managing a growing business. Kylie was a CPA and had spent last summer raising her husband's twin nephews while singlehandedly maintaining the financial records for half the town. Mia was glad she had friends who had already gone through something similar and could help her navigate the unfamiliar terrain.

"Okay," she said with a sigh. "Give me his number and I'll make an appointment."

Her friends left and, as much as she adored the two women, she was glad to finally be alone to come to terms with her new reality.

After securing the dead bolt, she grabbed the paper towel off the counter, sat down on her comfy old sofa and stared at the little test stick with the two blue lines. She was going to be a mother. Mia could hardly believe it. Growing up, whenever she'd complain about not wanting to audition for a certain play that had nothing to do with dancing or not wanting to move to an entirely different state because her mother had it in her head that Mia could land a talent agent if she would only take up acting classes, Rhonda Palinski would tell her daughter that she didn't even know *what* she wanted.

And for the past few years, Mia had allowed herself to believe that maybe her mom was right and she didn't know what she wanted out of life.

Putting the stick down, she stroked her still-flat belly. She knew with a certainty she hadn't felt in years that she wanted this child more than she had ever wanted anything. She'd always lived her life for others, having her dreams diminished or jerked out from under her feet. But this baby was hers. And nobody, not even GP What's-his-name, could take this away from her.

She reached into her sweater pocket and pulled out the gold and onyx cuff link, looking at the initials.

GPM.

The morning following their lovemaking she'd almost made it down to the lobby when she'd spotted a small bit of gold winking at her from the corner of the elevator. When she'd picked it up, she remembered the way he'd had her body pressed up against the mirrored walls, her hands pulling him in closer and slipping under his suit jacket—which had gotten in her way. She'd heard a thunk right before the ping of the elevator alerted them that they'd reached her floor. But he'd scooped up the fallen case along with his discarded coat before they exited and fatefully made their way to her room.

Mia didn't wear much jewelry and had no idea what the cuff link was worth, but its potential monetary value wasn't what made her slip it into her satiny pocket that morning. She should've turned it in at the front desk lost and found. And if she hadn't been completely embarrassed by her lack of inhibitions and the threat of discovery, maybe she would've.

She thought about the careless way he'd left them at the bar and his annoyance at his father's idea of a gift, telling herself that GPM probably didn't care about the things anyway. Sneaking away from the elevator, she decided that having such a small memento would help her remember that she was still a woman with passion and life left in her.

Even Prince Charming had kept a glass slipper. Of course, unlike the smitten royal, Mia had no intention of traipsing around the countryside trying to find its owner.

She traced her finger over the gold-embossed letters.

If she thought about the man she'd left naked and asleep in her hotel bed, or the way he'd made her body come alive, responding to his skillful touch and his adoring mouth, she would lose all rational thought and make a pathetic attempt to take Maxine up on her offer to have Chief Cooper perform some miracle and attempt to track him down.

No. Things would be better if she just forgot about him and their night of sensual lovemaking. She reached for the little wooden treasure chest Maxine's son had given her for her birthday three years ago. She put the cuff link inside then snapped the box closed, along with her heart.

She doubted that a man like GPM would even want to be found. He'd seemed to have his own share of problems he'd been trying to escape from and probably wouldn't appreciate having any long-lasting reminders of that night, let alone an unexpected paternal responsibility. In fact, he'd most likely been more than relieved to have found Mia long gone the morning after.

Really, she'd saved them both from an awkward situation.

She'd never been the type of woman who had casual sex with strangers she'd met in bars. Heck, she wasn't even the kind of woman who went to bars, or slept with many men, for that matter. Her actions that night had been so out of character for her that her first instinct the next morning was to run and hide before pretending that it had never happened.

From the moment she'd driven her five-year-old Prius

away from the hotel, she'd forbidden herself from ever thinking about GP again.

Yet she couldn't help remembering how, as they'd walked down the deserted hallway, her plastic key card quivering in her hand, she'd known that she was making a conscious choice.

When they'd stood at her door she lifted her face toward his and saw the passion in his eyes, dimmed only slightly by a furrowed brow, as if his own set of second thoughts was playing out in his mind. Then and there she decided that maybe he needed her just as much as she needed him.

It had taken her two tries to get the key card inserted and she remembered letting out a breath when the little green light signaled that the lock had finally released, because for once in Mia's life, she had followed her physical urges—and her heart.

But now it was time to return to reality.

Getting off her sofa, she walked across her tiny apartment and opened her patio doors looking out onto Snowflake Boulevard, the main street leading through Sugar Falls. *This* was her reality. This town was her safe haven and home now. She took a deep breath of the cool mountain air, wanting to inhale the familiar sights and scents as if she could absorb enough of the environment into her brain so that she could push aside all thought of her carefree and careless night in the anonymous big city.

Because that was the key. Anonymity. She'd thought about leaving her telephone number for him, or staying a couple more hours to share breakfast and possibly something more.

But no matter how much she might want to see her

mystery lover again, or how guilty she might feel for keeping this baby a secret, she knew she wasn't ready for that kind of intimacy. She was just now allowing herself to put down roots and come out of her shell. All it would take was one bad relationship to put her right back to square one.

And that was a chance she just wasn't willing to take.

Garrett wasn't quite sure what to make of Cessy Walker. The older socialite had kindly volunteered to fill in at the front desk until he hired a nursing staff, but she didn't seem like the best fit for a small-town physician's office. After all, she was dressed in a designer wool knit pantsuit—Garrett recognized it as a staple brand from his last stepmother's closet—and enough pearls to sink a life raft.

"Have you ever worked in a doctor's office before, Ms. Walker?"

"Please, call me Cessy. Not in an office per se, but I did chair the Boise Children's Hospital black-tie gala back in eighty-nine and we raised over fifty thousand dollars for a new sports medicine wing."

"And tell me again why you want to work here?"

"I figure I needed to be doing something a bit more stimulating with my time. I tried to do that volunteer patrol program with the police department, but Cooper got all bent out of shape when I played my Barry Manilow CD on the squad car's loudspeaker."

Garrett bit the inside of his cheek, all too familiar with the eccentric personalities of the bored elite. Apparently, even small towns such as Sugar Falls had their share of overprivileged do-gooders looking for something to spice up their daily routines. The woman was sincere enough and probably had good intentions, but he really didn't need her help. If his first patient wasn't coming this afternoon, he would've politely declined her offer to act as a quasi-receptionist. But before he could make a decision one way or the other, she continued talking.

"I can see by your expression that you're a bit shocked at my resourcefulness when it comes to entertaining. My third husband used to look at me the same way. But just between the two of us, it didn't take a party-planning whiz to realize that the Labor Day parade was going to be a major snoozefest with that Mae Johnston running the show. Personally, I think the townspeople enjoyed me adding some festive music and pepping things up. But afterward, the chief was concerned other townspeople might follow suit and utilize public resources in an *un*authorized manner." Ms. Walker made it sound as if *her* Fanilow utilization was completely authorized. "Anyhoo, Cooper suggested that you might need some temp help, and since I know everyone who's anyone in town, I figured I would be an asset to you setting up shop and establishing yourself with the crème de la crème of our town."

Hmm. It sounded to Garrett as if Cooper wanted his wife's former mother-in-law out of his hair and had dumped her into his lap. He'd met her a couple of times when she'd brought her grandson to visit Cooper at Shadowview and had an idea that she was used to getting what she wanted. But he was new in Sugar Falls and, as much as he prided himself on his independence, it couldn't hurt to have an established and well-connected member of the community give him her bedazzled seal of approval.

Plus, he was about to ask for a favor himself, so keeping Cessy Walker busy would make the chief of police indebted to him.

It had been over eight weeks since that night in the hotel, and he hadn't been able to get the woman from the bar out of his mind. He'd tried everything he could think of to look for her—everything from calling the hotel the following day to try to find the guest who'd been staying in room 804 to researching dance performances in Boise hoping to come across her picture. He'd even spent a few evenings sitting in the hotel bar the following week, closely watching every brunette that walked through the door—but always ended up at a dead end. The more time that went by, the colder her trail would get. It was time to call in the big guns.

"All right, well I appreciate your helping me out just for the next couple of *days*." He purposely paused to emphasize that her receptionist skills—or lack thereof—would only be temporary. "My first patient is a referral from a friend and she's coming in an hour. Have her fill out these forms and get copies of her insurance card. Technically we're not open for business yet, and I don't expect many calls in the next few days, but if you could answer the phone and take down messages for me, that'd be great."

"No problem, Doc. And keep in mind that I can only volunteer for the next two weeks. I go on my sabbatical after that."

He couldn't imagine what a woman like Cessy Walker needed a sabbatical from. But he wasn't going to ask because he had a feeling she'd tell him.

He took a seat behind the battered desk he'd found online. Garrett wasn't in the habit of using money he hadn't earned himself, and he'd already dipped into his trust fund account to finance the building and splurge on his top-of-the-line medical equipment. While he wanted to make his patients comfortable, he didn't really see the need for wasting money on decorations or frivolous extras when it was surgical equipment and state-of-the-art radiology machines that he needed most. But hiring a full-time professional staff just jumped to the top of his to-do list.

He probably should've made a telephone call, but he didn't want his new "receptionist" to overhear his very personal conversation. So he fired off an email to Cooper, listing as much information as he could think of about the mystery woman from the hotel. He told himself that if she wanted to be found, she would've left her contact information. But the more time he spent recalling every little detail about that night, the more obsessed he became with locating her and seeing her again.

Maybe he was romanticizing it. Or maybe he didn't like the lingering feeling of rejection. Although he'd grown up a pampered rich kid, it wasn't as if he was some spoiled brat who only wanted things he couldn't have. Most likely, it had been a one-time experience and, if he met her again in person, none of that sizzling spark would be there anymore.

But what if it was?

He clicked Send and then slammed his laptop closed. This whole search was probably the most futile endeavor he'd ever embarked upon. And it would probably only give Cooper extra ammunition for busting his chops. Garrett needed to focus and get back to work.

He was putting away supplies and arranging one of his exam rooms when he heard his first patient arrive. She was early and he wasn't quite ready. Besides, he didn't want to look too eager—as if he had nothing more important or doctoral to do with his time.

Cessy Walker's voice carried back to him as she greeted the patient. "Mia, you're going to just *adore* Dr. McCormick. He's a family friend and is known to be the best orthopedic specialist in the state. He'll have your knee all fixed up in no time."

Okay, that might be a bit of an exaggeration, but his suddenly fragile ego could use the boost. Also, technically, he was a friend of the new husband to Cessy's former daughter-in-law, but in a small town such as this, he figured everyone had some kind of connection with everyone else. The woman might not be experienced as a receptionist, but perhaps she'd been right in declaring herself an asset to his growing practice.

He looked at his stainless steel watch. It would probably take a few more minutes for the patient to complete the insurance paperwork, so he went back to puttering.

After about ten minutes, he heard murmuring, and then Ms. Walker's voice again. "Great. Follow me on back to the exam room."

Garrett was shoving his left arm into the sleeve of his white lab coat when his receptionist walked in and handed the file to him.

"Doctor, Mia Palinski is here to see you," Cessy said then walked out, leaving Garrett face-to-face with his first patient.

But instead of sticking out his hand to introduce himself, he froze when he recognized the midnight-black hair, the pale blue eyes and the graceful body he could never forget.

Chapter Four

No, Mia thought. *No, no, no.*

GPM was here in Sugar Falls? And he was her doctor? How had this happened?

"It's you," was all he said. She stood there, stiff and numb, drinking in the sight of him, at a complete loss of what to say without looking foolish.

"You live here in Sugar Falls?" he asked when she remained silent. His eyes hadn't stopped their constant perusal of her. "How could this have happened?"

His words mirrored her own thoughts so exactly that the nervous giggle she'd been trying to swallow almost bubbled out. But then he smiled as though Santa had just delivered a long-sought-after Christmas gift to him and a familiar cold panic spread through her. Mia reached for the file, the one containing all her personal information, including the fact that she was now carrying this stranger's child, and tried to yank it from his hands. The hands that had so skillfully brought her body to life just two months ago.

Judging by the way he was gripping the manila folder, she probably would've had better luck ripping a present away from a child. She dropped her arms instead, the instinctive response of flight winning over her urge to fight.

She inched backward, calculating an escape route in her mind. The exam room was in the farthest corner of the building and if her knee was in better shape, she could probably make it out of his office in less than three seconds.

But then she recalled that the self-appointed socialite of Sugar Falls was sitting right outside and had a penchant for spreading her unsolicited opinions around town. Of course, it wasn't as if Mia was going to be able to hide her pregnancy much longer, but she would've at least liked to keep the baby's paternity somewhat secret.

Which brought her back to the question: How had this happened? What in the world was he doing here? And how was she going to deal with the consequences of her actions?

"Miss," he paused and looked down at the file still in his hands. "Palinski? It is miss, right? Not missus?"

His eyes seemed to be pleading with her to assure him that she wasn't married. Was he hoping that if she was single, she'd be up for a repeat performance? She didn't respond only because she didn't want to feed his unrealistic expectations.

Of course, he'd find out the answer soon enough since he was still holding on to her medical history, which clearly listed her full name, insurance information and, unfortunately, her address. But that didn't mean Mia had to show her hand just yet.

"Why don't you step inside so we can talk—" he looked pointedly at her feet, which were now completely backed into in the hallway "—more privately."

Being alone with this guy was the last thing she wanted. But it wasn't as if she could hide from him if he was truly setting up shop in Sugar Falls.

At least, not yet. Plus, Mrs. Walker would be right outside the room, probably with a stethoscope pressed against the door, and could hopefully intervene if things took a bad turn.

Mia took a deep breath. Really, she knew better than to project her one bad experience onto other men. She needed to think logically. GP or Dr. McCormick or whatever his name was was a reputable surgeon. Her best friend's husband—the chief of police, for crying out loud—had been one of his patients. Chances were he wasn't some obsessed sociopath who, several weeks after meeting her, decided to uproot his whole life and move his medical practice to Sugar Falls, Idaho, in order to stalk her.

Besides, she'd already let down way more than her guard with him before.

Maybe that was what she was really afraid of. She'd already proved that she couldn't trust herself alone in a room with him.

He put his hand on her elbow and Mia immediately flinched and pulled her arm away. He looked surprised and a bit offended by her response, and she felt so stupid for being there in the first place. She swallowed a gulp of air and entered the room, turning around quickly so that she wouldn't have her back to him or be susceptible to a surprise attack.

Calm down. He isn't Nick. He's not going to hurt you. Even as Mia tried to reassure herself, she couldn't help but take inventory of her surroundings. Old habits died hard when she was thrown into an uncomfortable environment. Plus, she had more than just herself to protect now.

There was an exam table, which she had absolutely no intention of lying down on, a stool and a hard plastic chair that looked like the kind her elementary school would've thrown out a couple of decades ago.

For a guy with impeccable taste in shoes and scotch, he really could benefit from hiring Cessy Walker as a decorator rather than a receptionist.

"Do you mind if I close this?" He was holding the heavy birch wood door and Mia was grateful he was at least giving her the option of escaping. She nodded after checking to ensure there were no internal locks on the knob.

The room was small and they stood inches away from each other. The only way to put some distance between them would be if one of them sat down, but she didn't want to put herself at a disadvantage.

"Well, Mia Palinski, I didn't expect to meet you again."

"I didn't expect to meet you the first time," she said before thinking better of it. She was a natural peacemaker and hated confrontations. Plus, her mother had drilled politeness into her from a young age, warning her she never knew when she'd come across a potential talent scout or rich stepfather. "Sorry. This is all so unexpected and I'm not usually so flustered like this—not that you would know. We don't really know each other at all."

"As I recall, we never did officially introduce ourselves. I'm Garrett McCormick." He held out his right hand, his other still gripping her file.

"Mia Palinski," she said, sticking out her own to shake his. Yep, there was no forgetting those hands. He had on silver knotted cuff links this time and she wondered what it was about this guy that made him want to dress to the nines, even at work. "Wait. I thought your name was GP."

"How'd you know my nickname?"

"I could hear…uh…your father call you that when you were talking to him on the phone in the bar."

His eyes grew darker, from hazel to a cloudy deep brown, and she mentally kicked herself for bringing up a touchy subject.

"Well, only he calls me GP anymore. It's short for Garrett Patrick. But if he'd had his way, he would've just named me Junior."

"You don't really look like a Junior," she said, not sure she wanted to bring up the subject of overbearing parents again. Although, it was safer to talk about that than the big pregnant elephant in the exam room.

"I've tried my whole life not to feel like a Junior, either." That was pretty telling. And so was the fact that Mia's small hand was still wrapped possessively in his larger one. She snatched it back before wrapping both of her arms around her midsection.

The motion startled him and must've brought his attention back to the present. "So I've never really done this before," he said, still holding her file.

"You mean you're not really an orthopedic surgeon?"

"Of course I am." He gestured to the framed diplomas and awards he'd yet to permanently hang on the walls. So he'd gone to the Naval Academy at Annapolis, followed by med school at Dartmouth. Pretty impressive—if they weren't forgeries. But even someone as suspicious as Mia had to doubt that anyone would go so far as to fake a medical career in the military and then open a board-certified surgical practice. "I meant I've never had a relationship with one of my patients."

"We didn't have a relationship." It was best for her to make sure he understood that what happened between them was a one-time deal and there would never ever be an encore. "And maybe it's not such a good idea for me to become one of your patients."

Mia looked down then took a step back and tripped over the stool, which banged into the metal exam table as she lost her balance and tumbled to the floor. Her bad knee thudded against the wheel of the stool and she gasped in pain.

Garrett was beside her in a heartbeat, straightening her leg and asking where it hurt. When she didn't answer, he said, "Looks like you're going to be my patient whether you want to or not. I think you should let me help you up onto the table so I can take a look and see if you did any damage."

Unless she wanted to sit on the floor indefinitely, she would have to allow him to assist her. But instead of pulling her up, he reached behind her back and under her legs and lifted her toward his chest.

When he stood, all the blood left her head and was replaced with a spinning dizziness. She didn't know if it was the nausea that had been plaguing her, the stress of the situation or feeling him so close to her again.

Either way, she tamped down her instinct to wrap her own arms around his neck and reached toward the exam table to steady herself as she maneuvered her body onto it and away from him.

He stepped back, eyeing her as though she should be seeing a psychiatrist, not a surgeon. He rubbed his finger across his forehead and she remembered the gesture from the hotel bar.

"Why didn't you tell me you were a doctor? Or that you were opening a practice in Sugar Falls?"

"The subject never came up." His lips were clamped tightly and Mia realized he was keeping something a secret... *Oh, no.*

"Oh, my gosh! Are you married?" Her eyes darted to his ring finger, but it was still bare—just as it had been that night. Of course, that didn't necessarily mean anything.

"What? No, I'm not married. Are you?"

"Of course not. I already told you I was a miss." She tried not to sound offended at the suggestion that she would cheat on her nonexistent spouse with a stranger in a hotel bar. But she'd considered the same thing about him.

He opened her file and glanced at it briefly, almost as if he didn't believe her verbal answer and was looking for written proof. She held her breath, knowing what information he was about to read and then saw him do a double take when his eyes got halfway down the page.

Right where the question about pregnancy was.

"Oh, my God." He looked at her still-flat stomach. "How far along are you?"

This was it. She could lie and say she was further along to try to get him to believe that the baby wasn't his. But since he was actually going to be working in Sugar Falls, he'd see her regularly and figure things out when her baby was born nine months after the night they spent in the hotel.

"I'm in my first trimester," she said, giving a generic but truthful response. "My first appointment with the OB/GYN is next Monday so I'll know for sure then." She stood up, wanting to end this conversation before it could even begin, but her leg buckled and she had to hold on to the edge of the table so she wouldn't fall to the ground.

"What's going on with your knee?" he asked, still looking at the papers in his hand. This time, he didn't make an effort to help her back up, which was fine because she was balancing okay on one limb and she didn't think she could handle having him pick her up or hold her close to him again.

She'd almost forgotten her entire reason for making this stupid appointment in the first place. Her damn knee was getting her into more problems lately.

"I had replacement surgery three years ago, and it just never felt like it healed right. Anyway, it's been bothering me more lately and I thought I should get it looked at before the ba…" The word froze in her mouth when he looked back up at her. "But seeing as how this is probably some sort of conflict of interest or something, I think I'll probably just see a specialist down in Boise."

"Do you go to Boise a lot?"

He was inches away from her and his eyes were staring deep into hers, questioning her, challenging her to explain an answer to something he wasn't coming out and asking directly.

The back of her good leg bumped into the exam table and she realized she was trying to get away from his intent gaze. "Why does Boise matter?"

"It doesn't matter," he said and looked back at her file. What exactly didn't matter to him? Her driving habits to the nearest big city? Or the night they shared there?

"Why don't you let me take a look at your knee?"

"I don't think that's such a good idea…" She pulled herself up straighter and looked at the closed door, wondering how quickly she could hop through it.

"Listen, Mia. You can let me do my job and examine your knee, or we can talk about your obstetrician's job and whether your due date is anywhere close to nine months after September third."

He remembered the exact night they'd been together. And he obviously wanted to discuss it, yet he was being a gentleman and giving her the opportunity to talk about her injury instead.

She scooted her rear onto the exam table as quickly as she could, having never felt so grateful to have a bum knee as she was then.

Mia Palinski.

The woman he hadn't been able to get out of his mind for the past two months was now sitting in his office, tugging her leather boots down over a pair of tight black leggings.

And she was pregnant.

He'd dreamed about her disrobing in front of him again, but not in his barely established medical practice. And definitely not with Cessy Walker hanging out on the other side of the door. Garrett was a consummate professional, which was the only way he was going to get through this increasingly awkward appointment.

He was dying to ask her a hundred questions, but Mia looked at him as though he were a drug-resistant strain of some unheard-of disease.

What was she playing at? Most women in her position would be salivating at the good fortune of successfully accomplishing the oldest trick in the gold digger's handbook—getting impregnated by a famously wealthy man. Or in his case, the man reality television had once dubbed the most eligible doctor in Southern California.

He was usually so careful about using protection for this exact reason, but he was fast realizing that his brain and his body simply didn't react the way he wanted them to when Mia was around. Which was why he needed to treat her like any other patient. Not only would playing the doctor role force him to keep his emotions in check, but it might also make her more willing to talk and let her guard down so he could figure out exactly what she was up to.

He didn't want to resort to using their barely established doctor–patient relationship to try to get personal information, but she was pregnant—possibly with his child—and he deserved to know the truth. If he could get through performing an emergency spinal cord surgery on board a naval hospital ship during hurricane-force winds, then he could get through a routine examination.

Actually, there really was nothing routine about this at all.

He slowly touched her knee, and even through her black tights he could still feel the heat radiating off her. He concentrated on staring directly at her leg and not letting his eyes stray to her beautiful face to see if his touch could still bring her pleasure the way it had that night in Boise.

She was his patient. He needed to treat her as such.

But she was holding her body with such tension; she was as stiff as one of his father's favorite surfboards. And just like a fiberglass board, she might snap in two if he didn't handle her smoothly.

How could he get her to relax when he was so damn dismayed himself?

Go through the motions of the exam. Keep it steady. You're the king of control, McCormick.

"Where did you have surgery?"

"I had it on my knee."

Was she serious? He chanced a look at her, but her eyelids were squeezed tightly closed. He was barely touching her, so he doubted she was in pain. Was she truly that uncomfortable in his presence?

"I know the surgery was on your knee. I meant, where was your surgeon located? I would like to get your records from him or her and get an idea of what exactly they did."

"Right. Of course. It was in Miami. Dr. Ron Prellis."

"I don't think I've heard of him."

"He specializes in sports injuries. The team doctor referred me to him because they were trying to keep the whole thing quiet."

"What team doctor?" She was on a sports team? And why would they want to keep it quiet? Mia Palinski seemed to have a lot of things she wanted to keep under the radar.

"For the NFL."

"As in football?" That didn't make any sense.

"Yes. I was on their cheerleading squad after college."

Crap.

When she'd told him that she was a dancer, his first thought had been stripper. But then she'd made it sound like she was a professional dancer. Professional jersey chaser was probably more like it. While he couldn't believe he hadn't made the initial connection, he kept his mouth shut and continued the exam.

He felt some definite swelling, but he doubted she would be willing to remove her tights so he could get a better look.

"I'd like to get an MRI on your knee, but just to be on the safe side, we should wait until after the first trimester. Are you currently taking anything for the pain?"

"I used to take ibuprofen before I found out about the baby. But I've been too scared to take anything since then."

He sat back on his stool and let out a breath. At least she was taking healthy precautions with his unborn child's life.

His child. Possibly. He was going to be a father.

"I take it you plan on keeping it, then?"

"My baby?" Her eyes grew even more icy with the question and she wrapped her arms around her midsection. "Of course I plan on keeping it!"

He'd noticed that she'd referred to the child as *hers*— not *theirs*. Did he get any say in this? Should he? She hadn't denied it that the baby was his, but if he could keep her talking, maybe she would give him confirmation. "Were you planning to tell me about it?"

She looked away quickly, but not before he'd seen the guilt flash in her eyes. She was probably planning to wait to tell him when the due date grew closer and there was nothing he could do but sign a hefty child support agreement.

"Even if I'd wanted to, I really didn't have any way of contacting you. Up until now, I didn't know your real name or how to get in touch with you."

Wait. Did she just say even if she'd wanted to? Implying that she had no intention of telling him about the baby? He braced his feet on the floor. If he could roll his stool back any farther from the exam table and her duplicitous mind, he would have.

"You know, if you would've stuck around that morning instead of sneaking off like a common criminal, I would have been more than happy to provide you with my name and contact information." He couldn't help the accusing tone of his voice.

He wanted to lash out at her and blame her for orchestrating this whole mess. But if he was being honest, he was more upset for letting her fool him in the first place.

She must have realized his exam was over because she sat up and reached for the boots she'd discarded before climbing up on the table. "I didn't sneak off."

"Well, you didn't wake me up to say goodbye and I certainly didn't find a note anywhere thanking me for the good time."

She reached for her boot on the floor and must've thought better of swinging it at his head because she shoved her foot into it instead.

"Did it ever occur to you that maybe I was embarrassed? Or that perhaps I wasn't well rehearsed in one-night-stand protocol because I've never done anything like that before?" She stood up and stomped her leg as she tried to get the zipper unstuck, then sucked in a tight breath.

"Hey, take it easy. No wonder your injury has been aggravated again."

"Look, I think it's in everyone's best interest if I find a different doctor. You don't need to worry about my knee anymore and you certainly don't need to concern yourself with my baby."

"Wait, Mia. Please." He moved in front of the door. He would never physically restrain a woman, but at this desperate moment, he wasn't above impeding her escape route. "We really need to talk about this."

"What's there to talk about?" she asked.

"Are you kidding me? I'd say there's a whole lot to talk about. First of all, you can barely walk—you're visibly in pain. Even without an MRI, you probably have a loosening of the device components. It sometimes happens a few years after surgery when the artificial replacement is faulty or doesn't graft properly to your bones. Which means you might eventually need a revision surgery. But I can understand if you want to go see another specialist. Second of all, you're carrying my child. I mean, it *is* mine, right?"

Her head whipped up as if he'd slapped her. "Of course it's yours."

"You can't blame me for asking," he said. "Up until an hour ago, I didn't even know your name, let alone your relationship history. You've had almost two months to get used to this whole pregnancy idea, so forgive me for being a little slow in wrapping my head around everything that's just happened."

She gave a barely perceptible nod, but her nostrils flared slightly, indicating she was still on edge with him. But at least she could acknowledge that he wasn't trying to be confrontational.

"I'm still trying to get used to it all myself. Like I said, running into a former one-night stand and having him find out I'm pregnant with his child isn't something I've had much practice at."

"Fair enough." Garrett heard the office phone ring and was reminded that they still had an audience out in the waiting room. "Look, maybe we should take some time to think this all through and then meet later. Somewhere in private and figure out where we are going to go from there."

Mia lifted herself up to her full five-foot-four frame and arched a perfectly sculpted black eyebrow. "How private? I think I made it pretty clear that I don't normally engage in…you know…what happened at the hotel in Boise. So I hope you're not expecting me to hop right back into your bed."

"First of all, I think it was *your* bed we were in." Although, as discombobulated as Garrett felt, he couldn't help but be intrigued by spending another night with her. *Don't go there, McCormick.* "And second of all, unless you allow me to give you a shot of cortisone for the pain, you'll be lucky if you can hop anywhere."

She sat back down and he opened up his cabinet, pulling out a clean syringe and small glass vial. He turned his back while she removed her black tights and, he assumed, shoved them into her purse. She closed her eyes, while he injected her knee with the pain reliever, then turned around again and busied himself in his cabinets as she pulled her boots back on—her legs remaining bare.

When it seemed that they'd both gotten their emotions under control, he finally said, "I just meant we could meet someplace that didn't have the town busy-body sitting right outside the door."

"I prefer the term 'town socialite,' Dr. McCormick," Cessy Walker shouted from a location that was much closer than the reception desk.

"Sugar Falls is a small place. It's pretty hard to go anywhere without seeing someone who doesn't already know your business." Then Mia raised her voice a few octaves. "Which is why I'll know exactly who to blame if any of this leaks out."

Garrett heard a sudden increase in volume over the computer's desktop speakers.

"Why don't we meet for dinner tonight?"

"I can't. After school, I teach two ballet classes and then I'll have rehearsals for the Christmas pageant until eight."

Garrett remembered the small sign on the pink Victorian building downtown. He'd passed by it several times when he'd been driving into town to check on the progress of his office remodel. "At the Snowflake Dance Academy?"

If women had hackles, Garrett would've sworn that he'd just seen hers rise. "If you didn't know anything about me, then how'd you know about my studio?"

And here he'd thought they were making progress. Maybe the cortisone wasn't as effective as he'd thought it would be. "It wasn't a difficult deduction, Mia. I know I haven't been here long, but that's the only dance place in town. At least, that I've seen."

She wrapped her cardigan sweater tighter around herself and let out a small breath. Jeez, did this woman think he was some kind of creepy stalker?

"Well, if you can't meet me tonight, then what about breakfast tomorrow at the Cowgirl Up Café?"

"Nope. The Quilting Club meets there on Wednesdays."

God forbid they bring the attention of the Quilting Club upon them. "Is there any place we can go where there won't be a swarm of townspeople?"

She bit her lip. "I guess we could meet at my place."

"Great. When?"

"On Saturday. My last class is at three. So any time after five should guarantee us some privacy. But come to my apartment above my studio. I know our situation will come out eventually, but the longer we keep things anonymous around town, the better."

Anonymous? That's how they'd gotten into this predicament in the first place. Yet, he was too much of a gentleman to point that out. "Okay, your apartment on Saturday. I'll meet you there at six, just to be safe."

Mia nodded and left the exam room, still limping, but at least she wasn't on crutches. The doctor in Garrett wished he could have finished his examination and made a better recommendation for her treatment. But the man in him was relieved to be alone for a second to get control of his thoughts. There was something about that woman that turned his brain to spaghetti, and he needed all his wits about him if he was going to take control of this situation.

He slumped down in his stool and rubbed his palm over his forehead. He couldn't believe it. He was going to be a father. This wasn't what he wanted, and it definitely hadn't happened the way he would have planned if he *had* wanted it. But he couldn't help but feel a small kernel of anticipation. Not at all the unknowns that lay ahead—he was too pragmatic to see this as an actual blessing—but at this chance for familial redemption. He always knew that when he became a dad, he would break the overbearing cycle of parenthood that he'd been subjected to.

Cooper had assured Garrett that once he moved to Sugar Falls and the locals embraced him as one of their own, he wouldn't have to worry about the potential celebrity ramifications that tended to follow his family name. After all, if his building contractor, who Garrett soon figured out was baseball legend Kane Chatterson, could hide out in this small, tight-knit community, Dr. Gerald McCormick's long-lost son should be able to fly under the radar, too.

But all it would take to blow his cover would be some tourist with a smartphone and a fondness for reality shows about plastic surgery makeovers spotting him in the quaint ski resort. But maybe that was what Mia was hoping for.

Suddenly, the Quilting Club and some low-level town gossip didn't seem so bad.

Chapter Five

Mia had been kicking herself the past couple of days for not clarifying that she'd actually meant she'd meet Garrett McCormick at her studio, not her apartment.

Of course, where the meeting took place was probably the least of her worries.

At least she now knew the name of her child's father. And so did her friends, who were aware that she'd be seeing him tonight. They'd convinced her that she was perfectly safe with the reputable doctor and that she would've looked paranoid and suspicious if she had called him and changed the location of their rendezvous.

Sheesh. She needed to stop thinking of it like that, of *him* like that. This was a formal discussion and she'd keep things as proper and as professional as she could. There would be no drinking, no sultry piano music, no dim lighting. In fact, she'd been debating all afternoon

whether or not she should take a quick shower before
he showed up or whether she should play it casual and
stay in her work clothes.

At five-thirty, she suddenly decided that she wanted
to at least look physically put together, because her spinning emotions had her feeling like a mental wreck on
the inside. As she stood in her bathroom blow-drying
her long dark hair, she considered everything she'd been
able to find out about him so far.

She'd done an internet search on him the moment
she'd gotten back from his office. She'd already known
he'd been in the navy and was licensed to practice medicine, but not much else. The name was common enough
to land several hits and she'd even been directed to a
website for some reality shows on Med TV about rich
plastic surgeons in Southern California, but that Dr.
McCormick was in his sixties. She'd found a couple of
articles published by Garrett McCormick in a medical journal. Other than recent developments in roboti-
cally assisted surgeries, she hadn't been able to narrow
anything down. At least there weren't any glaring articles about serial killers or other criminals with that
same name.

Of course, Mia knew all too well that narcissistic
spoiled jerks, especially ones such as Nick Galveston,
with wealthy families, usually kept their sociopathic
personalities well hidden. Even though Garrett's office
was sparsely furnished, underneath that white lab coat
he'd worn, his clothes reeked of fine taste and fortune.

A firm knock sounded at her front door and she took
one last look in her bathroom mirror. *Please don't let my
baby's father be anything like Nick Galveston.*

Her soft-soled flats didn't make much noise as she

crossed her small living room to let him inside, but honestly, she couldn't hear much over the pounding of her heart. She almost lost her nerve when she looked through the small peephole and saw his hazel eyes and freshly shaved jawline.

Why did he have to be so handsome?

She took a deep breath, just as she used to do before a big performance, steeled her spine and swung the door open. But she must've been standing a little too close because she yanked the doorknob right into her hip bone.

"Ow," she said, trying not to double over as she rubbed the spot just below the waistband of her jeans.

"Are you okay?" he asked, coming quickly to her side. But she wasn't comfortable with his attention focused anywhere near the location of her injury so she sucked up the pain and pretended she couldn't feel the throbbing ache or the sting in her pride.

"Yes, I'm fine. I just misjudged how far I was from the door. Come on in."

Her apartment was a small one-bedroom and, up until this moment, she'd never felt cramped by the lack of space in the tiny entryway.

She gestured him toward the white-and-blue sofa upholstered with a soft paisley print, and tried not to worry about how he might perceive her eclectic decorating skills. Most of her furniture and accents were funky pieces she'd picked up at nearby antiques stores and came in a multitude of shades of blue and painted oak. She'd moved around so much as a child, she'd always been drawn to furnishings that were old and had a deep history. But she also had an artistic streak that extended beyond dancing and she liked the abstract hodgepodge of it all—the uniqueness that was reflective of her personal style.

"I feel silly showing up to your house empty-handed like this," Garrett said, before taking a seat. "But, I wasn't sure what to bring. It didn't really seem like the occasion for flowers, and, well, you probably aren't drinking much champagne these days."

She probably shouldn't have been drinking champagne two months ago, either. But Mia kept that thought to herself. "Please, don't worry about it. Speaking of beverages, can I get you something?"

"What do you have?"

That was a good question. In her angst over having him over to her house, she hadn't thought about what she would do with him once he got there. She didn't entertain people other than her friends and she hadn't been to the market all week so her inventory wasn't exactly up to par.

"I have water. And ginger ale."

"I'll take the ginger ale."

She grabbed the liter bottle and two glasses and carried it over to the small round coffee table she'd painstakingly sanded and painted the color of a pale robin's egg. She should've planned for a better seating option because she couldn't very well sit down on the sofa next to him. That'd be way too intimate. She didn't have any chairs besides the ones pushed into the dining room table and it would look suspicious if she hauled one of those over here. She spied the white tufted ottoman and decided that was better than nothing.

Mia tried to casually move the overstuffed footstool out of the way by using her left calf, but her attempt at nonchalance was rewarded by a sharp pain in her Achilles tendon when its clawed wooden foot tripped her up.

She sucked in a whispered curse as she plopped ungracefully onto her impromptu seat. "Are you sure you're okay?" Garrett asked.

"Yep," she said, although it came out more like, "Whepppp."

He rubbed his forehead as though he was pondering whether or not to believe her. He must've opted for the politest choice because he didn't say anything else.

Instead, he shrugged out of what looked to be a cashmere coat and laid it over the back of her couch before pouring them both a drink. He was dressed in a soft gray sweater, definitely just as pricey as the starched custom-looking button-up shirt she'd seen him in before. But this time, there wasn't a cuff link in sight.

Relieved to have something to do with herself, she reached for her ginger ale and gulped it so quickly, she inhaled tiny carbonated bubbles into her nose. She let out a small sneeze before he had even raised his own glass.

"Are you coming down with a cold?" Garrett leaned toward her and put his cool and smooth hand to her forehead.

Mia jerked away as if he'd burned her and almost toppled off her backless seat.

"Whoa." He relocated his hand to her shoulders as if he could help steady her. Why was he always touching her? "Are you okay?"

She scooted toward the center of the ottoman, causing his fingers to fall away. "I'm fine."

"If you say so."

"Sorry, I'm usually much more graceful than this."

Which was true. She was a dancer, after all. But after tripping in his office and now tonight, she had to conclude that there must be some sort of hormonal imbalance wreaking havoc with her body because she was all kinds of thrown off by his nearness.

"I think it's safe to say we're both a little out of sorts." He smiled at her, probably in an attempt to be reassuring, but it didn't quite reach his eyes. It was probably the same smile he gave to wounded soldiers when he had to tell them they needed major orthopedic surgery—which was pretty apropos considering she felt as if her future was being amputated.

"Speaking of hands, uh, I mean…" She trailed off since they hadn't been speaking of anything to do with his hands. Instead, she reached into the little wooden treasure chest on the coffee table and pulled out a small gold circle. "One of these fell out in the elevator, uh, that night."

His brows lifted and his eyes grew darker when he ran his finger over the onyx stone. "Thank you for returning this to me. I'd wondered where I lost it."

Her face had to be the most unflattering shade of red. "I found it when I was leaving the morning after and was kind of in a rush to get out of there." Her stomach, which had been acting queasy all week, was threatening to take center stage if she didn't calm down and relax. "Anyway, I thought you might want it back."

He angled his torso and slipped it into his hip pocket, thankfully not mentioning the last time he'd shoved it away. "I never should have left them on the bar in the first place. I was being stubborn and perhaps a little bitter toward my father when I pulled them out. I was glad when you reminded me to take them and then, well, one thing led to another and I got a little careless afterward. I kicked myself for it after the fact, but it was one of many recriminations I carried from that night."

Recriminations indeed. At least she now knew he'd regretted their lovemaking.

It should make what she was about to say a lot easier. She'd rehearsed exactly what she was going to tell Garrett several times these past three days, but now, with him sitting in what used to be her cozy and safe living room, her mind had just exited stage right.

She could hear the retro clock on the kitchen wall ticking in a steady cadence and felt each awkward notch of the second hand push them further into an uncomfortable-silence territory.

"Have you had dinner yet?" he asked.

"Uh, no. Why? Are you hungry?"

"Actually, I am. I skipped lunch today because the MRI techs, who were supposed to set up my equipment yesterday, didn't show up until this afternoon. So I've been at the office all day."

"I would offer to fix something to eat, but I haven't been to Duncan's Market since, well, since I saw you last and I've been trying to avoid too many public places until…" She trailed off, her excuses sounding lame to her own ears.

"Oh, I didn't expect you to cook for me. I just thought maybe we could go grab a bite to eat. Maybe it would help lighten the mood if we had something else to do besides talk about…you know. But, if you're worried about being seen in public with me, I could pick up something to go and bring it back here."

"I'm not afraid to be seen in public with you." Okay, that was only partially true. She might not be afraid, but

she definitely didn't want her personal business broadcast all over town just yet. And having a meal in public with him was tantamount to a front-page article in
the *Sugar Falls Advocate*. "But getting takeout sounds
good."

Great. If she couldn't even have dinner with the man,
then how was she going to raise a baby with him?

"There's that Italian restaurant about a block from
here. What's it called? Patrelli's? I hear they have excellent lasagna and these amazing garlic knots. Why
don't I call in an order?"

The thought of garlic made Mia's stomach do another
cartwheel and she quickly clapped her hand over her
mouth. But it was just a false alarm. She took a small
sip of her drink, hoping it would be enough to quell her
nausea and her sketchy nerves.

Unfortunately, Garrett was instantly alert. "What's
wrong?"

Of all the random men she could've accidentally gotten pregnant by during a one-night stand, why did she
have to choose a doctor who was trained to be attuned
to even the slightest physical discomfort? She almost
giggled at the absurd thought, but didn't want to risk
choking on her beverage. It wasn't as if she'd known
he was a doctor at the time.

"Sorry." She waved him off with her hand. "I'm just
getting a little firsthand experience with the wonderful world of morning sickness. Unfortunately, it's been
taking place in the evenings and usually centers on all
things smelling of garlic."

"I could pick up something else?"

"No," Mia said, a bit too loudly perhaps. "I can just

order a salad or something. And maybe some plain bread."

Ever since seeing Garrett again, all she'd been able to stomach were peanut butter sandwiches. Of course, that wasn't much different from what Mia usually wanted to eat. Her friends constantly ribbed her about her peanut butter obsession, but when one grew up with a mother who thought anything with more calories than a celery stick would cause her young daughter to balloon into a whale overnight, one tended to indulge in the foods she missed out on during childhood.

In fact, her mom used to keep a postcard of a large cartoon hippo ballet dancing in a tutu taped to their refrigerator door. At first, eight-year-old Mia had thought the image was humorous, but Rhonda Palinski had intended it to be a deterrent for anything her daughter might be tempted to put in her mouth that could jeopardize her dancing career. That picture moved each time with them and had graced several kitchens before Mia went to college and found it on top of her leotards in her suitcase with a note attached suggesting she affix the dancing hippo to her dorm room fridge. She'd torn it up and thrown it away before her ballet shoes had even been unpacked.

As if the unpleasant memory conjured up the woman herself, the apartment telephone rang and Mia's posture became even more erect. Only one person ever called her landline.

"Do you need to answer that?" Garrett asked.

"Nope. It's probably just a wrong number or a telemarketer. Most people who need to get ahold of me call my cell phone." That was true. She'd had the home line installed only when she'd first moved to Sugar Falls.

She'd still been traumatized after the Nick incident and her peace of mind dictated she have several means of access to call 9-1-1.

When the answering machine clicked on, she prayed that this time, it truly was just a telemarketer. But the second she heard the raspy smoker's voice, she should've known she wouldn't be so lucky.

"Mia, baby, it's Mom. I've been trying to call your cell phone all week but you haven't been answering. I just wanted to make sure we're still on for our Thanksgiving plans… Hello? Hello? What in the…"

The message continued to record as Rhonda Palinski pushed a series of buttons on her end of the line then abruptly disconnected. Several seconds later, the phone rang again.

"You know what?" Mia jumped up suddenly, knowing that her persistent mother would just keep calling and leaving messages until Mia answered. "Why don't we just walk over to Patrelli's and place our order?"

Maybe if she put on a thick scarf and hat, she wouldn't be as recognizable walking with a good-looking man down Snowflake Boulevard. The phone began ringing again. Even if she was recognized, it was less risky than staying in her apartment with him like a sitting duck, waiting to see what her mother said next on her machine. She was relieved to see that Garrett was now rising and following her lead, even if the amused expression on his face suggested he was enjoying her awkward discomfort. She'd made it to the wrought iron coat rack by the door and was just finished bundling up before the outgoing greeting started all over.

"Baby, it's Mom again. Your machine cut me off. Anyway…" Mia rushed Garrett outside and slammed her door behind them, effectively cutting off Rhonda's voice.

"So does your mom know about the baby and everything?" he asked as they made their way down the wooden staircase attached to the back of her building.

"Not yet. I need to tell her, but I've been putting it off. I guess I've been putting a lot of things off."

"Speaking of that…" He turned toward her and, sensing the direction of his thoughts, she wondered if maybe they should go back upstairs and have this conversation. "I still can't believe you were just going to have my baby and not even tell me."

Nope. It looked as if they were going to do this right here, in the dimly lit alley behind the Snowflake Dance Academy. "Garrett, I thought we went over this in your office. How could I tell you when I didn't even know you or where to find you?"

He buttoned up his coat, but his hazel eyes didn't look away from her. "You're right. There's no sense in looking back at the past. What's important is that we figure out what we're going to do from here on out."

"What *we're* going to do?"

"You can't seriously expect me to not want to be a part of my child's life."

"Actually, I didn't really know what to expect. It was never my intention to get pregnant that night in Boise, and I'm guessing raising a child with a complete stranger wasn't what you had in mind, either. So I completely understand if you want to pretend none of this ever happened and walk away. I'm more than capable of handling this on my own. No strings attached. You're off the hook." She shoved her hands in her pockets, but not because it was cold. She just didn't want him to see her crossing her fingers.

"Walk away? From my own child? Nope. That's most assuredly not going to happen. So back to what *we*— meaning you and I together—are going to do. I've been doing a little bit of online research about co-parenting and shared custody. If we do things right and put the baby first, there's no reason why we can't work together to raise a well-adjusted and happy kid."

"You want to co-parent?" She had never even heard of the term before. Mia's own father had bailed the minute he'd found out his mistress was pregnant. Actually, he didn't bail so much as he'd simply gone home to his wife and his real children. Maybe Dan Perez had co-parented with the mother of his legal offspring, but he certainly hadn't done so with Rhonda Palinski. "What does that entail?"

"Well, we would share custody. You get the baby half of the time and I get him or her the other half, and we make decisions together about what school they'll go to and who has to pick them up from sports class and that kind of thing. I mean, we live in the same city now, so it shouldn't be that difficult to coordinate our work schedules and pass off back and forth to each other."

Share her child? Was he delusional? Did he actually think she'd leave her precious son or daughter with some guy she barely knew? He made it sound so simple. Yet they were talking about an innocent human being. Not a basketball.

"But we don't know each other. What if you're a completely unsuitable father?"

"Me? I'd make a terrific father. I'm well educated,

I have a stable job and income, and I've been around kids before."

"What kids?" She remembered him mentioning that he had a strained relationship with his own dad and wondered if that extended to the rest of his family.

"I did a couple of rounds in the pediatric unit when I was doing my residency. And I found one of my old textbooks on childhood development when I was unpacking some boxes in my office." Even in this alley with the orangish glow of the light poles, her face must've reflected all the skepticism she felt because he squared his shoulders defensively and asked, "What about you? What if *you're* a completely unsuitable mother?"

"Garrett, I'm a dance teacher." Mia started walking, but not to get away. She needed to move around in order to redirect her normally nonexistent temper. "I work with children all day, every day of the week."

"Fair enough." He kept pace beside her as they turned the corner of the building and made their way along the main sidewalk. "But what if you end up being like one of those spiteful women who becomes bitter and vindictive and uses our child to punish me?"

Mia had never been prone to violence, but she had also never had her morals or her potential parenting skills called into question by a virtual stranger. She stopped and pulled her hand out of her coat pocket to point her finger at him. "I would never use another person, let alone my own child, to punish anyone. But even if I were the type who *was* like that, we don't have an invested emotional history so it's not like I'm some bitter ex. We didn't exactly have the kind of relationship where one would establish those kinds of feelings toward each other."

He rubbed his forehead, then reached out and took her hand in his own. What was up with him and this whole touching thing? It must be something they taught in medical school because Mia surely wasn't used to so much constant physical contact.

She also wasn't used to the heat that shot from her fingers, up her arm and deep into her chest. So then why was she so mesmerized by it?

Uh-oh. She was feeling that weird bubbly champagne thing again. If she'd had any control over her brain, she would've yanked her hand back. But he was using his thumb to stroke her palm, and the last thing she wanted to do was make a scene now that they were on the main street through town—or to lose his comforting warmth. So she kept walking, letting him hold her hand as if they were a couple of lovers on a leisurely evening stroll.

"Listen, Mia. We barely know each other at all. We certainly don't know what kind of parents we'll be, let alone how we'll get along in a couple of years. But I hope that we can both agree that deep down, we want what's best for our child."

She glanced at him as she nodded in agreement, and his lips split into a full grin. This time, his expression matched his eyes. Now, *this* was a reassuring smile.

"So we've got a couple of months before Pipsqueak gets here to learn everything we possibly can about each other and how to successfully co-parent."

There he went with that co-parenting mumbo jumbo again. But he was right in the fact that they would have to learn about each other and how to manage being in each other's lives for the next eighteen-plus years at least.

"Okay, co-parenting rule number one." She felt her

frown lift and her guard ease just a smidge. "We are not naming this child Pipsqueak."

They reached Patrelli's, and Garrett smiled as he pulled open the heavy oak door leading to the crowded Italian restaurant. Looking into his eyes again, Mia remembered why she'd let this man lead her back to a hotel room. Or maybe she'd been the one doing the leading. Either way, if she wasn't careful, the whole world would see just how eager she was to have him smile like that at her again.

At least on a Saturday night, Patrelli's was mostly filled with tourists since most of the locals knew to avoid the busier places on the weekends.

"Mia, what a surprise!" Mrs. Patrelli, the matronly woman who owned the restaurant with her husband, greeted them as they walked inside. "We're packed tonight, but we might have a booth opening up in a few minutes. I'll move you to the top of the list."

"Oh, no, Mrs. Patrelli. Please don't do that. We just wanted to put in an order to go."

The fortyish-year-old plump woman with short, dark curly hair looked at her and Garrett skeptically before pulling a pad of paper out of her black apron and taking their order. Hopefully, Mr. Patrelli wouldn't take too long in the kitchen because the normally pleasing smells of marinara sauce and yeasty dough were already playing havoc with Mia's sensitive stomach.

"I'll bring you both some Chianti while you wait."

"Actually—" Mia put a hand to her tummy "—I'm not really feeling up for any tonight. Could you just bring me a ginger ale instead?"

"But you and your friends always have wine when you eat here. You love the house Chianti. There's only one reason a passionate woman like you wouldn't drink wine and that's if she's…" Mrs. Patrelli paused as she studied Mia carefully before turning her appraising eye to Garrett. She looked back and forth at them several times and Mia could see the moment the Italian woman made the connection. "I'll go get your ginger ale."

"Great." Mia slumped into an empty seat by the hostess stand as Mrs. Patrelli bustled off to the kitchen. "She totally knows."

"Knows what? About you being pregnant?" Garrett sat beside her, his arm immediately going around her as if to comfort her. "How can you tell?"

"Mrs. Patrelli has seven kids. I'm sure she's pretty astute about things like that."

"Is it bad if she knows? I mean, it's not like everyone won't find out eventually, Mia."

"I know. I guess I'm still just trying to get used to the fact that we're having a baby."

His expression softened. "We. I like the sound of—"

"Oh, my gosh, GP!" a beautiful blonde shrieked as she walked by carrying a toddler covered in pizza sauce and still eating half a slice. "I barely recognized you without the tailored suit and stiff collar. How in the world have you been?"

It took Garrett several moments to identify the woman who had just intruded on one of the most important conversations of his life. With her nose job and cheek implants, Cammie Longacre looked less like the girl he'd known in high school and exactly like every other debutante-turned-housewife he'd grown up detesting.

He could feel Mia trying to scoot her chair away,

but Garrett's arm around her shoulder was frozen—as if the shock that had been lying dormant in his body the past couple of days had just formed a glacier inside him. He could see Cammie's lips moving, and he even caught the words "senior class," "your dad" and "thought you'd disappeared off the face of the planet." But he couldn't make himself respond.

At least, not until the former yearbook editor for Newport Hills Prep Academy sat down next to him and leaned in closely before snapping a picture of them together on her smartphone.

"They're not going to believe it," Cammie said before looking over to Mia. "And I just couldn't help overhear you guys are pregnant! How exciting."

Realizing his former classmate must have overheard Mia's admission, he went into auto-pilot and switched over to damage control mode.

"What are you doing here, Cammie?" he asked, then wanted to kick himself for sounding so defensive.

"My husband and I brought the kids up to kick off the ski season." Just then, a man who looked as if he was still president of his college fraternity walked over with two laughing children under each of his arms. "Chip wanted to do Telluride again this year, but let's face it. All the good spots in Colorado and Jackson Hole are becoming so commercial lately. A friend of a friend recommended Sugar Falls and we decided to try out something new."

"Us, too," Garrett said capitalizing on her line of thinking. If he could convince this woman who'd led the campaign to vote him Most Likely to Model For Brooks Brothers that he was simply on vacation, then word about his permanent whereabouts would be less likely to leak out. He squeezed Mia in closer next to him, hoping she would play along. "We just love hitting the slopes, but there isn't any good snowboarding where we live in…Miami."

He'd blurted out the first city that had come to his mind, which was what he had been researching after Mia had sat in his office and told him that she'd used to be a professional NFL cheerleader.

"I should have known you were living on the coast somewhere. And snowboarding, too! You've finally turned into a beach boy, GP. Just like your dad." Her youngest child let out an unhappy wail before throwing his half-gnawed pizza crust to the floor. Being compared to his father left Garrett feeling like that piece of chewed-up bread lying on the ground. "Well, that's our cue to get going. Maybe we'll see you guys at the Snow Creek Lodge this weekend. We can catch up and I'll fill you in on what's happened to everyone since graduation."

"Sounds good." Garrett waved to the departing family, forcing a smile when what he wanted to do was crawl behind the hostess stand.

He waited until Cammie and her brood were well out the door before chancing a look at Mia.

She held her jaw firmly clenched, her eyes staring at the faded poster of Venice affixed to the wall across from them. Someone as naturally beautiful as Mia couldn't possibly be jealous of a woman like Cammie, could she? Or maybe she was embarrassed that he hadn't introduced her to his old classmate. Either way, he needed to get back into her good graces. "Look, I know what I just said to that woman might've sounded crazy, but trust me. It was for the best."

"Why would you let her think we were together? Or suggest we were living in Miami?"

Was that what had Mia so on edge? The fact that someone might actually believe they were a couple?

"Actually, I believe she overheard *you* practically announcing to the restaurant that we were having a baby." There went his defensive tone again. Perhaps Mia had set this all up.

"But Miami? I'd really prefer people didn't connect me with that place."

He almost laughed at her impractical concern. Anyone with a computer could figure out where Mia used to live. It really couldn't be that big of a deal. Clearly, she didn't understand the potential risk of having someone from his hometown recognize him.

Or maybe she understood it too well.

"Listen, when she snapped that picture, it caught me by surprise. The last thing I want is for her to broadcast on social media where I'm currently living. Florida was the first thing that popped into my mind since the other day you'd mentioned that you'd lived there."

"Why wouldn't you want anyone to know you've moved to Idaho?"

Was she serious? Maybe she was hoping for the camera crews to show up and for their unorthodox relationship to be broadcast to every major tabloid in America, but Garrett would be damned if he'd let the paparazzi find out about his child. "Let's just say that I value my privacy."

Something that looked like understanding flashed in Mia's pale blue eyes, but it was so unexpected, Garrett wasn't sure he'd interpreted it correctly. He hoped she did understand because this was one child-rearing issue that wasn't up for negotiation. The sooner she realized that in order to make this co-parenting thing work she would need to keep their relationship out of the press, the better.

He was relieved when she nodded and said, "I'm glad we're on the same page."

She brushed her long dark hair away from her face and he thought back to her not wanting to be seen together in public. Maybe she had something to hide, too. He wondered whether she'd be willing to sign some sort of confidentiality agreement—especially if he tossed in a decent amount of money as an added incentive to keep quiet.

God, that sounded so cheap and tawdry. As if he was trying to buy her off in order to keep his child a secret. What kind of man did something like that?

A desperate one.

"So, for now, we're just keeping this whole baby thing between the two of us?" he asked.

"Well, us and Mrs. Patrelli," she said, one corner of her lip lifting slightly. He liked seeing her smile and realized that during their brief encounters, he hadn't seen it too often. "And probably Cessy Walker. Oh, and my two best friends."

"What?"

"I had to tell them about you when Maxine called the hotel room the morning after and you answered the phone." So that *had* been someone looking for her and more than likely hell-bent on calling security to protect her. "They were also with me when I took the pregnancy test. But that was before I knew you were going to be living here and would want to be…uh…involved."

Okay, he could handle a couple of locals knowing

about them. After all, he'd figured he'd have to deal with as much when she'd limped out of his office the other day. He nodded and realized his arm was still resting along the back of her chair. If he moved it just an inch, he'd be able to feel her shoulders pressed firmly against him again.

"And Kylie and Max might've told their husbands. Which means your buddy, Chief Cooper, probably knows, as well as Dr. Gregson. Didn't you work with him when you were stationed at Shadowview?"

"I didn't know you were best friends with their wives." Yep. Word was going to get around Sugar Falls awfully quickly. "Anyone else?"

She opened her pretty pink lips to answer but was interrupted by the theme song from *Jaws*. She looked at the screen before pressing a button to silence the ringer. "Not yet, but I can tell you who isn't going to be happy when I *do* finally tell her," she said, flashing the screen at him. "My mother."

"Maybe you should take that."

"I'll call her tomorrow. Look, my tummy isn't doing all that great and I'm not really feeling up for dinner anymore."

"Oh. Okay. Should I cancel our order?"

"No. You take it to your place. Where is your place, by the way?"

"I've got a room at Betty Lou's Bed-and-Breakfast. But eventually, I'd like to find something here in town. Maybe one of those old Victorian homes to remodel."

"That sounds pretty permanent." He looked at her sideways. That was the point, wasn't it? She stood and he picked up his coat. "Where are you going?"

"To walk you home." Did she really think he'd be so ungentlemanly as to let her find her own way home?

"It's only a couple of blocks. I walk it all the time."

"So then you won't mind if I walk it with you."

"But what about your lasagna?"

"What about it? I'll come back for it."

He held open the door for her and they walked quietly down the street lined with gas lanterns and a heavier-than-normal amount of foot traffic, probably due to the weekend tourist crowd. If she wasn't feeling well, he didn't want to make her talk, even though there was still so much to say.

When they were almost to her building, he could no longer stand the silence between them. "So when do you see the obstetrician?"

"My first appointment is Monday afternoon. Why?"

He had a feeling the shy and reserved Mia wasn't going to like what he was about to say. But this was his future, too, and he wasn't going to take a backseat for any part of the process. "Should we take your car or mine?"

Chapter Six

Mia couldn't believe she was actually allowing Garrett to accompany her to such an important and intimate doctor's appointment.

But lately her emotions had been zooming up and down on the rickety roller-coaster tracks that were her nerves. So on Saturday night, when Garrett had asked in such a way that gave her no wiggle room for extracting herself gracefully, her already foggy brain couldn't come up with a good reason to deny him the simple request.

Besides, this child was his, too. As much as she'd wanted to keep the experience to herself, to keep the whole child to herself, she couldn't in good conscience do something so selfish—to either Garrett or to her unborn baby. Unless, of course, he proved himself to be untrustworthy or a bad father. In which case, she would pack up her son or daughter, along with the rest of her life, so quickly that nobody—not even her mother—would ever find them.

She kept her Prius at a steady and safe pace, which was more than she could say for her pulse rate, as she drove down the mountain highway toward Boise. Garrett sat quietly in the seat beside her, his fingers intertwined tightly together. They'd barely exchanged more than some simple pleasantries when they'd met in the back alley behind her dance studio after lunch. But that was for the best since Mia wasn't very good at making small talk.

"I could have driven us, you know," he said again for at least the third time.

"Yes, you mentioned that. Thank you for offering, but I feel more comfortable in my own car." *And in control.*

He fiddled with his seat belt before returning his hands to their original position. If Mia hadn't seen him so confident in several other situations, she would think that he was just as nervous as she was.

She saw the black cuff links, the ones with his initials secured at his wrists. "I see you're wearing your father's gift."

He clasped his hands together and held them in his lap. "I am. I was pretty angry at him that night I first met you. And you'll probably see me angry at him again in the future. But I decided to channel his words about remembering where I came from into something less bitter. Or maybe I'm a sentimental moron. I really don't know. Anyway, do you mind if I change the radio station?"

Mia frowned. But not because the guy didn't totally hate his father. That was actually a good thing. She was annoyed because this was her favorite CD, the one she'd once planned to use for her audition to the MFA program at Hollins University in Virginia. She'd just saved up enough money for the first year of tuition when she'd had to undergo reconstructive surgery on her knee. Nothing had been the same since then. "Do you have something against Mozart?"

"It's just so slow and tedious. It's making me really antsy and tense."

"Really? It's supposed to be soothing. I read an article that said babies can hear everything in utero, so I try to pick classic pieces for him or her to listen to whenever possible."

"The Rolling Stones are a classic." He shoved his sunglasses higher on his nose. At least he didn't just reach for the knob and change the station. Which was something that some of the entitled guys her mother had encouraged her to date in college would have done.

She glanced at the blue shirt that clung to his chiseled torso, his tailored khaki pants and his expensive loafers. Garrett dressed like the trust fund preppy types Rhonda Palinski insisted her daughter latch on to for financial security. But he'd also been in the military—and underneath those expensive clothes, she knew he had the well-muscled physique to prove it—so he didn't walk around town acting as if he owned everything in it, including her.

Plus, the fact that he'd been so standoffish with that woman who'd recognized him at Patrelli's was another thing she hadn't expected. At first, Mia had thought that Garrett's chilly response was due to his embarrassment of being seen with her. But when he wouldn't release her hands, as though he were holding on to her as he would a lifeboat in a stormy ocean, she realized that something else about Cammie Perfect Teeth had Garrett spooked.

Mia wouldn't characterize Garrett as being rebellious, but she'd definitely recognized the look in his eyes as the other woman had talked endlessly about the people they'd known in high school and running into his father. It was a look she'd seen reflected in her own mirror too often, such as right before she'd defied her mother by getting her nose pierced after college. But his hazel eyes had also held a fierce determination, like a cornered animal not willing to give himself or his starched collars up.

So who was after Garrett McCormick, MD, and why?

But before she could solve that mystery, she needed to get through her first obstetrician appointment.

She pulled into a parking spot in front of the three-story medical office building near Boise State University, but didn't dare look at the well-dressed gentleman sitting beside her. Maybe she could just try to pretend he wasn't there. She took a couple of deep but subtle breaths. Mozart hadn't been the least bit helpful thus far.

"You ready for this?" he asked, not looking entirely ready himself.

"No," she said. Yet, she opened her car door, determined to swallow her own uncertainties and discomfort for the health of her unborn child. They walked silently across the full parking lot. He was probably just as lost in his own thoughts as she was.

He held open the large glass doors for her and then found the suite number on the directory near the elevator. She could tell he was equally anxious, but at least he was being solicitous.

Almost too solicitous. When they walked up to the receptionist, it was Garrett's voice that announced them. "Mia Palinski to see Dr. Wang."

The lady behind the desk was wearing scrubs printed with storks and handed her several forms to complete. But before Mia could take the clipboard, Garrett said, "Here, let me help with that. I'm a doctor. And the dad. Not *her* dad. The baby's dad."

The woman laughed, as if she dealt with nervous expectant fathers every day. Which she probably did. Next, she handed Mia an empty plastic cup and pointed to the restroom before saying, "Can't help with this one, Dr. Dad."

"Honestly," Garrett whispered as they walked toward the chairs in the waiting room, "I can't really help with the forms, either. Besides what I memorized from my own medical charts, I still don't know much about you. I guess I just wanted to feel useful."

Mia's spine tingled, but not out of apprehension. He'd memorized her medical history? Not that she could blame him. She would look through any records she could to find out as much information about him as possible. In fact, she'd talked to her best friends' husbands at length yesterday, quizzing them on everything they knew about Garrett.

Kylie's husband, Drew Gregson, was a psychologist at Shadowview Military Hospital and assured Mia that her baby's father was a well-respected doctor who treated his nurses and staff well and had a reputation for being professional.

Cooper could also vouch for the man's military record and skills as a surgeon, but she could tell the police chief knew more than what he was admitting. When it came to a personal background check, all he would tell her was that Garrett had a clean criminal record and was a trustworthy guy.

Drew was trained to notice abnormal behavior and Cooper was a good judge of character. They were two of the few men Mia trusted implicitly, which was what had ultimately swayed her decision to allow Garrett to be a part of her pregnancy.

But after she'd left her urine sample and changed into a plain cotton gown, Mia had to wonder if the small confines of the obstetrician's office, with all the pictures of women's reproductive organs on display, was the best place for her and Garrett to get better acquainted.

He offered to take Mia's blood pressure, but the nurse pointed to the chair in the corner and told him that he could either sit out of the way or out in the waiting room.

"Well, she could certainly work on her bedside manner," Garrett said when the medical assistant left them alone to await the doctor.

"I thought she was sweet and more than capable. Besides, you're not her patient so she probably doesn't care too much about your bedside requirements."

Garrett crossed his arms and, as if by silent agreement, they looked everywhere around the room except at each other.

At least he didn't show too much interest in the posters or the life-size model of a uterus. Instead, he kept checking out the medical equipment and even commented on the newness of the ultrasound machine.

Dr. Wang, an older woman with a short, messy ponytail and bifocals, finally entered and relieved some of the tension. "Congratulations, you two. The urine sample was positive, so let's take some measurements and figure out when exactly this baby will be arriving."

Garrett must have taken that as his cue to leave his seat of exile and hover around Mia as the doctor performed her exam.

"Aren't you the curious one," Dr. Wang said, lifting her wiry eyebrows high above the rim of her glasses.

"I'm in orthopedics," he said. They spoke briefly about medical school, the people they both knew at Shadowview Military Hospital and the differences between joint replacements and fetal development.

Mia wanted to wave her arm and call out, *Hello! I'm the one with the baby inside me*, but she was so accustomed to not trying to draw attention to herself that she remained still and quiet, trying to absorb the fact that she was truly and officially pregnant. It was one thing to see a couple of lines on a plastic stick. It was quite another to lie back in a sterile room with two doctors conversing about due dates and trimesters and fundal height measurements.

Somehow, everything was so real yet so surreal at the same time. Mia felt as if she was the cute and cuddly kitten in the poster tacked to the ceiling, looking down at the nervous and excited woman lying on the exam table.

Whoa. A fleeting moment of déjà vu replayed in her mind as she remembered having this same out-of-body experience when she'd entered the mirrored hotel elevator with Garrett and watched him pull her into his arms.

It was as though she knew this was her. But at the same time, it couldn't possibly be her.

"What's that?" Garrett asked when Dr. Wang pulled a small instrument out of her lab coat pocket.

"This is a fetal Doppler," the obstetrician said. "We're going to try to hear your child's heartbeat."

Mia tensed when the doctor opened the hospital gown and exposed her abdomen. She lifted her arm up so it lay across her face, hopefully hiding the blush spreading on her cheeks. Garrett had seen her much more intimately than this, plus, he was in complete medical professional mode and would hardly observe her body as anything other than for its basic anatomical purpose.

"Are you okay?" He rubbed her forearm, causing her to move it away from her face and make eye contact with him.

"Yep," Mia replied, her jaw stiff. "It's just cold."

When the quick-paced whooshing noise filled the small room, Garrett's hand slid along her arm, until it was locked tightly around her fingers above her head. Instead of looking at the doctor, he looked at Mia. His hazel eyes had turned dark green and slightly misty. "Is that it?"

She felt her own eyes grow damp and couldn't stop her fingers from squeezing back. "I think so."

That was *her* baby moving inside *her* body—dancing to its own pulse and synchronizing its heartbeat with hers. Her throat grew tight and she felt the wetness of a happy tear trickle toward her ear. She pulled Garrett's hand tighter, moving it to just below her chin. She was so relieved he was there and that she wasn't experiencing this wonderful moment alone. She'd never heard such a beautiful sound in her life. Not even Mozart could top this.

Garrett's other palm moved toward her bare stomach

and it felt like the most natural thing in the world when his thumb traced a circle around the small monitor.

"Can you believe it?" His grin was full of pride and awe, but it was also contagious. "That's our Pipsqueak. Can we see him on an ultrasound?"

His eager voice reminded her of a kid who'd just been given a brand-new toy and was already tearing into the packaging trying to get it out. For a skilled surgeon, he certainly wasn't exhibiting an ounce of impulse control at that moment.

"We can." Dr. Wang pulled the bigger machine over. "But as of now, I'm estimating you to be at ten weeks. So we won't know just yet whether your Pipsqueak is a boy or a girl for another few weeks."

"I can't wait," he said, then removed his hand only when the doctor pushed it away to squirt a cold lubricant on Mia's belly.

"Being a parent takes lots of patience," the obstetrician said. "Making it through the next several months will be your first taste of that."

I can't wait. The words he'd uttered without thinking ricocheted inside his head all the way back to Sugar Falls. Along with the fact that what he'd said was true.

He didn't know how to be a father or how to co-parent, for that matter. And he assuredly didn't know this woman who was carrying his child. But when he'd heard the thrilling wish-washing sound of his baby's heartbeat, he knew with a deep certainty that he'd never been so excited for anything in his life—not even for that plane ride that had taken him from his family home to his future dorm room at Annapolis.

And just like joining the navy, Garrett knew this

journey of fatherhood would have its ups and downs and that in no way would it be an easy road. But for some reason, he was no longer looking at the situation the way a third-year resident dreaded getting deployed to a combat zone.

"Why are you smiling?" Mia asked as she steered her little hybrid car onto the interstate.

"I can't stop."

"I know. Me, neither. Earlier in the exam room, I was thinking that this whole experience is so surreal."

"Exactly. It's just so crazy, you know? I should be scared to death of what the future holds. But I'm not. It's a weird sensation for me because usually I like order, I like rules. It's why I joined the navy."

"I thought you joined the navy to get away from your father."

"Well, partly. But I could've gone anywhere to get away from him. The navy was both a physical and an emotional escape for me. Growing up in my family was like being on an eighteen-year concert tour with Jimmy Buffet. I became a surgeon because I'm good at remaining steady when there's chaos all around me."

"What about your mom? You've never mentioned her."

He looked at Mia, something about the emotional experience they'd just shared making him decide to open up a little. "She died of breast cancer."

"That must've been very sad."

"I was two when it happened so I really don't remember much about her."

"I'm sorry," Mia said, but Garrett didn't want to end their day talking about something depressing. He fingered his cuff links, the ones that now had a little more sentimental meaning to them than they had that night he'd lost one.

"So that ultrasound was pretty amazing, huh? Pip-squeak looked pretty healthy in there."

She smiled at him. "I'm happy you're excited and, for what's it's worth, I'm glad we're off to a good start with this whole co-parenting thing."

"Me, too."

They'd had a relaxing drive back from Boise, neither one of them talking much, but neither one of them on edge, either. Something had happened in that doctor's office that had allowed them to accept the fact that they were embarking on a special journey together, and that they were going to be partners in whatever happened from here on out.

Sure, Mia still hadn't given him any indication that she was willing to let him see too much of who she was, but at least she hadn't insisted on playing that "soothing" classical music on the way home. In fact, Garrett had been surprised to discover she actually had a couple of classic rock stations preprogrammed on her car radio.

They were listening to Crosby, Stills, Nash & Young when Mia parked the small vehicle in an assigned spot behind the building housing the Snowflake Dance Academy. He thought about her warmly decorated apartment above it and hoped she'd welcome him back there again before the baby was born. At some point, they would need to get to a familiar place where they would feel comfortable in each other's presence. Yet after the miracle he'd just been a part of, he didn't want to rush anything that would force them together.

But he didn't want to go back to his empty and lonely room at the bed-and-breakfast, either.

"Thank you again for letting me go with you to the first appointment."

"Honestly, I was a little surprised that you'd want to."

"Why would that surprise you?" Did she think he planned to be some sort of deadbeat dad?

"I just figured with you being a man of science and a doctor and all that, it wouldn't be too thrilling for you."

"I probably would've thought that myself a few months ago. But it's different being the one on the other side of the curtain, so to speak. When I'm the doctor, it's all about business and caring for the patient and being the one in charge. Plus, I only have a basic fundamental understanding of childbirth from medical school since I've never been too interested in that field before. I guess it's more exciting when it's your own child—your own future—at stake."

"I can understand that." She nodded toward the freshly painted Victorian building that housed her studio. "When I watch my students perform their routines in a recital, it just feels like a job well done. But then I get a glimpse of their parents sitting in the audience, holding up their cameras and leaping up to applaud when it's over, and I think about how much more invested they are than me."

A tiny knock sounded at the driver's side window and she turned her head to smile at a little girl wearing a heavy pink coat over her pink tights.

"Hi, Madison," Mia said as she exited the car.

"Hey, Miss Mia." The six-year-old pulled a finger out of her left nostril then smiled, revealing two missing teeth. "I've been practicing my kick ball chains all week and my mom brought me over early so I could show you before the other students get here."

"I can't wait to see them. We have about fifteen more minutes until class starts so give me a couple seconds to get inside and then I'll watch." Mia pulled a bobby pin out of her own sweater pocket and used it to straighten the girl's lopsided bun. He'd seen her in work mode for only thirty seconds, but she seemed pretty invested in her students so far. She turned to Garrett. "Tap class starts at five, so I better get going."

She put her hand out, but must have thought better of the formal action after the intimate afternoon they'd just shared because she pulled it back and then drew the edges of her cardigan tighter around her waist instead.

They weren't quite at the hugging-goodbye phase, but he'd like to think they'd at least gotten past the hand-shaking stage. As Dr. Wang had suggested, he would try to be patient over the next seven months. Too bad he wasn't ready to go back to the B and B just yet. "Actually, do you mind if I come inside for a second and use your restroom?"

Okay, so maybe that was just an excuse to linger and gain more of a glimpse into her world. But who could blame him? He *should* see the environment where his child would be raised part-time. She'd had the opportunity to see him at work, so why shouldn't he be afforded the same?

"Sure," she said, shrugging her shoulders. He followed her inside to where another instructor was conducting some sort of hip-hop dance class.

So she had employees—legitimate ones, not just a socialite sitting behind a reception desk in a start-up orthopedic practice—working for her. Business must not have been too bad.

As soon as their feet hit the parquet floor, Mia's steps

picked up speed and she lifted her hand in a halfhearted wave toward several parents sitting on folding chairs in an alcove off to the side of the main dance floor. But she didn't stop to make small talk, or to otherwise introduce him to anyone. Either she was hoping nobody would pick up on the fact that his truck had been parked in front of her studio all afternoon and, therefore, surmise that they had been together. Or she thought he must really need to use the bathroom.

While he was washing his hands, the bass pounding through a mounted wall speaker down the hall came to an abrupt halt. He checked his watch and assumed the hip-hop class had just finished. Maybe if he took his time in here, he'd get the opportunity to watch her in action teaching a class.

But a loud knock on the door, followed by a young voice yelling, "Mommy, I really gotta go and I don't wanna be late for Miss Mia," threw a wrench in his stall tactics.

Garrett walked slowly out of the unisex restroom, tempted to stop by the wide-open doorway of what must've been Mia's office. Maybe he could slip in there and take a look around, find out some more information about her.

Oh, come on. What was he thinking? When had he become such a spy? He'd never had to dig up information on women before. Of course, he had never been that interested in another woman before.

Whoa. He needed to back up. Obviously, he wasn't interested in Mia as a *woman* woman. He was merely interested in her as the person carrying his child.

Be patient. He reminded himself of Dr. Wang's

words yet again. He would find out what he needed in due time.

He passed her office, for now, and hung back against the wall behind some folded-up floor mats. She had thrown her hair up into a knot on top of her head and was dressed in the same leggings she'd worn to the obstetrician's office. But she'd removed her outer sweater and his eyes were drawn to the scoop neck of her leotard. Her throat and upper chest were on full display and his mind took him back to their magical night. He remembered the feel of her collarbone beneath his lips as he'd trailed kisses along its silky-smooth ridges and the way her skin had tasted when her body had arched up into his arms and she'd pulled his head down lower.

A sudden burst from the speaker right above his ear brought him back to the present. Mia had put on some jazzy swing music and was now watching the little girl from the parking lot tap her little heart out. After she applauded the girl's solo performance, she called out, "Okay, my dancing butterflies. Let's get started."

Several other six-year-olds click-clacked their way out onto the floor and Mia led them through a series of toe shuffling, heel tapping and arm spinning.

He watched her try to stifle a giggle when one little girl spun too much and landed on her rear end. He also watched her soothe that same little girl when her two younger brothers, who were sitting and observing from the sidelines, roared with laughter during a second fall.

He wondered if Mia even knew he was still there. That he was watching her. He hoped not because right that second, she was more at ease than he'd ever seen her—even that night in Boise. She was clearly in her element and hadn't been lying when she'd said she was used to being around children.

When she started a conga line of sorts, the dancers followed her as she wove back and forth along the wooden floor. But the few stragglers at the tail end got separated and when the last butterfly ran to catch up with her classmates, she slipped in her metal-plated shoe and Garrett watched her go down awkwardly on her right ankle.

He was by the girl's side before Mia had even turned around—getting there before the poor child's mother, whose scream stopped the entire class and put an end to the conga line. The little one was crying and Garrett could tell by the odd angle of her foot that this was more than a sprain. He immediately went into emergency mode. His first job was to stabilize the patient. Someone else could deal with the flustered parents and everyone who crowded around to see what had happened.

"Honey," he said to the girl, but loud enough for the distraught mom to hear. "My name is Dr. McCormick and I want to help you. What's your name?"

"Madison," she said through trembling lips. Her mom stroked her hair as she knelt on the other side.

"Okay, Madison, I'm going to put my hands on your leg and check to see how strong your dancing legs are." Madison nodded but didn't make an effort to wipe away the fat teardrops spilling down her rosy cheeks.

Mia leaned over him and said, "What can I do to help?"

He pulled his keys out of his pocket and handed them to her. "I have a small bag in the backseat of my truck with some splints and a first aid kit in it. Can you get it for me? Also, we're going to need an ice pack." Then, so he wouldn't alarm his young patient, he said, "Wow, you've got some pretty sturdy bones and trust me, I've seen a lot of bones. That's the kind of doctor I am."

"Okay, class," Mia said. "Dr. McCormick is going to take good care of Madison, so let's call it a wrap and finish early tonight. I'll see all you butterflies next Monday."

Several parents herded their children toward the exit and Garrett was glad Mia was helping to draw their attention away. He didn't need the other students, who looked to be still shaken up from the injury of one of their own, to make his patient any more anxious.

"Do you have a skel'ton at your doctor office?" Madison sniffed her nose.

"I do, but it's not a real one."

"My friend Chelsea had a skel'ton at her Halloween party and I was the only girl who wasn't afraid to touch it."

"You know, that sounds very brave. In fact, I think you're being pretty brave right now."

He gently removed the patent leather shoe from her foot, trying to be mindful of the swelling that had already started.

"Owie, owie, ow!" Madison yelped, but she didn't release any more tears. She was a tough one, all right.

"Mom," he said, looking at the mother, who was still trembling. "Is her pediatrician close by?"

"Uh…" Madison's mother looked lost, as if she couldn't understand what he was asking. He repeated the question. "Not really. She's in Boise, but we've seen Dr. Suarez before for emergencies."

Garrett had met the older town doctor who had one foot out the retirement door and most likely wouldn't be able to do much more than stabilize the little girl until she could be seen by a specialist anyway.

Mia returned with his medical bag, which she placed on the floor beside him. "I'll be right back with an ice pack."

"Thanks," Garrett told her before turning back to the concerned mom. "I'm an orthopedic surgeon, so this is my forte. My office is only about five minutes away from here and with your permission, we can at least take an x-ray so little Madison won't have to sit around doctors' waiting rooms for the next few days."

The woman ran a plump hand through already frazzled hair. "My husband is out of town for business right now and there is no way I can take off work this week to take her to a bunch of appointments. Do you think it's bad?"

"Until we get to my office and do the x-ray, I can't be one hundred percent sure. Judging from the swelling and what I can feel, it's most likely a clean break. She'll need a cast just to help the bones stay in place while they heal, which we can take care of tonight."

"Like a real cast?" Madison looked hopeful. Why was it that children thought having their bodies restrained in plaster was an adventure? "One that my friends can sign and stuff?"

Garrett smiled at her. "Yup. But first, I want to take some pictures of your leg to see if you even need it. And if you do, I'll make you the most beautiful cast your friends will ever lay eyes on. How does that sound?"

She nodded enthusiastically and wiped her still-damp face.

Mia handed him the ice pack before walking toward a group of lingering parents and children who seemed reluctant to leave without ensuring their classmate was in good hands.

Thank God Mia was there to handle the onlookers so that he could focus on his patient. He spoke with Madison's mom about driving the girl over to his office as he put a temporary splint on her ankle and then wrapped it to keep it in place.

When he was done, he lifted the six-year-old and carried her out to her mother's older minivan and got her strapped in before getting into his own truck to lead the way to his office.

It wasn't until he pulled away from the curb that he realized he hadn't even said goodbye to Mia.

Chapter Seven

Mia was worried Garrett's office would be locked by the time she'd finished her last class of the evening. But when she pulled her Prius into the dark parking lot, she saw his truck and Mrs. Rosellino's van parked in front of the building and made her way inside.

She'd sprained her wrist once in junior high and she remembered her own mother fluttering around the gymnastic mats and yelling for someone to call an ambulance. It might have been the first time her mother had actually been more concerned with her daughter's injury and subsequent pain than the fact that Mia would be missing out on practice. That whole week her mom had babied her, making her grilled cheese sandwiches and buying two gallons of chocolate peanut butter ice cream so they could pig out on the sofa and watch *Dirty Dancing*, *Grease* and old Fred Astaire and Ginger Rogers movies.

After that, it was back to celery sticks and rice cakes and two-hours-a-day dance workouts. But for that one week, Mia herself, not her talent or her career or her future, had been Rhonda Palinski's main concern. She'd seen the same caring transformation with Mrs. Rosellino tonight. So maybe there was something more to these stage moms than she'd been giving them credit for all along.

She hadn't even realized that Garrett was still at her studio when little Madison had slipped and done a number on her ankle. It wasn't until after he'd carried the injured little girl out to her mom's car that it had dawned on her that he must've stayed to watch her class.

Why would he have done that? Really, why would he have done any of the things he'd done today? Such as, why had he gone with her to her doctor's appointment and then asked the doctor for his own printed set of ultrasound pictures—which he'd folded carefully and slipped inside his leather wallet with a designer logo on the front. Aside from his fashion sense, the man wasn't fitting any of the rich-playboy stereotypes she'd had him pegged for. What else would he do to surprise her?

Even though the front door had been open, the reception area was dark and empty. She saw lights on in the back and made her way toward the exam rooms.

She tried not to think of the last time she'd been in this hallway or the panic that had gripped her when she'd realized that Garrett was going to find out about the baby. She also didn't want to think about the way he'd smiled at her when they'd heard that same baby's heartbeat earlier today. Or the way he'd opened up more about himself during that car ride.

So much had changed in less than a week… How much more would change over the next seven months?

"Miss Mia!" Madison squealed when she got to the doorway of the same exam room she'd been standing in when Garrett had made that fateful discovery.

"Hi, sweetie," she said to the little girl. "I would have come earlier, but I had to teach my yoga class. I knew you'd be in excellent hands with Dr. McCormick, though."

He looked up from the bright pink fiberglass material he was carefully wrapping around Madison's foot. She could see the surprise in his hazel eyes, but he was probably too professional to comment on her unexpected arrival.

"Dr. McCormick says that I'm his first patient ever to get to have a pretty pink cast. I can't wait to show it to my friends at school tomorrow." Madison's excitement was short-lived when she frowned and added, "But he says I can't do any more tap dancing until my leg gets better."

"Maybe you can come to class and be in charge of the music? Or help me pass out the props? I'd love to still be able to see you, and I know the other girls will be pretty impressed with that fancy pink work of art you've got there."

Madison turned a pleading gaze to Garrett. "Can I, Doctor?"

Garrett finished his task, then stood up from his stool and said, "I think being a dance teacher's assistant would be a perfect job. As long as you promise to always use your crutches and get right back to tapping as soon as the cast comes off."

"I promise," the girl vowed and Mia gave her a high five.

"I had crutches like these once," Mia said before helping the little girl off the table.

As Garrett provided Mrs. Rosellino with a list of instructions, Mia helped Madison practice on the new crutches and tried not to think about the year she'd spent using the blasted things. It had been the most painful and demoralizing time in her life.

But for a six-year-old with a bright pink cast, it must seem like a wonderful adventure.

"Thank you so much, Dr. McCormick." Mrs. Rosellino followed her hopping daughter toward the front door. "We were so lucky you were there when it happened."

Please don't ask what he was doing there in the first place, Mia silently begged the woman, even though a little while ago she'd been wondering the exact same thing.

But this was Sugar Falls and, of course, any little detail outside the norm was cause for speculation and gossip. She and Garrett were still getting used to this whole co-parenting thing and their new unorthodox relationship. Mia didn't need the added bonus of unwanted opinions and assumptions to get in the way of their goal.

Wait. Did they even have a goal, besides raising a healthy, well-adjusted child? They hadn't really defined their own roles yet and Mia was hoping that once they decided to do so, it wouldn't be with an audience.

"Why were you there, anyway?" Mrs. Rosellino asked.

Ugh! There it was. Mia knew the question was coming, but had hoped for a lucky break—just this once.

"We had just come from the obstetric..."

"He was using the bathroom," Mia interrupted loudly. Maybe too loudly because the woman slowed her pace to turn back and tilt her head, looking side to side at each of them.

"I know!" Mia tried to make her pleasant surprise sound believable. "It's pretty, random, huh? I guess we were lucky that Dr. McCormick was in the right place at the right time."

Madison's mom probably didn't buy that dumb explanation any more than Mrs. Patrelli would have. But instead of asking more questions, she started walking again toward the door.

Garrett caught Mia's eye before giving her a wink and adding, "I seem to have a knack for being at the right place at the right time lately."

Mia's feet locked into place and she couldn't have commanded her body to move if she'd wanted to. Had he seriously just winked at her? Sure, Mrs. Rosellino hadn't seen him do it, but only a fool wouldn't have caught the implication in Garrett's tone.

Or the reminder that he *did* seem to have a habit of walking into her life just when she least expected it. And each time he did, the man turned her whole world upside down.

"I'll see you next week, Madison." Garrett touched the girl's lopsided bun as she maneuvered herself through the door. "Make sure you tell your mom if your leg starts hurting or if you think something is wrong with your cast so she can bring you back sooner."

"I will," the girl said as she hobbled toward the parking lot. "Thanks, Doctor."

Mia finally got her shocked muscles moving but had

to pause again when she realized that the way Garrett was holding the door blocked her from exiting unless she slid her body against him to pass through.

Her brain was telling her to follow the Rosellinos to the parking lot—not only to diminish the appearance of suspicious activity, but to prevent her from having to be alone with the man who had a tendency of showing up everywhere she didn't want him to be. It had been an emotional day—really, it had been an emotional *week*—and she didn't think her nerves could afford even the simplest polite conversation.

But her tired and taut body was telling her that if she so much as chanced the slightest contact with the hero doctor, she would wind up melting like smooth and creamy peanut butter left out too long in the sun.

For the thousandth time she asked herself why he had to be so good-looking. And so strong and capable. She had never needed a man before, and she had no intention of becoming susceptible to one now, when her emotions and hormones were spinning in a fast and reckless pirouette—one she knew she could maintain for only so long until she spun out of control.

"So, thanks again for taking care of Madison," Mia said, deciding she had no choice but to wait until he moved out of the way enough to let her pass.

"No problem. I'm glad I found that pink fiberglass wrap in my supply closet." His face turned toward her, but his body stayed firmly planted in front of the door.

"So you're still not unpacked?" She saw a breeze ruffle his brown hair, causing it to stray away from his perfectly combed part.

Sheesh, wasn't the man cold? The November night

air was coming in through the open door and Mia had been in such a hurry to drive over here after her yoga class, she hadn't even bothered putting her sweater back on.

"Nope. I really hadn't anticipated having many patients these first couple of weeks while I was getting situated." He looked down at her camisole, and Mia felt her nipples grow tight, but not because of the chilly temperature. "But for some reason, I keep having beautiful dancers show up at my office."

Mia wrapped her arms around her torso despite the fact that his gaze had just launched a sudden influx of heat to her bloodstream.

"Well, technically, the last dancer didn't show up here." Because at this exact moment, with the way he was looking at her, she wasn't sure she wanted to know why he had been at her studio.

"If we're going to be technical, I should probably also clarify that the first dancer is the only one whose beauty has completely affected me. In fact, it's wreaked havoc on my normally sound code of ethics."

He let the door close, which brought him close enough to her that she had to lift her face up to his. She watched his eyes trail down her neck and stop at the spot where her collarbone dipped into a small V. *Stop this, Mia. Now's your chance to walk away before this conversation gets dangerous.* But she didn't stop. Instead, she asked, "Why your ethics?"

He stepped closer, yet her body defied her brain once again and she didn't step back.

"Because for the first time in my life, I am deeply tempted to kiss one of my patients."

Her breath caught in her throat. "But I thought we established that it would be best if I saw a different surgeon about my knee. So, I'm not really your patient anymore."

"Thank God," he said before lowering his head toward hers.

She gasped when his lips touched hers, and opened her mouth to draw in air, but instead drew in more of him. Her arms followed an instinct of their own and soon Mia was plastered against him like a hot pink cast, matching each thrust of his tongue.

It was as if her mind had gone on vacation, leaving no instructions or provisions for her body—a body that had clearly remembered his kiss and was suddenly desperate to make up for lost time.

He never should have kissed her again.

As part of his rigorous naval training, he'd had to skydive out of a plane traveling at high altitude. All it had taken was one simple jump—more of a step off the cargo door ledge, really—and he'd been spiraling down in a free fall, feeling the air rush out of his lungs. He'd known that kissing Mia again would have that same effect on him. Unfortunately, this time he hadn't had the foresight to pack a parachute.

And as much as he liked order and organization, who could plan anything when confronted with this kind of temptation? One minute she'd been standing there, her skimpy camisole showing off her perfect body, and the next minute he had her wrapped up in his arms, claiming her mouth as if it was his own personal oxygen mask.

Mia moaned, but Garrett's brain wasn't so high up in the clouds that he mistook it for one of pleasure. He pulled back quickly. "Did I hurt you?"

"Just your height," she said before leaning down and rubbing her knee. He drew in his brows and she added, "I haven't been on my tiptoes that long since my last ballet audition several years ago. I guess the pressure was too much for my injury."

"Oh," he said. "I forgot you were wearing heels last time..." He let his voice trail off, not sure it was wise for either of them to be reminded of what had happened the last time they'd shared such a passionate kiss.

"I should probably be going," Mia said, her arms doing that wraparound protective-stance thing she tended to do any time he got within a couple of feet of her. Her eye tic was back, as well. Did she honestly think he was going to hurt her?

"Right. It's been a pretty emotional day for you. For *both* of us."

"Yes!" She seized upon his lame excuse a little too quickly and he wondered if he would have preferred that she deny it. That she correct him and say she wanted to kiss him because she'd been aching for him these past couple of days—hell, these past couple of months—just as badly as he had been for her.

But Garrett didn't do awkward conversations. Not with his family and definitely not with the women he normally dated. Which, he should point out, he and Mia certainly were not doing.

Still, it would just be more comfortable all around if she left now and they pretended this little lapse in lust had never happened. So he waited until she opened the door—he should've been gentleman enough to open it for her, but he couldn't trust himself to let her walk by him—and allowed the cold breeze that rushed in to cool his emotions and his libido, before he spoke. "Okay, so take care. I guess I'll see you around town."

Her response was an over-the-shoulder wave that she threw out while darting across the parking lot before quickly getting into her car. Hmm. Her knee clearly didn't seem to be bothering her anymore. Or maybe she just wanted to get away from him that badly.

After watching her drive away safely, he turned and sat down heavily in one of the chairs in the waiting area. Mia Palinski was truly unlike any other woman he'd ever met. On one hand, it was refreshing considering he'd spent the past ten years avoiding women like Cammie Longacre—women who would just want him because of his family's money and his father's notoriety. But on the other hand, it was also quite perplexing because he just didn't know what to make of her. He hoped that she was a solid, trustworthy person who had his and his child's best interests at heart. If not, eighteen years was a long time to have to engage with someone who was only looking out for number one.

On Thursday night, Garrett found himself sitting in Cooper's living room, getting ready to play poker with Mia's best friends' husbands and some other men he'd met since he'd moved here. Actually, he'd known both Cooper and Drew Gregson from the Shadowview Military Hospital—way before he'd even learned Mia's name, let alone that they were married to her friends. So it wasn't as if he could be accused of trying to infiltrate her ranks in an effort to spy on her. But, hey, if the guys wanted to provide a little background intelligence on her during their weekly poker game, Garrett wouldn't stop them.

Besides, the only thing he'd been able to find out about Mia on his own so far was an article on the internet about her being attacked by some sort of stalker back when she'd been a professional cheerleader. But it was weird that there wasn't more information on what exactly had transpired or who the attacker was. There were no court documents, no police reports, no media statements. At least none that his limited research capabilities could find.

Someone must have paid good money to keep that incident under wraps because in Garrett's former world of reality television, the spotlight would have shown brightly on something like that, and there would have been no end to the bad press.

Being attacked would explain why Mia was so jumpy, but it only left him with more questions. It also made him think that someone with some deep pockets had helped that situation go away—which usually translated into a cash settlement of some sort.

Mia certainly wasn't flashy or living a glamorous lifestyle, but maybe she'd blown her monetary award already and was patiently awaiting her next meal ticket to arrive. And arrive he had. Hell, Garrett had practically been delivered to her on a room service cart.

The shuffling of cards brought him back to the present.

"So the buy-in is a dozen chocolate-chips and six maple-pecans." Cooper made the announcement while looking around at the men who were pulling cookies from Maxine's famous bakery out of cellophane wrappers and stacking them neatly on the green baize-covered table.

Luke Gregson, Drew's twin brother, walked in the door with his own set of identical sons and said, "We got to the bakery right before closing, but by the time these two hungry monkeys got their little hands on the bag, all I have left are some cranberry-orange ones and those pumpkin-nutmeg things left over from last week."

The eight-year-old boys still had their mouths full and gave Luke a chocolaty hug before running off to Cooper's stepson's room to play with Hunter. The former navy SEAL looked as if he certainly had his hands full. And judging by the tired look on the man's face, Garrett was sure glad Mia's obstetrician had heard only one heartbeat.

The men were on their second hand when Kane Chatterson, Kylie's brother, who'd done the renovation of the old lumber mill for Garrett, came in through the door carrying a white sack from Domino's Deli.

"I hear congratulations are in order," Kane said as he passed out sub sandwiches. Garrett looked around the room to see who the former baseball pitcher was talking to, but all eyes were on him. Realizing what they were talking about, Garrett was surprised that he didn't feel any need to hide it. In fact, he was glad the secret was finally out.

"Word travels fast." Garrett took a sip from his bottle of beer, wondering who had spilled the beans.

"That it does," their host and the police chief said. Cooper knew about Garrett's family because, well, he was Cooper and tended to find out anything he wanted. Hopefully, he also knew what would happen if the rest of the world found out. But his next comment allayed some fears. "At least you can rest assured that it will end at the city limits signs. This town protects its own."

"Maybe." Kane shrugged, not looking entirely convinced. Garrett had confided in him about his identity as well, once he realized that the man was also performing his own disappearing act to avoid the limelight. "Time will tell."

"So everyone in Sugar Falls knows? I wonder how Mia will react to that." Garrett casually moved his sandwich to the side and ate a snickerdoodle—the poker cookie with the highest value and the closest proximity—hoping nobody noticed his subtle attempt to fish for information.

"I heard it from Donatella Patrelli, who just hired me to add a bathroom on to her house," Kane said.

Alex Russell, who owned the sporting goods store, folded before adding his own two cents. "I heard it from Jake Marconi's dad, who stopped by the store to pick up the new basketball team uniforms. He told me Mia was at his gas station filling up the other day. I guess she went inside to pay and when the person in line ahead of her opened up the beef jerky dispenser, she threw up right in front of the snack cake display. Said his wife knew then and there she was in the family way."

"The twins told me about it." Luke reached inside the deli bag and pulled out a container of hot peppers. "They found out at school from some little girls in Mia's tap dance class."

Drew laughed. "Word on the street is that you were

quite the hero at her studio the other night. One of the kids broke her ankle and Dr. McCormick was hiding in the wings and sprung into action."

"I wasn't hiding in the wings."

"Then what were you doing at a dance class for six-year-olds?" Cooper asked.

"I was using the restroom. So how long has Mia been a dance teacher?"

"Really? The Snowflake Dance Academy was the only business in town where you could find a place to go?" Nope, Cooper wasn't going to make things easy for him.

And here, Garrett thought *he'd* be the one getting answers tonight. Man, he should've known better than to become friends with a former MP who'd been trained to interrogate terrorists.

"Okay, so I had gone with Mia to the baby's first doctor's appointment in Boise on Monday and I used the bathroom when we got back from the long drive."

"How was it?" Luke asked.

"Her bathroom? It was fine."

"Not the bathroom, Doc. The first appointment. When Samantha was pregnant with the twins, I was on deployment and couldn't go to ours. But she'd recorded the whole thing and I must've watched that ultrasound video five hundred times."

"I'll never forget ours, either," Drew said, even though his was probably just several months ago. "The only thing keeping me from passing out when the doctor told us Kylie was having two girls was hearing my father-in-law whooping and hollering on the other side of the door. Kane, your old man has the loudest voice on the planet."

"At least he was happy. You should hear him when one of his pitchers gives up a walk." Kane finished his beer, then looked at Garrett. "Anyway, I just wanted to say congrats. I came to play cards, not to listen to the Daddy Train toot its own horn all night."

It was true. Garrett was entering an exclusive club for fathers, and the ones sitting here with him were as proud as could be. And he was now among their ranks. He remembered the thrill that had shot through him earlier this week when he'd heard his baby's heartbeat. He'd also remembered Mia's mad dash across the parking lot later that night when she was trying to get away from him after he'd kissed her.

"Well, Kane, we *could* talk about how the high school varsity team still needs a pitching coach this spring." Alex looked at the quiet baseball player, who shook his head once before going back to the refrigerator for another round of beers. "What about you, Doc?"

"What about me?" Garrett asked. "I'm not a pitching coach."

"No, but the high school also needs an athletic trainer. They have a couple of students volunteering now, but if you wanted to take on the team doctor role, you could oversee things. It's only on Friday nights for the football games right now, but eventually they'll need someone to help out with the other sports."

He thought about his office, which was practically unpacked and ready to go as soon as he got some new patients. Mia certainly wasn't blowing up his phone wanting to spend time with him, and this poker night constituted the extent of his social life. It wasn't as if Garrett had much else going on right now. Besides, the more time he spent with people who knew Mia, the more information he could find out about her.

"Sure. Why not?"

Chapter Eight

Mia didn't go to all the local football games, but she helped the varsity cheerleaders choreograph their bigger performances and had come with Maxine and Kylie to watch the halftime show tonight.

This was her last weekend of freedom before her mom showed up on Monday for a weeklong visit. She didn't know how she was going to get through Thanksgiving if her mom found out about the pregnancy before then. And knowing Rhonda Palinski's nose for drama, the woman would surely find out. Especially if she spent at least five minutes in town, where everyone else seemed to have already clued in.

As Mia walked with her friends toward the stands, the small marching band blasted out a loud rendition of the Sugar Falls High School fight song. She turned toward the field and saw a man dressed in track pants and an SFHS Huskies hooded sweatshirt bent in front of one of the players, unwrapping tape from the teenager's wrist. A bubbling blast of energy shot through her veins and Mia recognized the feeling—the sensation she got only when Garrett McCormick was close by.

That couldn't be…

"Watch where you're stepping, little mama," Kylie said when Mia stumbled over the first row of bleachers. She forced her head straight and concentrated on watching what she was doing, rather than looking behind her to see what her body already knew.

He might not be dressed in one of his fancy button-down shirts with his perfectly creased slacks, but there was no doubt of exactly who it was.

What was he doing there? It was bad enough that several of her students' parents had congratulated her this week on her pregnancy, and even worse, that most of them asked her directly if the father of her child was also the handsome new doctor in town. But did he have to flaunt it to everyone by showing up at the same events she did? No wonder the flames of gossip had been fanned into a citywide forest fire. They'd barely been seen together, but all it had taken were a few slips and a handful of sightings for suspicions to become facts.

"Nachos?" Maxine lifted a yellow goop-filled paper boat up under Mia's nose, causing her to gag.

"No, thanks. That processed cheese smells horrible." So did the popcorn Hunter was eating, as well as the hot dog Kylie was stuffing in her mouth.

"I was like that several weeks ago," her pregnant friend said around bites. "Couldn't stand the smell of anything. I think I lost ten pounds my first trimester.

Then I hit twenty weeks and lately it seems like I can't *stop* eating."

But Mia couldn't blame the sudden queasiness in her tummy on pregnancy-related nausea alone. She'd eaten anything she'd wanted to just fine since she saw Garrett on Monday evening. Well, almost anything. There *had* been that unfortunate beef jerky incident at the Gas N' Mart earlier this week. Otherwise, it was only when he was around that her stomach did backflips.

She narrowed her eyes. "What's Garrett doing down there on the sidelines?"

Kylie licked the mustard off her fingers. "Drew told me he agreed to help out as the team doctor and athletic trainer of sorts."

"Why? Is he trying to drum up business or something?"

"Wow. That doesn't sound like our sweet, even-tempered Mia," Maxine said, a tortilla chip paused on its way to her mouth. "What's got you in such a snit over Dr. Dreamboat?"

"Really?" Mia lifted her brows. "Is *that* the nickname we're going with?"

"Well, Dr. Handsome got taken when Kylie married Drew, so we wouldn't want to get the two men confused. Anyway, spill it. Why are you so on edge around him?"

"Besides the fact that I barely know the man but now have to 'co-parent' with him since I got knocked up after a one-night stand?"

"Hey, Mom." Maxine's eleven-year-old son leaned in to be heard over the loud trombones below. "What's a one-night stand?"

The blonde cookie baker pulled some cash out of her purse and shoved it at Hunter. "Here, sweetie, go to the snack bar and buy Aunt Mia a Sprite. And a king-size package of peanut butter cups."

"We shouldn't give her those until she tells us what's going on between her and Dr. Love Muffin," Kylie suggested.

Mia shuddered under her down-filled coat. "Suddenly, Dr. Dreamboat doesn't sound so bad. Okay, you two, I'll tell you but you have to swear not to say a word to your husbands." Her two friends held up their forefingers in a number one and touched the tips together. It was a gesture from their cheerleading days they always used to secure a solemn promise.

Mia told them about Garrett's reaction to hearing the heartbeat and how his excitement only intensified her already overwrought emotions. Then she filled them in on how she'd gone to his office that same night to check in on Madison Rosellino, which resulted in them sharing that passionate kiss.

"Boy, when we dared you to live a little, you sure took the ball and ran with it," Maxine smiled.

"Don't remind me of that text," Mia said. "If I wasn't a more responsible adult, I'd totally blame you both for this situation."

"So what did you do when he kissed you?" Kylie wanted to know.

"I kissed him back."

Kylie rolled her eyes. "Duh. Obviously. Then what?"

"Then we stopped kissing and I ran off."

Maxine dropped her shoulders and actually looked crestfallen. "Oh, Mia, you can't keep running forever."

A loud whistle signaled the end of the first quarter and Mia knew she would need to make her way down to the field soon to help get the cheerleaders ready for their halftime routine.

"I know that. Especially now that I'll have a little one who needs more stability than what my own mother gave me. But it would be so much easier if I didn't have to deal with its father."

"Would it?" Maxine asked. "I raised Hunter pretty much by myself until Cooper came along. Believe me, single motherhood is just as unglamorous as it sounds."

Her friend was right. She'd seen Max struggle financially and emotionally when she'd been raising her son on her own. And Lord knew Rhonda Palinski hadn't provided an award-winning example of single parenting. But Mia was used to being alone. She'd learned early on from her absentee father that men didn't stick around long. Therefore, she'd always been resolute in her determination to never rely on one for anything.

At least she *had* been until Garrett had taken her hand, first on Snowflake Boulevard and then on Monday in the obstetrician's office. When she was with him, it was so easy to get lost in the belief that everything was going to be okay, that he was strong enough and capable enough for both of them.

Which was why she was now trying to avoid the guy like her mother avoided carbs. He might make her body crave more, but nothing good could come of overindulging in too much bread—or too much Dr. Dreamboat.

Halfway through the second quarter, Mia made her way down to the field and was standing on the dirt track talking to the young cheerleading coach when Garrett spotted her. They hadn't talked all week and she was still embarrassed about the way she'd let herself come unglued in his arms.

She'd heard of doctors, specifically surgeons, having a God complex, thinking they could do no wrong. She didn't necessarily get that vibe from Garrett, but he'd admitted he liked control and order. Not to mention, there was definitely something about the way he carried himself that led her to believe that he was used to getting what he wanted. And clearly, his actions thus far demonstrated that he did not want her as anything more than a vessel to carry his child.

On Monday night, she'd expected him to run after her, or show up either at her studio or her apartment to try to win her over. That's what persistent men did when they learned she was unobtainable. Especially spoiled rich guys like Nick who weren't used to anyone telling them no. The jury was still out on whether Garrett was spoiled, but she could tell by the way he dressed and the new four-wheel-drive platinum-edition truck he drove that her baby's father was definitely living off more than what most naval officers brought home in their paychecks.

Judging by the fact that Garrett hadn't pushed her further that night or sought her out since, she had to assume that he was equally embarrassed by what had happened in the doorway of his office and no longer had any romantic interest in her at all.

But as he turned and walked toward her, seemingly heedless of the empty paper cups and the gravel crunching under his top-of-the-line cross-trainers, Mia realized that he was looking at her as if *she* was the very thing he wanted. Just like the tiny dirt pebbles lining the track, Mia's heart threatened to crumble with his every step. If she let him get too close, she might not be able to put those fragments back in pace.

"Hey," was all he said when he finally stood in front of her.

"Hey," she responded. "So, you're the new team doctor?"

"I'm just kind of helping out for now."

"How's it going?"

"Well, our defensive tackle was a little wobbly there during the first quarter because he'd heard a rumor that some girl he likes might be asking him out. But he threw up in the trash can behind the bleachers and I think everyone's in good shape now. What are you doing on the field?"

"I helped do some of the cheerleaders' choreography—" Before Mia could finish, four teenaged girls in matching cheer uniforms and bouncing ponytails interrupted them.

"Excuse me, Miss Palinski." The cocaptain spoke for the group. "Sophie wanted to know if at the end of our routine, we could all hold up these signs we made asking JoJo Patrelli to go to Sadie Hawkins with her?"

"Is JoJo Patrelli the defensive tackle?" Garrett whispered and Mia nodded.

"That should be fine, as long as you wait and do it *after* the final basket toss. I don't want any of you getting hurt during the stunts. Right, Dr. McCormick?"

The man looked completely confused about why the teenaged girls burst into a fit of giggles when he smiled at them. Did he not realize that a couple of the adolescents and many of the grown women in town would probably have lovesick crushes on the handsome single doctor?

"So." He rubbed his forehead as he spoke with the

cheerleaders. "You're holding up signs to ask a boy to go to a dance with you? Is this a thing now?"

"Come on, Garrett." Mia stood up straighter. "Why shouldn't girls be able to ask out a guy? We're all about gender equality here in Sugar Falls. Besides, it's for Sadie Hawkins. It's a tradition."

"No, I know what Sadie Hawkins is. I meant, is it normal to ask someone out in such a public way?"

"Oh, totally," Sophie said and the girls all agreed and launched into some of the most memorable invitations. And bless Garrett's patient heart for listening to them go on and on.

There were thirty seconds left on the clock when one of the girls turned to her and said, "So are you going to chaperone Sadie Hawkins this year, Miss Palinski?"

"Yeah, who are you going to invite this time?" another girl asked as she wiggled her head toward the new team doctor.

Garrett's eyebrows went into high alert and he crossed his arms across his sweatshirt. "Yes, Miss Palinski, who *are* you going to invite to Sadie Hawkins this year?" All the girls giggled again at his obvious ploy.

Cornered by cheerleaders? Her own kind turning against her? She'd have to think twice before giving this squad her best moves again. "I, uh, wasn't going to go this year because of my bad knee, Dr. McCormick. But if I was going to ask someone, I'd probably ask Mr. Cromartie again."

"And who exactly is Mr. Cromartie?" She saw him clench his jaw and narrow his eyes as he looked at the crowd in the stands. The girls giggled even more and she wondered if Garrett had any idea how jealous he appeared at that moment.

Mia pointed out the eighty-year-old coffee-skinned man with a thatch of bushy white hair and a long conductor stick. "See that gentleman leading the marching band out of the stands and toward the track? He knows his way around music and the dance floor."

"Hmm," was all Garrett said, but he did allow his shoulders to drop.

"Don't worry, Dr. McCormick," Sophie said. "I'm sure you could find another woman to ask you to Sadie Hawkins if you want to go."

The referee signaled for halftime and the girls took off running to gather their pompoms and their signs.

Mia and Garrett were left on the side of the track alone. She tried not to smile at the idea that he might have been a little peeved that she would go out on a date with another man. She wanted to ask what it meant, but she didn't want to embarrass him. Or hear him deny it.

Say something, her brain commanded. But a whiff of his musky citrus cologne mingled with the night air and she found herself staring at the light pulse thrumming along his neck. "So, I scheduled another ultrasound for next month."

If she hadn't been standing in front of a crowd of a hundred or so people, she would've slapped her palm to her forehead. She was such an idiot. Couldn't she have come up with a better conversation starter than that? In fact, why did she even need to speak with him in the first place? She should've run off with the cheerleaders.

"Oh, good." His hazel eyes lightened and his lips softened. "Let me know the date and I'll clear my calendar."

Great, now she was stuck going to another doctor's

appointment with him. How did she completely lose all sense of subtlety every time she talked to the guy?

Ever since she'd been a teenager, she had trained herself to be skilled at avoiding men and their advances—not that Garrett was making any real advances toward her—so that she could focus on her career. It had started when her mother refused to allow her to date in high school because time spent with boys was time not spent practicing. Then, when she'd gone to college, she'd gone out with a few guys, but they always seemed to want her to be their personal cheerleader just as she was finally learning to be more independent, so it was just easier to keep them at a distance. She used to be savvy enough to speak casually with the opposite sex and not lead men on or otherwise invite them into her life.

Maybe this self-imposed exile she'd been under since she'd moved to Sugar Falls had caused her to completely fall out of practice.

The band launched into a drum line performance and Mia watched the football teams hustle off the field. But Garrett still stood in front of her, as though he didn't see sweaty jocks in full pads running right past them. She took a deep breath. "So, is that your cue?"

"What? Oh. Yes. I better follow them to the locker room and make sure nobody has any sprains or concussions."

"Yeah, and I need to get the cheerleaders set up for their routine."

If they were business associates, this would be the part where they shook hands. If they were lovers, now would be when they kissed. But they were neither of these things. Plus, they were standing on a high school football field in full view of the crowded bleachers.

The wind picked up and blew a strand of dark hair

into her eyes. Garrett reached out and pushed it back behind her ear. Then he rubbed his thumb along her cheek. She remembered from her high school science class that physics dictated bubbles were supposed to rise up. But the ones tingling inside her made their way clear down to the core of her womanhood. Those hands were surely going to be the death of her.

"Okay, so I'll see you around," she said then did an eight count as she forced her legs to walk slowly away from him.

It was almost the same thing he'd said to her when she'd left his office on Monday, and she hated the way it sounded tonight as much as she'd had then. The implication was that they had no need or desire to speak to each other except in passing. The truth of the matter was that she was afraid of everything she wanted to say to him—like the fact that no man had ever been able to make her feel as if she was on the edge of a cliff, about to free-fall into the unknown.

But at least this time she hadn't run from him. That was progress.

The following Tuesday, Garrett was craving a hot home-cooked meal. Since his arrival in Sugar Falls, he'd been living on stale muffins and the whole grain cereal offered at Betty Lou's B and B, which was turning out to be more of a bed place and less of a breakfast place. While eating like that was fine when he was on deployments or too busy in surgery to make it to the mess hall, he was now a full-fledged resident of the Potato State and intended to partake in some skillet-cooked home fries. Plus, he'd heard the Chamber of Commerce met at the Cowgirl Up Café on Tuesdays and now that his practice was almost up and running, it was time to establish himself as a permanent part of the business community.

Plus, he hadn't seen Mia since the football game on Friday and knew her mom was supposed to be arriving any day, if she hadn't already. Garrett was curious to find out if Mia had told her mother about the baby, and there was no better place to accidentally run into her than downtown Sugar Falls.

He entered the restaurant, which was housed in its own gingerbread-shaped cottage across the street from Mia's dance school. He should have known by the purple exterior of the building that the inside would be just as eclectic.

Apparently, a rodeo queen with a penchant for do-it-yourself crafts had gotten some great deals on every horse riding–themed picture from each flea market west of the Mississippi, and then thrown them up on pink-and-white-striped walls. Stirrups and bridles had been spray painted in glitter and tacked up alongside the equestrian art. The long and winding rope spelling out "Cowgirl Up" behind the counter seating area was an interesting touch.

He doubted Cammie Longacre or any of her interior design friends would have thought to use old cowboy boots planted with cacti as centerpieces on all the wooden tables of varying sizes, shapes and years of origin.

But he was a business owner and he was here to meet with the Chamber of Commerce, not to research decorating tips for his sparse office.

"So we finally get to meet the infamous new doctor in town," an older waitress wearing a zebra-print apron said. The woman had dyed red hair teased clear up to heaven and a tight lime-colored V-neck shirt plunging clear down to—well, the opposite of heaven.

If he hadn't left his sunglasses in the truck, he would've pulled them down until his eyes could grow accustomed to the bright and vivacious surroundings. But he could hear a grill sizzling, and the smell of bacon and maple syrup told him that there was a reason this place was packed with locals clamoring for a delicious hot breakfast.

Many of the customers' faces turned to look at him and Garrett's heart dropped, thinking they'd found out exactly why his name was semifamous. But the waitress's coral-painted lips smiled to reveal a slightly crooked tooth and she held out her hand to him. "I'm Freckles and I own this place."

"Nice to meet you, Miss Freckles, but you'll have to fill me in on how I earned the title of infamous."

"Oh, darlin', it's just Freckles. And everyone in town has been talking about how you finally got our sweet little Mia to come out of her shell."

Come out of her shell? Even a remote mountain town like Sugar Falls had internet access. Didn't they know that their sweet little Mia had been an NFL cheerleader? She'd most likely danced on a Jumbotron in front of over seventy thousand screaming fans, as well as on the living room television sets of millions of people watching the games from home. That didn't seem too shell-worthy to him.

At least Mia had proved to be pretty sweet. So far.

Just then, the subject of their conversation walked in the door.

"Speak of the devil," Freckles said then sashayed behind the counter to get a coffeepot.

Great. Now Mia would think he was gossiping about her around town. Which was exactly what he would have done if she hadn't shown up and interrupted the question he'd been about to ask the café owner.

"Hey," he said, sounding like the same idiot he'd been when he saw her a couple of nights ago at the football game.

"Hey," she responded, but didn't really smile. Her eyes scanned the room as she pulled off her jacket, probably hoping they didn't have any witnesses to yet another awkward and unexpected meeting.

Of course, by now everyone was most likely aware of the fact that she was carrying his child. As far as he knew, nobody had made any sort of huge announcement from the gazebo in Sugar Park, the grassy square in the center of downtown. But these people weren't stupid. They'd eagerly picked up the clues about one of their beloved townspeople's delicate condition and word had spread down Snowflake Boulevard like an avalanche.

She was wearing another one of her soft wraparound sweaters over tights and a tank top and he wondered how the men in this city didn't go wild seeing her walk around in her dance clothes.

Garrett rubbed his forehead before firmly shoving his hands in his pockets. He needed to put those things away before they were tempted to reach out and touch her again. "So, did your mom make it to town yet?"

She looked toward the several tables that had been pushed together. "Yes. She arrived last night and I'm already about to move in with Maxine and Cooper for the rest of the week."

"Did you tell her yet?"

"Tell her what?"

"About the baby?" His voice dropped to a whisper. "About me?"

"Not yet, thank goodness. But I don't know how much longer I can keep it a secret."

"Why would you want to?"

She took a step back and looked at him as though he'd just asked her why she would want to drive on the right side of the road.

He should clarify what he meant, but Maxine was waving them over to where the rest of the Chamber of Commerce members were sitting. There were two empty chairs between her and Kylie, who had offered her CPA services to Garrett right after the football game. Although, he had to wonder if Kylie was actually interested in helping him file his taxes, or whether she was hoping to get a glimpse into his personal financial records on behalf of her best friend.

Everyone sat down and Garrett noticed most of the businesspeople left the seat closest to Mia open. They all seemed friendly enough toward her so he had to deduce that they weren't treating her as a pariah so much as allowing him the option to sit next to her.

He was going to have to work extra hard at keeping his mouth closed so he wouldn't stick his foot in it during the breakfast meeting.

"Let's get started." Cliff Johnston, the mayor, called the meeting to order. "Weather reports show that the ski season is starting early this year and with the holiday weekend about to start, we need to get a game plan locked down for how we're going to handle an increase in tourists."

A jingle interrupted and drew everyone's attention. Kane Chatterson pulled open the door to the café and was about to walk inside when something outside on the street caught his eye. Garrett watched the man pull his cowboy hat lower, turn right around and walk quickly down the road.

That was odd. Was everyone in this town avoiding someone? If so, then maybe they should think twice about eating at one of the busiest local restaurants.

But less than a minute later, Garrett saw what Kane was fleeing from. A sixty-year-old man wearing a loud Hawaiian print shirt and flip-flops in forty-degree weather would normally stand out on his own. But when that man also had a shaggy gray ponytail topped off with a red Angels ball cap and held open the door for a guy carrying an oversize video camera with a boom mike attached, it was hard not to take notice.

"Oh, no," Garrett muttered, wanting to duck under the table.

"What's the matter?" Mia whispered before glancing toward the door. When she spotted the camera, a shocked look shot across her face.

Why? Hadn't she set this up?

Whether she had or not, there was really nowhere for him to hide. He would have to weather this situation with the leading members of the Sugar Falls business community by his side, being allowed full access to the spectacle that was about to be unleashed.

"GP," the man said as he opened his arms up wide— to create the most dramatic display possible, naturally. "I've been looking all over this backwoods town for you."

"Dad, what are you doing here?" Garrett stood up, hoping to direct the focus away from the table—and from Mia—and the curious stares aimed at them. "And why in the world would you bring a camera crew with you?"

"One of your old friends from high school swung by the office the other day and said she'd found out that you were having a baby. I wouldn't have believed it myself until she showed me her social media page with a picture she'd posted of you with your arm around this pretty young thing here." His father turned to Mia and held out his hand. "Hi, I'm Dr. Gerald McCormick. I'm GP's dad and the soon-to-be grandpa." He shook his head ruefully. "Wow, that word really made me sound old. Anyway, I agreed to give the network an exclusive interview with my reclusive son and the touching journey of his transition from rebellious teenager to elite navy surgeon and father. It's going to be an award-winning piece and if we're lucky, we might be able to talk them into a spin-off. Nice cuffs, by the way."

Garrett looked down at the monogrammed cuff links and shook his head, trying to let go of the rage building inside him.

"Oh, my gosh." Mia's face went pale and instead of shaking Garrett's dad's hand, she gripped the armrest of her wooden chair tighter, her eyes glued to the huge video camera. That was one reaction he wasn't used to seeing women exhibit when they suddenly had the lens turned on them.

"Dad, I told you way back when I was eighteen that I wanted to be as far away from your reality shows as possible. Nothing's changed. Why do you think I moved out here?"

But before his dad could answer, Garrett heard Freckles' loud, countrified accent.

"My stars! If it isn't Dr. McCormick from that plastic

surgery show on TV. I woulda recognized that lucky red cap anywhere. I'm Freckles and I own the Cowgirl Up Café. I gotta tell you, I'm a big, big fan. I never miss an episode of the new season. It would be a real pleasure to serve you in my restaurant." She set her coffeepot down on an empty table and reached out to shake his father's still-outstretched hand. Which made Garrett all the more surprised when the waitress said, "But I'm going to have to ask you to leave your camera outside."

"Thank you for the compliment, ma'am," Gerald Mc-Cormick said and tilted his head humbly. Garrett knew that look. His dad may look like a beach bum, but he was a determined man who could—and had—talked a woman into signing a prenuptial agreement mere minutes before she walked down the aisle. The older, sassy waitress didn't stand a chance. "My crew and I will just be a second and then we'll be out of your way."

This was his father's usual way of minimizing the video presence, trying to get everyone to act natural and forget the cameras were even there. As if Garrett could ever forget.

A man Garrett had seen tying his horse to the hitching post in front of the restaurant stood up. Garrett hadn't been formally introduced to the old coot, but he knew Scooter and his old mare were permanent fixtures around town. "I think you misunderstood Miss Freckles, Doctor. She said that your man here would need to wait outside. See, us backwoods types don't take too kindly to cameras filming us here in Sugar Falls."

"But I'm not filming *you*." His dad's teeth smiled brighter than the puka shell necklace around his neck. Uh-oh. This wasn't going the way his father must have anticipated, and Garrett couldn't help but relish in the man's sudden shift of power. "I'm filming my son."

"Seems to me like the young doc here doesn't really want to be filmed," Freckles said. "And seeing as how he's now one of us—what was it, backwoods types?— I think it's best if you gentlemen skedaddle on outside. But let me know if you want to order some biscuits and gravy or one of my famous maple-glazed cinnamon rolls and I'll be happy to box it up for you."

Garrett glanced at Mia, who now had her face completely turned away from the camera and was slowly lifting an open menu higher in front of her.

Enough was enough. He needed to get his father out of here. But before he could tell his old man to hit the road, several more business owners rose from their chairs without much fanfare and slowly found their way in front of his and Mia's seats until they'd fanned out around them, forming a human barrier of sorts.

Garrett blinked several times. Never in his life had he seen anyone—besides himself, that is—stand up to famed television producer Gerald McCormick. Yet these small-town strangers were pulling rank around not just Mia, but Garrett, as well.

It was a nice gesture, but honestly, Garrett didn't need anyone to fight his battles for him. He scooted his chair out from the table, but before he could walk toward the chaos, he felt a sharp tug on his starched oxford shirt sleeve.

"It's best not to make a big scene and draw more attention in this direction," Maxine whispered. "Besides, they've got this under control."

It was true. Nobody uttered a single rude or threatening word. In fact, they were being just as cordial as one would expect small-town folk to be. A woman Garrett recognized from the local market asked for an autograph, distracting his old man even further. "Make it out to Marcia Duncan, please."

"Is this thing still running?" Jonesy, a cowboy who was usually seen riding his horse around town with Scooter, stood directly in front of the camera, thereby ensuring any footage contained only the image of his dusty, sweat-stained Boise State cap. "You know I was Special Forces back in 'Nam. They should do a reality television show about us vets."

"Special Forces? You don't say." Garrett could now only hear his dad's voice, which had taken on a note of frustration, but couldn't see much around the growing group of protective townspeople. He didn't dare look at Mia to see how she was reacting.

"Yep," Jonesy continued. "Learned a lot of life skills back in the corps. Did you know they taught me over a hundred ways to kill a man?" Okay, so maybe that was a bit threatening. But the cameraman lowered his equipment and shook his head toward his boss. "Anyway, just wanted to come on over to meet you and say I'm really looking forward to watching your show next season."

When the offending camera was finally switched off, the crowd opened up a little and Garrett was able to move closer to his dad. "Listen, son, I'll be in town a few more days. I'm staying at the Snow Creek Lodge if you want to give me a call."

"I'll talk to you later, Dad. But not with cameras nearby."

"I'll take whatever I can get. But just to give you a little warning—my producers weren't the only ones that got wind of you resurfacing and the pregnancy rumors. Besides me, nobody knew you were actually living in Idaho. Yet. All I'm asking is that you talk to me before the rest of the media figure things out and you have news vans parked up and down this charming little main street."

Garrett knew he'd had good reason to be suspect of Cammie Longacre when she'd spotted him with Mia in Patrelli's. This had the potential to be a media debacle of epic proportions. But before he could think of his next step, the horseshoe-shaped wind chime tinkled above the door and a fifty-something-year-old woman with bleach-streaked hair and a rhinestone-studded denim jacket walked in. She yanked her dark glasses off her overly made-up face so quickly, they got stuck in one of her giant fuchsia hoop earrings.

"Oh, my!" the newcomer said, still trying to get untangled. "Nobody told me they were filming in Sugar Falls."

"Mom?" Mia suddenly spoke up. "What are you doing over here?"

Chapter Nine

Seeing the cameras had been shock enough for Mia, but hearing her mother's forced cheerful voice was more than even she could bear. How many embarrassing introductions was she expected to endure in one morning?

Or puzzles, for that matter. From what she'd been able to piece together in the past five minutes, the father of her baby's father was some sort of reality television mogul with a sense of fashion that was best described as *surftastic*. When the man called his son rebellious, Mia had to cover her mouth to keep from bursting out in nervous laughter. Gerald McCormick could easily be referring to his son's preppy appearance, but most likely he was discouraged that Garrett didn't share the same media objectives.

In fact, judging by his reaction just a few moments ago, Garrett seemed to be just as freaked out about being caught on camera as she was. Sure, he had Hollywood good looks and she'd correctly assumed that he came from money. But she knew firsthand that people didn't relocate their lives from Hollywood to a town so small that horses took up parking spaces.

Instead of answering her question, her mother was chatting up the famous plastic surgeon and Mia's stomach dropped. Rhonda Palinski had always kept her acrylic manicured finger on the pulse of the entertainment industry and clearly recognized Garrett's dad.

Mia's posture was so stiff, her solid oak chair felt like a sagging life raft. Why hadn't she stayed home this morning and told her mom about the baby?

Now that the woman was here in the flesh, it wouldn't be long before she figured out that not only was she going to be a grandmother, she was going to be a grandmother to a baby with a famous pedigree that obviously came with its own publicity.

This was a nightmare and Mia needed to wake up—and get the heck out of there. And by there, she didn't just mean the Cowgirl Up Café. She meant the town of Sugar Falls. It'd been easy enough to run before. She looked at the distance from her seat to the kitchen.

"Simmer down, Mia," Maxine whispered. "Don't get spooked and do something you'll regret."

How could her best friend be so calm?

"That's your mom?" Garrett had the audacity to ask, as if today's version of "Surprise Your Offspring at the Chamber of Commerce Meeting" was reserved for him alone.

"Yep. Looks like it's turning into one big unhappy family reunion around here," Mia said under her breath. Her eyelid began to shudder and she couldn't stop her foot from tapping on the tacky turquoise paisley carpet. Oh, no. The nervous twitching was spreading to her other extremities.

Her mother, most likely sensing she was about to miss her prey, finally looked her way.

"Mia, the dance studio was closed when I went by so I knew I'd find you here." Rhonda looked down at the barely touched bagel smeared with peanut butter. "Eating, of course."

Don't think about the dancing hippo. Think about sure-footed bunnies hopping their way to freedom. "Mom, I left a note telling you I'd be back after my meeting."

"I know. But when I saw the news vans, I was worried sick." Funny, her mom didn't look too sick. Or too worried. "I thought maybe Nick had gotten out of prison and come after you again."

"Who's Nick?" Garrett asked at the same time Rhonda Palinski stepped around Scooter, the kindly old man who'd quickly jumped up to protect both her and Garrett's privacy. "So, what's going on with all the cameras?" she asked.

That figured. Her mom was so worried that instead of rushing across the street to check on her only child, she'd gone straight toward the celebrity limelight, her large knock-off designer tote bag bumping into the nervous twenty-year-old kid holding the video recorder at his side.

A loud crash sounded when the expensive-looking equipment dropped onto a table. Several cowboy boot–shaped water glasses exploded on the ground, sending ice and shards of glass every which way. When the last dish clattered to the floor, the only sound in the room was her mother's familiar, "Oopsie."

How the clumsiest woman in the world could have given birth to a daughter whom dance teachers had praised as "graceful" and "fluid" and "mastery in motion" was beyond Mia. Then again, she herself hadn't been too poised lately. Maybe that branch hadn't fallen too far from the genetic tree after all.

"Is she drunk?" Garrett asked.

"No. She's always been a bit accident prone. And extremely dramatic." Mia leaned toward Kylie, figuring she had precious few moments during the crash's aftermath to sneak out while everyone's attention was diverted. "Listen, I really need to get out of here."

"Done," Kylie said as she slipped her keys into Mia's hand.

"No good." Freckles, who had made no move to assist cleaning up the spill, spoke out of the corner of her heavily painted lips. "Your and Maxine's place will be the first place they look. Doc, you and Mia meet me in the kitchen. On the rack by the back door, I've got a spare set of keys to Cessy Walker's lake house. She's in Vegas this week for that Barry Manilow show and I'm supposed to be house-sitting. Nobody will look for you two there."

"Thanks," Garrett said as he edged his seat back and reached for Mia's hand.

Wait. What? Did he seriously expect her to take off with him? She was trying to get away from the guy and this crazy cast of characters he'd just drop-kicked into her life. Well, not Rhonda. That one wasn't his fault. She would have to shoulder the blame for that particular character.

"I'm not going with you," Mia said quietly, but firmly. She glanced between the scene her mother was causing by gushing all over Garrett's famous father, and the remaining customers still shuffling around their table, just waiting to pounce again if there was a problem.

"I'm guessing you didn't drive yourself across the street, so unless you want to risk having *Med TV's* executive producer and your, uh, mom—" a bright flash shot through the restaurant and Dr. McCormick Sr. was now squinting his eyes closed as her mother tried to snap a selfie with him "—follow you back to the dance studio, you might want to think about sneaking out the back door with me."

"If you don't wanna go with the doc here," Scooter said, his dirty Stetson in his tan, weathered hand, "then you're more than welcome to ride Blossom on back to my cabin. She's a real sweet filly. After we distract these folks a bit more, I can hop on the back of Klondike with Jonesy and meet you out there."

Jonesy nodded then shifted a wad of tobacco from one cheek to the other.

Mia weighed her options, but she needed to act fast. Since she'd never ridden a horse, escaping out the back door with Garrett seemed like the lesser of two evils. At least for the time being. She'd have one of her friends come get her as soon as the coast was clear.

"Thanks, Scooter, but I think it's in Blossom's best interest if I go with Dr. McCormick." The older man widened his eyes and Mia clarified, "Junior. Doctor McCormick *Jr*. But we will definitely take you up on that offer of distraction."

The two cowboy buddies turned back toward her

mother and Garrett's father. "Forget vets. You know what you should do a television program on?" Scooter asked way too loudly, but succeeded in getting everyone's attention. "Rodeo cowboys!"

Jonesy sniffed then added, "Let me tell you about the time…"

Mia didn't wait to hear the story. She silently counted to three then said, "Let's go, Junior."

He stood up and pulled her behind him as several townspeople drew closer together to form a blocking wall that they passed behind on their way to the kitchen.

"You know, I hate being called that," Garrett whispered as they slipped by the short-order cook flipping pancakes as if he hadn't noticed that all hell was breaking loose in the dining room.

Mia didn't respond, but neither did she let go of his hand. Apparently, this was another crazy mess they'd have to wade through together. She watched Garrett grab the keys hanging on the small rack by the back door. He glanced out into the alley before ushering her outside.

The frigid air penetrated her cotton sweater and tights and Mia was reminded she'd left her heavier coat inside. And her purse.

As far as escape attempts went, this one was certainly the least and worst planned. Sheesh, even when she'd snuck out of the hotel room in Boise, leaving Garrett sleeping in the big king-size bed, she'd had the good sense and the forethought to take her belongings with her.

They walked between two Victorian structures, and when they'd made their way around the front corner of the building, he paused and she pressed up against his back so she could peek out onto the street, as well. There was an empty white van parked next to the hitching post where Blossom and Klondike stood drinking water out of a tin trough. She spied her mother's red convertible Camaro across the street—the one that still had Florida vanity plates reading DNCEMOM. Otherwise, there wasn't much traffic on Snowflake Boulevard. Yet.

Had his father really said that there would be more news vans coming soon? The ingrained instinct to hide overwhelmed her. It felt as if she'd left her stomach behind in the alley as they ran to his fancy truck and he held the door open.

She waved him away, but he practically stood at attention, waiting for her to get situated inside the fully loaded cab. Good manners were nice and all, but they needed to hurry.

"Do you know how to get to Cessy Walker's house?" Garrett asked when he finally climbed in and started the engine.

"Flip a U-turn and head north toward Sweetwater Bend." Mia's seat belt had barely snapped into place when he gunned the big truck across the double yellow lines. She looked behind her, making sure nobody else had exited the café. She could see him checking out his rearview mirror, but her own nerves told her to keep a lookout, as well. By the time they turned off the main highway, Mia had a permanent crick in her neck and an ache in her knee.

"I think we made it." He let out a breath, but didn't decelerate or otherwise look relieved.

And why would he? Just because they'd temporarily escaped the eye of the storm didn't mean they wouldn't be affected by the aftermath. When she'd lived in Florida, she'd learned that devastation caused by hurricanes lasted long after the harsh gale winds blew through.

And now they would be stuck doing damage control together.

She pointed out the turn to Cessy's gated community. With shelter in sight, Mia finally asked, "Why didn't you tell me your dad was some famous television producer?"

"Are you kidding?" He punched in the code written on the tag attached to the house keys, then looked at her incredulously as they waited for the ornate gate to swing open. "How did you *not* know that?"

"Why in the world would I even suspect that?" Even as she asked the question, several comments he'd made in the past came back to her and things began to click in place.

"Didn't you at least look me up on the internet? I looked *you* up."

He'd researched her? Had he found out about Nick? She didn't want to know. "I did a little bit of research. I even saw a link to your dad, but I guess I was too blind to see the connection. Or maybe my brain just didn't want to see what was right in front of it all along."

He drove through the gate then waited for it to close behind him, one side of his mouth quirked up in disbelief. "Why would you not want to see that? That's usually the first thing that draws women to me."

"Constant media attention and an absolute lack of privacy actually *draw* women to you?"

"Isn't that what drew you?"

She could feel her brow furrowing as she shook her head. "Your sad eyes, your boyish smile and the way your strong hands circled around that crystal glass of single malt scotch were what drew me to you. But trust me, it didn't matter how sexy you were or how my body responded to you. If I would've known who you were, I would've bolted in the opposite direction so fast I'd still be running."

He didn't respond for several seconds. He just stared at her, his hazel eyes trying to read her face as though he was debating whether or not to believe what she'd just said. Either that or he was debating whether or not to kiss her again.

And God help her if he opted for the latter because even after the hellish morning they'd just had and her claims to the contrary, she really didn't think she could run too far from him. Or those lips.

"If that's the case, then you are the exact opposite of pretty much every single woman I've known my entire life."

"Oh, come on, Garrett. I find that extremely difficult to believe. Sure, there may be some women out there who would love that type of public life—my mom, for one—but most rational ladies I know wouldn't want anything to do with that kind of constant exposure."

He took his hand-tooled wingtip off the brake and resumed driving toward Cessy's house. But every few hundred yards, he would look over at her, as though the tooth fairy had just fluttered into his truck with him and he couldn't quite accept the realness of the situation.

She pointed to a large craftsman-style home with a huge wraparound deck that looked out over Lake Rush. "That's it up ahead."

His four-wheel-drive tires crunched along the Ushaped gravel driveway. "Do you think there's room to park my truck in the garage so it can be out of sight?"

"Probably." She took the keys out of the cup holder in the center console. "I'll go in and open the garage. I might have to move Cessy's car and park it out front."

"Wait," he said, reaching out and wrapping his fingers around her upper arm. "Are you really willing to hide out here with me? I mean, how do I know that you're not going to be calling the paparazzi the moment we get inside and blabbing out our location?"

She stiffened her back, trying not to be insulted by his question. None of his behavior this morning had been the reaction she'd expected from him when she'd first spotted his famous dad and the cameraman today.

The second she'd heard his father say "GP," her first thought was that Garrett had lied to her. She'd been right and he was some spoiled rich guy used to getting what he wanted. Her second thought was that he'd gone just as pale as she had, if not more. Then he'd told his notorious father to get out.

At first, she'd assumed that he didn't want it found out that he'd gone slumming with some has-been cheerleader and was now expecting an illegitimate child. But she'd quickly seen that his disgust was directed at the camera and his anger aimed at the older guy dressed like some big kahuna. Several comments he'd made in the past were finally adding up.

"First of all, my only other choice would be back at my apartment with my mother. Second of all, why is it so hard for you to believe that I want nothing to do with any of that forced notoriety, Garrett? From what I saw back at the café, you weren't too thrilled to be in front of those cameras, either. So if that's the case, clearly it would stand to reason that there are other people in the world who aren't any different from you—people who would detest the intrusion just as much as you do. I'm not even sure why you hate it, but let me assure you that some of us have a lot more than just our privacy to lose."

His eyes narrowed. "Is this the part where you decide to tell me about whoever the hell this Nick guy is?"

He still didn't know whether he was buying it. But he had to admit she'd looked downright petrified at the thought of having her whereabouts disclosed on television. Then, when her mom had walked in and made that comment, Garrett recalled that article he'd read on the internet. The one about her stalker.

If they were going to lay all their cards out on the table, now would be the time. He held her gaze, willing her not to clam up now.

"Okay. I'll tell you about Nick. But let's get inside the house first. I'm freezing."

He looked down at her skimpy attire and mentally kicked himself for shutting off the truck and its heater. "Fair enough."

She jumped out and ran up the front porch steps. Damn, he would never get tired of watching her body in motion. She sashayed through the large redwood door and slammed it closed behind her.

The garage door slowly lifted and he saw the taillights of Cessy Walker's red coupe back out into the driveway. Once Mia had it parked along the side of the house, Garrett pulled his truck inside. He had to park at an angle to make the extralong bed fit, and he cursed himself for purchasing such a useless vehicle.

Sure, when he'd bought it, he'd just come home from

a two-year assignment in Afghanistan and he'd been missing some of the luxuries he'd grown accustomed to stateside. Being stationed just outside Boise, it hadn't seemed like that much of a splurge at the time since he'd needed something for the rugged mountain landscape, but with the hint of the luxury he preferred.

His whole life he'd tried to do everything the exact opposite of his old man. When he'd started junior high, his dad took him back to school shopping at Tommy Bahama. So when it was time to go to high school, Garrett begged to attend an elite prep academy with uniforms so he could wear a coat and tie. His dad drove an old VW bus, so Garrett bought a used Buick for his first car. But blood ran thicker than premium unleaded and extra starch, and he wondered if he would ever be able to escape his connection to his family.

And now that he had his own child on the way, he wondered how he would feel if his son or daughter turned out to be the opposite of him. Deep down, he knew he would still love him or her and would never give up on his offspring.

He looked at his cuff links, then unfastened them and dropped them in the center console before rolling up his shirtsleeves. There were a lot of ways he was exactly like his father, and persistence was one of them. Garrett's clothes and the car he drove didn't make him who he was. But how could he prove that to Mia?

Mia reentered the garage and held open the mudroom door for him. He jumped out of the truck and followed her inside. They bypassed the kitchen and entered a living room three times the size of the Cowgirl Up Café.

Speaking of going overboard on luxury, Cessy Walker's decorating bill had probably eaten up a large chunk of her monthly alimony payments. Vaulted wood-planked ceilings with exposed beams arched high above his head and huge unadorned windows faced the crisp blue lake outside.

Her overstuffed sofa was covered in a soft taupe-colored suede while chairs and throw pillows in matching beige tones filled up the living room. Several pottery vases were lined up along a glass-topped coffee table that had the same square footage of his sleeping quarters on board the *USS Bowler*. The vases were probably more expensive than the rest of the furnishings in this entire room. But they were ugly as sin. Hopefully, Ms. Walker wouldn't bring up any more suggestions for decorating his office.

Mia walked over to the thermostat and pushed some buttons before finally giving up. "I can't figure this stupid thing out. It's too high-tech for me."

"Maybe I should make a fire," he said, nodding toward the wide hearth made entirely out of river rock.

"That would help. I'll check the kitchen to see what the food supply is like. I hope we don't have to stay here too long because if I know Cessy, there's probably only expired carrot juice and a fifth of vodka in the fridge. If we're lucky, we might find some frozen diet meals and a bag of Snickers miniatures in the freezer."

Mia left the room and he walked toward the fireplace, noticing there wasn't a log to be seen. He looked around the room again and then stuck his head behind the screen before realizing it was a gas line with a hidden light switch to turn it on. He flipped the toggle and a roaring fire shot to life.

That was easy.

His cell phone vibrated in his pocket and his first

thought was that his dad had probably just come to the conclusion that he had vanished and was already on the hunt.

But when he looked at the screen, he saw Cooper's number pop up instead. "Hello?"

"Hey, Doc," his friend said. "It looks like you've been found out. Maxine told me about your old man showing up at the café. She said you and Mia hightailed it over to Cessy's place to ride out the storm."

"I was right about the provisions," Mia said, walking back into the room holding a spoon and a small container of peanut butter. "But at least she had this in her pantry. Oops, sorry," she whispered when she saw him on the phone.

"It's Cooper," he mouthed and watched her settle in on the floor in front of the fire. She took off her shearling-lined boots, then winced before lying on her back and stretching one leg up into the air. She pointed a toe before bringing her shin all the way to her forehead. Man, she was flexible. He'd remembered that from when they'd made love that night in the hotel room. He watched her, mesmerized as she put that leg down and raised the other one up for the same stretch.

"Did you hear me, Doc?"

"I'm sorry. What was that you were saying?" Garrett turned his back so he could concentrate on the call.

"I asked how persistent your father was. As in, how long do you think you're going to have to hide out before he gives up and takes his camera crew home?"

"I don't think it should take more than a couple of days."

"A couple of days?" Mia yelped from the floor. Garrett looked back at her to nod, but she was now sitting up with her legs in an open position, her torso leaning forward and her back arched.

Aw, hell. How was he going to last a couple of hours alone in this house with her, let alone days?

He walked toward the back deck and opened a sliding glass door, needing to cool off.

Cooper continued. "Well, Mia left her purse and cell phone at the Cowgirl Up. The ladies think that if she plans to be there for a few nights, she might want a change of clothes. Kylie's going to hit Duncan's Market and grab some groceries for you guys and Max is going to pack her an overnight bag. They'll meet up and bring some stuff over later. What about you?"

"What about me?"

"Do you want me to swing by your condo and grab some gear for you, too? I mean, Cessy has a pretty extensive wardrobe and I know you're a sucker for the designer clothing. But I don't think you two wear quite the same size."

"Oh, yeah. I guess I probably will need some clothes. Thanks, man."

"No problem. So how's Mia doing?"

"I think her knee is a little bit sore."

"I wasn't talking about her knee, Dr. McCormick. I meant, how is she doing considering the big blowup at the café earlier?"

How the heck was he supposed to know? She'd seemed flustered at first, but then she'd gotten a little attitude in the car when she'd insisted that not all women were after his money or his notoriety. Actually, he'd liked seeing her square her shoulders and challenge him. But at this second, he really just didn't know what to think.

He looked back toward the fireplace. Mia had removed her sweater and was lying on her back, her arms extended above her head and her feet out in a wide V.

"I'm not entirely sure. She looks pretty fantastic, if you ask me." A heat rose up Garrett's cheeks as he realized he'd just confessed exactly what he'd been thinking. "I mean she's…uh…stretching right now and… Aw, hell. You might want to tell Maxine and Kylie to just hurry up."

Garrett pulled the phone away from his ear so that Cooper's sudden burst of laughter wouldn't pierce his eardrums, then discontinued the call when he realized his buddy's loud guffawing wasn't going to stop anytime soon.

He returned his cell phone to his pocket before rubbing his forehead. "Your friends are going to be here any minute with some clothes and groceries and stuff." His voice sounded unusually scratchy to his own ears.

Mia sat up and he suffered a moment of guilt for bending the truth. Really, nobody would be here for probably a couple of hours, but he needed to tell himself otherwise so he didn't put either one of them in a compromising position.

"Then we might as well relax while we wait for them."

Relaxing and letting down his guard was the *last* thing he wanted to do. "Why don't you tell me about Nick?"

There. Hearing about a former lover would dim any man's desire.

Her blue eyes grew darker, and her lips turned down slightly. But she nodded and stood up. "Okay."

Her bare feet padded over to the sectional sofa. He

waited until she was settled in one corner and then sat on the opposite side of her, wanting—needing—to keep his distance.

She ran a hand through her long dark hair, then deftly wrapped it into a loose knot on top of her head—as if she were preparing to get down to business. "Nick Galveston was a guy I met when I was cheering in Miami."

"Nick Galveston? Where do I know that name?"

"He was the punter for the team I cheered for a few years ago." Aha. She'd been involved with a professional athlete. Maybe he'd had her pegged right, after all. But he sat silently, keeping his forming opinions to himself. "I'd never really met him, but he called me out of the blue one day. Said he'd seen me during one of the halftime routines and had bribed someone in the admin office to get my personal number."

He nodded, but she wasn't looking at him anyway. She stared straight ahead at the fire, seemingly lost in her recollections. "I told him that there was a strict rule against players and cheerleaders fraternizing off the field. And honestly, even if there wasn't, he certainly wasn't someone I would normally date anyway."

"And what kind of guys do you normally date?"

"Lately?" Her head whipped back toward him and he saw the flash of sadness in her eyes before it was replaced with an air of defiance. "Not *any* kind of guys. Actually, back then, I didn't date much, either. I was focused on my career."

"Your cheerleading career?"

She looked at him as if he was a bunion on her foot. "No. On my dance career. I was planning to attend Florida State to get my master's, but my mom had been pressuring me to audition for an NFL team and I needed to earn some money to cover my first year's tuition. Anyway, even if I *had* been in the market to date, it surely wouldn't have been with some spoiled, rich playboy who'd paid someone money to break the rules just to obtain my number."

"So, you have a thing against rich guys?"

"Not because they're rich." She looked down at his shoes before quickly refocusing her gaze on the vaulted ceiling. "I don't like them because of their sense of entitlement."

Why did he have the feeling that she was lumping him into this same category?

Whoa. He needed to check himself. Mia'd been on the cusp of opening up and he'd put her on the defensive. While she was cute when she got riled, he needed to stop acting like a jealous lover and more like a compassionate listener. "So this dirtbag… I mean, this Nick guy was pretty entitled?"

"That's okay. You can call him a dirtbag. Lord knows Kylie and Maxine have called him way worse. I have, too." She put her elbows on her knees and propped her chin in her hands, her resignation obvious. She took a deep breath before continuing. "But he was even more creepy than entitled."

She leaned forward to reach for the jar of peanut butter on the coffee table and sucked in a breath, grabbing her knee instead.

"Are you okay?" He was by her side in an instant.

"I think so. I'm pretty sure I just tweaked my leg when we were running to your truck earlier. I was stretching it out, but it's still pretty tender."

"Here, let me see," he said, then sat next to her and

pulled her leg onto his lap. He kneaded the muscles around her knee, not wanting to put too much pressure on her tendons. "Feel better?"

She nodded then leaned toward the container on the glass table again, but Garrett was quicker and handed it to her, along with the spoon she'd brought from the kitchen.

"Thanks." She lifted the edge of her mouth shyly, but Garrett could tell the smile wasn't heartfelt. He had a feeling telling this story was harder on her than he'd anticipated.

"Maybe we should talk about this later. It's kind of been an emotional morning and…"

"No." She held up her spoon to interrupt him. "You need to know and I'm supposed to be able to talk about it and put it in my past."

She unscrewed the lid of the container. "I'm also supposed to watch the extra calories during the first trimester, but since I tend to use food as a coping mechanism, well, I figured I might just need a spoonful of PB reinforcement."

He watched as she took a bite, mentally steeling herself for the conversation, and decided she was much tougher than she looked. He could sit here all day, watching the emotions cross her face. But when he heard her take in a resigned breath, he knew he wouldn't have to.

"Anyway," she continued, "the first couple of times he called, I was polite, but told him no. After that, he had roses delivered to me at one of our rehearsals. I was mortified and my choreography coach was wondering who had sent them. So, not wanting to get in trouble, I refused the bouquet and sent the deliveryman on his way. When I got out to my car the next night after practice, there were torn flowers and stems all over my car."

"That *is* creepy."

She bit her lip and nodded. He kept massaging her knee, more for support than pain relief now. "Things just progressed from there. All season long, he called me and drove by the practice field and the studios where we had our rehearsals. I changed my number, but then he started escalating. He got bolder, coming over to talk to me during the games while I was on the sidelines. During the last game of the season, he missed an easy kick, causing a fumble and the team lost. He ran over to me afterward, screaming that I had distracted him and that because I was all he could think about, he hadn't been able to focus."

Garrett could feel her leg tensing and knew her whole body was reliving the fear and stress of the verbal attack. He wanted to relax her and remind her that she was safe now. But he also needed to keep her talking. Not only because he needed to hear the rest—but because he sensed she finally needed to let it out.

"Where was security during all this? Where were the managers and coaches? Did everyone see this happen?"

"The station had cut to commercial break already and, did I mention that it was Nick Galveston?" She took a bigger bite of peanut butter, as though she was using the food to wash the jerk's name off her tongue.

"Yeah, you said that. He's some self-absorbed football player. Big deal. They… Oh, wait. You mean he was Neville Galveston's son?"

"You guessed it." She pointed the cleaned-off spoon at him. "His father's a big deal in the Florida business world and was a big sponsor at the time. Since the season was over and I was planning on going back to school for my MFA anyway, I didn't make a big deal of it. Plus, his coach assured me that he would be going to mandated counseling."

She shook her head. "Looking back, I wish I would have at least filed a formal complaint."

"So Nick was your stalker? He was the guy who attacked you?" Her neck angled back in surprise, as if she thought she'd been able to keep this awful episode completely hidden before now. "See, I looked you up online, too. But I could only find one article and it was pretty brief. Sorry for interrupting. Go on."

She took a deep breath. "A couple weeks later, I came home to my apartment. It was dark and I hadn't seen or heard from the guy in a while and thought I was safe enough. But out of nowhere, here comes Nick. And he glares at me with such hate in his eyes. Crazy hate." He felt her whole body shiver. "I'd never seen anybody look like that at another human being before. I couldn't move, couldn't blink. I didn't even see the golf club he was holding. He told me that if I wasn't going to be his little dancer, then he'd make sure I never danced again. That's when he swung at me and smashed my kneecap."

"That son of a…" Garrett wished he had access to a nine iron and a dark room with the bastard trapped inside it. But he could still feel the tenseness in her leg and he realized he'd stopped massaging and was gripping her tighter. "Sorry."

But she didn't seem to hear him, so lost was she in her terrifying memory. "I screamed and one of the neighbors ran out, but not before he hit me several more times. One was to the back of my head. I was in a coma for a week." A tear trickled down her proud, high cheek-bone and she shook her head, as if she could shake loose the pain she'd been holding inside. "After I woke up, I found out about my knee and I knew it was all over. My dancing career, my whole life. Everything."

Neither one said a word for a few seconds and he could tell the dam holding back the rest of her tears was threatening to come loose.

"They caught him, though, right?" he asked, trying to divert her.

"They did. It helped that I lived at a complex with video surveillance in the parking lot so the cops had everything on record. They charged him with attempted murder and he pled down to assault with a deadly weapon. He's serving time and his dad paid off the right people and everything was kept hush-hush."

Mia shuddered, then used the edge of her knitted sleeve to wipe her face. Garrett had to exhale and count to ten to get his anger in check. He could only imagine the toll that kind of event had taken on her. Years had gone by and he could still see the way it had impacted her.

It really explained why she was so skittish and looked at him sideways any time he walked in the room. He used to wonder if she was pretending to be coy, but there was no way to act out this kind of anguish.

He was a healer and not at all prone to violence. But he had never wanted to hurt anyone the way he wanted to hurt the man who had crushed Mia's leg. Her dreams. Her trust...

"It's okay. He can't hurt you anymore. I've got you now," he said and pulled her into his arms. Her body shook as she finally let out a small sob, but she allowed Garrett to hold her as the dam inside her finally broke, to let him absorb all the hurt she'd been hiding for way too long.

Chapter Ten

Mia hadn't told the story to more than a handful of people, including the police officer who'd taken the initial report, and her best friends when she'd first moved to Sugar Falls.

She had expected to cry her way through it as she usually did, especially considering the hormonal imbalance she'd been experiencing lately. But she'd never allowed herself to be this vulnerable before. Especially not in a man's strong embrace. When she finally had her tears under control, she wiped her face and scooted away from Garrett, but her knee was still awkwardly draped across his lap.

Yet for some reason, she didn't feel as embarrassed as she had before. Although she'd gone through an awful lot of peanut butter and her tears had left a damp spot on the shoulder of Garrett's shirt where she'd been crying, Mia felt emotionally drained, but also surprisingly stronger.

Talking about Nick with Garrett was like getting a root canal. Now that she'd gotten to the core of her problem and eased some of the ache, her nerves were still throbbing, but more out of a sense of relief.

"So everything worked out in the end, then?" Garrett asked. His hands had dropped back to her leg, but this time, they were a bit higher on her thigh.

"I never thought of it that way before." She angled her head. "But I guess if it hadn't been for that incident, I wouldn't be sitting with you at a mansion on Lake Rush right now. At the time, I was in such a dark and scary place. Not only from being stalked and attacked, but also from the surgery that had taken longer than expected and the fact that my knee had never healed quite right. Kylie and Maxine thought I should get a second opinion, that I shouldn't rely on the team doctors whose best interest was their franchise and keeping things out of the news. But afterward, I just wanted to get as far away from it all as I could."

"So that's why you moved to Sugar Falls?"

"Yep. My best friends were already established here and there was no way I was going to move back in with my mom. Ballet had always been my goal, not living in some small remote town in Idaho, teaching dance classes to little kids." She shook her head ruefully. "Spending day after day explaining to parents that it's okay if their child isn't the best one on the stage as long as they were having fun was never my dream. But dreams have a way of changing."

He nodded and took the empty jar of peanut butter from her, setting it down on the table in front of them. Her leg was still across his lap, and the movement caused him to shift in a way that brought his free hand farther up her thigh. "But at least you no longer have to worry about that bastard following you around."

Mia shivered. "Actually, last year I had a feeling someone was. I've never really been able to shake that sense of unease, and then I got a letter from the parole board advising me that Nick might get an early release due to budget cuts and the fact that he was a first time offender. Cooper called in some favors from a buddy with the Florida Department of Corrections and when they searched his cell, they found a bunch of recent pictures of me and the dance studio and my apartment. The jerk had hired a private investigator to look me up."

Garrett's hands stilled and when she finally chanced a peek at him, she realized his jaw was unusually rigid. She'd seen him look at his father in frustration, but she'd never seen him look so intently furious. For a moment, she wondered what kind of anger he was capable of.

She reached out and rubbed his arm. "Hey, don't be so upset. The parole board found out and denied him. Plus, they're watching him more closely now."

"I just hate what he did to you. What he put you through. No human being should have to go through that."

"I know. I used to run around afraid of my own shadow. I still do sometimes. But now that I have a little one to think about, I can't keep living my life in fear. I have to be strong for both of us."

Saying it out loud made it ring even more true.

He looked at her face, then at her hand on his biceps. She felt his muscles flex ever so slightly, and her thumb slipped into the ridge along his muscle. Underneath those starched custom-made shirts, Garrett McCormick was solid as a rock.

She glanced down at his fingers, which were still on her thigh, commanding herself not to move, even as the rest of her was bubbling up inside, wanting to feel more of him.

The morning had been intense, to say the least, and now she'd just let down this huge emotional wall in front of him. If she truly knew what was good for her, she'd jump off this sofa and never look back.

"So you're not afraid anymore?" His voice was deeper and she knew he was equally aware of their proximity—both physical and emotional.

"Of you? No. Two months ago—heck, even two weeks ago—I would've been terrified to be in the same room with a strange man. But ever since I met you in that hotel bar, my entire body feels at peace around you. Even when my brain is trying to tell it to stay on high alert. And now, for some strange reason that I can't explain, being with you gives me this sense of empowerment. It's made me realize that I'm tired of running. Tired of being afraid."

It was the truth. She could have told this story to anyone, but it was Garrett who made her feel safe. It was Garrett whom she'd chosen to open her heart to. And if she was being one hundred percent honest, it was Garrett whom she loved.

She felt the weight of her hair slip loose, so she reached up to unclip it from its makeshift knot, allowing it to tumble down her back. And like the heavy raven locks, her stored-up self-consciousness followed suit and she relished the freedom.

She brought her hand up to his smoothly shaved cheek and watched his nostrils flare slightly when she traced her fingers along his jaw, behind his ear and toward the back of his scalp.

His close-cropped hair prickled at her fingers like spiky little speed bumps, warning her to proceed with caution.

Screw that. She was done with caution. *No more living in the dark*, she vowed, right before pulling his head down to hers.

When her lips touched his, she was no longer tentative or ashamed. She was eager and reckless and on a mission to make up for lost time. There had been so much she'd given up and so much more she'd never allowed herself to experience. But not anymore.

Just as she'd done in that hotel bar on the night she'd met him, she set her inhibitions free and exploded in his arms. His hand traveled up to her ribs, and her skin couldn't contain her any more than a glass bottle could contain the bubbling champagne released by its cork.

His mouth wasn't enough. She needed to feel him, needed to get closer.

She brought her other leg up and maneuvered herself into a plié before straddling his lap. Her lips caught his groan and heat shot through her core when she felt his zipper pressed against her thin cotton leggings. He grabbed her hips and pulled her tighter against his arousal until she was the one moaning.

She threw back her head as he kissed his way down her neck and along her collarbone. When he pulled down the spaghetti straps of her sports tank, she released him long enough to yank the entire thing over her head, not wanting to keep him or his incredible hands away from her aching breasts any longer.

He rewarded her by drawing one tight nipple into his hot mouth, before kissing his way over to the other one and loving it equally.

"Garrett, you make me feel so good." He paused and she opened her eyes, wondering what she'd said wrong.

"I couldn't remember if I'd even told you my name that night we met. But afterward, all I could think about was making love to you and hearing you scream it out."

She put her palm to his face, cupping his cheek, and whispered it again. "Garrett."

"That sounds even better," he said before slipping his hands inside her waistband.

She reached for the buttons on his shirt, but when the first one proved too difficult for her restless fingers, she yanked through the rest. The sound of tearing fabric didn't cause her to slow down as she pushed the material off his shoulders and ran her hands over the well-formed pectoral muscles of his chest.

Bringing her lips back to his, she moved with him when he leaned forward to shove his shirt off. The light hair on his chest tickled her breasts and when she arched up, he used her leverage as an opportunity to push her black leggings down to her thighs.

Twenty-five years of dance enabled her to maneuver her limbs effortlessly as he removed the rest of her clothing while she remained firmly in place on his lap.

Now that she'd decided to take control of her life, she wasn't about to waste a second.

Raising her body slightly, she allowed him to kiss the sensitive area just above her rib cage while he unbuckled his pants. But before he could take the time to remove them, she came back down until the tip of his erection was situated directly below her.

She paused, relishing this small act of power. She was in charge now.

Briefly, she thought of the dark fear that had ruled her life for too long. And she remembered the dark hotel room where they'd once made love. Then she pulled her face back, taking in the bright light streaming in from the vast wall of windows. She needed to see him, needed to watch him.

When she finally allowed herself to slide down over his hard shaft, it felt as if she was claiming him, claiming her life.

"Aw, Mia. My sweet Mia," he whispered.

He'd been right. Hearing her name cherished by his lips was something she hadn't realized she'd missed out on the last time.

She moved slowly at first, letting her body become accustomed to him once again. She watched his lids grow heavy, heard his breathing become more shallow and rapid. He held her waist firmly, but didn't try to manage her movements.

"I don't know how much more I can take." His voice was ragged and his hands trailed down along her backside until they fully cupped her bottom. Mia took him deeper and quicker, her eyes never leaving his face.

It was like focusing on the brightest spotlight in the theater as she danced in sync—her pirouettes becoming faster and faster until she didn't think she could hold her spin any longer. When he gripped her tighter and her muscles contracted around him, she finally let go as though she was floating off the stage and twirling through the air without a cable.

Garrett held Mia to him until they both got their breathing under control. But the woman who had been so graceful just a few moments ago, defying the laws of physics with her balancing and flexibility, was slowly toppling over like an untied satin ribbon on a well-used ballet shoe.

And he was falling with her.

As they drifted to their sides and nestled into the cushions, he pulled a brown throw blanket off the back of the sofa and wrapped it around them. She had straightened her legs, but he could feel her breasts pressed firmly to his chest, her stomach softly resting against his.

His child was growing there.

As a medical professional he knew what they'd done hadn't endangered their baby. But he wondered what kind of father didn't even bother to fully remove his khakis before so thoroughly ravishing the mother.

Actually, it felt more as if *he'd* been the one ravished. Mia had seemed intent on taking the lead and for once in Garrett's life, he'd allowed himself to sit back and let someone else take control. He was learning that as much as he'd fought to establish his independence from his father and take charge of his own future, he couldn't micromanage every single detail.

He would have to start getting used to relinquishing power some of the time, especially to Mia, who had just proved herself to be more than capable of leading him to paradise.

He kissed her forehead and her sigh was the last thing he heard before drifting off into a blissful sleep.

Which was better than what woke him.

"Okay, you two, company's here," Maxine's voice called from the closed-off kitchen before two sets of distinctly male laughter echoed through the room.

"Oh, no." Mia pulled the blanket over her head. "I forgot they were coming over."

So had Garrett. Which wasn't like him. Enough of this reckless leisure. He needed to get himself back in charge.

But not until they got dressed. He gave her one last kiss and sat up, watching her walk around the room gathering their clothes as she tried to keep the blanket wrapped around her.

"Here." She tossed a wrinkled wad of cloth at him before pulling on her top and leggings. He put his arms through the sleeves, not taking his eyes off her. Watching her wiggle into the tight, stretchy fabric was almost as pleasurable as watching her remove it.

She looked at his shirt, which was hanging open, its buttons probably scattered somewhere in the sofa cushions or along the hardwood floors. She gasped then blushed. "I'm so sorry I ripped it like that."

He grinned. "I'm not."

She glanced around the room. "Did we miss anything?"

He stood up, revealing the fact that he was still wearing his pants and that they hadn't wasted time when it came to disrobing. He chuckled when her blush got even deeper.

He attempted to tuck his shirt in so he would at least look presentable and then thought, why bother? Surely the couples politely hiding out in the kitchen already knew what they'd been doing in here.

"They're going to know," Mia said, their thoughts on the same page.

He looked pointedly at her still-flat belly. "I don't think it's much of a surprise to anyone that we've made love." She returned his appraising look and he couldn't help but add, "Your top thingy is on inside out."

She slapped her hand to her chest, then quickly threw her sweater on over the whole ensemble.

He chuckled at her embarrassment, and then to his surprise, she joined him. They were looking at each other, giggling, and Mia finally walked up to him and tried to straighten his shirt so the button holes at least lined up. But when he felt her fingers on his bare skin, he couldn't help but pull her in for another deep kiss.

"It's been five minutes," Cooper called out from the kitchen. "We're coming in whether you're dressed or not."

Kylie was the first to emerge through the door. "I've had to pee since we turned in the gate," she yelled before doing some sort of running waddle toward the bathroom.

Maxine rolled in a suitcase behind her and Mia walked over to her friend, her posture erect and her chin high—as if they had absolutely nothing to be ashamed of. And really, they didn't, seeing as how they were two grown, consenting adults. But he still felt a small thrill of pride that she wasn't humiliated to be caught in such a flagrant situation with him.

"Sorry to intrude like this," Drew said, ever the diplomatic psychologist. "We did bring steaks, though, as a sort of peace offering."

"Actually, we brought half of Duncan's Market with us," Cooper said, gesturing his thumb toward the kitchen. "We weren't sure how determined your parents were going to be so we wanted to make sure you two were well stocked to ride out the storm."

Kylie came out of the bathroom just then. "Thank goodness. I'm starved."

"You're always hungry," Maxine said.

"That's because I'm eating for three. Why don't I whip something up?"

"No," several voices, including Mia's, shouted. Apparently, the redheaded CPA was not known for her prowess in the kitchen.

"Cooper knows how to work Cessy's grill, so why don't the guys go outside to barbecue the steaks, and us ladies will take charge making the side dishes?"

Garrett didn't like Maxine's suggestion only because he could see a light dusting of snow on the deck already and knew it would be freezing outside. But he wanted to give Mia her space and figured she would probably like some time alone with her girlfriends—hopefully, not to talk about him.

Thirty minutes later, they were sitting around Ms. Walker's dining room table, which looked as if it could seat the entire marching band from Sugar Falls High School, along with their instruments. Even the teak-and-bamboo-filled mansion in his father's house didn't have anything this ostentatious.

Speaking of his father, Cooper brought up the Botoxed elephant in the room. "So what's the plan for getting Dr. McCormick and his television show out of town?"

"Maybe you can just arrest anyone walking down

the street with a video camera," Kylie suggested before spearing a piece of filet mignon.

"As much as I'd like to, I can't. It's a public area. Plus, the chamber of commerce isn't opposed to some free publicity. But the mayor did say that if things get too crazy in town, it could diminish our reputation as a... what were his words... 'A tranquil and idyllic vacation destination.' So suffice it to say, it's in everyone's best interest if we get them to leave as soon as possible."

"Does that include my mom?" Mia asked. "She doesn't have a camera, but I'm sure she would be the first one lined up to offer an exclusive interview."

"Your mom didn't seem that bad," Garrett said. "A little clumsy, maybe, but relatively harmless."

"Clearly, you don't know my mother. What she lacks in grace, she more than makes up for in tenacity."

Maxine passed the bowl of mushroom risotto to him. "If you think *my* ex-mother-in-law is persistent, Ms. Palinski could run circles around Cessy Walker and be on the phone with every talent agent in Hollywood while she was doing it. No offense, Mia."

"Trust me, none taken. It's true, Garrett." She looked at him briefly before piling her plate full of spinach salad. At least her appetite was back. "My mom's biggest goal in life was to make a name for her only daughter by any means necessary. She can be a hammerhead shark when she makes up her mind about something."

"So what's the goal for you two?" Drew asked. "Once we figure out what we want to achieve, then we can formulate a plan to make that happen."

Garrett knew Kylie's husband was great at his job treating soldiers with PTSD, and this was one of the first rational ideas he'd heard all day.

"My short-term goal is to stay out of the news and off my father's television show," he said. "I'd been doing pretty well at it, too, until one of my schoolmates publicized my personal life. My long-term goal is to get my medical practice up and running and live a relatively quiet and peaceful life up here in Sugar Falls."

Everyone but Mia laughed as if this was the funniest idea they'd ever heard. "What?"

"You're about to have a child," Drew said. "I don't think your life is ever going to be quiet or peaceful again."

Not that Garrett had been around too many kids, but surely it wouldn't be all that bad. So far, Mia and he seemed to be on the same page with this co-parenting thing. Although, after this afternoon on the living room sofa, Garrett wasn't exactly sure that he wanted to keep his distance from her too much. It wasn't as if he believed in marriage or happily ever after, but they were getting along really well so far and if what they'd done a couple of hours ago was a perk of parenthood, then he'd be a happy father, indeed.

"Mia." Cooper reached for a piece of hot French bread and slathered it generously with butter. "What about you?"

She shrugged. "I just want to have a happy and well-adjusted baby. I want my knee to get better, or at least as better as it's going to be. I want to teach dance without my mother constantly telling me I'm settling. And I want to make sure that Nick Galveston never gets out of prison or finds out where I am."

And there it was. The reason why she could never truly be with Garrett.

If he was in her life, he could guarantee every single

one of those things *except* Nick finding her again. Or her mother issues. Everyone had to deal with wacky parents, so she was on her own with that. But if his famous father and the media's obsession with exposing his whereabouts brought Mia or their child into danger, he would never forgive himself.

Chapter Eleven

"Okay, so here's what I suggest," Kylie said after dinner as she brought out a tray full of Maxine's cookies with ice cream sandwiched inside.

Garrett didn't take one as she passed the tray. He hadn't been able to eat much at dinner. But now that he'd resigned himself to the fact that he and Mia couldn't ever be together, his appetite was completely gone.

She continued. "My brother, Kane, had to pull a disappearing act back when he was leaving Chicago so the press wouldn't constantly hound him about whether or not he would be able to play baseball again. He told everyone he was going to Scottsdale, Arizona, for surgery and some R and R."

"But I'd prefer not to go anywhere," Garrett said. He'd been on the move since he'd been eighteen. He was finally at a point where he wanted to put down roots.

Where he wanted to stop running. "I'm trying to get my orthopedic clinic up and operating and I can't do that from Scottsdale, or anywhere else."

Mia pulled her cookie apart and started on the ice cream first. "I have dance classes scheduled and the Christmas pageant I'm working on. I mean, I could probably get you ladies and a couple of my other teachers to cover for me, but I can't just leave all my students hanging indefinitely."

"No, that's not what I'm saying," Kylie said as she took two ice cream sandwiches off the tray before passing it on to her husband. "I meant you *tell* everyone you're going somewhere and leave a fake trail of bread crumbs for them to follow. They take off to look for you and when it's all clear, you two resurface and go back to living your ordinary lives."

"Like a red herring!" Drew took only one dessert, unlike his wife.

But then they'd still be living with the threat of being discovered again. Garrett thought of Kane and the way the famous baseball pitcher had ducked out of the Cowgirl Up Café when he'd seen the cameraman coming. The whole point was to *stop* hiding out.

"We'll tell them that you eloped," Cooper suggested and Garrett almost choked on his ice cream.

"Nobody will believe that I've run off to get married. Even my dad knows me better than that." He didn't see Mia set her uneaten cookie on her plate or look down at the napkin in her lap.

"Not if we make them believe it," Kylie said. "I can sell anything. First, you guys call them and tell them that with all the pressure, you decided to just run off to Aruba or Bali or somewhere for a babymoon."

"What in the heck is a babymoon?" Cooper asked.

"It's when the expectant parents go on vacation as a sort of last hurrah before the baby gets here. Drew and I are going back to Reno for ours. It's a totally romantic thing to do."

Several voices chirped into the conversation to discuss the fake destination for their fake plan—a plan Garrett thought was absurd at best.

"Reno was the most romantic place they could come up with?" he whispered to Mia.

"That's where they got married," Mia whispered back. "But they were both drunk and didn't remember it, so they're going to go back and renew their vows."

He glanced over at the unlikely couple—a straight-laced, bespectacled psychologist and a sassy redhead with a penchant for high heels. Maybe it wasn't the most orthodox of marriages, but it seemed to work for them. Besides Cooper and Maxine, Garrett had never seen a couple more in love with each other than Drew and Kylie.

The psychologist stroked a loving hand over his wife's extended stomach. Seeing the glow of pregnancy reminded Garrett of where he and Mia were going to be in just a few months. And even though they'd just made love and he was feeling closer than ever to her, the fact remained that there were still so many unknowns. Plus, she was somewhat, in a sense, hiding out from that Nick guy, and Garrett's father was on a full-blown crusade to expose both him and Mia to the world. Or at least, to his adoring viewers.

The couples continued to discuss the types of clues they would leak to the press, and the plan was sounding more asinine by the second. Gerald McCormick may look like an old, sun-weathered surfer, but he was a smart and savvy man. He would be waylaid for only so long before he and his television crews ended up right back in Sugar Falls. And as long as that possibility was an issue, Mia would never truly be safe.

"Listen, guys." Garrett held up his hands, quieting the dramatic crowd. "My not being completely up-front with my father about my feelings is what got us into this mess. I'm not going to lie to him or spend my life hiding out. I'll get in touch with him tomorrow and speak with him one-on-one."

Even as Garrett said the words, he knew there was no guarantee that any conversation he'd have with his dad would have any long-lasting effect. He needed to provide Mia with a bit of security, no matter how temporary it might be, but that didn't mean everything would be lollipops and rainbows after that. As much as he wanted to, he wouldn't be able to protect her privacy forever.

And he couldn't bring himself to be the person who was constantly putting her in jeopardy of being exposed to the press or the reason why she needed to live like a hermit. She'd eventually resent him and he'd end up hating himself.

Nope. It could never work out between them.

Once he explained things to his father and they got rid of the immediate threat, then Garrett would need to figure out a way to let her go—for her own safety.

"Hi, Mom," Mia said into her cell phone after her friends and their husbands left.

"Don't you 'hi, Mom' me." Rhonda wasted no time. "The entire Sugar Falls Chamber of Commerce knew my baby girl was pregnant before I did. And then you just left me there with that big shot producer trying to figure out what was going on and how we could put a positive spin on it."

"I'm sorry I took off like that and didn't tell you myself. It's just that things with Garrett and the baby have been so sudden and unexpected and I was trying to get everything in order before I shared the news with you."

"Who's Garrett?" Sheesh, was her mom serious?

"*Garrett*, Mom. You know the man from the café?" *The man who is the father to your unborn grandchild?*

Okay, so she left out that part at the end, but it was a fact Mia *couldn't* afford to forget. She watched the subject of their conversation as he stood at the kitchen sink, doing dishes and looking more sexy than domestic.

"Oh, you mean GP? Dr. McCormick's son?"

"Uh, yes, he *is* Dr. McCormick's son. But his name is Garrett and he's also a doctor."

"Well, I don't care what you want to call him, Mia. He's loaded and his dad has a lot of connections in Hollywood. If you play your cards right, you could land some sort of dance school reality show. Even if you can't dance yourself, you might be able to make something of your career."

The old Mia would've winced at the careless remark. But the new and improved and empowered Mia was going to speak up for herself.

"Mom, I like my career just fine. You know that I don't care about that show business stuff."

"Well, you *should* care. Do you have any idea how many jobs I lost hauling you around to audition after audition? How many know-it-all dance teachers I had to kiss up to in order to get you enrolled in their classes?

And for what? To have you bust up your knee and get knocked up? I did not sacrifice my entire life for you to sit around and play Holly Homemaker out in the Idaho wilderness." Mia listened to the familiar rant, one hand nestled over her own baby, as if she could cover its ears from the harsh and unfair reprimand. She'd never asked her mother to make those choices. "But at least this time, you landed yourself a good catch. You're finally making some lemonade out of those damn lemons you've been hauling around."

"You're right, Mom. I've always made the best of things, even when you coerced me into everything you wanted me to do. And I'm making a lot more than lemonade this time. I'm going to be an amazing parent and I am very excited about this baby."

There was a long silence on the other end of the line and Mia had to wonder if her mother even heard what she'd just said. She could see the woman pinching the bridge of her nose, trying to think of a different way to get what she wanted. "Gah, I can't believe I'm going to be a grandmother already. You're going to lose your figure, you know."

"Probably."

"Well, at least your father-in-law will be able to do a tummy tuck and boob lift afterward. Wait. You and GP *are* getting married, right?"

She doubted it. But she didn't want to bring up his comment at the dinner table while she was trying to convince her mom that she had her life under control.

"It's Garrett, Mom, and we haven't gotten that far."

"Are you taking your prenatal vitamins?"

The maternal question tugged at Mia's heart and she

was reminded that her mother really did love her, in her own selfish way. "Yes, Mom."

She could hear her mother sigh on the other end of the line. "I worry about you, you know? I've always wanted what's best for you."

"I know that." She really did. The problem was that Rhonda Palinski wanted what *she* thought was best for her daughter and wasn't willing to listen to anyone else's opinion on the matter. Mia squeezed her eyes closed. She was not going to get emotional right now. Not here. "But you have to trust me that this is what's best for me and for your grandchild."

"I know. And I do trust you, even if I never stop worrying about you. As a parent, you'll learn that it's hard to just switch off the caring button when your own baby grows up. Speaking of which, do you know whether we're having a boy or a girl yet?"

"Not yet."

"M'kay, but don't forget that a lot more boys have been getting into dance now. So don't worry if it's not a girl. We can still work with him and make sure he gets a good background in ballet and tap, but we might have to enroll him in gymnastics pretty early on. Thank goodness GP's family can probably afford private lessons."

"You know, that's a great idea. If you see Garrett's dad before he leaves town, make sure you run that idea past him."

One of Garrett's brows shot up and she wondered if he could hear the other side of the conversation. Sheesh, she hoped not. She swallowed a pang of guilt for purposely unleashing her persistent but well-meaning mother on her child's grandfather. But really, if they were both going to interfere in their grandchild's life, then Rhonda and Gerald would have to duke it out between themselves first. At least it would keep them occupied and off her back.

"Anyway, Mom, I'm not coming back to the apartment tonight. I'm going to be staying with a friend." She chanced a look at Garrett to see if he had any reaction to her mentioning her plan to spend the night with him, but he was scrubbing a pan with the same concentration he probably used in the operating room. "Maybe we can meet up tomorrow and catch up?"

"Of course. Bye, baby girl," her mom said, then disconnected.

Mia let out a breath and set down the phone. Talking to her mom was like getting her eyebrows plucked—painful, but thankfully necessary only every few weeks.

Plus, some positive things had come out of their conversation, so it hadn't been a complete failure. She'd stood up to her mom and reminded her that Mia was now calling the shots in her own life. Nobody else.

Now, if she could only figure out what to do with her baby's dad.

Garrett had clearly said he wasn't the type to run off and get married. Sure, they could co-parent all they wanted to, but where did they draw the emotional line? After what she'd experienced on the sofa earlier, Mia didn't think she would be happy with such a casual relationship. Either they were a couple or they weren't. As much as her behavior lately suggested otherwise, she wasn't a woman who would allow herself to be used at a man's whim.

They didn't need to make any decision tonight, but she would have to bite the bullet soon and tell Garrett that their child would eventually need stability. Whether they provided that individually or together was a choice they would both need to be comfortable living with. Once that choice was made, though, she wouldn't be jumping back and forth between roles.

It could wait until after he talked to his father and they hashed out their issues. She picked up a dish towel and started drying dishes so she would be forced to stop staring at him and wondering what he was thinking.

She wanted to know whether he was doing any of this for her because he thought that was what she wanted. She'd already had to face her world—the town of Sugar Falls and her mother—with the announcement of her pregnancy and the paternity of her child. But he had yet to face his world, which would be much more judgmental and unforgiving.

She wanted to tell him that things in his life would be so much better once he explained his feelings to his dad. But Mia was just barely learning how to take control of her own life. How could she try to tell him how to control his? Then she would be no better than her mother or Dr. McCormick Sr.

But just as her friends had once dared her to come out of her shell, maybe Garrett just needed a push in the right direction.

It wasn't that Garrett was nervous about talking to his father. He just doubted the effectiveness of their conversation. He'd overheard most of Mia's phone call with her mom and was proud of how well she'd handled herself and how she'd stood up to the woman. But putting Rhonda Palinski in check was probably an afternoon frolic in the kiddie pool. Dealing with Gerald

McCormick was like being dunked into deep, shark-infested waters.

Garrett watched Mia as she put dishes away and wondered if she doubted him as much as he doubted himself.

She'd been quiet as she'd helped him clean up the kitchen, and Garrett was trying not to draw attention to how useless he felt.

Normally, he was a proactive man—someone who got stuff done. People entrusted their lives to him. Hell, he had been an officer in one of the most elite branches of the military. Sitting back and waiting until the camera crews left town so that he could confront his father made him feel like a coward.

Even if it did mean guaranteeing the privacy of the woman he loved.

He stroked his forehead. It was true. He loved her. He didn't know how that had happened or when he'd let his heart even consider the possibility. But this gut-twisting agony and the decision he knew he had to ultimately make was definitely because of love.

Watching his father bring wife after wife into their lives had done nothing to cement the concept of matrimony in Garrett's young mind. In fact, before his twelfth birthday, he had sworn off the idea of marriage altogether. He told himself it was a sham, that it was for suckers, or that it had a failure rate to rival any property division percentage his former stepmothers had ended up relinquishing. If his beach-loving, ultrasuccessful father couldn't make it work, then how could he?

But Garrett wasn't a failure and he sure as heck wasn't his father. He knew that he could make a marriage with Mia work. But the unfortunate irony of the situation was that now that he'd finally realized it, he would never be able to make it happen.

After the kitchen was back in order, Mia walked around the house making sure the outer doors were secured and bolted. He wondered how often she'd followed this same procedure in an effort to ensure her safety. All Garrett had to do was avoid some cameras if he didn't want to be seen. But a few photos or some video footage never truly endangered him. What did it feel like to live in a state of fear such that her very life depended on whether or not she locked a door?

Maybe there wasn't much of a threat with her attacker now in prison. Still, he couldn't marry her and risk exposing her and their child to unwanted attention, but he also couldn't live without her.

He was so angry at his selfish father for putting them in this situation and he was just as pissed at himself for not telling his old man where exactly he could stick his reality show and its ratings sooner.

When he'd been surprised at the restaurant earlier, he'd reverted to his standard operating procedure. It had always been easier to just take off and leave. But what worked back when he was a teenager no longer felt like an effective solution now that he had so much more to lose.

Mia yawned as she made her way toward the stairs. "I'm exhausted," she said, reaching for her suitcase.

"Here, let me carry that up for you." Garrett jumped out of his chair. He needed to feel somewhat useful. "Any idea what the sleeping arrangements are like upstairs?"

"I, uh, well." A pink blush spread up Mia's neck and blossomed over her cheeks. She hadn't been ashamed earlier when she'd taken charge of their lovemaking on the sofa. Tonight, a lot of questions had arisen in his mind about which direction their relationship should be headed in. And he was willing to bet she'd been thinking about some of the same issues.

In his heart, he knew they would have to end things eventually. But maybe for just one more night, the magic could last a little bit longer. He wrapped an arm around her and pulled her toward him before kissing her deeply. When he felt her respond, he knew she'd come to the same conclusion as him.

"There's a guest room at the end of the hall," she said breathlessly.

It was all he needed to hear. He lifted her into his arms and had to remind himself to go slowly. To savor every detail of tonight. Because when this was all over, he would have to let her go.

He carried her past both the master suite and one that was decorated as if a slew of adolescent boys stayed over frequently. By the time they made it to the guest room, Garrett wasn't concerned about who normally slept where in this house or whether there were even sheets on the bed.

And by the time they finished making love and fell asleep in each other's arms, Garrett wasn't concerned about anything beyond the people inside this lake house.

But the sun streaming in through the windows was a cruel reminder of everything in his life he hadn't concerned himself with before now. His cell phone vibrated and he saw a text message pop up on the screen from Cooper.

Just saw your pops walk into the Cowgirl Up Café. He was driving a nondescript sedan with plates registered to a rental company. I called the Snow Creek Lodge and confirmed that his crew checked out earlier this morning. So my guess is he'll be on his way out of town after breakfast. I'll keep you posted.

Garrett should be thrilled. He should be elated that he finally had the chance to confront his father without anyone video recording what he needed to say. But what about the next time his old man came to town? And knowing his dad, there would be a next time.

"Morning," Mia said, stretching like a cat in the sunlight. Man, that woman could sure move her body into the most alluring positions. But her smile fell and she asked, "What's wrong?"

He answered by handing his cell phone to her so she could read the text.

She sat up, her beautiful shoulders poised perfectly straight. "But this is good news, right?"

"Is it?"

"Didn't you want the chance to talk to him alone?"

"I honestly don't know what I want."

She pulled the thousand-thread-count sheet higher under her arms. "Do you want me?"

This was it. This was his opportunity to tell her that he didn't. His opportunity to let her go. To keep her safe.

She didn't deserve to be lied to, but she also didn't deserve to keep living in fear. This was a woman who'd done everything in her power to protect herself. So why couldn't he make the decision to do whatever he had in his power and do the same?

"You know what? You don't need to answer that." She stood up, letting the sheet fall to the floor as she walked toward the door.

It was on the tip of his tongue to tell her exactly how much he wanted her. But maybe it was better this way. Why give her false hope?

He resisted the urge to rush after her, to stop her from reaching the suitcase she'd left downstairs. He'd already dealt with having her sneak out of his life once, and this time she wasn't sneaking.

Damn it.

He stared in anger at the black screen mounted to the wall.

Television and his father's stupid shows had shaped his life, but he couldn't allow it to shape Mia's. She deserved to live her dreams, even if it completely ruined his.

He walked to the hallway, but when he heard the zipper of her suitcase, followed by the sound of little plastic wheels rolling along the hardwood floor, he froze.

She was leaving. And he had to let her go. For her own safety and peace of mind. Outside, the engine of Cessy's Lexus shot to life. Garrett didn't know if it was the powerful engine or all the frustration he felt toward his father that was causing the roaring in his ears.

Mia might be gone, but it was still up to Garrett to keep his old man from making things worse.

Chapter Twelve

Mia wasn't one hundred percent sure that taking Cessy Walker's car had been the best idea. She couldn't even operate the CD player, let alone figure out how to turn off the squawking GPS, which was directing her away from Sugar Falls and toward the shopping mall in Boise.

Yet she'd had no other choice.

Hearing Garrett's deafening silence after she asked him if he wanted her had been worse than taking a golf club to the knee. But seeing the aching look in his hazel eyes had been a crippling blow to her heart.

She knew his answer. And she knew how to fix this. She hoped.

Mia ignored the blinking triangle on the screen and drove straight to the Cowgirl Up Café.

As much as she wasn't looking forward to the upcoming confrontation, she didn't want to cower and she didn't want to be protected.

She made a right turn onto Snowflake Boulevard and took a deep breath just as Barry Manilow belted out about being ready to take a chance again.

Her brain flashed back to that stupid text her friends had sent her when she'd been sitting in that bar in Boise.

Even though she'd had no intention of accepting their dare, that one spark of confidence had changed the entire course of her life.

And now some crooning love ballad stuck on Cessy Walker's car radio was daring her to put her love on the line.

Garrett better not be pissed that she was about to fight his battle for him. But seeing the way he'd looked at her back in the bedroom, she knew he'd go to battle for her if the situation was reversed.

Now all she could hope was that the stubborn man would come to his senses and follow after her.

The downtown city street was a bit more busy than usual and she'd had to drive around the block twice before she'd become impatient and created her own parking spot.

By the time she walked across Sugar Park, a spot opened up right in front of the restaurant.

Garrett's truck pulled in at an angle and Mia was relieved the cavalry had arrived. Or else he'd come to stop her.

"What are you doing here?" Garrett said after doing a double take of her walking toward him.

She stood up straighter, hoping her initial instinct had been right. "When I asked you if you wanted me, your eyes gave me your answer. I'm pretty familiar with the I'm-doing-this-for-your-own-good look. So I decided to rescue you before you made the mistake of attempting to rescue me."

At his confused expression, she went on. "I planned to catch your father before he left town."

"You were coming to see my father?" Garrett asked, walking toward her.

She tried not to think about the fact that they were having what should be a private conversation in a very public location. But that seemed to be a habit between the two of them.

"Yes. I figured you'd end up confronting him and decided that maybe I could talk to him beforehand and convince him to hear you out this time."

"I don't know if that would be enough, Mia. I've been over it several times in my head and I'm not sure anything could convince him that I don't want my life— our life—to be on TV."

"Is that why you were so miserable last night?"

"You moaned my name out loud several times. I hardly think I was miserable."

She blushed, hoping the two horses tethered out front were the only ones who'd heard him. "I meant is that why you were in such a quiet mood in the kitchen after dinner?"

"Partly. I was angry because I shouldn't even have to explain all of this to my dad in the first place. But I was also sad because I knew that anything I did would be temporary anyway because it's not like I can be with you permanently."

Her legs grew shaky and her throat threatened to close up. But she wouldn't cower anymore. Hell, she'd already driven Cessy's prized Lexus into town and parked it illegally in front of City Hall. Mia was invested at this point and wasn't going to back down.

"Why not?" Was there something she didn't know about preventing them from staying together? Had she misread the protective look in his eyes?

"Because of my father."

"He doesn't want you to be with me?"

"He probably doesn't care either way as long as ratings go up. And him going after those ratings is the problem."

She still didn't understand his line of reasoning. She knew he was strong and that he'd rebelled against his father plenty of times—albeit, his idea of a proper rebellion was up for discussion. So now what was different?

"Do you want to be with me, Garrett?"

"Of course I do. I've been half in love with you since that night we first met in Boise. The other half of me followed suit the minute you limped into my office."

Her heart did a little kick ball change at him finally saying it out loud. "Then what does Gerald McCormick have to do with whether or not we're together?"

"Mia, don't you see? If you marry me, you'll never be fully safe from the limelight. You worked so hard and sacrificed so much to get away from Nick, that all it would take would be one camera to start all that drama back up again."

"Maybe. You're right that I got away. And if I have to, I'll get out of it again. But not by escaping. If it comes to it, I'll face things head-on." He didn't look persuaded. "Listen, Garrett, yesterday, after I told you about my past, something powerful came over me. You know what that was? It was the realization that nobody but me was in control of my life. My mom, God bless her misguided heart, tried to shape me into the person she wanted me to be and then that whole thing with Nick crushed my spirits and I went into hiding. But from the second I met you and opened myself up, not only in that hotel room, but also in the doctor's office when we heard the heartbeat and then yesterday when we ended up at the lake house, I knew that I no longer wanted to stay in that world where I was scared, little Mia."

"But what about the baby? How do we keep it safe?"

"How does anyone keep their child safe? There're going to be accidents and there're going to be mistakes. We protect our child as much as we can and we love it unconditionally. But we also need to allow him or her to experience things. Last night, my mom reminded me of how much she'd sacrificed for me. But I never asked her to do any of that. In fact, it was an overwhelming responsibility she'd burdened me with at such a young age. Her happiness was always dependent upon how well I'd done at a rehearsal or performance. I would never put that kind of pressure on our child. So while I don't condone the whole television producer lifestyle, we can't keep our baby in a bubble forever."

He looked down the street toward the park in the center of town, where two young children were climbing on a slide. "I always hated having my childhood exposed to the whole world due to the life decisions of my father. You're right. Forcing our child to live some secret existence based upon our choices would be no different. But what if I can't keep you two out of the public eye?"

She stepped closer to him and wrapped her arms around his waist. "See those kids playing in the park without a care in the world? I want this baby to have the freedom to do whatever it wants. And I also want you and I to be able to have the freedom we need, too. So I figured I could go inside the café to talk to your dad and explain things to him…"

"Whoa. If anyone's going to explain things to my old man, it's going to be me. Lord knows I've tried to make him see things from my point of view for the past twenty years. But, like you said, it's not just about me anymore. My whole life I've been talking big, but my actions have been to say my piece and then take off to avoid any further conflict. It's the only way I knew how to take control of my world. But I don't want to just talk anymore. I need to stand my ground on this one and make sure he listens to what I have to say."

"If you tell me that part about falling in love with me again, I'll listen to *anything* you have to say."

He pulled her closer and when his mouth claimed hers, she felt his resolve and his promise that they were going to stand together on this and claim a life neither one of them had thought possible.

Garrett held Mia's hand tightly as they walked into the Cowgirl Up, the jingling horseshoe wind chime not slowing him down.

He saw his father sitting all alone at a turquoise upholstered booth in the back corner of the restaurant. But before he could march over there, his friend greeted him.

"Figured this is where you'd end up," Cooper said from his seat at the counter beside Mia's two best friends. The man had an uncanny knack for knowing what people were going to do before they even did it. Hell, it seemed everyone in Sugar Falls, especially Mia, knew his mind. "I knew you would be by first thing this morning. We can't all keep running forever."

Garrett remembered when Cooper was recovering from a major career-ending surgery. He'd had nowhere to go, then found a home in Sugar Falls. It was a good reminder that some people came from more broken homes than he had. Gerald McCormick wasn't abusive or absent. He was just a pain.

"I think I've known that for a while now, but it's still nice to see we've got someone in our corner."

"You've got a lot of someones in your corner." Garrett looked at Kylie, who was speaking around a mouthful of cheesy hash browns. "Drew assumed the same thing and that you'd show up here. He had a group therapy session this morning, but he asked me to come and take notes."

"I'm just here for the fried chicken and waffles," Maxine said, then shoved something drenched in syrup into her mouth. "And for the fireworks."

"Thanks, guys," Mia said and squeezed Garrett's hand. Not that he needed the reassurance, but it felt good to have her by his side. To know what he was fighting for.

He took a deep breath and squared his shoulders as they approached his father's table. Lights, camera, action. It was showtime.

"Dad," he said. "We need to talk."

"GP." His father wiped his mouth on a paper napkin, then indicated the bench seat across from him. "I hoped you'd come find me once the cameras left. At least this time you didn't have to fly halfway across the globe to make your point."

Garrett allowed Mia to go first and slide in. He hoped she wouldn't think less of him if he lost his cool.

"That's the length I was willing to take if it meant keeping as far away from your show as possible."

"You and your new friends made that pretty clear yesterday, son."

"But I should have explained why. My whole life, it was easier to just avoid you and avoid the argument. But now I need to make you see that it's a lot more than just me trying to steer clear of the cameras." He looked at Mia. "Do you mind if I tell him?"

Garrett waited for her to nod her assent before telling his father about Nick Galveston and the potential danger Mia could face. Gerald McCormick listened and even asked about her knee and the possibility of having another surgery to fix the lingering damage. The man might be a showman and a fast-talking, famous television producer, but he was still a doctor first.

"You know, I'm just thinking out loud here, and I'd have to run this by the network, but maybe we can do a segment on this jackass Nick. Domestic violence can ruin a lot of people's lives and if we do a documentary on these kinds of lowlifes and expose them, we can help other women out there who may be victims."

"I think that would be a wonderful idea," Mia said. "But not for me. It's taken me a long time to move on with my life, and I wouldn't want to have to relive it all over again. Especially on television."

His father tilted his head to the side as if he understood what they were saying, but couldn't figure out why they would feel that way.

"Look, Dad, I know you love being on TV. It's your

life and I get that. But what you've never been able to understand is that it's not for me."

"Oh, son, I knew you *thought* it wasn't for you, but I figured you'd eventually shake off this whole nomadic lifestyle and see the opportunities that I'd worked so hard to provide for you. Growing up, you and I, well, we never really had anything in common. You were so studious, so damn formal. You saw the world in black-and-white and looked down your nose at me every time I couldn't make a marriage work."

"I wasn't trying to look down my nose at you." Garrett felt somewhat chastised. He'd never stopped to think that his father had also felt the strain of his failed relationships.

"I know you didn't try to, but you were such a serious little boy. A lot like your Grandpa McCormick, you know. He always thought I was too flighty. He used to tell me there was more to life than being a hippie surfer. I could've gone pro on the long boarding circuit but instead I became a surgeon and it still wasn't enough for him. So, I decided, why not show him that I could have a successful career and that I could have fun doing it? When you went to med school, I thought, 'Maybe GP and I have more in common than either of us realized. Maybe he's going to follow in his old man's footsteps.' I mean, after all, if you hated me so much, why would you have become a surgeon, too? I guess I just thought if I gave you enough time, you'd come around."

"I'm thirty-six years old, Dad, and I can assure you that I'm not going to come around. At least not as far as reality television goes. Please understand that I never hated you. I hated the constant shows and the paparazzi. And I really couldn't stand that one producer you had a few years back—the pushy dude who tried to sneak into the base hospital."

"Yeah, I'm sorry about that. I never authorized that one. I hope you know that I would never risk getting you in trouble or putting you—either of you—in danger."

Garrett released the breath he hadn't realized he'd been holding. "I hoped as much. I love you and I know that deep down you wanted what you thought was best for me. But just like you're not Grandpa McCormick, I'm not *you* and I can't live my life in front of the cameras. It makes me feel like a spectacle in a three-ring circus."

"I'm not going to apologize for my career." His dad took a sip of coffee. "I enjoy what I do and I enjoy how I live. But I am sorry if I ever made you feel like you couldn't be what you wanted because of me. When your grandpa tried to pigeonhole me into joining the family practice, I promised myself I would never do to my children what he was doing to me. When I gave you those cuff links, it was like a peace offering telling you that if you came back into my life, you could wear whatever the hell old-fashioned clothes you wanted to."

Garrett thought about the gift, what the gesture must've meant to his father, and how he'd almost left that black case on some hotel bar in Boise. But Mia had saved the cuff links—twice. And she'd saved him from himself.

"I appreciate that, Dad." Garrett put his arm around Mia. "We made the same promise for our child not too long ago."

She met his eyes and they shared a silent reminder of the fresh bond they'd recently forged.

"I hope you two will be able to keep that promise. I

wish I would have, back when you were younger," his dad said before rubbing his eyes. "I also hope that you'll give a vain old man a chance to know his grandchild."

"Of course we would." Mia smiled. "And when this baby grows up, if he or she wants to be on one of your shows, then we'll cross that bridge when we get to it."

His dad let out a small chuckle. "That's more than fair. Listen, son, I've always wanted the world for you. When you joined the navy, I was as proud as a father could be. I know that my world isn't what you wanted back then. And now I understand that it most likely never will be. I don't get it, but I guess my own father never really got my decisions, either. Maybe, though, if you change your mind, just consider the possibility of doing a guest appearance?"

"Nope."

"How about we broadcast the wedding? Maybe if this stalker dude knows Mia's married, it will help keep him off her back. If not, I'll call Neville Galveston my damn self and threaten to expose his crazy son to the world. I didn't spend years cultivating my media connections for nothing."

Garrett looked at Mia. "Actually, that's not necessarily a bad idea. But not filming. Just pictures. You can choose which wedding photos we release to the press."

"Slow down." Mia lifted her hand. "I hate to point out the obvious here, but you haven't even asked me to marry you yet. Who says I'd even be willing?"

He hadn't thought about the possibility that she might say no. Or might not want to get married. Of course she would be reluctant to enter into a serious relationship with someone after what she went through.

But he would give her the choice.

He looked at the crowd of diners and how everyone—especially their friends—had somehow moved their tables and chairs so they were all closer to the rear corner of the restaurant where he and Mia had confronted his father.

Hell, he'd spent the last half of his life trying to avoid being a spectacle and now he was on center stage. Well, if he was going to make a scene, then he'd make it a huge one. After all, he was Gerald McCormick's son. Showmanship was in his blood.

He scooted off the edge of the bench and dropped to his right knee. He picked up Mia's hand and spoke loud enough for the whole café to hear. "I love you, Mia Palinski. Not only can I not live without you, I wouldn't want to. I know that I'm not perfect and that a life with me might not be what you've dreamed about. But I promise that if you marry me, I will try my hardest to be perfectly right for you and to make some new dreams come true."

"That's not a proper proposal," his dad said, shaking his head. Seriously? Here Garrett was, exposing his heart for the first time—in a public forum, no less—and he was getting criticized? "Nope. There was hardly any flair, and to be honest, it was a little lacking in production value. A woman like Mia is an artist. She needs a grand gesture. Something significant that she'll remember for the rest of her life."

"Well, this is my first proposal." Garrett looked at his father in disbelief. "You've done what, six of them so far?"

"At least give her a ring."

"I don't have a ring," Garrett said, patting his pockets and looking around at the crowd behind him.

Freckles tried to pull a behemoth monstrosity of pink and purple stones clustered into the shape of a peace symbol from her finger. "Y'all can have this one. My third husband gave it to me, but we were just common-law married and he left me for some hippie gal living on a commune outside of Billings."

Mia was shaking her head at him, and he didn't know if she was turning him down altogether or just object-ing to the peace ring. She was sucking in her cheeks, as if she was trying to suppress a giggle, and her eye wasn't doing that nervous blinking thing so he hoped she wasn't saying no to him.

"Here, kiddo," his dad said, sliding a platinum band off his pinky. Except during filmed surgeries, he'd never seen his father without it. "This was the ring your mom gave me when we got married. She was a good woman, and I never was able to find another one to take her place."

The metal was warm in Garrett's hand, and even though he couldn't recall any memories of his mother or her love toward his father, it somehow felt perfect. He held it up between his thumb and forefinger. "Will you marry me, Mia?"

She smiled and the sparkle in her blue eyes lit up the restaurant. "I love you more than I could have ever thought possible. I didn't think I had any more dreams left inside me. But being with you has been exciting beyond my wildest imagination. I *will* marry you, GP, Garrett, Dr. McCormick or whatever your name is." He grinned as he placed the ring on her finger. "And just for the record, that was the best proposal I could've hoped for and, hopefully, the last one you'll ever make."

She moved across the seat, and when she threw her

arms around his neck as he knelt in front of her, he kissed her for all the world to see.

Then he lowered his head and kissed her abdomen, thinking of his child growing there. Several cheers pierced the air, and Maxine and Kylie were the first to rush over to Mia and offer their congratulations.

Garrett rose to his feet and was the recipient of numerous handshakes and backslaps. But behind him, he heard Freckles talking to his father.

"I'm sure glad you two were able to work everything out. But just remember that if you ever decide to start filming them again, I'll be on the horn with Mia's momma so fast, you'll have the clumsiest broad from Florida knocking into your set before you can even say 'roll tape.'"

"I'll take that under advisement. Now, Miss Freckles, have you ever considered being on TV? You've got a personality that our viewers would eat up."

"Sure, darlin', as long as it's not one of your plastic surgery shows. After all, you can't fix what ain't broke." Several shouts of laughter floated through the restaurant and Garrett couldn't help but join in.

"What about the other news vans that might find out you're here?" Cooper asked.

"Don't worry about those guys," Gerald McCormick said. "I'll put out a press release saying you guys ran off to Bali or something. Send them all on a wild-goose chase."

"Hey." Kylie wiped her mouth. "That was my idea!"

Garrett pulled Mia in close to his side and planted soft kisses along her jawline until he reached her ear.

"Actually, I was thinking about that babymoon we haven't gotten to yet," he whispered and felt her shiver in his arms. "I know we'll probably need to figure out where we're going to live together eventually, but I was thinking that since Cessy Walker's house is still available for the next couple of days…"

He raised his eyebrows and asked, "What do you think?"

The woman who was about to become his wife and the mother to his child smiled brighter than any star over the Hollywood Hills, but it wasn't for the cameras or for the crowds. It was only for him. "I think that you can't fix what ain't broke."

Epilogue

It was Thursday night and Mia sat with Maxine and Kylie at their usual spot in Patrelli's. Well, technically, Kylie had to sit in a chair outside their booth because the tall redhead was almost full term and her stomach wouldn't fit between the high-back seat and the table unless she was angled sideways.

Now that Mia was in her second trimester, her morning sickness was long gone and she was craving Italian food as if it was going out of style. In fact, as soon as the waitress showed up, she planned to order a double batch of garlic knots.

Her phone buzzed and Mia looked down at the screen, trying not to blush at the text message Garrett had just sent her.

"So, what should we throw first, Mia?" Maxine asked, thankfully interrupting the direction of her thoughts. "Your baby shower or your bachelorette party?"

"I vote for the baby shower first," Kylie said. "The bachelorette party needs to wait until after I have the twins. I barely remember Maxine's and I'm not going to miss another one."

"I doubt there will be time for a bachelorette party. Now that Garrett's practice is up and running, we wanted to get married before I became too big to waddle down the aisle," Mia said, then looked at her very pregnant friend. "Not that you waddle, Kylie."

"You can say it. I own my waddle. Man, I can't wait for these two little girls to finally get here. Even if it *does* mean I'll have my hands too full for any more wild and crazy nights."

Mia smiled, looking forward to it, too. "Anyway, we were just thinking of doing a small, quiet wedding at the courthouse."

Both of the ladies gasped and then craned their heads around the restaurant as though they hoped Mia hadn't been overheard.

"What are you two worried about?" she asked. "My mom's back in Florida and Garrett's dad started filming a new season in California. I doubt they can hear me."

"That's not who I'm worried about," Maxine said. "If I were you, I'd be really careful not to let Cessy Walker hear you talking about quiet weddings at the courthouse."

Kylie nodded. "That woman doesn't believe in small or quiet anything."

Mia let out a small chuckle. "I know. Garrett says she's still showing up at his office once a week and trying to play receptionist. Maybe I should take some pity on him and give her some wedding-planning duties to keep her out of his hair."

Both of her friends looked at her as if she'd just announced her plans to walk down the aisle naked. Although, after the text message Garrett sent her a few minutes ago, she knew her husband-to-be was anxious to get her naked as soon as she got home tonight.

But before she could think about what she and Garrett would be doing later on that night, Mrs. Patrelli made her way to their table carrying two waters and a glass of cabernet for Maxine. But Maxine held up her hand. "Actually, Mrs. Patrelli, I'll just have a ginger ale tonight."

"But you always have wine with…" The restaurant owner trailed off and glanced at Kylie's protruding belly and Mia's slight rounded bump then back at Maxine. Kylie let out a loud squeal and Mia clapped her hands when they realized the reason their best friend wasn't drinking.

"Well, I guess I'll just save this for after all you ladies have your babies." Mrs. Patrelli returned the stem glass to her tray, even though the woman looked as if she was about to drink it herself. "Let me assure you, when the three of you get to the toddler years, you're gonna need it."

The women laughed and Mia thought about how far they'd come since first meeting in college. They'd gone from cheerleaders, to single career women, to a trio of devoted friends. They'd embarked on many journeys together, but none of them had warmed her heart as much as this one. They'd all found love and, judging by the next stage of life awaiting them, there was so much more to come.

But those adventures were still a little ways off. For now, Mia was looking forward to tonight's gossip session, and then going home to cozy up to her husband-to-be.

* * * * *

MILLS & BOON®

Desire™

PASSIONATE AND DRAMATIC LOVE STORIES

A sneak peek at next month's titles...

In stores from 10th March 2016:

- **Take Me, Cowboy** – Maisey Yates *and*
  His Baby Agenda – Katherine Garbera

- **A Surprise for the Sheikh** – Sarah M. Anderson *and*
  Reunited with the Rebel Billionaire – Catherine Mann

- **A Bargain with the Boss** – Barbara Dunlop *and*
  Secret Child, Royal Scandal – Cat Schield

0316/51

MILLS & BOON®

Helen Bianchin v Regency Collection!

MILLS & BOON®

Why not subscribe?
Never miss a title and save money too!

Here's what's available to you if you join the
exclusive **Mills & Boon® Book Club** today:

◆ *Titles up to a month ahead of the shops*
◆ *Amazing discounts*
◆ *Free P&P*
◆ *Earn Bonus Book points that can be redeemed
   against other titles and gifts*
◆ *Choose from monthly or pre-paid plans*

Still want more?
Well, if you join today, we'll even give you
50% OFF your first parcel!

So visit **www.millsandboon.co.uk/subs**
to be a part of this exclusive Book Club!

MILLS & BOON®

Why shop at millsandboon.co.uk?

Each year, thousands of romance readers find their perfect read at millsandboon.co.uk. That's because we're passionate about bringing you the very best romantic fiction. Here are some of the advantages of shopping at www.millsandboon.co.uk:

* **Get new books first**—you'll be able to buy your favourite books one month before they hit the shops

* **Get exclusive discounts**—you'll also be able to buy our specially created monthly collections, with up to 50% off the RRP

* **Find your favourite authors**—latest news, interviews and new releases for all your favourite authors and series on our website, plus ideas for what to try next

* **Join in**—once you've bought your favourite books, don't forget to register with us to rate, review and join in the discussions

Visit **www.millsandboon.co.uk**
for all this and more today!